PR

"Gripping, horr ... ntinues to be a winner ... ."

Seanan McGu ... or of the InCryptid ... Daye series

"Moore has laid the groundwork for a trilogy that promises to be loaded with terrifically grim fantasy storytelling. There is a lot of swift, merciless violence in this book, mingled with an undercurrent of very welcome, if very dark, humor. All of it together takes me back to what made me giddy about epic fantasy way back when."

Barnes & Noble Sci-Fi & Fantasy Blog

"James A Moore is the new prince of grimdark fantasy. His work is full of dark philosophy and savage violence, desperate warriors and capricious gods. Exhilarating as hell."

Christopher Golden, New York times bestselling author of Snowblind

"*The Last Sacrifice* is brilliant, devious, dark and compelling. This is epic fantasy at its very best. Highly recommended!"

Jonathan Maberry, New York Times bestselling author of Kill Switch

"*The Last Sacrifice* is dark and violent with no punches pulled. The worldbuilding is epic in scope but focuses on a select few individuals to flesh out the story."

San Francisco Book Review

"With *The Last Sacrifice,* James A Moore has triumphed yet again, delivering a modern sword and sorcery tale to delight old and new fans of the genre. With its intriguing premise, stellar cast of characters, and flavorful horror elements, this is damn good stuff."

Bookwraiths

"From living mountains to the secret behind the veils of a nation, Moore pushes and pulls the story through questions and answers, keeping the reader on their toes. For me, *The Blasted Lands* is more immersive and thrilling than some of the fantasy masterpieces. Moore shapes a story which appeals to fans of all types, showing how fantasy can be a grand equalizer."

Literary Escapism

"The end of the book had me on the edge of my seat, wanting more. I will definitely be reading the next book in the Seven Forges series as soon as it comes out."

Avid Fantasy Reviews

"Wow, that twist. In some ways I think I should have seen it coming, and I kind of did, but *Seven Forges* just lulled me into security and BAM! Craziness!"

On Starships & Dragonwings

"*Seven Forges* is an excellent, enjoyable, and thoroughly entertaining fantasy debut into a new world of swords and sorcery, complete with romance, intrigue, and danger."

Attack of the Books

"I thoroughly enjoyed *Seven Forges* although I was left speechless by the ending and left wondering for days whether there was to be another book in the series. There were so many threads of stories left open that I need to know what happens next."
The Bookish Outsider

"James A Moore dedicates *Seven Forges* in part 'to the memory of Fritz Leiber and Robert E Howard for the inspiration.' Moore is far more than an imitator, though. He does some fresh, counterintuitive things with the genre conventions. More than once, he startled me into saying out loud, 'I didn't see that coming.'"
Black Gate

"Moore does a fantastic job of building worlds and characters in *Seven Forges* as we hop on board the train that is about to meet its doom."
Troubled Scribe

"The race of the Sa'aba Taalor are the newest and freshest I've read in decades. Where many writers will have gods who are nebulous and unreachable, many of Moore's gods respond immediately. I think I like his creatures the best – the Pra Moresh. Here Moore's horror roots allow him to really shine. His descriptive prose and keen eye for the horrific proves that he's a master architect of the gruesome and prognosticator of fear. If you have yet to try these, then do so on my word. You'll thank me for it."
Living Dangerously

BY THE SAME AUTHOR

The Tides of War series
The Last Sacrifice • Fallen Gods • Gates of the Dead

The Seven Forges series
Seven Forges • The Blasted Lands
City of Wonders • The Silent Army

The Blood Red series
Blood Red • Blood Harvest • Blood of the Damned

The Chris Corin Chronicles
Possessions • Rabid Growth • Newbies

The Serenity Falls Trilogy
Writ in Blood • The Pack • Dark Carnival

The Griffin & Price series (with Charles R Rutledge)
Blind Shadows • Congregations of the Dead • A Hell Within

Alien: Sea of Sorrows
The Predator: Hunters & Hunted
The Haunted Forest Tour *(with Jeff Strand)*
Bloodstained Oz *(with Christopher Golden)*
Buffy the Vampire Slayer: Chaos Bleeds
Cherry Hill
Deeper
Fireworks
Harvest Moon
Homestead
Under the Overtree
Vampire: House of Secrets *(with Kevin Andrew Murphy)*
Vendetta
Werewolf: Hellstorm
The Wild Hunt
Slices *(stories)*
This is Halloween *(stories)*

JAMES A MOORE

Gates of the Dead

TIDES OF WAR, BOOK III

ANGRY ROBOT
An imprint of Watkins Media Ltd

20 Fletcher Gate,
Nottingham,
NG1 2FZ • UK

angryrobotbooks.com
twitter.com/angryrobotbooks
To kill a god

An Angry Robot paperback original 2019

Cover by Alejandro Colucci
Set in Meridien by Argh! Nottingham

Distributed in the United States by Penguin Random House, Inc.,
New York.

ISBN 978 0 85766 746 5
Ebook ISBN 978 0 85766 747 2

Printed in the United States of America

9 8 7 6 5 4 3 2 1

This book is dedicated to Thomas Sneigoski and Steve Bissette, for the friendship.

CHAPTER ONE
TURBULENT TIDES

Brogan McTyre

To the south of the shoreline the sky was sunny and the sea was calm. In all other directions, clouds had devoured the daylight and waves chopped and foamed rabidly. Brogan McTyre stared at the end of the world and realized again that it was his doing.

Well, his and the gods. That was why he meant to kill them.

To be fair, the gods started it. Their servants came to his home while he was away and took his family to be sacrificed in their names. He did not reach his family in time to save them, but he made sure the gods knew of his anger by murdering great numbers of their servants and selling the rest as slaves.

They'd demanded his family for sacrifice and he'd failed to stop them. He'd fouled up their attempts enough, however, that the gods in their miserable hiding places decided to end the world. They'd offered punishments in the past, but never one so extreme.

They were unforgiving of his sins and he, in turn, was unforgiving of theirs. The only thing to do was to end their feud as conclusively as possible and he intended to do just that and walk away as the sole survivor of their personal war.

"Will you stand there all day, you daft fool? Our ride is here." Anna Harkness's voice cut across his silent, angry thoughts and he looked her way.

"I've just helped kill a god. I can have a few moments, can't I?"

"That was hours ago, Brogan. We've more to do if we're going to finish this while there's still a land to call home." She smiled as she said it, but the smile barely reached her eyes. He understood. The land they'd been born and lived most of their lives in was in ruin. Most of the largest cities, and surely the smaller towns, were gone, destroyed by the storms looming so close to Torema, the southernmost city in the Five Kingdoms. What was left was looking more like a warren of drowned rats than a proper city.

He snorted bitter laughter and shook his head. The ship waiting for them was a small boat ride away. The smaller vessel would surely be sunk in the rough seas, but the larger looked like it just might hold water long enough to get them to their destination, the warren of rats that was currently drowning.

Torema was a very large city and even from a distance, and past the approaching storms, he could see the smoke rising in columns from the shoreline. The city was alive and probably holding every person who could find their way from any other eastern part of the continent. From the west would hardly matter. There was nothing the westerners could do to get to the closer side of the land. The mountains had been shattered, hadn't they? Brogan knew and had watched the entire incident and quite possibly was responsible for that part, too.

For one small stretch of time, he had been joined with the essence of a god. That was done now, but he was forever changed by it. He had sought and now had the ability to touch the gods.

"Brogan!" Anna's voice had taken on a waspish edge. He looked at the stunning woman and was glad for a moment that she was Desmond's concern and not his. Desmond Harkness was a fine man, a deadly warrior and one of Brogan's friends. He was also the husband of Anna, who had journeyed with Brogan to help him achieve his goals. She was a good woman, and lovely, but she was also a powerful distraction if he let her become one. He was doing his best to make sure that didn't happen.

When she was yelling at him like that, she made it easier.

"Fine!" The clothes he wore were borrowed from Anna's bag, the one that seemed to hold endless wonders. The colors for his tartan were wrong. The boots were slightly too tight and the vest smelled of Desmond. All of that was better than going into a battle situation naked, and that would have been his other option. When Walthanadurn, the dead god he'd connected with, rose from the mountains and fought his own murderous daughter, he'd been kind enough to send Brogan and his companions across the lands in an instant rather than let them die in the fight.

Brogan's clothes did not make the journey. Everyone else was just fine, but part of the ritual to summon a dead god had required painting Brogan's naked form.

Jahda, a very tall man he'd never met before; Faceless, a very large creature of unknown origin; and Roskell Turn, a substantially smaller Galean sorcerer, had all made the trip. Faceless even carried Brogan's axe, but his clothes? Nowhere to be found. The same with his horse, which he hoped had somehow avoided the catastrophe. Anna had made the journey as well, which was good, as Desmond would surely kill him if she did not.

Anna yelled a third time and, finally, Brogan nodded and gathered his few remaining weapons. If all went according to his wishes, the rest of his friends would be waiting with a ship in Torema. If not, they'd have to improvise, because reaching the gods in order to kill them would require some travel time.

Brogan headed for the small boat and the group that was already climbing aboard. There was a lot of fighting to be done. There was a lot of killing to accomplish. The gods had to pay for all they'd done and Brogan had to be the one to make them do so.

He climbed into the sturdy boat and settled himself, staring at the overcrowded bay of Torema as they started toward the ship waiting for them. Soon enough the gods would be held accountable for their actions. That was enough to know for the moment, but, oh, he longed to feel them dying at his hands.

The ocean's breeze was cleansing and cold against Brogan McTyre's skin, and the sun was very nearly blinding. After his time entombed in a mountain he welcomed the sensations.

The waters were rougher than he'd expected and colder, too. This far south the ocean was often warm to the touch, but now the waves felt rimed with frost.

Across the waters he could see Torema coming closer. The city had been called many things over the years, complimentary and condemning alike, but he had always found it mildly repulsive. There were too many people for his liking. He preferred the small areas, like the town where he'd built his home so many years ago. The home that he doubted he would ever see again under any circumstances. Kinnett held nothing for him any longer. His wife, his children were gone, and they were the only reason he'd ever needed to return.

Anna Harkness walked closer and he looked her way for a brief moment before staring back out at the waters. If he didn't look for too long, she didn't become distracting.

In hindsight, starting a war with the gods might not have been the wisest choice, and yet he found he still did not feel guilt or shame over the matter. Brogan liked to think of himself as a good man, even if the facts often disagreed.

Now the gods sought him and his companions as sacrifices. For all he knew the rest of his friends were already dead or captured. All he truly knew was that the world was suffering the price of his deeds and that he needed to make it right before the world ended.

If that meant slaying all of the gods, then he intended to do just that.

And now, thanks to the actions of his recent

companions, he at least had a glimmer of a chance. He had journeyed to find a dead god, and with the help of Anna and the Galeans – a people who studied the secrets that the gods once revealed to a single woman, who dared to ask the right questions – he had spoken with that god and for one brief moment shared consciousness with them.

Gods, it seemed, never quite died completely. He intended to rectify that situation if at all possible.

Brogan half-listened to the conversation between Jahda and the captain as he looked at the coastline coming their way.

Torema was partially concealed under a miasma of smoke and filth. Too many people crowded into a vast area that was still too small for their needs. The captain of the barge taking them to the city was a squat man with bad skin, a balding and badly sunburnt head, and a penchant for gossip. He'd made it clear that war was kissing the city. There was no way around it. Too many people fought for the same land, desperate to escape the inevitable.

There was nowhere left to go. All any of them had to do was look at the land to the north of the city, and the towering storm front crushing that land, and they could understand the desperation.

He was certain of it. There were things in those clouds. Be they gods or giants, something churned and moved those lightning-strewn forms and cast ruination down upon the lands.

All this, he thought. *All this is my doing. My anger caused this, justified or not.* There was no guilt. There was no regret. One thing he knew was that if the same circumstances came again and he had a chance to save his family from the hunger of the gods, he would do it all again.

It was too late for that. Now he had to make certain that the rest of the world survived his decisions.

Or he had to die trying.

The waves grew rougher and Brogan moved his body to keep his balance as the barge rose and fell with the shifting waters.

Next to him Anna moved to get a better look at the city. Her husband, near as they knew, was still alive. He might even be waiting for them.

He hoped so, for her sake. Desmond was a good man and Anna deserved a good man. She was a good woman.

Still, he looked her way for a moment with thoughts that had nothing to do with Desmond and everything to do with his friend's wife.

Not far away a figure that seemed formed of wood stood on the deck and looked toward the city. Faceless was what he called the thing. The shape of the creature was changing slowly. It was taller than him, and it had been a nearly featureless doll of a shape when first seen, but the longer it stayed around him and the other humans, the more it began to resemble them. His rough feet had changed enough that it now had toes and a discernable heel. The hands were different as well, developing individual digits and even crudely formed fingernails. The face was mostly the same. There was a hint of a shape, smooth enough save where the two deep pits in that rudimentary skull were positioned where eyes should be. Now and then there was a glint of light from those pits, but mostly they were dark.

If Faceless was bothered by the motion of the sea, he did not let it show.

Stanna

The air above Torema stank of smoke, desperation, disease, and death.

Though no official word had been given there were already several funeral pyres burning and they would not get smaller as time went on. Throughout the vast, overrun city there were groups gathered who took the dead from the streets or from any who offered them up and dragged them to the great pyres. It was grim work, but there was little choice in the matter.

The cemeteries in Torema had been inhabited by the living. There were camps, and lean-tos, and new communities gathering in the places of the dead. Headstones had become walls for makeshift homes, and actual tombs were now the foundations on which people placed their tents. There was no more room for corpses when the living demanded real estate.

And so there were mountains of dead flesh burning in places where stones could be gathered to stop the worst of the flames from spreading. Stray dogs and cats lingered in those areas, possibly mourning their dead people, and just as likely waiting to see if anything edible might fall free of the conflagrations.

Not far from the closest of the pyres, Hillar Darkraven walked with Stanna. Both women were dressed for trouble and sported armor and weapons.

On most any day that was true, but currently Stanna looked deadlier than usual.

"We've held back the worst flows, but people are still coming in. There is simply no way to stop them." Stanna spoke calmly. She was not aggravated by the situation. You haul enough slaves for a decade or so and you develop a pragmatic way of looking at the world.

Hillar nodded. "You can only do what you can do. My people tell me that there are worse problems coming."

"Worse? How so?"

"The remaining armies of Giddenland are heading this way. They've gathered as many people as they can and it doesn't matter if they are trained, the citizens of Giddenland are now soldiers."

Stanna looked toward where Edinrun once stood. "Then we will lose."

Hillar shook her head. "I have a few tricks. When those are used up it will be you and yours who have to defend."

"Yes, well, about that. I've heard tales that we have another threat and this one is just as bad."

"What other threat?"

"Beron of Saramond." Stanna frowned and pointed to the far west. "He's already gathering an army of people to cut through Torema. They are willing to work with him because he promises them the city. All the people at the edges, too far out to push their way in alone. He's recruiting them and offering them real estate. A place to call their own and food, besides."

"Really? Where will he get all of this?"

Stanna looked at the shorter woman. In fairness Stanna had never met a woman who came close to her height or physical prowess. "Beron is a slaver. He has been called the slaver king more than once. His was the First House in Saramond. He was in charge of the entire trade and that includes all that I did. I answered to him." She frowned. "At least, I was supposed to."

"Did you decide not to answer to him?"

"When the Undying claimed his slave women as their own I let them have them." Stanna shrugged and looked to the skies. They were dark with smoke, and clouds, and pregnant with the promise of a hard downpour. The city was not in good shape and that wasn't going to change. The world was ending, after all, and that meant that even Torema was likely to fall.

"I wouldn't argue with the likes of the Undying myself," Hillar agreed.

"Thing is, I can kill the likes of Beron. I tried killing one of the Undying. Cut his head clean off. He came back."

"After you cut his head off?" Hillar seemed a little taken aback by the notion.

"They *are* Undying."

"Well, yes, but I rather hoped that was all rumors and misdirection."

"Not this time. Took one of my friends with him the last time he showed up. I see him again, I'll try to kill him again."

"You're determined, aren't you?"

Stanna frowned. "I don't intend to be killed the

same way, is all."

"How did your friend die?"

"Last anyone saw he was rising into the air and moving away faster than arrows can be fired."

"That fast?" Hillar looked around. She was not exactly afraid so much as suddenly very wary.

"I'd suggest not offending the Undying."

"I'd rather avoid the idea, actually."

"In any event, Beron is coming and he's gathering an army of riff raff to fight with him."

"Why should that be a problem?"

Stanna looked around and then spit on the cobblestones. "The people he's choosing have nothing. That means they have nothing to lose and everything to gain. The only saving grace we might have is that ex-slaves are likely to avoid walking by his side."

"There are a great number of ex-slaves in Torema. An even larger number of slaves."

"If it was me, I'd change that."

"Why?"

Stanna stared at her benefactor for a moment and then gestured at the city around them. "Free the slaves and you'll have loyal followers. They'll be grateful. If Beron frees them, they'll be loyal to him." Stanna looked around again and squinted toward the north. "Slaves serve through fear. You offer them something better than fear and they'll serve you well enough. Long enough to fight off the armies coming your way with any luck."

"Two armies against us."

Stanna shook her head. "Three."

"Three?"

"The people of Hollum are penned up in the western area. They don't want to be. Sooner or later they'll see an opportunity and they'll attack."

"Gods! Attacks from three sides?"

"Only safe place to be soon will be the docks. And believe me, others will see that, too." Stanna looked toward the waters and the shifting island of ships and boats that dominated the area.

"There aren't enough ships to save everyone."

Stanna shook her head. "The only people anyone ever cares about saving are themselves."

"You think so?"

"I promise you the people in Hollum paid dear for the privilege of riding in wagons. They either owned the wagons, or bought the right to be on them, and paid with most of what they could carry."

Hillar stared at her for a long time without speaking.

Stanna continued, "You run this city. You own half of everything or more. You are paying me and mine to keep your city safe, because you can afford to. But if you had to leave Torema right now, this instant, what would you take with you?"

"Everything I could carry and more besides."

Stanna nodded her head, and felt the growing wind run across the shaved portions of her scalp. "And where would you take it? Do you own any ships?"

"At least a dozen of the ships in the harbor are mine."

She nodded again and ran her fingers through the thick red hair that remained across the top of her head. "And the people who run those ships? Think they'll leave their families behind to let you carry your possessions?"

The wind was picking up again and the clouds from the north held over them like a vast tidal wave suspended in time. Stanna shook her head and the increasing breeze threw aside the crimson hair that tried to block her view. "You've a dozen ships and papers to prove it. No one will care. Not a bloody soul. They'll kill you and everything you own to get on one of those ships and head away from this."

She gestured toward the clouds above and as she did the rains started in again, thick, fat drops that chilled the skin.

"What would you recommend?"

"Forget Torema. Gather your soldiers, your trusted ones, and get to your ships before everyone realizes that the city is doomed. And it is. You know it as well as I do."

"And would you have a place on one of those ships?"

"I find safety is the finest currency known to any living being. I'd be there. Invite me and I'll stay by your side and keep you safe. Leave me behind and I'll find another ship to call my own."

Stanna looked down to the docks, far below. The waves were crashing harder now and most of the boats, large and small alike, lifted with those waves and stayed safe, while the docks themselves were battered and half-submerged.

"Only decide soon, Hillar Darkraven, before the fates decide for you."

CHAPTER TWO
FIRST THE GODS

The He-Kisshi

The sky raged. The storms seethed. The winds roared and the rain dropped in fat globules that hit like rotten fruit and soaked everything they touched in a matter of seconds. Lightning peeled back the clouds and thunder roared its fury into the skies above Torema.

And in the heart of that furious conflagration the He-Kisshi roared, too.

Eleven of the Undying wailed their fury and sorrows into the air, suffering a loss that none of them had ever thought possible.

Their sibling was dead. Uthl-Prahna would not be reborn, would not come back, would not be saved, no matter how much they might beg for a return of one of their own. An Undying had died, and there was no removing the great wound that bled into their beings as they considered the loss.

One of the voices they'd always heard was gone. Just gone.

Murdered by Brogan McTyre.

Worse still?

One of the *gods* was dead. Destroyed. Cast down by McTyre and the god he'd touched with his very being.

Oh, his death would be the greatest triumph of their existence.

They looked down upon Torema from their places in the clouds and wailed their sorrows into the furious storms.

Torema did not care. The humans had no love for the gods or their servants: they feared them, as had always been the case. Uthl-Prahna had cast its fury over the world on several occasions, and was the first to work as the executioner of the gods, when the need arose. Of all the He-Kisshi, certainly it was Uthl-Prahna who tracked the deviants best. It had sought and found Brogan McTyre and, in the end, had paid the price for that skill.

Murdered by the very creature it sought. The song of the He-Kisshi no longer sounded the same, no longer had the proper balance. The Undying roared and howled their agonies out and then threw those very sorrows down upon the city, shattering the skies with brilliant lances of lightning and crashes of thunder that could never equal their suffering.

Far below them the humans fled, trying to find places to hide from their fury. The desire to kill them all was a living thing, but they knew better. They could not simply kill the beings below them. The gods had decreed that the humans had to suffer before they could die and already the First Tribulation was ruining them.

Ohdra-Hun looked to the west and saw the growing crowds of humans, thousands upon thousands, that gathered there, seeking a way to force themselves upon the city. From this distance they looked like a puddle growing at the edge of the city, but it knew that would not last. The mass of people would, when they were certain of their leaders, move and try to crush Torema. To the north was more of the same and to the east as well. Different factions, and though it did not study their actions, it understood humans well enough. Blood would flow across the hills and streets of the city in the very near future. The deaths would come hard and fast, and the gods would feast on every death that happened, even those not directly meant for them. That was the advantage of gods: their actions set other actions in motion and in the end those new actions worked as well as proper sacrifices. They were not as satisfying, but they were just as effective. The living would gather and fight and the dead would feed the needs of the gods long enough for them to finish their work. This land, this place, was destined to die and in the dying would once again serve the gods.

In the process, all those who had ever wished harm on the He-Kisshi would die and that was enough for them. They would savor the end of the humans here.

There were other places with humans. There would always be more fodder, but there were only eleven of the Undying left.

Down below them the winds howled, and the seas surged and threw themselves madly at the places where the humans dwelled, and the mortals below them trembled and knew fear.

The He-Kisshi saw this all and knew it was good.

Harper

Laram and his red-haired love held each other as the ship rocked beneath them. The waiting was the hardest part.

Mearhan Slattery clutched Laram's beefy arms as if he were the only anchor she could find in the whole of the world, and at that moment it might well have been a true statement. Harper watched the way they held each other and allowed himself a thin smile.

It wasn't a time for romance or merriment, but a time for worlds to end and civilizations to crumble.

The ship moved, as the waves grew worse. The first mate called down from the top of the ship to get directions and Harper looked at the Slattery girl again. "Mearhan, which way?"

The girl shook. She was scared and had every right to be terrified out of her mind, but that wasn't a luxury they could consider. The young woman was a Scryer, a messenger for the gods. They'd taken her with them so that they would know what the gods wanted and could be prepared. She could pass on the words of the gods and she could hear them when they spoke, but there was little control over how the words came to her and apparently the gods were being unkind of late. They did not speak so much as they screamed.

The gods were furious that Brogan McTyre and his cohorts were still alive. As one of those cohorts, Harper was glad to disappoint, but he also knew that all of the men who'd helped Brogan in his time of need were being hunted, with an eye toward making them replacement sacrifices for the failed attempts with Brogan's family. Four deaths, twenty deaths, it hardly mattered to the gods as long as they were indulged.

A few hours earlier Mearhan had fallen over, screaming in agony. She'd thrashed and moaned and would likely have clawed her own eyes from her face if Laram and a few others hadn't restrained her.

When she could finally be calmed and had recovered from her fit, Harper got the words from her lips that one of the gods was actually dead. Murdered. She spoke only in a whisper and only to him. That was for the best. The people around them might not have received the information well, and no one wanted to let the crew of the ship know that they were hunted by all five kingdoms and the gods themselves. Well, the remaining gods, at least.

The gods were saying that Brogan was close by and that was important. More important still was that they meet up with him as quickly as possible, and thus the urgency for moving into the open sea from the bay of Torema. There were armies, several of them, looking for Brogan and his companions. If they found them, no matter how good they might be at fighting, the sheer numbers of people hunting them would overwhelm any possible skills and they'd be taken to offer up to the gods.

Even their friends and the people who would usually aid them would turn on them. Why? Because the gods were ending the world and if Brogan and his companions were not offered up as sacrifices, none of the people they knew would have a place to call home any longer. Loyalty was a lovely thing, but so was staying alive.

Mearhan looked his way with misery in her pale blue eyes. "Head south. There are three ships on the waters from Kaer-ru. The one you want is sporting a red sail."

Harper smiled, nodded, and walked toward the ladder. "Red sails. Find it, please."

Lendre smiled and his head bobbed up and down rapidly. Harper trusted him not at all. He smiled back just the same.

"Thank you, Mearhan. Get rest if you can. We've a long path before us."

And so they had. First they had to reach Brogan, preferably before he made it to Torema, and then they'd likely be sailing directly into the storms to the north in an effort to find the gods. The Gateway was the only place Harper had ever heard of that led to the gods, and even that knowledge was mostly rumor. A few small facts, and a great number of tales told in secrecy by his father who, like Harper, had worked for the gods in one capacity or another for most of his life. Had the man been alive, Harper suspected his father would have either disavowed him or killed him. One does not betray the gods, after all, but Harper had no choice. Brogan McTyre and his family had cared for Harper after his bloodline passed. They'd been like blood and one did not betray blood.

Again guilt twisted at his guts. He'd been jealous on several occasions of Brogan's perfect wife and lovely children. He'd made his half-hearted bitter prayers to the gods that they balance things out. He'd wanted to have all that Brogan had, a family and the love of a good woman, but it had never worked out. There was a part of Harper that wondered constantly if the gods had taken Nora and the twins and even young Braghe as an answer to his prayers. What a horrid thought. How very like the fickle gods to answer exactly the wrong prayer and see it as simple convenience.

He would never know the answer, of course. Was it his wishes that brought an end to Brogan's family? Only the gods knew for certain and they had never spoken to Harper even once in his life.

Once on the deck Harper took a moment to look around. The Kaer-ru islands were visible in the distance. Between here and there were close to fifty vessels moving across the ocean. Most of them were headed toward the islands and away from the bay and the vast overflow of people facing the apocalyptic storms coming their way. That was inevitable and if Harper could have found someone to bet against he would have gleefully spent his entire fortune betting that it would only get worse. The reason he'd flat out purchased the ship he was standing on was because he knew the rest of the ships in the bay would be leaving and heading south. It was that, or die. The land was gone. There was nowhere left to go but to the sea.

And nowhere to go on the sea but to the south if a soul wanted to avoid the raging oceans.

There were other lands. Harper knew that, but had no idea where they might be. Captain Odobo claimed he'd been to all of them. That was a lovely thought, as they might need to flee the gods and in so doing they'd need a new land, if not an entirely new world.

The red sail was visible on the waters between the Kaer-ru and the ship.

Harper stood on the deck and watched as the ship came closer. He never quite stood still and his eyes looked everywhere they could to make sure that all was well with his world.

Well, as well as could be when the world was being murdered.

Captain Odobo came closer, followed by his shifty second in command.

"I say your friends are there. The one you worried about the most, he is with them." Odobo spoke casually about the situation.

"I have my doubts." Harper shook his head.

Odobo reached into his purse and pulled out four small coins. They were enough to pay for a night with the very finest whores at the finest of the brothels in Torema. "Fancy a wager?"

"You're on," Harper smiled. He could play along.

They waited together and Odobo spoke to his second in their native tongue, one of the few with which Harper was only passably capable of communicating. He spoke most of the major tongues in the land, but the Kaer-ru had small islands as cities and states and while they were often familiar there were differences. He was fairly sure he was called a fool at least once, but had no reason to show that he knew that. Instead he gazed at the approaching barge. It was large enough to survive the harsh waves and that was a good thing, as some of the surges were enough to throw unfortunate fools from the decks where they stood.

Not too much later Harper had to hand over his coins. The form of Brogan McTyre was impossible to miss. His clothes belonged to Desmond, but the stance, the expression, and the flaming red hair all belonged to Harper's best childhood friend.

There was something different about the man, though at this distance Harper couldn't have begun to guess what it might be. He was the same height, the same heavily muscled build. His eyes were as brooding as they had been since his family was slain, and his expression was just as it always was these days, a grim set to his mouth that bordered on an angry scowl.

There was a thing standing near him. It was not human, though it stood like a man. It was not wooden in nature, but the skin resembled bark that had been smoothed and oiled with only a modicum of efficiency. It stood taller than Brogan by most of a foot and it turned its head with quick motions, almost birdlike in their stuttering speed. There was much to see in Torema and he doubted that anyone in the city had ever seen the like, which meant in turn that the creature had probably never seen Torema or anything quite like the coastal city that was currently drowning in humans and their waste.

Brogan saw him, and smiled. The expression took a decade away from the man's features. Harper would have given nearly anything to keep that joy on his best friend's face. He knew well enough that there was nothing he had that would mend what Brogan had been through; he'd been there, hadn't he? He'd watched as the family of the man who was his brother in many ways was murdered and he'd helped with the revenge.

It wasn't the blood. Harper had killed more people than he could recall. He'd seldom felt a bit of guilt over it, either. Raiders tried to take the caravan and he cut them down with arrow or blade as he saw fit. It was what he was paid for and he knew well enough that the very same men would have killed him given the chance. They might not have liked it any more than he did, but sometimes life required that you deal in death. It was the nature of the world and few knew that better.

He'd dealt with the Grakhul and the He-Kisshi before the latter came for Brogan's family. He'd taken their coin and served them as best he could when they required his services. Just like his father before him.

That was the part no one talked about. Old Volkner had always sneered at him when he was growing up. He understood that working for the Undying was not the sort of work a man did without getting stains on his soul. The bastard had known his father well enough. They'd shared more than a few drinks, and after his father passed, Volkner had stared at Harper as if he were the very essence of evil distilled into something dark.

Volkner and a lot of his ilk had always looked at Harper as less of a man, solely because his family was born into work and servitude with the He-Kisshi. Sometimes the Undying needed to get information they could not achieve on their own. Nothing to do with the sacrifices – that was why the Grakhul existed. Harper and his family, for generations back, had made deliveries to the Undying. They'd captured notes on some occasions and on others they'd sought and found rarities that the He-Kisshi needed for whatever reason. If there had ever been a dire need for any of what he'd found and delivered, it was a surprise to Harper.

Trinkets, most often. A ring found in a flea market, or a lock of hair to take from someone's bedroom in the night. There was usually an element of risk, yes, but the He-Kisshi did not hire the members of Harper's blood for their more dangerous abilities. They hired them to purchase, or steal, and then deliver, nothing that was more valuable than a memory. It might be that those who lost the items missed them. It might be they never noticed. Whatever the case, the Undying wanted those things and paid well. Sometime in the past they started dealing with Harper's family.

Harper shook the thoughts away and looked at Brogan again. There were strangers with him, though none stranger than the tall thing that stood at his side. And Anna Harkness was with him, too.

Anna, whose husband, Desmond, was not with them and might well no longer be alive. Harper had seen friends taken by slavers. He had no notion if they were alive or dead and no way to find out.

Telling Anna that Desmond was among the captured would not be a pleasant task.

Odobo called out to his helmsman and waited as he smoothly steered the ship around in an arc and then raced alongside the other vessel.

Brogan looked up at the higher deck where Harper stood and smiled again. "Come to get us?"

"Oh yes! It's time we were on our way, my friend." He looked away for a moment to the vast black clouds rising in the north, to the brilliant flashes of lightning that danced inside them. "It's going to get worse before it gets better."

Crewmen from the ship tossed ropes down to the low-riding barge and Odobo spoke to his counterpart on the other vessel. In moments the two ships were joined together and Brogan and Anna were the first to climb between them, scaling a plank that was dropped from one to the other.

As soon as Brogan was on the deck, Harper walked over and hugged his brother hard. He nodded to Anna, conscious as ever of the fact that Desmond – even when he was away and possibly dead – was a jealous man and a fearsome opponent.

"Desmond was captured, Anna. He was taken by slavers." He did not hide the facts. He did not lie to her. He wanted to soften the blow, but that had never truly been his way. "We don't know where he is, or if he is alive."

Anna looked hard at him and slowly nodded her head. "Time will tell. For now there is nothing we can do about the situation in any event." Her voice barely shook, and her lower lip hardly trembled. She looked away, irritated at what must have surely been a mote of dust in her eye. Truly she was a strong woman. But he'd known that all along.

Brogan spoke softly. "First the gods. Then we find Desmond. You have my word, we will find him if he is alive to be found."

Brogan looked away, studied the clouds, his eyes shifting and squinting as if he might find some secret hidden in the depths of that massive storm.

He spoke again, but it was barely a whisper. "First the gods."

CHAPTER THREE
SACRIFICES

Myridia

Myridia stared out at the sea with a sense of dread that she could not understand. The ocean had always been her home as surely as the land, and here, on the far side of the continent from where the gods had started their destructive rampage, the waters were calm and promised nothing but easy fishing and pleasant weather. The fishing was true. The weather was deceptive, but still, as servants of the gods, the Grakhul seldom had to worry about the destructive forces the gods amassed.

The trouble seemed to come from the north. She looked that way and saw nothing amiss. The weather was calm. The seas unmarred by disaster.

The rest of her people worked. She would join them soon enough but for the moment she had to worry about what it was that filled her with such a deep and abiding dread.

Brogan McTyre had killed her world. Her life mate

was gone. The gods had leveled the land where she'd been born, and raised. The man who'd tried to save his family, and failed, had destroyed her people in retaliation, killing the men and enslaving the women and the children. The gods had ordered the women to come to the Sessanoh, to restore the place called the Mirrored Lake and to prepare for sacrifices again. There had never been a time in her life when Myridia did not follow the orders of the gods and there was no reason not to listen now, but that dread kept circling around in her heart and mind. It was not the end of the world she feared. It was something different. Something she could feel and yet had no precedent for.

Lyraal walked toward her, the wind ruffling her pale hair. Her sword was held in the usual position, wrapped in linen and carried over both shoulders. The other woman, who should have been the leader as far as Myridia was concerned, looked out over the ocean for a long moment before speaking. She was always wiser that way. That was only one of the reasons Myridia would have preferred to defer to her. "We are as prepared as we can be. The Sessanoh has been sanctified in the eyes of the gods. All we can do now is wait."

Myridia nodded her and then answered, "There is something wrong. I can feel it in my guts." She placed her hands on her abdomen and looked at her friend and second in command.

"Others feel it, too." Lyraal shrugged. "I feel nothing, but I am not a cautious sort." She touched the hilt of the heavy sword over her shoulders, one finger tapping the oiled leather wrappings. "We should all remain prepared. It is too easy to think we are safe from danger this far from anyone else."

Myridia sighed heavily and nodded. "Best we be prepared. Double the sentries. No one stands alone."

Lyraal looked into her eyes for a moment and slowly nodded. "I'll see to it." The woman pointed at Myridia with her chin. "You see to being prepared yourself. When the gods make the demands, we must be ready to offer them what they require. We are the last chance this world has, Myridia."

"Yes, I know." She also knew why her friend was speaking to her like she might be a simpleton. She'd allowed a troupe of humans close and before all was said and done those humans, possessed by something else, had tried to kill them and partially succeeded. Her own sister was dead now and that death weighed heavily on her. Bad choices had been made because she was frightened and lonely. That could not happen again. She had to be stronger than the others if she was going to lead them, and as the gods had decreed she should be the leader, she would listen and obey. That was her place in life. The gods made demands and she made certain those demands were answered in kind.

Something had happened the day before. Something vast and terrifying had occurred to the north and east. Though they were far from the Broken Swords Mountains, they'd felt the earth shake, had seen the waters off the shore vibrate with unseen violence. That was not the source of her growing dread, but she suspected the two were likely connected. Everything was connected in the eyes of the gods. The He-Kisshi had not yet shown themselves and she worried about that, too. The Undying were the messengers of the gods, the voice with which the gods spoke to the Grakhul and she had already caused enough troubles. She wanted advice. She wanted to be told how to handle the dread that threatened her and her people.

Myridia did not wear a crown and she did not want one. She had no desire to lead her people in anything, and yet here she was, chosen by the gods.

She prayed they had not made a mistake as she once again turned to the northern waters and sensed something coming her way

Bron

He burned. Every inch of his flesh, the blood in his veins, the teeth in his mouth and the eyes in his head, all of him burned and in the burning was remade.

Flames sculpted new nerves, new sinews, and the very hairs on his head. The pain was incandescent and he glowed along with it, screaming in uncountable agonies with his newborn throat and howling his pains to the god that made him anew.

Sometimes a king had to suffer for his people.

Was he a king?

Yes. He believed that he was.

Did he have a name?

Yes, though it took time to remember it. Bron McNar. He was the king of Stennis Brae and he'd offered himself to Theragyn, the demon, for a chance to escape the fate the gods offered. What choice did he have? The gods had gone mad and torn the world asunder. His home and his castle were besieged by storms and ice and the infernal He-Kisshi had come into his home not once, but twice, and made threats, demanded that he kill his own blood if he wanted his people spared for another month.

He breathed in fire and coughed out something dark that soured the air around him.

The pain was impossible, but he endured. He had no choice. This was the test that Theragyn had given him. He either endured, or he failed his kingdom. He endured or he died.

In the end, he endured.

Bron walked out of the flames and into gloriously cool air. He breathed out the heat and sucked in fresh, painless breaths.

The pain faded as quickly as an ember tossed in a pail of water cools.

Parrish looked at him and smiled softly. "Welcome to the fold, Bron."

The words were genuine. He stared at the other king, once his enemy, and nodded. There was an awareness inside of him that had not been there before. The world itself looked different to Bron and he saw with more colors than he had ever noticed. Every sense was keener. He could smell more than he should have, and his hearing, which had never been all that good after he was struck on the side of his head by a very heavy shield, was sharper than he'd ever thought possible.

"Give yourself a moment, Bron. It will take some adjusting to."

Bron nodded without speaking, looking down at

his arms. They were covered in the same markings that covered Parrish and the other Marked Men.

His discomforts, the signs of a man who had lived a long and often violent life, were gone. His muscles did not hurt. His scars did not sting, and his knees no longer carried the perpetual ache that had haunted him for years.

"Impossible."

"Nothing is impossible for gods, Bron. Theragyn is a god." Parrish shrugged his shoulders. "He has remade you. Just as he did me. Close your eyes and think of the north."

He did as he was instructed and saw the ruin of the Broken Swords in his mind. The vast mountain range was shattered. The stone and crystal that had once been the barrier that protected Stennis Brae from eastern attacks was gone. The vast spine of the range was crippled and where the highest spires of stone had been there was now a gigantic hole filled with water, and the shape of something long dead and impossibly large rested in that turbulent sea, half-submerged but riding atop a form he could not clearly define. Two corpses of impossible scale, where once had been mountains.

Stennis Brae should have been ruined in that moment. He could see where the castle he called home had been, and where the towns around his vast keep had rested, but there was no sign in that spot of any structures.

They were to the west, beyond the mountain range instead of nestled within it. The growing horror he'd felt was washed away with that simple knowledge.

Bron dropped to his knees and looked around him at the stone interior of the place simply called the Cauldron by Parrish and his new god alike. The stone tower was impressive from the outside, but impossible from within. He could see miles of stone passageways ahead of him and behind, interspersed with trees the likes of which he had never seen before and firepits that lit the world for as far as he could see.

None of that mattered. He could close his eyes and see his kingdom, his people, safe from the devastation that had literally shattered mountains and felled gods.

Parrish put a hand on Bron's broad shoulder.

"Now you understand. Now you can see why I turned my back on the gods of old. They are weak and they are tired. Theragyn grows stronger by the day."

Bron nodded but did not speak. The world was too new, too fresh and his people were safe.

Whatever Theragyn demanded would be his so long as the god could accomplish that. He swore it silently and felt the god's sigh of satisfaction.

Light and flame flared into a tower of fire a dozen steps away. Within that conflagration flesh burned and a man screamed. Whoever he was he tried to suck in a fresh breath and inhaled heat and fire.

A moment later the flames faltered and the body of King Pardume of Saramond crashed to the stony ground. He did not breathe. He did not move. His flesh was burned and blistered and his skin was not Marked.

Bron stared down at the dead man and shook his head.

"What happened to him, Parrish?"

Parrish looked at the smoldering corpse and sneered. "He was weak."

Bron nodded and said nothing more.

Beron

The restless masses stood behind him and Beron allowed himself a smile. Lightning shattered the calm and thunder followed shortly after, a wild storm, a fury that was terrifying.

He knew exactly how that storm felt. It was time. Behind him they stood, waiting for a single gesture. He would not disappoint.

He raised his sword and pointed toward the city's center. Nothing more needed saying.

They moved and followed him as he started riding forward. Those few that still had horses rode at the front. It was a sight to behold, really. He had led many people into combat before, but never so many followers.

Some had weapons. Others found whatever they could use. Impossible numbers marched with him as he stormed toward Torema proper, and as his horse moved faster, they began to run.

He called out, "Ariah!" and the people around him took up the demon's name as their own chant.

The first person to stand in his way had no part in the battle that he could see, but the man was in the wrong place, and so he killed him with a swing of his sword. The blood that hit the blade seemed to hiss and smolder, though he could not have proved that in the excitement. All he knew, all that mattered, was that the man died and in so doing fed Ariah.

And Ariah was so very hungry. Gods, it seemed, could be nearly insatiable.

A small touch of each life given to the god was granted to Beron. Every death made him feel stronger and bolder and so he charged harder into the fray, his sword and spear both tasting flesh and stealing lives.

And all around him the rabble grew bolder as well, screaming out the demon's name as they bashed in heads, or cut throats. It wasn't long before the people ahead of them grew wise enough to flee, running away from the massive tide of people determined to take the city at any cost. The waters washed down from above and Beron saw the growing crimson stain that ran through it.

Small wonder then that Beron grew bolder still, and sought to take all that he could possibly want.

When he finally met resistance, he was genuinely surprised.

Torema had no army. That was something well-known by one and all. Though there were certainly guards of a sort, they did not wear uniforms and they most certainly did not move with military precision.

The Avenue of Kings – a road named for wealth, not for any sovereign – was as wide as any street in the entire town and moving down it was easy. A dozen men on horses could ride in formation and not block the cobbled street, and yet, just ahead of him the passage vanished, lost behind a collection of wagons and debris.

"Wagons? Is that all you have?" he called out, making certain that his associates could hear his contempt for the barrier.

Rather than answering with words, the fifty or so men behind the wagons rose into view and loosed bolts and arrows from whatever weapon was available. The crossbows did their work and the bolts plunged deep into flesh, often pushing through armor. The arrows did their work as well and it was one of those that cut the throat of the horse Beron rode.

The beast let out an astonishingly human noise and then fell forward, throwing Beron from his saddle.

For a big man he was very nimble and Beron rolled as he was thrown. The sword stayed in his hands, but the spear clattered into the street.

More arrows cut through the air and more bolts followed. Beron stayed low as he moved forward and the people behind him did their best to follow his lead, though it cost several of them their lives.

The mob that followed him faltered, and Beron scowled.

Easy to be brave when there's no resistance. He had to show them courage, or they would run. Beron reached his spear and lifted it, looking toward the barricade ahead of him.

One throw was all he would get and he knew it.

He hurled the spear at the closest bowman and watched the weapon cut through the air with a flawless trajectory. He'd have bet good gold that his aim was off, but the spear struck his target just the same and the keen tip of the thing cleaved through a rusty breastplate and hammered into the heart of his foe.

He did not wait to see if anyone noticed. There was

no time. Beron ran forward, screaming Ariah's name, and let his sword take care of the next enemy. The blade was true and split a man's face in two, carving a bloody swath down to the breastbone.

A turn, a swing and the next in line fell.

Beron reached for the haft of his spear and looked toward his enemies, a savage grin on his face.

Most of them were cowed. Behind Beron the people who followed him once again took up Ariah's name and made it a battle cry.

"Tear it down!" He bellowed the words and they listened, charging at the wagons and the barrier of street carts and debris that blocked them from taking control of the city.

It was glorious!

For all of three minutes. He drove forward and slashed and stabbed and if he should have felt exhausted by the constant motion, Ariah's Grace kept him going. He gasped for air, he blocked and parried and cut into his enemies, and his heart remained steady instead of hammering away and his eyes remained keen and his blades did their work.

The wave of followers surged against the barrier and shattered it with ease, pushing the wagon to the side, hurling vases and furniture out of the way as easily as Beron himself threw his spear.

As soon as they broke through, however, the far better-organized defenders took to the task of killing them. There were arrows, of course. And spears. Swords aplenty. The people using those weapons were skilled and absolutely determined to stop the would-be invaders.

Ariah's name stopped coming from a thousand throats, and Beron watched on, more outraged than shocked, as his forces were driven backward. Some retreated, but most died for their troubles. There were no uniforms, no banners. There were weapons and shields, all of the things missing from the forces he led, and there were orders called harshly by a voice that was familiar enough to make the end of his assault feel like a complete betrayal.

"Stanna!" The woman turned and looked his way, her expression as grim as he felt.

There were plenty of people he'd fight without hesitation, but Stanna was not one of them. She was a terror in combat and even if she were unarmed – which she was not – he'd have hesitated.

Stanna swung the Bitch, her well-used long sword, with all the ease of a dagger, and headed for him. "Retreat, Beron! I've no desire to fight you."

"Then let us pass!" He spat the words and she shook her head, smiling. Around them, her forces were cutting his people apart.

"Hillar says to keep you out and she pays me well. No choice in this."

"We served together for years."

"Aye. And you would do the same if the tides were reversed."

She had him there.

"Stand aside, Stanna. I don't want to hurt you."

She nodded. "I don't want to be hurt, and yet, here we are."

There was no choice. Beron charged forward, his spear in one hand, the sword of Ariah nearly singing in his grip.

Stanna's heavy boot caught him square in the testicles while he was looking at her sword. The impact was enough to send him staggering back and the damage done to his nethers came up like a wave and had him vomiting a second later.

"Hunn. Ah." It was all he could say.

Stanna did not wait for him to recover. Her body slammed into him even as her sword knocked Ariah's blade aside. The force of the blow dropped Beron into the street, to wallow in the stew of his own puke, and the muck, and blood of his followers.

Ariah's sword clattered in the road and one of his followers grabbed the blade before Beron could muster the strength to move.

The pain passed through him in pulses that left him half-blind and dry heaving.

Stanna's sword came down upon his neck and sliced deep even as he saw Ariah's human form at the edge of his vision.

There was nothing to say as he died.

CHAPTER FOUR
BLOOD, LIKE RAIN

Stanna

Stanna had no idea where Beron's head had fallen. She looked. He was an ally once and she wanted to see his ashes burned properly, but there was no sign of his head and she'd been watching as the blade cut through his neck. The man's skull didn't fall free and roll away, it simply vanished.

There would be time to look later.

Around her the people she'd hired stormed into the crowd and cut them down with haste. There were a lot of Beron's followers and she needed them retreating. There would be no attacks tolerated. The outcasts would not be allowed to make a move against the city, not until Hillar said they could and that would never happen. Besides which, there were other armies she had to deal with.

The fool who'd grabbed up Beron's sword came for her, screaming and swinging wildly.

Stanna stepped aside as he ran past where she'd

been and then smashed the side of his head with the Bitch's pommel. He fell hard and flopped to the ground, twitching. A dent in his skull told her he'd not be getting up any time soon.

Temmi stalked past her. The younger woman carried a much smaller sword and short spear. She held them in the proper way and Stanna nodded her approval. Her young lover was learning well, though she also sported a few cuts to show where her enemies managed to cause her harm.

A man charged from behind her, intent on bashing Temmi's head in with a wooden post made into a weapon. As the girl was momentarily busy stabbing another fighter in the shoulder, Stanna took it upon herself to cut down the one who was trying to sneak in for the kill.

Her sword nearly severed his head, and he dropped his weapon and flopped bonelessly into the rising waters.

They were rising, too. The entire field of battle was on a slope, and the waters were coming down so fast that they were rapidly making their own stream. It wouldn't be long before the current was strong enough to lift bodies.

Even as she was considering how to break the spirit of her enemies, they started to retreat. Encouraged by the sight of their enemies running, her followers let out a bellow of their own and gave chase.

Stanna did not strike anyone else. Instead she kept watch for possible sneak attacks but there were none.

When she looked at the ground around her she frowned. Something was wrong.

"Ah. How in the name of the gods?"

Beron's body was gone now, missing as surely as his head.

The waters were not nearly strong enough.

Stanna suppressed a shiver and looked around again, paying closer attention. In the closest alleyway, something white and very nearly hairy squatted in a narrow corner between two buildings. She squinted and tried to make out what it was, but the rains were too violent and the image was blurred.

"Enough."

She shook her head and then swept the long hair out of her eyes. She'd cut the stuff down to the skin in most places and contemplated hacking away the rest of it to stop it impeding her view any longer.

Interlude: The Sisters

The soldiers in civilian attire milled around for a few moments and then followed Stanna's call. There were two more armies at the very least, which would likely be trying to take the city. They all needed to be dealt with and soon.

When they were gone and the bodies of the dead lay across the ground, spilling more of their cooling blood into the waters running toward the bay, Ariah's child pushed her hand through the layers of silk that held her suspended against the brick walls of the alleyway.

Her claws allowed easy purchase on the surface that held her and she carefully moved herself to the ground, stretching her limbs and shivering in the unexpected waters. She was cold. That would likely never change until Ariah remade the world in his image.

She had started off as one of the Grakhul and then been altered into a nightmare of metal and withered flesh. She had been seeded, fertilized by the altered He-Kisshi, turned into a larva that looked remarkably like she had when she first appeared in the world, but that was done now. After gestating within her cocoon, the creature took on a final form that was green, glorious and freed of traditional flesh.

She looked around her and saw with eyes that were entirely different than what she had known before. The effect was momentarily disorienting. The water ran over her feet, chilling, but not harmful.

In the distance she heard a new sound, a deep, thrumming rattle that sang to her. One of her sisters was now awake. Before she could respond she heard another similar sound from a different location. They were all awakening.

It was almost time.

Ariah would be pleased.

Interlude: The Blood Mother

Theryn looked out at the continuous rain and scowled. All the wealth in the world changed nothing if they could not leave their new homes.

Being of sound mind and substantial fortune, the Blood Mother of Hollum had managed to procure very fine rooms for her and her chosen when they rode to Torema. Had the rains stopped she'd have been content with that.

The rains were not stopping and her seconds paced like a pack of starving mutts looking at a fresh roast just beyond their reach.

Naza glanced her way and very nearly growled. "We cannot stay here."

Theryn looked at the heavy scar tissue that covered most of her lieutenant's face and hands, and nodded. Naza was a deadly enemy to have and her skills were undeniable. She no longer wanted to be here.

"We need a ship."

Choto snorted. "I already have one waiting, but it won't wait forever. The city is doomed. We need to leave."

"There are guards on us. They expect us to leave."

Kemm peered out the window before answering. "So we pay them or we kill them, but either way there's no longer a Torema in a few days and if it sinks, we sink with it."

Choto gestured to the four chests of gems they'd already procured. They had more wealth than they could ever use. They had no intention of getting rid of it, either. There were other lands and they needed to reach them. Wherever they went they could make their fortunes all over again if they needed to, but it was easier to start with a strong bargaining position than to reacquire it.

Rik did not speak. He dared not. He was barely allowed to live. Having betrayed his Blood Mother for the benefit of his true love, he was in a dangerous position, especially since the girl he loved above all else was Tully, who was currently wanted by Theryn for her treacherous behavior in the past.

Tully claimed she had never betrayed Theryn and Theryn was inclined to believe her, but her actions spoke of a different situation. If she was innocent of stealing from the Blood Mother, she should have stayed in Hollum and proven her innocence.

Whatever the case, Theryn was not completely willing to forgive either of them yet. They needed to be reminded that loyalty was rewarded and foolishness was punished.

Theryn looked around the suite of rooms they now lived in. It was enough for ten. She was not satisfied. She had spent her entire life building her own army, the union of thieves in Hollum, and at the end there was nothing left of it but a scattering of the finest thieves and cutthroats in the world.

And that union would be moving on.

"Why are we discussing anything? The money is ours. Go kill them and let us be about the business of getting to your ship, Kemm."

Her lieutenants smiled, even Rik. A moment later she was alone in the room and listening to the rain fall in sheets outside her very lovely prison cell. She rose gracefully and headed for the window.

"They'll not have all of the fun."

Because of who she was, because of what she did and because, somewhere out there in the city, Tully had the ear of important people, there were thirty guards around the building. Some were in plain sight and others pretended to be doing other things. Directly below them there were four men who played at cards and genuinely never seemed to sleep.

The windows opened to let in the cooling breezes from the ocean, though just now those very winds seemed a bit too chill.

Theryn crouched on the sill for a moment and carefully set her hook into the wooden frame, making sure it was properly secured before she used the silk line to drop down toward the window below.

It was open, as she knew it would be. The men in that room sat together playing cards and speaking softly. Like as not they'd heard at least a few of the words coming from the room above, were trying to make sense of the Hollum dialect. It would have been easier for them if they were members of the Union of Thieves and could understand the coded phrases that had been used in the conversation. Suspicion did nothing to make their case.

There were actually six men. Four of them played cards. Two were asleep on narrow cots. The one facing the window stared at her with wide eyes as she descended her nearly transparent rope.

"What in the hundred hells?" He was fast, she gave him that. The man pushed back his seat and was standing before her feet touched the open windowsill.

She was faster. The dagger slipped from between her fingers and streaked through the air, flawlessly driving into his left eye.

The guard fell back, a scream stuck on his lips. Her second throwing knife sliced the ear of the man on the left, but he was moving too quickly and the damage was minimal. He hissed and continued to rise, his hand grabbing the club he'd rested against the table.

Amazing how many people felt a club was a poor

weapon, but Theryn knew better. She'd taken more than one blow from them over the years and had suffered a broken wrist defending herself from one in the distant past.

Because she knew better than to underestimate the danger the club presented, she moved fast and drove the business end of one of her blades into the wielder's throat.

By that time the other two men had managed to get out of their seats, though one of them was still fighting to draw his own dagger from the sheath at his waist. The same blade she'd killed his friend with drove through his temple even as he finally got his weapon free.

The last of the conscious men let out a battle cry that nearly shook the walls. The blade of her free hand smashed across the bridge of his nose and broke it. He backed up, blinking furiously as the blood started spilling from both nostrils. While he was busy trying to recover his senses, she stabbed him in the neck three times and then stepped back before he could hit the table and then the wooden floor.

Thunder shattered the momentary silence.

The two men rolled from their cots, ready for combat. Even if they had been sleeping, they were very obviously seasoned fighters. Both took proper stances and one of them slid sideways, moving to bar her from escaping the way she came in.

There was no consideration of trying to talk her way out of the situation. Theryn was not called the Blood Mother because of her skills in raising children.

The man to her left, trying to block the window,

was nervous; he could see the dead around her and knew exactly how quickly she had taken them out.

The man to her right nodded, to himself, she assumed, and reached for the whip on his belt. Not a perfect weapon for close quarters, but it would do the job if he could strike first.

Theryn slid across the floor, using one foot to propel her and raising the other higher, kicking at the man's head.

He reached for her leg, prepared to block, and while he was thus distracted, she threw the dagger at his face.

The blade punched through his cheek and clacked audibly against his teeth.

He let out a loud yelp and reached for the pain in his face, dropping his whip and his dagger alike, which was when she drove her fingers into his eyes and temporarily blinded him.

Her hands grabbed at his ears and hauled him forward. He moved with her, the sudden pain making him momentarily docile, and she used him as a shield between her and the man blocking the window.

It was a well-timed ploy as the guard had been coming for her and now was forced to hesitate. She could see him considering which was more important, stopping her or avoiding the death of his partner.

The man in her hands thrashed, pushing against her, and she slipped away, letting him flail.

He was a perfect distraction.

Theryn's next attack was not a knife, but a thin needle. The weighted tip stuck in the neck of the man near the window and he hissed at the sudden pain.

And then he died. The poison was expensive, but it was useful.

By the time he'd hit the ground, Theryn had her arm around the neck of the last man and was choking the life from him. He could not breathe and her arm was positioned to cut off the blood flow to his head. He struggled for a few seconds and then collapsed. She lowered him to the ground and kept her grip. The sounds of his neck bones breaking were like a lover's song for her.

She checked the apartment one last time and then left through the doorway, moving into the hall and then down the stairs to street level. By the time she walked outside the rest of her crew was with her. There were no words. They moved back up the stairs and gathered their belongings.

The ship was waiting. The rains were falling harder, and as far as she could tell the world was ending.

Until it did, she would fight and kill to keep what was hers.

And if she happened across Tully before then, she'd peel the flesh from the foolish girl.

CHAPTER FIVE
WAR

Tully

Tully stared at the long ranks of horsemen and decided she could find better things to do with her time. Most of her friends were within arm's reach but she found that didn't matter much. She started to back up and felt Stanna's hand on her shoulder.

"None of that. Just wait right where you are."

Tully looked at the larger woman. "They've horses."

Stanna nodded her head. "Aye."

"And armor."

Another nod. "Oh, yes."

"And there are a lot of them. A damn sight more than I expected."

"There always are."

"So why am I supposed to stay here?"

"Because we have to direct them the right way."

"And where is that?"

"West of town."

"And how are we going to do that?" Tully frowned.

Seemed she knew all the answers a few minutes earlier, but watching the numbers of soldiers increase, all rational thought tried hard to escape her.

They had not yet started their charge into the city, but the armies of King Opar were impressive even from a distance. They stood at the northern edge of the valley that swept down to Torema. The slope was gentle enough but rains were washing down in a constant torrent and Tully wondered how the horses would fare.

In the long run, she figured it didn't matter much. The horses could fall down and their sheer weight would crush the city.

"How many do you suppose there are, Stanna?"

"Ten thousand or so."

Temmi, ever the optimist, replied, "More like seventeen thousand or so. Plus there are probably supply wagons. Not that they'd have much left to them after all that traveling. I expect they'll be ready to plunder."

The storms cut loose with a barrage of lightning and a nearly constant drum roll of thunder to follow the light show. The rains, already heavy, grew worse.

Tully shook hair from her face. "Why don't we just go find that ship you were talking about and get away from this place?"

Stanna looked at the growing tide of soldiers looming over the city and frowned. The angle wasn't perfect, but they could all tell that the soldiers ran as far as the eye could see. They were waiting for something, and all the runner had told Stanna was that there were more soldiers still coming.

Stanna tilted her head and closed her eyes for a moment, then she nodded. "Right. We're leaving. Head for the docks."

Tully turned her head so fast she felt a hot flare of pain in her neck from a muscle protesting. "Really?"

"Really. There's nothing here to fight for. We're leaving town."

Temmi frowned. "What about your word to Hillar Darkraven?"

"I fought one war today. Don't want to do a second. Or a third." Stanna shrugged her massive shoulders. "And like as not, Hillar is taking this time to prepare her ships for leaving."

Before Temmi could respond, and judging by her expression she was ready for a long argument, horns sounded in the distance. The sound was repeated in several locations to the north of the city and the armies of Giddenland moved forward with frightening efficiency.

There was nothing of the scattered remnants they'd fought earlier. These soldiers were armed, armored, and well-trained.

Temmi looked to Stanna and nodded. "Right. Let's be off then."

Stanna looked to one of her lieutenants. Tully recognized him. Rhinen, of the dark hair and the blue eyes. He had a nice smile half-hidden under a thick, mutton chop mustache. Stanna said nothing, but made several gestures with her hands.

Rhinen nodded, then looked to Tully and smiled, before calling his people to arms. All around them the ex-slavers and the citizens of Torema moved as a unified front, sliding around Stanna and her closest companions.

Stanna turned her horse toward Torema and started to ride. Tully and Temmi followed, but Tully kept looking over her shoulder, frowning as the forces moved to meet the enemy.

"Are they not retreating?" She had to yell to make herself heard as the army that had gathered behind them surged toward the invaders.

Stanna shrugged. "This is their home."

"What about us then?"

Stanna skewered her with a hard glance. "Did you not say you wanted to leave?"

"Well, yes, but–"

"Then we leave. Before this gets worse – and it will only get worse."

"What about Rhinen?"

Stanna shook her head and frowned. "He will live and retreat, or he will die. I cannot say."

Tully turned her head several times. Then she shook the thoughts away and frowned. She was starting to think like Niall Leraby and that was a mistake. It was time to look out for herself; that, if nothing else, she had learned from the Blood Mother. The rest would have to sort itself.

Behind them the sounds of combat began.

Tully looked over her shoulder and saw the horsemen from Giddenland charging down the slope, rain waters splashing at the hooves of their horses and banners hanging limply in the torrential rains.

She knew the plans, of course. The notion was to hit from the east and drive the invaders to the west.

They couldn't hope to defeat those numbers, but if they could move them west, then the Giddenlanders would take care of the Hollumites left to their own devices on the other side of Torema.

No. There was no reason to stay. It had all been said before. Torema was doomed. The only wise choice was to flee into the ocean and the only way to do that was to get on a ship.

The war was a lovely distraction. It let those with the right connections or money reach the ships first. Currently Tully had the right connections. She counted her blessings and moved away from the battle.

A voice in her mind said she was a coward. She ignored that voice as best she could.

Brogan

The winds railed against the ship and the waves lifted and settled around it, but the vessel was well-built and despite all of that, Brogan was comfortable for the moment.

There were discussions. They were inevitable. All things considered, he was surprised by how many of his companions had made it to Torema in the first place, especially when one considered how many wanted them dead. Perhaps it was a sign that the gods did not control everything as much as he believed. Perhaps it was mere dumb luck. He could not decide.

Anna was not pleased. Nor would he have expected her to be happy. Her Desmond was among the missing and there was simply no way to know if he were alive or dead. Despite her many abilities she could not simply cast a spell to see if he were among the living – there might be Galeans who could find out for her, but that was not one of her skills – and any attempt to locate him would simply point at where he was, not whether or not he still lived. That helped not at all, as they were on the move and there would be no time to go back to find him.

Some things took precedence, no matter how much they might wish otherwise.

First they had to finish this impossible war with the gods and then they could go looking for loved ones. That fact stood true, but was not well-liked by anyone.

Brogan thought of all of these things as he ate the food offered him. There was little that was fresh, but at least the captain of the ship had some fruit that hadn't rotted away.

"So, where to then? Where do we go from here?" Anna pointed to the city in the distance. "We do not need to be there."

"No." Brogan shook his head. "We do not. We need to go north."

"North is where the worst of this is." She looked his way, frowning.

Harper spoke up. "North is where the Gateway is."

"The Gateway?"

"The Gateway to the gods. It's a very large stone arch in the waters. We've seen it. It exists and according to what I learned as a child it is a doorway to the realm of the gods."

"So you plan on facing the gods?" The expression on her face said she knew it was a foolish question.

"I do." Brogan set down the fruit and reached for the cup of water next to his plate. "There's no choice in the matter. I have to end this."

"Is there no way for others to join you?" That came from Harper again.

"You can join me, but I don't know as it will do any good." He shrugged. "I'm supposed to be able to touch the gods now, but I don't think it's a trick I can share."

If anyone disagreed with him, they kept their mouths shut.

"I have to go north. That does not mean the rest of you do." He gestured with his free hand. "There are lands to the south. Some islands to the east of the Kaer-ru, as I understand it. They might keep you safe from the gods, at least for a time."

Before the conversation could go any further, Captain Odobo and his first mate knocked at the door to the cabin and opened it without asking.

Odobo smiled and bobbed his head nervously. Several men with swords, together with some 'thing', looked his way in response. Mostly he fixed his gaze on Faceless.

"I beg pardon. I do not mean to interfere, but the weather grows worse and I need to know where we are going."

Brogan looked around. He'd assumed the man already knew. "North. Up along the shoreline and north."

"The weather is bad there. The seas are violent."

"And yet that is where we need to go. If you are not up to the task, we can try to find another to captain the ship." Brogan was not in the mood to debate anything at all with the man. He had places to go and little time to discuss the matter with anyone.

"I do not know if the ship can survive."

"She seems seaworthy to me." Though he'd have admitted to knowing very little.

Harper interjected, "Do your best, captain. But if he says north is the direction then that is where we must go."

Odobo looked around and nodded, before his gaze once again found Faceless and stayed there.

"As you wish. I fear there will be little we can do by way of supplies."

"There are fish in the sea. We will not starve," Anna spoke up. "There are ways to purify water and I know a few of them. We will not die of thirst."

Odobo nodded again. "The waves from the north are greater than most would expect. I have recently been north of here and it is only through the grace of the gods that we survived."

Brogan felt his jaw clench.

Jahda, the tall man who'd joined them in the mountains, one of the Louron and, if he'd heard properly, the closest thing the Kaer-ru had to a king, spoke softly. "Do you know who I am, Captain Odobo?"

The man looked his way and slowly nodded, his smile faltering.

"We have reasons to go north. You have been tasked with getting us there safely. Do you believe you can do this?"

Odobo hesitated for a moment and finally nodded his head. "I can take you there. I merely warn that there are dangers."

"Your concern is noted, Captain Odobo." Jahda moved closer. "Just the same, we must go north."

The first mate looked ready to ask a question, but Odobo silenced him with a glance.

"If we must go north, then we shall go north. I think it best if we make landfall one last time for supplies, just the same." Odobo spoke firmly, but with deference.

"If we must, then we must, but it will have to be a very quick journey. We have a great distance to travel." Harper spoke calmly, but Brogan knew better, the man was annoyed at the very least.

"I merely think it best that we have full supplies."

"You were supposed to have stocked those already." Harper's expression was civil, but barely.

"We can go without, I suppose." Odobo did not sound pleased, and something about that tone bothered Brogan more than he'd have expected. It was a simple thing, really, to read most people, but the captain was not open. He did not share his words easily and his face was masked, even when he was smiling.

"No." Brogan stood up. "Perhaps it would be better to head to Kaer-ru. The supplies are likely better and there isn't so much risk of being attacked."

"Attacked?" Odobo's voice was loud, possibly louder than he meant it to be. He looked at Brogan with hard eyes. "What do you suggest?"

"People have grown desperate in Torema. The situation is dire. The people there might well try to overrun a ship in an effort to get away."

The expression on the captain's face was enough. It was relief and something else.

Still the man nodded. "Yes. The Kaer-ru would make more sense. Of course." He nodded his head several more times and smiled broadly. "I shall make the arrangements then."

Jahda spoke, and this time his voice carried an edge. "Make certain that you work quickly with the arrangements. Time is no longer our friend."

"As you say, Jahda." Odobo smiled and moved for the deck. His first mate followed him like a shadow.

When they were out of the room Jahda spoke softly again, barely above a whisper, but just loud enough to be heard by those close by. "I do not trust that man."

Harper nodded. "Nor I, but he was the best I could find. When we get to Kaer-ru I might seek another captain."

Jahda crossed his arms and lowered his head, a brooding expression shadowing the broad features that seemed better suited to smiling. "You should have him go to Louron. The docks there have several captains I would trust."

"Louron it shall be." Harper nodded a second time and headed for the deck. "I'll pass that on."

"Tell him the supplies can come from my personal stores. There will be no need of bartering. I shall gladly offer up whatever is needed."

Harper nodded again and moved faster. In a moment he was gone.

Anna watched him go, her eyes narrowed ever so slightly. It was not an angry expression as one might suppose, but a thoughtful one. Brogan had seen it several times in recent days and had come to know the difference.

Five feet away from him Faceless moved and headed up the flight of stairs, toward the deck above them. What his reasons were, was anyone's guess.

All of them watched the strange creature move and waited until he was gone before anyone spoke.

It was the Galean, Roskell Turn, who said it first. "I do not trust that creature."

"Why is that?" Brogan studied the well-dressed stranger.

"I cannot read its face. It has no face to read. How can I ever know what it is thinking?"

Brogan nodded. Anna mirrored the gesture.

So far the creature had done no harm, it could even be argued that the thing had been beneficial, but there was no way to know something that had no face and almost never spoke.

The ship shuddered in the impact of a wave that struck the side instead of being cut by the prow. To the last they were staggered by the impact, and Brogan scowled.

"If we truly have to add supplies, we need to be swift about it. The seas aren't likely to get calmer."

No one had an answer to that at first, but finally Jahda spoke again. He said, "We should check the ship's stores."

Brogan nodded his head again. "I've no idea how much a ship should have for supplies, but I know roughly what we'll need for this journey." He hoped that wasn't a lie. The only true measure he had was how long a wagon ride would last, heading that far north and how much would be needed to feed those who rode with it.

Horses, less than pleased to be on a ship in a turbulent sea, took half of the storage space. The rest was dry goods and barrels of water.

"Why are there horses in the storage area?" Brogan asked that question as soon as he found the rest of his crew, most of whom were currently trying their luck at resting in the rough waters. A few of the lads looked positively green.

Laram looked at him and shrugged as he rose from his cot. "Harper thought it a shame to leave trained horses behind; besides, we have no way of knowing what we will encounter once we get where we're going."

Next to him on the cot, the Scryer he'd fallen for lay in a very nearly fetal position. Her eyes were closed and her skin was even paler than usual, covered by a patina of sweat.

"Is she sick then?"

"Something happened with one of the gods. Whatever it is she won't say, but it's left her in this shape."

Brogan nodded, knowing full well that one of the gods was dead, slain in an effort to get to him and Anna before they could find a way to access the mind of Walthanadurn. It had been a matter of moments to decide if they would die or they would live and, in the end, a dead god buried in a mountain had decided they should live.

"Will she be all right?"

"She says the gods are screaming. It's all she can

hear most times. They are enraged."

"The gods are angry. That's not a new thing."

Laram nodded, never taking his eyes off Brogan. "Do you think we'll survive this?"

"Who can say? All we can do is try."

Anna spoke up, "We'll survive. We have no choice. If we fail the world ends. All of us die."

Laram looked her way and nodded. His eyes explained how much he grieved for her loss.

Brogan looked away – he had enough grief of his own. He had enough of pain and loss and misery. He preferred, especially now, to focus on anger. Grief would slow him down, but anger, properly held in check, would feed him and offer its own cold comfort.

Rather than face any more of the grief offered to Anna, he shook his head and moved toward the upper deck.

Enough.

Enough of sorrow.

The air was cold and bit at him, and he welcomed it. Better a hard, wet, chilled breeze than the stillness of the caves.

The sound of steel clashing against steel was one he was very familiar with and Brogan turned his eyes toward the noise even as he finished climbing to the deck's damp surface. His hand reached for the axe without conscious thought and he watched on as Harper knocked a man's blade aside with his longer sword and shoved the poor bastard back against one of the ship's masts.

True to form Harper's second, shorter blade lashed out and ended the man before he could defend himself.

The mutineers were not waiting in a line, however, and even as the blood flowed from Harper's latest victim three more men were doing their best to rush him.

Faceless grabbed one of them and hurled him over the side of the ship as if he weighed nothing. The man let out a yelp and a moment later hit the hard surface of the water at an awkward angle.

That was all the time that Brogan took for looking. Near as he could tell it was the whole crew of the ship that was attacking. Many of them stood aside, waiting to reach for Harper.

Rather than consider whether or not he might be in the wrong, Brogan strode forward and buried the blade of his axe in the neck and shoulder blade of the closest crew member. His foot kicked out and the blade came free, dripping meat and crimson fluids.

The second man in line had time to look his way before Brogan used the haft of the axe to shatter his face. Step, turn, strike and retreat, and the third fell.

Captain Odobo was the one who came for him next, all pretense of docile personality washed away, replaced with a hard stare, a scowl and a long blade that was just shy of being a proper sword. The man was good with it, too. His thrust would have gutted Brogan had he been a second slower in stepping back.

Swords were elegant weapons. Those that were well-made were good at deflection, thrusting, slicing and stabbing. Sadly the knife in Odobo's hands was close enough to prove that point. Brogan went on the defensive, parrying and blocking as best he could, while the captain tried to either gut him or carve away a few fingers.

Brogan ducked a hard thrust and moved in before the man could pull back the blade. His hand caught the sword arm's sleeve and held tight even as his axe swept in sideways and slapped the captain across his face with a hard steel surface.

Odobo grunted and tried to pull back, but Brogan held tight and shifted his axe enough to allow a proper cut at the bastard.

The blade caught the captain in the face and opened a wound from his chin up to his eye, narrowly missing taking the organ out in the process.

Odobo screamed but did not stop fighting. His free arm caught Brogan's tartan and pulled it tight as the man fell backward.

A moment later Brogan lay on the deck trying hard to understand how he got there.

Odobo would have had him if not for Faceless. The bastard came in hard and fast, his now freed sword aimed at Brogan's chest, and Brogan had long enough to acknowledge that he was as good as dead. Then the powerful strike was halted in mid-stroke as Faceless caught the sword arm and yanked Odobo backward with enough force to send the bastard flying.

He saw the look of shock on the captain's face, and then Odobo crashed into the railing. His body shattered wood and likely a few bones. The impact stopped him, but did not spill the bastard into the water.

Brogan got to his feet, nodded his thanks, and then went after the man with a vengeance. Odobo was getting to his feet when Brogan ran into him, knocking him sprawling across the deck. The axe came down hard and cut off Odobo's sword hand. He could have killed the man but he wanted answers.

Odobo shrieked and looked down at his ruined limb, eyes wide and unbelieving.

Brogan kicked him in the side of his head and watched him lying there, dazed and bleeding.

By that point Harper was cutting the throat of the first mate. Surely the largest saving grace was that Harper was dressed for cold weather, as there were several new holes in his cloak and a few cuts running the length of his heavy shirt, but surprisingly little blood flowing from any of those holes.

Faceless stomped down on the head of a crewmember with astonishing results. Enough blood exploded from the remains to have the rest of the crew surrendering in an instant, all of them staring at Faceless with expressions of absolute dread. The wooden deck was broken where Faceless had planted his foot, and within moments Jahda came up the steps and stopped in his tracks, staring at the bodies and the blood and then, finally, at Faceless.

Jahda said, "I was coming up to let you know that we have plenty of supplies. I don't think we need to head for Kaer-ru." He looked away from Faceless and stared at Brogan. "What has happened?"

Harper answered, "Captain Odobo decided that we could not be allowed to go north as we are harboring people whom the gods would see dead."

Brogan nodded, his questions answered that easily, and looked down at the unconscious man.

His hands caught the captain under each armpit and he looked to Harper. "Help me cast him overboard."

Harper nodded and moved toward the captain's sprawled legs.

Jahda said, "Is that necessary?"

"Was it necessary for him to try to kill Harper?"

"Harper could defend himself."

"If you can find a smaller vessel to take him, by all means let him live. If you cannot, I will not have him awaiting the chance to kill any of us while we sleep."

In the far distance the storms over Torema unleashed a fury of lightning strikes that lit the skies as surely as a clear day at noon. The blue-white light was brilliant enough to nearly blind anyone looking in that direction.

A moment later the thunder roared across the seas and the air blew colder than it had before.

Brogan swore to himself that it was not his imagination. Things were moving in those clouds. It seemed that shapes writhed and danced with the lightning and moved the storm closer still to the vast city.

Back to the more immediate problem. "The choice is yours, Jahda. But I will not have him on this ship. I will not let him kill any of the people here or risk him using other means than combat. This ship was his and he knows all the secret places where a danger might be hidden."

Jahda nodded.

"Also, did anyone else see things moving in the clouds just now?"

Jahda frowned. "I was not looking, but I will now."

And he turned toward Torema, his face a mask of concentration.

Harper spoke. "It isn't my imagination then. I thought I was seeing things."

Faceless spoke, and Harper backed away from the thing, scowling, worried. "There are shapes moving. They are not gods. They are not He-Kisshi. They are something else. A different creature."

"How do you speak without a mouth?" Harper's words were muttered, and Faceless did not respond.

Brogan asked, "What are they doing there?"

"They are directed by the gods. They work to destroy the city and the land. They are the punishment of the gods."

"And how do you know this?" Harper's voice was as calm as ever but Brogan was not fooled. His friend was unsettled.

Faceless turned his head with that quick, jerky motion he had and then tilted it. "I do not know. I simply do."

Harper said nothing, but he was as displeased by that answer as Brogan himself.

Jahda blinked and squinted as the next cascade of lightning bullwhipped the sky.

"There are things within those clouds. Or they are part of the clouds. Whatever the case, there are things there."

The men who followed Odobo mumbled amongst themselves until, finally, Brogan took note of them. "Which of you wish to stay with your captain?"

Not one of them spoke up.

"Which of you can pilot this vessel?"

Two of the men stepped forward.

"You will follow our orders and you will be rewarded with good pay, or you will defy those orders and I will offer you to him." He pointed at Faceless. "Do you understand?"

Both of the men nodded.

The first of them was a short, stout man with a clean-shaven face and a thick braid of blond hair. When asked his name he answered "Arumehn". The second was taller, and deeply tanned. His body was covered in freckles and his eyes were extremely light blue. What little hair remained on his head was as red as Brogan's. His name was Bramsen.

Brogan looked at each of the crew. "You have surrendered. If there is a boat, you may take your captain and go, if you prefer to stay here, you have the same offer. You are paid well or you are killed by him." Once again he pointed to Faceless and once again the men blanched at the notion.

Jahda barked at the crew in a different dialect, one unknown to Brogan. Within minutes three of the men had found a well-made raft and were preparing to lower it into the water.

Jahda explained. "I told them what you said, in a language they can understand. I also told them who I am, what people I come from, and threatened any who would betray us with a horrible death."

"More horrible than what Faceless did?"

"The death it offered was quick. I can promise a much slower death without any hope of mercy from the gods."

"And how is that?"

"I can take them where there are no gods."

Brogan nodded. "What a lovely thought."

Jahda stared at him for a moment in silence and then, "Is that what you seek, Brogan McTyre?"

"I seek a world where gods do not choose to kill my loved ones."

"That, I fear, will be a hard world to find."

Brogan nodded his head and looked to the storms again. "I expect no less. Still, one must have goals."

Thunder rumbled hungrily across the waves and the air grew colder still.

While he watched, the captain of the ship was lowered down to a few members of his crew. He continued staring as they moved the small boat away from the ship and bobbed along with waves that looked eager to swallow all of them.

He stayed there, deep in thought and staring, until the boat was lost in the distance.

CHAPTER SIX
UNANSWERED PRAYERS

Myridia

The pain in Myridia's guts grew worse and then stopped completely at almost exactly the moment Lyraal called out a warning.

She had been standing near the cliff's side and staring toward the vast structure they had just reclaimed. Her thoughts were turned toward the gods, the possible sacrifices they would have to make, and the real possibility that the world would end. There had been a time when reflecting on the gods had been a positive thing, but these days there was little Myridia could think of that made her happy.

The He-Kisshi had not returned yet to offer advice, or to let her know that the sacrifices were coming to her.

Instead there was silence from the gods and their servants alike.

If it was wrong that she felt abandoned, then she was wrong. There was nothing she could do to change her feelings at that time and, much as she disliked that fact, she had to live with it.

When Lyraal called out there was an odd note to her tone of voice, which had Myridia moving her way without even considering the situation.

Below, along the cliff that each of them had scaled to reach the Sessanoh, the waters seethed as if cast into a sudden storm. The waves, placid a few moments ago, hissed and crashed and within the waters she could see the impossible. There were white forms moving through the waves.

Pale figures with pale hair. As she watched several of them caught the rough stone with their hands and began to scale the side of the cliff.

And each of the figures she saw was male.

The last of the men from her species had been slaughtered by Brogan McTyre and his men. They were gentle, the men of the Grakhul, philosophers and dreamers and poets, but far more importantly they were the ones best suited for performing the ritual sacrifices to the gods. Though she had found copies of the sacred prayers and texts, and had been studying them since they arrived, Myridia still felt she was unsuited to the actual task put before her by the gods.

And here, just possibly, was the answer to her prayers. Perhaps the gods had been listening, after all.

Lyraal did not look quite as impressed.

"They are very healthy specimens, Myridia."

Myridia watched the men scaling the rough stone. There was no easy access to this Sessanoh. There was no need. For countless centuries the vast stone keep of the Mirrored Lake had waited for one sole reason, to act as a replacement for Nugonghappalur should the great hall of the gods ever fall. As impossible as the idea had seemed, the sacred land where she had been born and raised had been tainted and then destroyed by the actions of Brogan McTyre.

"Where do they come from?" Lyraal's words cut through her thoughts. The woman was eyeing the men with suspicion and had begun unwrapping her sword.

"If they are truly our kind, then surely the gods sent them."

The taller woman looked her way and frowned. "For what reason?"

"To make us complete?"

"Did the He-Kisshi mention these strangers to you?"

Myridia shook her head.

Lyraal shrugged. "Then I suggest we be prepared."

Without another word her second in command waved her arms until one of the younger girls noticed her and used gestures to tell the child to summon the warriors.

They came from every part of the vast keep and they came at a run, carrying whatever weapons they had acquired on their journey to the Mirrored Lake.

At the height of their time in the world, the Grakhul had numbered close to a million. That had been a very long time ago. Long before their murderer came along, the race had dwindled to a few thousand. Time moves on and so do the whims of the gods. Now less than three hundred women made up the sum of the species.

Unless one counted the long line of men climbing toward them from the waves.

That was the challenge, wasn't it? She had to know if they were truly Grakhul, and what they planned to do once they reached the women.

A gesture and the very best they had took the front of the lines, and waited for the men. Myridia's own sword, Unwynn, rested across her shoulders, the keen edge kept away from her bare skin.

"What is happening?" Memni was young and often foolish, but she could fight.

Lyraal tried to silence the girl but Myridia answered. "There are men who look like us coming here. We must judge if they are our kind or a trick sent to fool us."

"Why would anyone want to deceive us?"

"Why would anyone want to sell us into slavery, girl?" Lyraal's voice was harsh. "We will know when we meet them."

They didn't have long to wait. The first of the men climbed over the edge of the long precipice and looked at the gathered women with a slowly growing smile. He was a handsome one, with a strong jawline and a broad, athletic chest. His skin glistened in the daylight and his hair was long and left free in the breeze from the south.

Myridia stepped forward. "I am Myridia. I serve as leader here. What are you called?"

The blue eyes that regarded her did not share the warmth of his smile. "I am Urhoun. We have come from the north, summoned by the gods to take command of the Sessanoh and prepare for the sacrifices to come."

"The Sessanoh has been prepared and we are ready to serve the gods."

His eyes scanned her with obvious contempt. "Women cannot serve the gods in this way. You have wasted your time."

Lyraal cast a look toward him as if he had just insulted her heritage.

Myridia tried for diplomacy, but the place where her stomach had been aching now frosted over. She did not like the way he spoke and suspected the men would prove troublesome.

She was not wrong.

"We have been told what to do by the gods and we have done it." Myridia looked at the man and considered the various ways in which the situation might work itself out. After the time she had spent reaching the Sessanoh and the sacrifices she had made, there was only one answer that could come from the man that would satisfy her.

"We also follow the gods and they've told us to take this place and sanctify it properly." His smile fell away as more of the men climbed over the edge of the cliff and joined him. For the first time she noticed that each of them had a manacle on one arm – sometimes the left and others the right – and that each of the manacles had a length of chain running to the long blades they carried.

Every single one of the men was armed and ready for battle.

Myridia shrugged her shoulders and Unwynn fell comfortably into her grip.

"You have obviously misunderstood the gods, Urhoun. You and your men should leave now."

Not far away she saw Lyraal smile and felt a surprising level of joy in the knowledge that the woman approved.

There were five men on the surface along with Myridia and her fellow warriors.

"Take them." Myridia swept Unwynn into the air as she stepped toward Urhoun. The man's eyes grew wide. Apparently he expected her to bow to his might. He was sadly mistaken.

The man's blade was quick and he blocked her attack, though it cost him dearly to defend against her sword. He staggered back and reached the edge of the cliff, his balance lost. She kicked him even as she brought the sword around a second time and the man who'd challenged her authority fell over the side, dropping toward the waters below.

Lyraal's chosen target let out a scream of pain as her sword sheared through half of his forearm. He had tried to block her attack and failed. She pulled the sword back and the man dropped his weapon and stared, horrified, at the blood flowing from his arm. While he was so occupied, she brought her blade around again and drove the tip through his chest.

Not far away the other men who'd managed to scale the cliff realized how badly they were outnumbered and did their best to retreat. Two of them managed to dive back into the water. A third died with a pitchfork through his chest. Verla, the wielder of the aforementioned weapon, pulled the pitchfork back and left him bleeding on the ground.

"This is going to get very bloody." Lyraal spoke, but did not sound unhappy about the idea.

"Why are you smiling?"

"I have never answered to men and I don't plan to start now." She shook her head. "Where would they get this notion?"

Even as they spoke more men were scrambling over the side of the cliff and standing. The women were ready and repelled them as they climbed.

It might have been an easy task. It should have been easy, but Memni called out and pointed. "There are so many of them!"

With her heart thudding heavily, Myridia moved closer to the edge and risked a look over the side.

They had the advantage of being on the high ground.

The male Grakhul had the advantage of numbers. Near as she could tell somewhere around three hundred men were scaling the cliff directly below her and another two hundred or so were climbing to either side of the main group.

Easily two thousand more men were still in the waters.

Lyraal looked over the side and shook her head.

"We may not win this."

Myridia said nothing. She was too busy praying to the gods.

CHAPTER SEVEN
MOVING ON

Tully

By the time they reached the docks the flow of people trying to leave Torema had grown from a trickle into a flood. It was the armies as much as anything else. The sheer volume of people trying to seize the city proved to be a tipping point and the majority of the travelers who remained looked to the sea and saw the possibility of escape.

The only good news was Stanna and her closest allies. The men who rode with them were hardened and desperate. They wanted to live and they wanted to get away from Torema. That meant they followed Stanna's lead and currently she was leading with devastating sword strokes.

The Bitch drew blood with every strike and those confronting Stanna tended to find retreat was a wonderful notion. The horses smashed into anyone who failed to move fast enough and more than a score of people had been crushed under their mounts by Tully's count. Not that she was keeping count, exactly. It just sort of happened. She saw them and kept a tally even as she moved forward and added her own strikes to the bloody swath they made on their way to the docks.

Once there the situation was no better. People were in a panic. Some were trying to swim to the ships in the harbor, several with all they owned strapped to their bodies. Many valuables did not float, and what might have been as many as half the people trying their luck with that method sank beneath the violent waves.

And the waves were truly violent. The weather had turned sour hours before and the waters seemed higher than should have been possible. Water and mud and blood all washed into the bay, staining the waves in shades of black and red alike. Corpses bobbed along those very waves and among them people tried to tread water while seeking a haven on the ships. Stanna dropped from her horse and moved toward the farthest part of the docks, hacking her way through the crowds without any noticeable remorse. Tully and Temmi stayed close to her and followed in her wake, keeping the area open with threats and screams and the occasional jab of a blade. More of the slavers followed, just as determined to get out of the entire affair intact.

People, horses, dogs, goats and more cats than Tully knew could exist were all along the docks and seemed to gather directly between them and their goal.

Stanna knocked them all aside, excepting only a substantial ox that looked angry enough to defend itself. The ex-slaver was strong, but not foolish.

When they finally reached her destination, she let out a shrill whistle and waited. Within minutes a small boat came toward them. People all around them grew agitated, sought to get the favor of the man steering the thing, but Stanna shoved and cut her way through them as well. It was not a large boat. Tully eyed it dubiously, and considered taking her chances on the shore, but ultimately decided she wanted to risk living if she could manage it.

Still people tried. They begged, they sobbed, they cried and they fought. The slavers took on all challengers and Tully and Temmi joined in. By the time they'd climbed into the vessel, which teetered on the edge of sinking under their combined weight, Tully had half a dozen scrapes, one boxed ear, a split lip and a hank of missing hair to show for her battle. Others were in worse shape, but Tully was faster than most and excellent at dodging.

The people on the shore did not give up easily and several tried to swim out and climb aboard the boat, risking capsizing the entire affair. Stanna watched them all as they approached and warned each one off. Those who did not listen lost their lives to the woman's sword.

The motion of the waves was enough to make her feel ill, but Tully was still glad to take the ride. Back on the docks full scale warfare seemed to be the order of the day, with people being shoved into the waters, diving in, or trying in vain to find a way to the ships in the harbor. Even as she noticed that, she saw sails being lifted in the distance and oars cutting the waves as more vessels turned, ready to flee to the Kaer-ru.

As the docks slowly dwindled in scale Tully let herself look at the waters more and more. She had never been to the ocean before coming to Torema and now she rode across the waters toward a ship that looked as large as a building in her eyes.

A towering construction of wood, with three masts, the name *Wave Dancer* was painted on the side and a wooden figure of a winged serpent adorned the front. As they approached she saw Hillar Darkraven herself gazing down from the prow and looked on as the woman instructed the crew to lower a collection of wooden slats and ropes for them to climb.

Stanna went up first, and Tully followed quickly behind her with Temmi on her heels. The ladder had Stanna trembling, an unsettling sight to be sure, but for Tully it was the easiest part of the trip. When she once again had solid footing Stanna was as calm as ever.

The city was a smear in the distance from where they were, and the sky above it was black with smoke and clouds alike.

"Torema is finished," Stanna said. "It's dead and has no notion that it's dead."

"Oh, I think it knows." Temmi shook her head. "We had to fight our way across the docks."

Hillar said, "You made it here. We'll be on the way to the Kaer-ru in short order."

Not three seconds after she spoke another person called out and pointed into the waters.

There, barely visible, was a very small vessel.

And on that vessel were four men.

One of those men, battered and badly wounded, was named Odobo.

Within fifteen minutes of the captain pulling the four men from the sea, everything changed for Tully and her companions.

Daivem Murdrow

Torema burned. What did not burn bled, and what little there was that did not burn or bleed died in agony.

Daivem knew and understood. Some places are not meant to continue on and that was the case with Torema and everything to the east of the Broken Swords. She considered that for a moment and shook her head. Probably true of everything to the west of them as well. She had seen the giant that crawled from the mountains and then collapsed. She had watched the form beneath that giant as it died. She had been drawn to that death as she had been drawn to the angry soul of Niall Leraby, as a moth is drawn to a flame, though in the case of the thing that died with the – *God! It was a god and it killed another even as it fell!* – vast creature on what had once been the desert of Arthorne, that flame had blazed near as bright as the sun before it faded to a minor ember.

The staff in her hands hummed within her grasp, though she was surely the only one that would have noticed.

Niall Leraby's essence, his wraith, very nearly roared with anger. That was sometimes the case with those who seemed weakest in life. "Meek in life, courageous in death," was one of the sayings her brother, Darsken, had hammered into her when he was training her to become an Inquisitor.

The air was bitter cold, and the storms above raged and thrashed and the things that either dwelled within those clouds, or possibly created them, were nearly as angry as Niall.

"Do you ever calm down, boy?" Daivem spoke softly, though at that moment no one was quite close enough to hear her.

The Inquisitors spent most of their time in other worlds. The Louron were not from the Five Kingdoms though they had long had a place in the Kaer-ru islands. It was their blessing to know the Shimmer and to walk between worlds. It was a gift they used as best they could to help the dead when the time came, and much as she would have preferred to be in her homeland, she was here now, because the dead of the Five Kingdoms were so very angry and needed help. Niall was not the only one. He was merely the loudest.

Well, second loudest.

Niall could not speak in words. That gift died with his tongue. Had he a body, she could have forced that form to speak, but his body was beyond repair and fed the fat ravens where he fell from the sky.

But he could speak in his own fashion. He could thrust images at Daivem and hope that she read them properly and responded well. Mostly what he offered again and again was a memory of his body plummeting toward the ground as he looked up at the He-Kisshi that dropped him.

They had a history, he and that agent of the gods, and it was not a pleasant history at all.

"There's nothing I can do for you. I don't have the time or agency to hunt down things that serve the gods of this world. I can try to help you find peace, but that is all."

She tilted her head as he responded. "How? That I don't know, either. But we'll figure it out along the way."

Inquisitors were not common. The man who led the Kaer-ru was not an Inquisitor, though he had obviously been trained. Jahda understood what she did and why she was there, though he offered no guidance.

So she did what her kind always did and tried to puzzle out how best to give the dead their peace.

And all the while, Torema burned, bled, and died. She was far enough away to watch it happen without being involved in the conflict. Pardume, the king she had met before, wanted the city for his people and it looked likely he'd have it, but there were others to the west fighting back and they were as cornered animals in a burning building, desperate to escape no matter how they had to find a way out. For each one the soldiers cut down, two more were there with weapons of their own, or a plan to unseat the horsemen and take their beasts.

She did not know the Five Kingdoms well, but she knew that the people of Hollum were cunning and more likely to attack from the shadows than to simply attack.

"It is hard to fight shadows, especially when the

night falls." Another of her brother's sayings. She helped the dead in her way and he in his, but his words were often mottos she lived by.

The winds howled along the hill and sleet fell from the sky. She pulled her cloak tighter to her body and shook her head.

She had to leave this place, or be taken with it. The dead were a rising tide in the area, so many of them lost and scared, so many more, angry and seeking to lash out. She had not been there for the other towns and cities and as much as Daivem wanted to help, the notion also terrified her.

There was already so much held within her walking stick.

Each Inquisitor was trained in how to carve one of the sticks. They were more than wood and less than steel, and every one of them was unique and told a story that only the bearer could fully understand. In some of the lands she had been to, there were sorcerers who used long staffs that helped them focus their power. In others, wizards used wands. It was possible that those items were similar. All she knew was that Inquisitors had to deal with the dead. They employed necromancy in places where the dark magic was not allowed, and even in places where no magic was permitted. Their walking sticks helped with that and allowed them to shelter the spirits of the departed from the forces that could cause them harm.

There were limits, however.

There are always limits on power.

The dead could cause her little harm, but what she carried was more than the usual energies. Some part of a god lingered with her. Not by her choice, either. That entity had come to her without warning and she'd held the walking stick while it poured itself into the vessel.

What it was, what it wanted, she did not know. How long it would stay with her was another question she could not answer.

Through long weeks and months and years she had carved her story into the walking stick, each design a part of her that she placed in the wood, her hands guided by the Shimmer, perhaps, or by the dead. Currently she could feel the wood in her hand changing, moving without her careful touch, shaping itself at the whim of whatever it was that lay inside the vessel she had created the day she started walking the path of the necromancers.

She was not frightened by that fact, but she was very curious.

To her knowledge no spirit had ever been powerful enough to alter what a necromancer created.

Around her Torema burned, and bled, and died.

And in her hand a being of immense power bent the laws of reality as she knew it.

She looked toward the sea and considered her options.

Daivem had a long way to go, she knew that much. She simply had no idea what her final destination might be, or how she was supposed to get there.

For now that was a secret the dead around her intended to keep to themselves.

There are those who need boats and those who can cheat as they move around the world. The Louron were blessed with the Shimmer. What exactly it was, they could not say. Where it came from they could not hope to guess, but the Shimmer was kind to her people as long as they were not foolish and Daivem Murdrow was not known for being foolish.

She asked the Shimmer to help her and felt the twist in reality that always preceded the actual opening of a portal. To the naked eye the world was unchanged, save for a faint flicker of distortion that could be seen from the corner of the eye.

Daivem stepped into that flicker, into the Shimmer, and moved on, away from the dying Torema.

She had places she needed to go, if only she could figure out the way to reach them.

Brogan McTyre

"There. That is all that remains of Hollum." Roskell Turn's voice was conversational and his hand pointed to the darkness on their right.

"You're daft." Brogan shook his head.

The sky above them was dark as night. There was no sun, though if one looked far enough to the south spears of sunlight still punctured the caul that now seemed to cover most of the world.

The land was visible, though there was little to see but more darkness. If there were people out there, they had no fires burning. If there were towns or cities, they hid away amongst the ruins and floods.

"The city is gone. The floods took it." He paused. "And the storms. The very ones that are crushing Torema right now."

Brogan looked at the black shape of the coastline against the nearly black sky. No stars. No hope of a star. The wind roared along and blew colder than he could have imagined. It seemed nearly impossible that the ocean itself hadn't yet frozen solid.

"Hollum is gone? What about Adimone? What of Elannis?"

The smaller man looked out at the waters and shrugged. "All gone."

Brogan felt cold grip his heart again. He knew that he had done the right thing when he fought for his family and yet, now, he had his doubts all over again. It was one thing to think that the world is ending. Another to see the proof. The very shoreline was different. There was something…

"There should be hills here, yes?"

Roskell spread his arms. "The rains have washed them away. This is all that remains."

Brogan tried to speak, but could think of no words.

The Galean spoke before he could come up with anything worth saying. "The gods did not make the world, Brogan McTyre. They remade it in their image. It's written in the books of Galea. They fought and killed their predecessors, as you already know. And then they took the world and built it anew."

The man stroked his neatly trimmed beard and then pointed toward the land again. "The hills that were there are gone now, not because of what you did, but because the gods have decided it is time."

"You say I am not to blame?"

"No. You have your share of blame, but if it had not been you it would have been someone else. The gods have not been calm and that started long before you committed your misdeed."

Brogan shook his head. "No misdeed, Roskell Turn. I did what I had to do in order to save my family."

Turn nodded. "Then perhaps I could choose better words, but in the eyes of the gods you betrayed their orders and tried to take what did not belong to you. To them you and I and everyone else, we are but small parts of the whole and they rule over that whole. To have you disobey them is to have a leaf from a tree decide that they are wrong. Would you listen to a leaf?"

"I would not burn down the forest because one leaf dared fall."

"That makes you wiser than the gods in this case, Brogan. My point is that they would have found a reason for what they are doing. They might have waited another hundred years or a thousand, but they would have eventually decided to end the world because that is what gods do."

"I don't understand." Brogan clenched his hands into fists, angered by the notion that all he did was for nothing. If all he had gone through was as nothing, then surely all he did to rectify the situation he felt responsible for was nearly useless.

"You've seen a dead god – he died because the newer gods came along to kill him. I have read the stories they told Galea. Not all of them, but more than most. They rose up because the older gods locked them away, bound them to the world and forced them to suffer in their prisons for lifetimes without count."

Brogan frowned. "I thought that was the fate of demons."

The Galean smiled, but it was not a happy expression. "Just so. Now there are other demons who have been locked away, held at bay for endless lifetimes."

"So the gods are trying to do what then? Punish the demons a second time?"

"For the first time in our history, people have turned from the gods and sought other answers, Brogan McTyre. You have heard of the Marked Men?"

"Of course." He did his best to avoid them. They were relentless hunters and trackers who would stalk an enemy into the ground if necessary.

"Jahda spoke with their king, Parrish of Mentath."

Brogan sneered. He knew Parrish well enough and no love was lost between the kingdoms.

"Parrish admits to dealing with demons in an effort to gain power and to move away from the gods."

"Then why not punish Parrish?"

"Parrish is being punished. Everyone is being punished." Roskell touched the bench next to him and then the deck railing of the ship. "But Parrish is merely another leaf. The demon he turns to is a different story. The demon has grown in power, just as the gods themselves once grew in power. It has stayed in its prison, and studied, and learned, and become something else."

"What has it become then?"

"It has become a godling that seeks to overthrow the gods in control of everything."

The man had surely lost his senses. Demons were gods? Nonsense! Gods were gods.

"I have read over one hundred volumes of the books

of Galea. I have studied the gods in particular because they have a history that is fascinating. The gods are tired and, more importantly, the gods are angry. They have been waiting for a very long time to have their battle with the demons that would replace them and now you have given them a reason to strike."

"Then why involve people at all?"

"Some things I cannot answer. The gods gave Galea many answers, and told her many secrets, but in a lifetime I could not hope to know all of those answers, and why the gods care about mortals is one of the answers I could never find."

Brogan thought back to his family, Nora, and the twins, and little Braghe. His mouth pulled down, his teeth clenched. The gods wanted people? No, they wanted death.

"They like to make us suffer. They like to watch."

"For all I know, Brogan, that is true." Roskell looked again at the dark land mass. "This is also true, the city of Hollum used to shine in the night right there. The torches along the Street of Champions were lit every evening before the sun finished setting and you could see those lights along the edges of the trees and sometimes could even see their glow on the underbelly of the clouds."

Brogan turned to the north again, already knowing the answer to his next question. "Saramond?"

"Saramond belongs to the sea. The city is gone. Lost to the waters and all the people are dead. The end came too quickly there."

"Yet you say my actions did not do this?"

"Not alone."

"Then we should get to the Gateway as quickly as we can. The gods must be made to pay before they notice us and act on their own."

"What do you mean?"

"We are not hidden from the gods, unless you have managed to hide us when I was not looking. Sooner or later the He-Kisshi will come, and sacrificed to the gods or not, they will have their messages for us."

The Galean looked to the skies above them. In the distance a crackle of lightning strobed across the bottom of the clouds for a moment, revealing very little. "Then I hope you are very good with your sword, Brogan McTyre."

CHAPTER EIGHT
AS THE GODS DEMAND

Opar

If Edinrun was the jewel in the crown of the Five Kingdoms, then Torema was the gold that crown was forged from. The city had wealth, a population larger than any other city in all the land, and a history that was rich in tales of wonder and decadence alike.

Opar looked upon the city and shook his head, rain falling from the brim of his hat.

"We are done. There is nothing left." The voice came from his cousin, Rithman. Rithman was a hard warrior and for that reason he had been chosen to lead the armies alongside Opar. He was also trustworthy and that helped.

"There is nothing left to conquer or nothing left?"

Rithman nodded his head. "Yes, well, the latter is close to true." From where they sat the docks could clearly be seen and the harbor beyond, despite the rains. There were no ships left in the area. They had all fled to the Kaer-ru or possibly even to distant

Pressya. The seas were choppy with waves and the docks rolled back and forth as those same waves thrashed themselves to death against the land.

"Even if we had the time, we could not build ships from what is left, and I am hardly a ship builder." Opar scowled, and then unceremoniously spat phlegm across the cobblestones.

His father would have been horrified. His mother would have disowned him. As both of them were dead, and the world seemed in a rush to join them, he found he did not care.

"Have you considered begging mercy from the gods?" Opar turned, fully expecting to see his cousin with a foolish expression on his face.

Instead he stared into the cavernous mouth of a He-Kisshi and at the vast rows of sharp teeth that filled that maw.

He was suitably terrified. The Undying were not kind at the best of times and as they were currently speaking for gods angry enough to end the world, Opar felt justified in backing his horse away.

The creature floated in the air, its wings snapping softly on a breeze that spilled from the messenger of the gods and pushed the damp earth below it away in slow waves.

"Have I not already made my loyalty known?" Opar's voice shook with a blend of fear and anger. "Have I not obeyed every order I have been given?"

He resisted the urge to draw his sword. The creature was a messenger, not the source of his troubles. "Even as you have destroyed all that I ruled over, I have made the sacrifices that were demanded of me. I slit the throat of my own son for the gods!" His vision broke into shards at the memory. He'd ridden from Stennis Brae with his entourage and returned to his camp a hundred leagues away, while the other kings discussed how they would avoid doing what the gods demanded. Opar loved his son, loved his wives, but in the end had sacrificed his firstborn to appease the gods for another month.

That month was not yet gone, but his kingdom was shattered and the greatest city in the Five Kingdoms, the very heart of Giddenland, Edinrun, was gone just the same, ripped away from the world.

The hooded form tilted its head, the vast teeth falling into shadows as lightning shattered the skies above Torema yet again. "Your capital city is still there. It is placed where it will remain safe until all is done. Whether or not Edinrun is returned to you depends on you, Opar, king of Giddenland."

The creature's words confirmed what Daivem Murdrow, the witch woman from Louron, had told him. "Then stop toying and tell me what I need to do!" He bellowed the words before he could stop himself, knowing that they were a horrid mistake.

The clawed hand of the He-Kisshi caught his throat so fast that he never saw the move coming. A moment later the man who was one of the most powerful mortals to walk the Five Kingdoms was cast into the mud.

Opar turned his head, prepared to stand back up, but before he could even reach his hands and knees the winged shape moved past his horse and landed in the muck inches from his face. The great, clawed feet found purchase, and that same hand that had cast him aside grabbed the back of his tunic and cloak and lifted him easily into the air.

"You dare to raise your voice to me?" The words shuddered as they escaped the vast mouth. The lips of the Undying's "hood" peeled back, revealing the pink gums that surrounded the teeth, the nearly endless teeth that looked capable of biting through good steel.

"Forgive me! Please! I am a fool!" Opar had never once in his life considered begging, but looking at the messenger of the gods he remembered that he was merely human and that he ruled only because the gods permitted it.

For the second time he was cast across the cobblestones. As he rose this time around, the He-Kisshi came closer at a slower pace. Whatever anger it felt was now once again hidden behind the folded wings that made its cloak, and the teeth, the horrid, uncountable teeth of the thing, were lost in shadows.

The rains hammered down around them but with a simple gesture of its hand the wind stopped, the storm abated.

Rather than try to stand, Opar stayed on his knees and crawled in the filth, eager to please the Undying that stood before him.

"I am unworthy. I have trespassed where I dare not. Please forgive me."

"I am Ohdra-Hun. Never speak to me that way again, foolish man, or I will peel the flesh from your bones, and I will take days to accomplish the task. Do you believe me?"

The taste of mud and worse painted his tongue and

Opar licked his lips. He nodded, momentarily unable to think of the words to say that might spare him the wrath of the Undying.

Ohdra-Hun spoke again. "Beg the gods! Ask them how you might be spared! See if they are more merciful than I, their servant! Only do it now, before I change my mind!"

Opar, king of Giddenland, conqueror of all that remained of Torema, looked to the lightning-clad skies and called out, "How may I serve? How can I be spared this madness?"

The skies unleashed a flurry of lightning strikes at that moment. The buildings around the king of Giddenland were struck a hundred, perhaps even a thousand, savage blows, and the ground around him crackled with tongues of electricity.

Had he thought Torema dead?

Foolish, foolish man. Half-blinded by the white fire that poured from the sky, Opar saw the true death of Torema. Buildings shattered around him as lightning smashed through them and then exploded outward. Stone melted, wood burned, people, those foolish enough to think that they might, somehow, survive the chaos within the city, were incinerated if they were lucky or merely crippled if they were unfortunate.

The very ground split not a hundred feet in front of him, gasping out blue flames and was instantly filled with the run off from the nearly endless rains. The cobblestones shattered and were replaced with muddied trails of water that washed down toward the ruined docks in the distance.

The air vibrated with the endless roar of thunder. He felt the bones within his body shake and shudder as the sound overwhelmed every possible thought. Surely he should have been struck deaf. Surely he should have burned with the air, the ground, the buildings, but he remained unscathed.

The barrage continued, the fury of the gods finally, truly, unleashed before Opar's horrified eyes. His hair, wetted by rain, stood on end and he could see sparks spilling from one finger to the next as the world around him ended.

Opar looked on, too scared to think clearly, too frightened to even consider moving.

And after what felt like an eternity, the lightning moved, shifting toward the north and cutting a trench that led away from Opar, from the ruins of Torema to Opar knew not where. He watched on mutely, as the skies burned with that horrid, pale blue light and carved the world a vast scar.

Eventually that light moved too far away for him to watch.

Opar shook. He turned his eyes back to the Undying before him, and the creature loomed high above, looking down at him.

"Stand up." The words were a command and he obeyed without question.

He looked around as Ohdra-Hun gestured, and saw that amidst the ruins an army of statues stood. Those statues were flesh and blood, but frozen for a moment in time. His cousin looked where the closest building had been, his eyes wide, his mouth agape, water running down his face and then down his torso. He did not move. He did not breathe.

Below his cousin the horse looked ready to rear up in fright, but it did not move.

Around him the dead burned on, or smoldered as the rains extinguished their corpses. Not far away he could see other horses, other figures standing or caught frozen in the act of riding. Humans and equines alike were unscathed by the fury that had shattered Torema beyond all repair. They remained motionless while all around them buildings burned, and the dying cried or moaned in agony as they got about the business of suffering.

Every last one of those frozen forms sported the colors of Giddenland. Each horseman was his, every foot soldier obeyed his commands.

Ohdra-Hun spoke. "You are spared. The gods have granted you this blessing." One of those clawed hands pointed to the north, where even now he could see a trail of glowing embers that marked where the lightning had cut its swath across the land. "Follow the trail that is provided. Ride hard, as if your very life depended on it. When that trail ends, you will wait and you will be ready to kill for your gods."

The He-Kisshi stepped closer, until that hideous cowl was inches from his face and he could smell spices and rot spilling from the maw of the servant of the gods. Opar held his ground, though it was true he flinched back a bit.

"You have asked for mercy and been granted it. The blasphemers who defied the gods will meet you there. Be prepared to kill them. Do not fail, or I will be allowed the pleasure of killing you myself. Do you understand me, Opar?"

He could not speak. He dared not. What if he offended the nightmare standing before him? For the first time he saw the eyes of the He-Kisshi, an endless streak of small orbs all along that vile mouth. Eyes as those belonging to a spider, or some other hideous creature best not considered.

He nodded his head and bowed before the messenger of the gods.

When he could no longer stand the silence, Opar raised his head and looked around. The Undying was gone and, as he watched, his people began to move again, to blink and cough the water from their mouths and gain control of the horses that were spooked by the unexpected changes around them.

"Opar?" Rithman's voice was strained as he looked to towards him, his face a mask of dread. "What has happened to Torema?"

"The gods, cousin." Opar's throat hurt from the screams he never realized he'd let loose. "The gods happened. We have been spared and we will earn back their graces now, before the world ends."

As he spoke Opar reached for his mount and the horse, well-trained and worth every coin he'd spent on that training, waited patiently.

"We ride!" Opar's voice cracked, but the people around him heard and because he was a king, they obeyed. "We ride now! We ride to honor the gods!"

The king of Giddenland rode to the north and his cousin followed and so did all of his people, though some took a while to fully comprehend the level of death and destruction around them.

They rode, oh, how they rode, to get away from the corpse of dead Torema.

Tully

The men they'd fished from the waters were sailors, and one of them screamed a great deal as he was pulled aboard. The reason why was soon clear enough. His hand was gone, hacked away just above the wrist. He howled and yelled out in a language Tully did not know and finally a doctor was brought up from below decks.

The man was held in place while the surgeon worked hastily to first clean the worst of the shredded meat from the wound and then to cauterize it. Five people held the man in place as hot metal was removed from a fire and used to seal the bleeding flesh. By the time it was done the man sobbed but no longer tried to move.

One of the other sailors explained what had occurred and why.

Tully looked on and considered that the man responsible for ending the world was still alive. According to several of the people on the ship the man was wanted by the gods themselves, and a deckhand from Hollum said if the man was given to the gods the world would be spared.

Tully did not know if those words were true, but she suspected they had at least a seed of truth to them. She was not, however, among those invited to discuss the fate of the ship.

Neither was Temmi and that fact nearly enraged

the girl.

"We've been on this journey, we've both lost people to the gods and their games, and yet when it comes time to decide if we should hunt down the fucking bastard that started all of this, we are told to stay put." Temmi spat into the sea.

"There can only be so many people deciding where a ship goes, Temmi."

"Well, I volunteer to be one of them!"

"You aren't big enough, mean enough, or wealthy enough."

"I'm plenty mean!"

"Not so mean as the ones in charge, or you'd be over in that cabin and sharing in the discussion."

Lightning flashed and Tully looked into the skies above. "I'm for going below decks."

"Why?" Temmi frowned.

"Because I might have seen something rather large floating in the clouds."

"How large?"

"Undying large."

Temmi nodded. "Below decks. That's the place for me." They could say they were tough as long as they wanted and they'd proven themselves capable enough, but one of the He-Kisshi still wanted them dead, and Tully felt no need to advertise her whereabouts.

Before they made it to the hatch the rain started in harder, pelting the wood enough to make the water splash up in fits.

Once below deck they stayed together and moved to the room they were sharing with Stanna. There was no space on the ship to spare. Tully didn't mind the close quarters, though she expected the other two would like privacy from time to time.

"I still don't see why we can't be in on the discussion."

"Because we offer nothing special, do we?" Tully sighed and looked at her friend. "You are the daughter of merchants who delivered goods to the Grakhul. I am a cutpurse and pickpocket from Hollum. Yes, the He-Kisshi killed your family, which is a misery to be sure. Yes, I was chosen as a sacrifice and escaped. I'd just as soon not mention that to too many people. I may not be on the shortlist of people the Undying are actively hunting, but I'd rather they forget that I exist."

"I've proven myself."

Tully sighed. "Yes, you have. I'm wrong. Go right up there, head into the captain's quarters and demand to be heard. Me? I'm going to get some sleep. I'm tired."

"Come with me." Just that fast the indignant tone faded and was replaced with a slight note of begging and a dash of whine.

"Are you mad?" Tully shook her head. "You've Hillar Darkraven and Stanna both in that room and you want to go in and demand that they listen to you? Stanna is your friend. She'll likely listen, but right now she is here on the graces of the Darkraven herself, and we could all be tossed overboard if you offend."

The entire ship shuddered around them, and Tully was obliged to push her hand against the wall to avoid falling over.

"I'm going anyway." Temmi stood and shook her

head. "I've every bit as much a right as they to decide where we go."

"Temmi, think this through, please. The Darkraven has a long history of not liking the people who cross her. That history includes making examples."

"I don't intend to cross her, I just want to hear what they have to say and help convince them to do the wise thing."

"And what is the wise thing?"

"I'm not sure yet. I'm still thinking."

"You *are* mad. You've lost your senses completely."

"What are your thoughts? I figure we continue on until we hit another land and hope the gods decide they've made their point, or we actually please the gods and stop them."

Temmi headed back up the stairs and despite herself, Tully followed.

They reached the captain's deck at exactly the right moment to be too late. The leaders who decided what must be done were stepping out, engaged in pleasant conversation. There was Hillar, looking grim but still managing a brisk pace. There was Stanna, looking more like a hunter at that moment than anything else, and behind her–

"No." Tully's voice was very small as she stepped back and tried not to see what she was seeing.

Theryn, the Blood Mother, walked out of the door behind Stanna, surrounded by her seconds.

Theryn smiled as she saw Tully.

Tully did not smile back.

"Tully. So good to see that you are alive." If a cat had a voice as it found a wounded mouse to toy with, surely that was the voice of Theryn in that moment. She'd sought after Tully for so long, and now she had her in a place where Tully could not hope to escape.

Behind her Rik shook his head subtly and the others with Theryn smiled.

"I've no quarrel with you." Tully retreated a few steps as the rest came forward. Stanna frowned, Hillar pushed past, and those gathered around the Blood Mother spread out.

Theryn's smile did not change. She stepped closer, despite Tully's best efforts to avoid that very thing, and looked down on her. "Nor I with you. What matters a few gold coins when the world is ending?"

"I did not take your coins."

"So you have already told me."

Stanna stepped closer, turning her back to Tully. "This one is with me. Should you have issues, discuss them with me. She is under my protection."

Oh, the change was subtle, but Tully saw it. Despite the best attempts to hide her disappointment, Theryn's smile faltered a bit as she considered the larger woman.

Without even considering the risk, Stanna looked away from the Blood Mother and said, "We are changing course. We go after the men who started this war with the gods."

Temmi opened her mouth and then closed it, slowly smiling when she realized the powers that be had agreed with her assessment.

Tully's feet shifted themselves into a better position as Theryn and the rest moved past her, each of the Blood Mother's followers promising her she would die soon, either with an expression or a small gesture that would mean nothing at all to someone outside of the Union of Thieves.

Tully noted each and every one of those gestures and promised herself that they would die first. She'd make it happen though she had no particular desire to do so.

Just after Theryn passed her she saw shapes in the dark waters.

They were slender and pale, and moved as much like fish as they did women, but she could see the streamers of white hair, and enough of their bodies to know they were at least human in shape if not design.

The pale women glowed in the waters as Stanna and Temmi and then Hillar all joined her in looking. Not a dozen paces away, the Blood Mother and her ilk did the same.

The women were a sight to see. Their bodies undulated, their arms cut the water before them and their legs moved as well, so fast that they seemed to blur. The shapes moved to the north like a school of fish and even as they did so the ship started turning, moving to follow in the same direction.

"What are they?" Hillar frowned as she spoke.

Temmi answered. "I think they are Grakhul. I saw enough of them in the water over the years."

Stanna frowned. "Those are the women I held as slaves for Beron?"

Temmi nodded. "Best you surrendered them when you did."

"I do not argue with gods."

"You saved me when you fought–"

Stanna silenced her with a look. "That was a messenger. It was in the wrong."

Temmi nodded and kept her tongue.

When Tully looked away from the conversation the Blood Mother and her followers were gone.

They were not forgotten.

Myridia

The sun set, and eventually it rose again and still the men did their best to scale the stone cliffs leading to the Sessanoh. They had numbers and they had patience, but they did not have the upper hand, or spears to push back the fools who got too close.

Still, the work was exhausting.

"They will eventually get up here." Lyraal's tone was conversational, though she had been pushing back the army of men for just as long as Myridia.

"Yes, I know, but so far there is little else we can do to stop them." The Sessanoh had been prepared to handle sacrifices, but they had certainly had little chance to gather weapons, or even food and water. So far they were lasting, but the fish they needed to eat were down with the men, and the water they had came from the shallow mirrored lakes.

"The gods have not answered our prayers?"

Myridia looked to her friend and scowled. "Do you see any of the He-Kisshi here?"

"Well, yes." Lyraal smiled and pointed with her free hand even as she stepped closer to the edge and used the pointy end of her spear to send another man falling back with a wounded arm. They weren't trying to kill anyone, but they weren't playing nicely either and if the men fell the thousand or so feet to their deaths, then so be it.

Myridia looked and saw the odd, fluttering wings of an Undying as the creature descended and landed on the plateau where the vast stone fortress rested.

"You have called, Myridia of Nugonghappalur. I am here to answer your questions."

She bowed formally, but quickly, and gestured to one of the younger girls to take her place on the line.

"We are besieged." She pointed to the edge of the cliff leading to the sea. "Other Grakhul have come and decided that we are not fit to serve the gods. I do not want to harm them, but I also do not intend to bow before these men, who do not follow our ways."

"You do not intend?" The hooded head moved closer. "What if the gods decree it?"

"I–" She closed her mouth. There was no proper answer. "I will obey the commands of the gods, of course, but I will not assume that these men know that will better than you."

"I am Dowru-Thist. You are wise to call for an answer from the gods in these times."

She bowed again, formally. "I await the word of the gods."

Dowru-Thist turned its head and then looked up toward the sun above. The clouds were darkening near the mountains to the west, but the storms had not yet reached the Sessanoh.

She wanted to speak, but was wise enough to leave the He-Kisshi to do whatever it had to do.

That hooded maw moved closer again and she saw

the endless eyes that fixed upon her. "They come from Trant's Peak, and they have waited there in a great slumber for a time when the gods knew more of the Grakhul would be required."

She frowned and looked over to the edge as Lyraal drew her sword and thrust the tip downward. A scream followed and when the blade was lifted the tip was stained a dark red.

"They are to join us?" Her stomach fluttered at the notion. The men were aggressive and demanding, and larger than any of the men she had been raised with.

"Your men are gone. You and yours will need to either serve the gods as the vessels of new children, or offer your services in another way."

"But they are *men*, they are weak."

"They are Grakhul – they are like you but their men do not follow your ways. They follow older ways."

"How else can we hope to serve the gods?"

The He-Kisshi looked away and moved, studying the cliffside and the men climbing it. When it finally spoke it said, "Mate with these men and have strong babies, or find and kill Brogan McTyre before he reaches your old home."

"Nugonghappalur is dead. The gods destroyed it."

"It is destroyed, but the Lum-Hunnipih'ar still exists. It must be preserved."

The Gateway, of course. Myridia nodded her head. The home of the gods themselves was beyond the Lum-Hunnipih'ar, a place where no mortal was allowed to go and surely the madman who would kill a god and enslave a race would be foolish enough to try to reach the gods.

"The gods fear Brogan McTyre?"

"The gods fear nothing. They do not wish to let the blasphemer know where they dwell. They do not wish their world tainted by his madness." There was no anger in the words of the Undying, but there was a certain tone of reproach just the same.

Dowru-Thist continued, "You may stay here and serve as broodmares to the Grakhul who come, or you may serve your gods as warriors. The choice is yours."

She had only to look toward Lyraal to know the answer. "We would serve as warriors to our gods."

"So be it." Dowru-Thist stepped toward her and raised its clawed hands into the air. The winds changed in that moment, sweeping up the side of the cliff with enough force to push the women away from their positions.

"Gather your forces. Go to the courtyard between the sacrificial pits." The Undying moved away from her then and faced the cliff again, waiting patiently.

She did not defy Dowru-Thist, but instead called the others to her side even as she started toward the vast holes where the sacrifices were cast down to the gods.

"I don't understand." Lyraal looked at her, studied her as if searching for signs of an illness. "Why did you choose to leave here after all you struggled through to reach this place?"

"Those are not Grakhul men. They are aggressive, and they are demanding, and I do not wish to change myself to suit their needs. There are thousands of them and hundreds of us, and you already know that they would fight to see who could mate with the best of us rather than letting us choose mates." She sneered. "Dowru-Thist said it himself. We could fight or we could be 'broodmares.'"

Lyraal looked back toward the Undying and her mouth peeled open to spit a venomous streak of obscenities.

Myridia stopped her with a gesture. "We were given options. I chose the one I liked best."

"Did you choose because of how you thought I'd react?"

"No. I did this because Brogan McTyre murdered my mate. Because he locked the children in cages, and us in chains, and planned to sell us as slaves. He killed our men and ruined our world. He chose his family over everything else."

"And you blame him for this?"

"I might have thought to do the same, but that does not change what his actions caused. The world ends. Our world has already ended. You lost your man and I lost mine. We have traveled across foreign lands and been told that we have two ways to serve the gods. We can be used to make babies, or we can fight and kill the men who destroyed our world."

She looked down at the closest pit. Far, far down in that vast, smooth hole leading toward the seas she could hear the sound of waves splashing against the sides. The fall would likely kill any who decided to dive down. Cutting the throats of the sacrifices was a mercy.

"I knew that you would want to fight but did you think that I would want to have a mate chosen for me? That I would want to be used by a man I care nothing about?" Myridia shook her head. "I will kill Brogan McTyre with my bare hands if I can."

Lyraal smiled then and put a hand on her shoulder. "Excellent. Then we will kill the dog together."

"The dog and all of his pack." Myridia looked down into the depths, and only looked up again when the Undying came for them.

"Do you have faith in the gods?" Dowru-Thist spoke calmly enough, its arms folded so that it looked like a hooded man and nothing more.

"Yes, of course."

One hand reached out and pointed to the deep hole they stood closest to. "Then show your faith. All of you. Jump."

Myridia looked long and hard at that shadowy mouth. She waited for fifteen heartbeats, and then she did what she had to do.

She stepped into the pit and felt herself falling into the darkness.

CHAPTER NINE
SMALL SACRIFICES

Bron

Five days of hard riding brought Bron and his escort to the new location of Stennis Brae. By all rights the kingdom should have been destroyed. There was no doubting that. He and those who rode with him saw the ruined mountains, the shattered stone and splintered crystalline shards that littered miles of land around the remains of the Broken Swords. A vast pillar of stone that looked almost like a leg was wedged into that chaos, a thighbone, perhaps, and the dual bones of the lower leg.

The things a man fancies he can see. Bron spat at the very notion and rode all that much harder to find his kingdom.

He very nearly wept when he saw first Brixleigh and then Kinnett and the cairns of the Brundage Pass, all of which had been situated in the mountains. He did weep when he finally reached Journey End and saw his home Stoneheart, nestled exactly where it should have been, in the very center of the city.

It was impossible, of course, but there it was, all of it, all that he ruled over as a king.

Bron rode hard, pushing his mount to the very limit of endurance as he made his way home. The children, his beloved Maura, they were all that he could think about. That they'd have been dead without the demon Theragyn's help was something he did not miss.

The gods had tried to punish him for not sacrificing his son. The demon blocked that punishment.

Of course he would follow Theragyn.

Maura came to him and he clutched her in his arms, kissing her face, her neck and her hair. "You are safe. You are safe. I was so afraid you were gone forever."

She stared at him with awestruck eyes, and her lips trembled as she spoke. "Bron, the very city moved. The *kingdom* moved. I do not know how."

"I do. I have promised another our fealty." He pulled back just enough to look into her eyes. "The gods have betrayed us, but Theragyn, a new god, has offered us protection."

Oh, how wide her dark eyes grew as Maura shook her head. "Bron. We cannot disobey the gods."

"I have already done so. If I had not, you would all be dead right now and I will not accept that possibility."

Maura's hands clenched at the cloak on his shoulders. "You don't understand. You must not say these things."

"What else can I say, Maura? The gods betrayed us. They would have let the whole of Stennis Brae be shattered with the mountains."

Maura backed away, shaking her head, and her eyes looked down to the markings that ran along the backs of his hands and his fingers. "Oh. Bron. No. Don't do this thing."

"It is done. It cannot be undone and I would not if I could." He felt his lips press together. "The gods betrayed us, Maura. They wanted me to offer our Liam as a sacrifice or for me to let you die, or Hemma. I could no sooner offer any of you than I could the very sun. You are that important to me." And again he thought back on Brogan McTyre and understood all too well why the man had defied the gods.

Maura shook her head again and retreated.

"You do not understand, my love."

The shape rose behind her. He saw the dark hood, so much like cloth, and knew then why Maura worried so.

Bron stepped forward and grabbed his wife's shoulder, pulling her away as the He-Kisshi made itself known.

Had he seen this one before? He had no idea, but whatever the case it was as hideous as any of its ilk. The cowled mouth showed rows of teeth far back in the shadows cast by the sun. Amidst those teeth dark objects moved, so like worms, but part of the whole.

The He-Kisshi moved forward without seeming to walk. "The gods offered you mercy, and you have refused them."

"The gods wanted me to kill my own. I cannot do that. I will not."

The Undying shifted, craning that cowled head

and examining Bron with its countless eyes. "You are foolish, King Bron McNar. The gods do not often offer mercy."

"You are right, no mercy was offered. I will not kill my flesh to appease the gods who already make so many demands."

He was not conscious of reaching for his axe, and yet it was in his hand.

"You would threaten me?" The He-Kisshi came forward again, its voice shaking with suppressed rage, the same fury its kind showed whenever any dared disagree with the gods.

Bron's axe slammed deep into the belly of the thing, or would have if the folded wings had not been in the way. The hide was thick, and tougher than he'd expected. Rather than falling back and dying as he'd hoped, the monstrous thing screeched and charged forward, grabbing the king in its claws and lifting him easily from the ground.

Bron let out a yelp as he was lifted into the air and cast aside.

The He-Kisshi did not bother with him. It approached Maura instead and, even as she flinched back, the left hand of the beast caught her braided hair and yanked her closer.

"No! Don't you do it! Let her go!" Bron was fifteen feet away and trying to regain his feet even as Maura was hauled closer and that vast mouth opened wider to show the full horror of the teeth usually hidden from sight.

Two arrows buried themselves in that maw, and the thing let go of Maura as it gagged on the shafts buried deep inside its wet obscenity of a mouth.

Maura screamed and screamed, her eyes wide and terrified.

Two more arrows hit just as fast and Bron rose to his feet, looking for the source of the shafts, and spotted two of his men. More of them came from other directions, all of their faces set like stone, and more arrows were clutched and notched.

Bron shook his head and rose to his feet, clutching his axe in both hands. While the guards kept the monster busy, he took a solid grip and then charged. The weight at the back end of his axe smashed into the back of the creature's skull and dropped it to the ground as more arrows drove into the heap of screaming fur and teeth. Blood spilled from a dozen wounds and Bron lifted the axe again and brought it down on the back of the He-Kisshi's head, which obligingly split in half.

It was not dead, but that was just as well. Undying was the phrase and Bron had no doubt it was a truthful claim. He gave commands and they were followed. The guards came forward with bonds, hard ropes and thick straps of leather, and Bron was among them as they wrapped that hideous form in layer after layer of constrictive strands, as surely as a spider binds a fly.

Maura wept openly as he continued with the madness, and he knew it was madness, because in thousands of years no one had ever managed to kill one of the damnable messengers of the gods.

Bron said, "Do not try to kill the damned thing. Bind it, gag it, silence the beast, and then we hide it away."

Maura continued to cry, and as much as it hurt his soul, Bron ignored her.

The thing began to move. Blood seeped from the open wound on the monster's head and it hissed and roared as it strained against the heavy layers of bonds. By all rights it should have been too damaged to move, and far too weak to do any harm to the rope and leather surrounding it, but the ropes creaked and the leather groaned and Bron was terrified that it might break free.

Nells, one of the captains of the guard, looked his way and offered, "We could bury it. Seal it in the ground."

Bron considered and finally shook his head. "Bury it, yes, but leave the head out of the ground, that it might still breathe."

Nells nodded his head and barked orders.

Maura wept.

"Maura, love, enough. It's been done." He thought his wife stronger than that, bolder. She had fought alongside him more than once when they were at war with Mentath. She had proven herself.

"Bron. You still don't understand."

"What is it?"

Her eyes were tear-stained, and her teeth were clenched and her hands were pulled into fists. "I was not allowed to speak. They swore the children would die if I did, but now, after this, I have no choice." She stared at him, and fresh tears fell from her eyes. "Three of them arrived at the same time. I have no idea where they might have gone."

Did Bron know fear in that moment? Oh, yes. He

knew it and held it like a lover. "Find the Undying! Find them now!" Nells made sure the right ones listened. Some had to stay with the beast, lest it escape. Others ran to find the other He-Kisshi.

The king of Stennis Brae ran then, his heart twisting and screaming inside his chest. He ran for his son's room. Liam was so small, only a baby, not even five years of age.

His old legs worked better than they had in over a decade as he pounded through the long halls of Stoneheart, his boot heels echoing on the hard floors, and pushed his way past anyone who stood between him and Liam's chambers.

People who were unfortunate enough to bar Bron's way suffered bruises to flesh and dignity alike and he cared not at all. Much as he was a king who would listen to his people, he was even more a father who would fight for his children.

When he reached the door to the chambers Bron came to a hard stop, his eyes flying wide at the sight before him.

Liam lay sprawled across his bed, his eyes locked in an expression of terror that Bron would never forget, never unsee. His chest had been pulled open, heavy claw marks showing where fingers had dug deep before ripping the ribcage apart with terrifying, casual strength.

Blood covered the bedclothes, the bared chest, and the face of Bron's sweet boy. There was no breath within that body. There was no life to try to save.

The He-Kisshi held Liam's heart in its hand, other bits and pieces torn from the body glistening darkly around that tiny prize.

"And so your people are spared, despite your folly." The voice was barely above a whisper. "A wise man would call this a lesson and save wife and child from the same fate. Release your captive or I will show you how angry the gods can truly be."

His boy lay dead.

The monster that killed him stood before Bron and held his son's heart in his hand, the blood of his child spilling down that taloned mass. Those very claws pierced Liam's tiny heart in three places. He could never look away and forget that moment.

Not as long as he lived.

"Your gods demanded the death of my son?" The words were whispered. Bron's eyes narrowed.

"They're your gods as well, Bron McNar. You swore your allegiance to them. For decades they offered you shelter."

Bron moved forward and looked down at Liam's wretched little form. Already growing cold, even as those eyes of his stared blankly at the doorway, waiting, no doubt, for his father to save him.

"Your wife and daughter are still alive." The voice uttered a soft warning and Bron nodded. "Do not be foolish. You have already offended the gods by aligning yourself with Theragyn. That sin might be forgiven, but not if you do anything else to defy them."

Bron moved forward and rammed the head of his axe deep into that mouth, pushing with all of his weight, all of his strength, intent on forcing the whole of his weapon down that offensive throat.

He did not speak. He did not offer last words of defiance. He merely acted, and screamed his rage out into the universe.

The axe pulled free and it rose and fell again and again as Bron McNar roared his sorrows out for all to hear.

The third of the He-Kisshi did not wait to have a discussion.

The king of Stennis Brae had broken with the gods and tried to kill two of the Undying. He was not forgiven for his transgressions.

As Bron pulled the axe back he felt it torn from his grasp and hurled across the room. At his feet the bloodied remains of the He-Kisshi bled across the furs covering the floor of his son's chambers. On the bed his footprint marked where he had, unthinking, stepped on Liam's remains as he charged for the thing he'd slaughtered.

He had exactly enough time to realize what he had done before the claws of the third Undying sank into the muscles of his shoulders and pulled meat away from bone.

The mouth of the creature opened so wide that he could see little else beyond teeth and the deep, cavernous opening into the hellish thing's throat.

Those teeth bit down and ended Bron's world before his rage could fully become sorrow.

Perhaps that was a kindness in the eyes of the gods.

CHAPTER TEN
THOSE WHO FALL

Brogan McTyre

Brogan paced the deck of the ship as if begging the gods to notice him. He trod across the layer of ice that sealed the wood away from the waves, ignoring treacherous spots and patches of snow alike. The cold seemed to have no effect on him, despite the gusts of steam he let out with every breath.

Day and night were the same now. The clouds covered this part of the world, and the gods seemed content with that decision. There were no stars. There was no moon. There was only the endless night.

The ship supposedly rode to the north on the violent sea, but Brogan could not be sure. All he knew was that the waves surged along, and the ship had not yet been crushed by their force. Anna Harkness was certain, and for that reason alone he did not cut the throats of the remaining crew. Had she said that they led the ship anywhere else, he would have ended their miserable lives. No part of him forgave the mutiny. He was not completely certain he was capable of forgiveness any longer.

"You should stop pacing." Anna shook her head. "You're making the rest of us nervous."

"I need to do something."

"Try sleeping. You've barely closed your eyes since, well, since the caves."

He shook his head. "I can't sleep. I'm not tired. I can't stop thinking about what I have to do."

Anna sighed. She apparently was feeling the cold far worse than he, as there were several layers of furs and shawls covering her form. "You need to find a way to rest. I hear not resting the mind can cause madness."

Brogan laughed and shook his head. "You doubt I'm already mad? I aim to murder gods!"

"They'll likely have different ideas, Brogan." She shook her head again. "Can we even be certain we head in the right direction? This Gateway you speak of, is it something that can move? Is it a door that can be closed?"

He scowled as he looked at the woman. "You see? This is why I pace. Because, when I stop, people ask me questions like that! How am I to know? The gods have not seen fit to share their plans with me, nor have any of the Galeans I've met had an answer for that sort of question."

"That's more the sort of question for Scryers..." Anna's voice trailed off quickly and her eyes grew wide and round.

Brogan stared at her for a moment and forgot to pace.

"Right you are," he said. And then he was heading

for the stairs below decks, down where Laram's Mearhan still rocked and whimpered in slumber, her mind nearly overwhelmed by the anger of the gods.

"Brogan! No!" He ignored her words.

Laram was asleep, and Mearhan beside him, when Brogan entered the cabin where they slept.

"Wake up, Mearhan, I'd have words with you."

Laram opened an eye and looked toward Brogan. "She's had a rough spell, Brogan."

"Aye, I know, and yet I need to speak with her and now."

"She can't help you."

"She can, Laram." He stared into his friend's eyes and saw the anger there. It was a just anger and surely he would have reacted the same way had anyone come along and made demands of Nora.

"She's got the gods screaming in her head, Brogan. She can barely even hear herself speak. The gods are angry. One of theirs is dead."

"Yes. I know." He spoke carefully. "That is why I need to speak with her. I want the gods to hear me."

Laram's face worked. His flesh grew red and his lips peeled back and settled then peeled back again as he glared.

"I came to your aid, Brogan. I'd do it again, but she never asked for this."

Before Brogan could answer Mearhan looked up at Laram and said, "Let him ask. Might be we can end all of this before it's too late."

The girl's skin was deathly white and her hair stood out like a blood-soaked mat. She'd been sweating and her eyes were as shiny as ice.

"Mearhan, can the gods hear me if I speak to you?"

"Brogan, you fool, the gods have been looking for you, if you reveal yourself they'll hear you, but they might not listen." She tried to smile as she spoke, to make light of the subject, but she failed. Her lips were chapped and her hands shook.

Brogan crouched until he was closer to the height of the prone girl. He spoke as gently as he could. "Then let them hear this. I am coming for them. I've killed one of theirs already and I'll kill the rest if given the chance. If they stop this, I might show mercy."

The girl fell back, a laugh burbling past her clenched teeth. Her features shook as the muscles beneath her pale flesh trembled. Her body shuddered and twitched for a few seconds and then was completely still, save for the shallow rise and fall of her chest.

She lay motionless for over a minute, long enough that Brogan began to fear for her safety.

Mearhan did not stir, but her body rose up into the air, her head falling at an angle, her eyes rolling back to show nothing but the whites. Laram pushed himself away from her and gasped. And Brogan stood his ground, though he felt the hairs on his neck and arms rise.

Her head did not move, but Mearhan's lips twitched into a sadistic smile. Her eyebrows knotted toward the bridge of her nose and her soft, smooth, innocent face became a mask of anger and madness. The voice did not completely match the way the girl's lips moved, and there was an echo, as if the words came from far across a long cavern. "It jests. It makes light of our anger and our pain."

Brogan's head thudded with each pulse of his heart. "I've killed one of you. You killed all of mine. What makes you think your pain is more important?"

"We are gods." The words were hissed past those smiling lips. "You are nothing."

"I am Brogan McTyre." He spoke as he approached the girl, thinking only of the voice that mocked him. Laram stepped closer to him, thinking, no doubt, only of the woman he loved.

"You are nothing. You are a nuisance best dealt with sooner. The He-Kisshi come for you."

"Shit!" Laram screamed the word and stalked toward the stairs. "Gather your weapons, lads! The Undying are on their way to deal with us!" His words bounced off the walls below decks and were heard by all, and answered by nearly as many.

Brogan paid no heed. He focused on Mearhan and shook his head. "Call them. I'll see them as dead as the other one. I'll kill them all myself if I must." He felt his own mouth pulling into a smile as frozen as the girl's. "I'll find the ways to make your little messengers bleed and die. I'll make sure they suffer, too. And each of them I kill will be practice for when I reach you."

"Arrogance." That was the only word uttered as Mearhan's hair began to crisp near her pale scalp. The stench of burning hair was what made Brogan back away. The woman still floated in the air, her face still held that stiff, maddening grin. Her hair was blackening near the roots, and smoke rose fine and thin.

And then her red hair was burning. Flames danced and swirled around Mearhan's scalp. There was a wineskin on the ground not far from where the lovers had been sleeping. Brogan grabbed it quickly and tried to douse the flames, pouring the contents over the poor girl's head, but even as he did so her porcelain skin began to blacken and blister.

She did not cry out. The flesh hissed like meat in a hot pot, but the girl didn't seem to care.

She said, "You will die soon. The He-Kisshi come for you. You have wounded them and they will have your blood. But your soul belongs to us."

Her lips moved, and she seemed intent on saying something more for a moment, until her mouth caught fire. That was all there was to it. The blaze roared past her shriveling lips and the body of Mearhan Slattery fell to the ground. She landed on her knees and then fell forward, her entire head burning like a fresh torch as the flames rose and a thick, black smoke billowed from the crest of the Scryer's head.

Brogan stared on, horrified. He had never expected the girl to be injured because of his conversation. Part of him wanted to move, to try again to save her, but his muscles did not respond and his body was as still as a stone sculpture. Laram would be so very hurt...

He might have stood there until the body was gone and the entire ship was burning but calmer minds overruled that notion. Anna's hand on his shoulder did nothing. Laram's hand shoved him aside as the poor bastard sought to reach his love and quench the flames that cooked her down to her bones.

Laram screamed, his voice a wounded roar of inarticulate grief and rage.

Faceless moved past him and caught the burning

body of Mearhan Slattery, lifting the flaming form and carrying the shriveling husk amid a cloud of black smoke that filled the galleyway, heat harsh enough to dry the eyes of anyone that close.

Laram fell to his knees and screamed again, his eyes wide and his face as stunned as if he'd been struck by thunder.

Brogan followed the odd creature and coughed at the dark soot that tried to work its way into his lungs. His eyes watered and his throat burned but he could not look away, would not allow himself that escape. This was his fault and he'd see it through as best he could.

Did Mearhan still move? He could not say, but it seemed she might be alive yet as the body curled in on itself and flames belched out from where her eyes had been, and smoke rose from her ruined mouth and throat.

Faceless reached the icy deck and walked at the same pace to the edge of the ship. Once there it hurled its burden over the railing toward the sea.

Mearhan did not fall, but instead rose into the air and shook her flaming head. The skull that had been her face blackened and burned and the fires around her crackled and snapped in the wind, casting smoke shadows toward the south.

Despite the crash of waves and the air's howling fury, Brogan heard the words she uttered clearly enough. "You have chosen to fight gods, Brogan McTyre. We have chosen to notice you. Your death will solve nothing, but we shall revel in every eternity of your suffering."

Before he could say anything in response, the bones fell apart and splashed into the angry waves.

Lightning cut the clouds into shreds and thunder cracked loud enough to mute even Laram's screams.

Brogan stared where the bones had sunk and beside him Faceless looked down as well, its flesh blackened by smoke but seemingly unharmed.

A moment later Jahda was next to them, staring into the waves. The man spoke to himself and made gestures at the water.

"What are you doing?"

"I am offering her spirit peace."

"You can do that?"

The man stared at him for a moment. His dark eyes were wider than usual, but aside from that he seemed unaffected by the bizarre death of Mearhan Slattery. Brogan expected he would not be as fortunate.

Jahda said, "Only for the dead, Brogan McTyre. You will have to find peace on your own."

"There is no peace for me." Brogan looked down at the sea again and then headed for the deck. Laram would want words with him and, short of a blade he'd let the man have his say. "I think that peace is for the dead and I am not there yet."

Jahda spoke, but whatever words the Louron offered as comfort were lost to the winds.

Tully

The weather was getting worse, not better. That was to be expected, what with the world ending, but Tully could have done without the surging sea throwing their ship around constantly. Every time she thought she'd managed to find a comfortable spot the waves came along and threw the whole of the ship up and then down. What was not tied in place tended to find a new location and that included people.

Temmi sat nearby and hugged her knees in close to her chest as she rocked back and forth. As bad as Tully felt, her friend felt worse. She had crawled up the steps a few times to void her stomach over the side of the ship. Each time she came back down cold, wet, and paler than she'd been before, which was quite an accomplishment.

The both of them had their problems, but Stanna seemed no part of them. Currently the woman was lying on her back, snoring softly, the Bitch at her side and held as gently as a baby in her embrace.

Somewhere on the ship a small army of people had plans to kill her. They'd make it as painful as they could. That she had done nothing wrong was unimportant. She stood accused of stealing from the Blood Mother, and that was crime enough.

Temmi groaned and headed for the doorway to their cabin, crawling on hands and knees. Tully felt bad for her, but couldn't actually muster any sympathy. Temmi was inconvenienced, whereas she herself was soon to be dead. The world was ending, but she'd not be around for that part. Theryn would see to that.

Unless she managed to handle Theryn first. The Blood Mother was a killer. She had earned her title. One way or another, if Tully did nothing, her adoptive mother would see her dead and no one the wiser for it.

The ship groaned and rolled and Tully shook her

head. It was time to clear her mind and possibly thin the numbers that currently stood against her.

Tully did not brag to her friends or show her skills. There was no need. If they thought her merely a girl from a town known for holding too many people, then so be it.

When she slipped from the room, no one noticed. With careful steps and alert senses she moved into the ship and the darkness that was prevalent below decks. Some people held lanterns, occasionally someone came past with a candle, but mostly it was dark in the underbelly and she preferred that. Tully was at home in the darkness. She always had been.

The process of finding her targets would be a long one. It was a challenge to move through the darkness and stay wrapped in its embrace.

Still, she was very good at hiding herself from the light.

Her blades found her hands and pulled her fingers in close. She would be patient. It was time to hunt and no longer be hunted.

Outside of the ship the winds howled and the seas bucked and tried their best to throw anyone foolish enough to rest into a different spot.

Tully did not rest. She willed herself into darkness and then she waited.

Beron

Death was not kind to Beron of Saramond.

He'd known for a long time that Stanna was a possible threat, but he had not been prepared for how fast she was, and even knowing her size he was not prepared for her strength. She'd killed him and in short order at that.

The sword cut his head from his neck and he died. That was the end of it. There had never been much doubt that he would die violently.

Only death ended nothing.

There was darkness for a time and Beron welcomed the silence, but when the light and sound returned he was not where he had been. He was, instead, prostrate before a vast throne of thorns, and looking down on him from that throne was Ariah, the god to whom he'd promised his fealty.

"I am not dead?" He tried to move his body but could not. His face looked up at the lean, striking figure and despite his efforts he could not so much as make an arm twitch.

"No." Ariah looked down at him and slowly shrugged his shoulders. "You are very dead. I simply choose not to let you die just yet."

"I don't understand."

"Beron, I gave you power and you promised to win a war for me, but that has not yet happened. I offered you servants and still you did not succeed. I wanted Brogan McTyre and the men who ran with him delivered so that the world could be saved and you have failed me time and again."

If he could have lowered his head, he would have. He felt shame. It was not an emotion he was used to experiencing.

"I never meant to fail you, Ariah. You have offered so much." And it was true. Money was not all that mattered. The demon had shown faith in Beron when no one else would, had offered mercy and a chance at redemption when his world was torn apart.

"You have failed me, but you have always been faithful." The demon frowned in contemplation. "Still, I am tempted to offer you one final chance at redemption."

"All I am is yours, Ariah."

"At the moment, that is not very much." The demon lord leaned down. "You are little more than a seed, Beron. However, I have always been good with seeds."

Beron tried to shake his head. He didn't understand completely, but when Ariah reached down and lifted him in both hands he achieved comprehension.

There was no body to move. There were no hands to feel, or shoulders to shrug.

"What shall we make of you, Beron of Saramond?"

There was no body to shake with rage, but there was anger just the same, clear and hot and useless for the moment.

"Make me an instrument of your fury, Ariah. Let me kill them all in your name."

"Kill who, exactly?"

"Whoever you want killed."

Ariah nodded and smiled. "That is the best possible answer. I have given you weapons before. This time I shall make of you exactly what you suggested. You will be my weapon, and my shield."

Beron felt his gratitude rise like the tides.

"I am afraid this will be painful, my champion, but no weapon is complete until it has been forged in flames and purified."

The hands of the demon lord held tightly to Beron's skull and then the fingers of his master dug through flesh and meat alike, caressing bone and beginning the process of reshaping the first of the slavers into something new and deadlier than ever.

CHAPTER ELEVEN
THE GODS MAKE DEMANDS

Myridia

The gods had their ways and Myridia was grateful for them. She had dropped into the sacrificial pit because the He-Kisshi told her to. That was enough. That was all she needed. Still, as she stepped off the precipice there was that small voice that warned it might be the last thing she ever did.

The sacrificial pits had only ever served one purpose in her lifetime. They offered the sanctified to the gods. If the gods demanded her life, the lives of her sisters, then they could have them at any time, but Myridia believed they offered something more than an expedient death and she was right.

The skies above her were as black as the night had ever been, but when she rose to the surface she knew where she was immediately. This was home, or rather all that was left of it. Her home was gone. The cliffs had fallen into the waters and shattered the stone teeth she had known for as long as she had existed. Her people were gone, taken by Brogan McTyre, but even if they had remained it would not have mattered. The gods were unforgiving and they had taken her home away, destroyed it.

Lyraal and a score more of her sisters rose from the depths and looked around. There were no looks of celebration, only caution and, in a few cases, dismay.

Not far away the Gateway stood in the stormy seas, unaffected by the waves or the clouds. Lightning flickered in lizard tongues along the surface and from time to time that electricity snapped a finger into the skies and stirred the heavens. Looking at the vast opening within the stone arch she could see light, pure and blue, spilling out and painting the turbulent waves.

The home of the gods was on the other side.

The lightning stopped, replaced by darkness and silence.

Atop the Lum-Hunnipih'ar a shape rested, cloak-like wings fluttering in the harsh winds. When it spoke the voice was exactly as she expected. The He-Kisshi had come with them, or another of its kind waited; she could not be certain.

"Brogan McTyre comes here, riding in a ship that is strong enough to reach the home of the gods. If you would serve your gods, be ready for him. Know that he must not enter their realm."

Myridia nodded her head.

Lyraal spoke. "You have the gift of the elements, do you not? Offered by the gods?"

The He-Kisshi looked her way and nodded.

"Can you..." She frowned. "We have seen it in

the past. But not for a long time. Can you freeze the oceans? Make them solid?"

"Yes."

"If we are to delay the arrival of Brogan McTyre and his helpers, perhaps you can freeze their ship in place."

"I will consider this and discuss it with the gods." The hood turned a bit, revealing nothing but shadows. "They may not agree. Then again, they may."

Lyraal shook her head and ducked down into the waters, the expression on her face making clear that she was not happy with the answer given. Myridia did not go after her second. The He-Kisshi had not yet dismissed her.

"Can you say how far away they are?"

"They are days away. But before them they have sent an army of your sisters, corrupted and made anew by the demon Ariah. You must prepare for them first."

"What?"

The He-Kisshi spoke, and despite the wind and the crashing waves its words were clear. "The demon Ariah has perverted your sisters, changed them into different creatures, things that would see the gods thwarted. They would protect Brogan McTyre and his companions. You must stop them."

"How many?"

"Well over a hundred."

The odds were still in their favor, but without knowing what sort of changes had been made, or how strong the perverted demon-followers were, she could not safely guess whether or not they would be ready for the coming battle.

"I must prepare." She spoke only to herself, but the Undying nodded its head.

"That is wise."

The arms of the creature spread out and the wings unfurled and caught the harsh winds. A moment later the He-Kisshi was riding into the air and the lightning began lashing out at the skies again. None of the energies came near the waters or the Grakhul. The gods were merciful.

With that simple fact in mind Myridia stepped onto the islands of stone that held the arch above the waves. Within moments the rest of her people followed.

The gods made demands. They would obey.

And they would either win the war for their gods, or they would die for their gods.

For now, for a short time, they had an advantage and she intended to make the most of it.

Lyraal stared up at the skies, into the dark heaving clouds where the He-Kisshi had vanished, and frowned. Myridia said nothing. She understood already what was going through her friend's mind. The gods made demands and now the question was whether or not they would make the challenges before the Grakhul easier to handle.

Interlude: Daivem Murdrow

The ships, it seemed, all wanted to go in the wrong direction. Two had gone north, but most, piloted by people wise enough to look at the weather, seemed determined to go to the Kaer-ru and beyond. The islands certainly had an appeal to them, but Daivem had different plans in mind. She needed to go north, at least if she wanted to silence the screaming dead around her. And she definitely wanted them silenced. After a few hours of their wailing her head began to hurt.

In the end she only had one choice, really. She followed the soldiers who rode to the north. The rains were not as bad along the path, and her clothes were enough to keep her warm.

She called through the Shimmer as she walked, and hoped that her message would make it through. Her brother was the one who'd taught her the ways of the Inquisitors and she sought his guidance now. He would likely tease her about it, but she'd find ways to return the favor when the time came. In the meanwhile she needed his advice if he could offer it.

The dead wanted to be at peace. They could not achieve that goal under the current circumstances and she understood why. The messengers of the gods had, near as she could understand it, driven an entire city mad and then left those poor wretches to die. It was true that some of them still lived, shunted off into another realm of existence, but most died and they could find no solace so long as the insanity continued.

"Tell me Darsken, how does one calm the dead when they are insane?"

She spoke to her walking stick as if it might suddenly have answers. It offered none, but the dead she held with it were angry enough that if she listened she might even hear them without trying to.

The winds roared and the rain slashed down at the

ground, and the trees around her shook and groaned as they fought to stay standing. Water cut at the soil and the plants, and bit by bit the foliage lost its battles, lifting into the current and dancing away downstream to where Torema used to be. The city was dead. There was no way around that. Some few foolish people continued to stay, hoped that, somehow, the world would be made right, but from what Daivem had seen, the gods felt no reason to relent in their assault.

Daivem walked between the worlds, sliding through the edge of the Shimmer as she trod the land. Each step she took was more like a score of long strides and in that way she made up for her dawdling in the dead city as the rains grew worse still.

She had been in Kaer-ru when the gods made their final judgment on Torema and had seen the spears of lightning crash down and shatter the hills and the buildings and the people of the city. She had wandered the blasted landscape and done what she and hers always did. She had gathered the spirits of the dead that crawled, broken and dazed, among the ruins.

And now she moved on again, as was her lot. The message to her brother would find its way or it would not. He would respond or he would not. In any event she did not intend to wait on the possibility of an answer. Opar headed north and so she would join him, whether or not he was aware of the extra traveler.

She stepped back into the world proper as she rested for a moment, winded by the distance she'd traveled. The Shimmer was powerful and it allowed speedy transportation, but she also needed to see the world she traveled to know where she was walking.

Where are we going? The words were not spoken, but felt. They were a thought from a dead man and though words did not take place she understood the thought almost as if it were her own.

The words came from Niall Leraby, whose shattered corpse she'd found frozen in the wastes. Of all the spirits she had ever encountered his rage was the brightest. His anger had called her from hundreds of miles away and so she now found herself on a quest to find justice for him.

All he could show her was the image of a nightmare made flesh. One of the Undying. The creature was loathsome indeed, and she thought it possibly the most unpleasant image she had ever encountered. She had not yet seen one in real life and if she never did, she was fine with that notion.

"We go north. We seek to find the man who caused all of your suffering."

I would see him dead!

"He fights against the creatures that killed you."

I–

"Yes. It's not always easy to choose, is it?"

Why does he fight them?

"I do not know. I only know the gods demand his death and the Undying want the same."

Niall Leraby's spirit brooded and Daivem let it be. She had other matters to consider, including what to do with Niall and the other spirits. They were angry at the Undying and those creatures served the gods themselves. Therefore the dead were angry with the gods. She had never faced off against a god before and that was considered a wise choice.

Not far away from her, one of the vast evergreens let out a groan and then a louder one as the mud beneath it gave way. The great tree shuddered and crashed to the ground only a dozen feet behind her.

Daivem moved faster, the winds whipping her cloak around and threatening to pull down her hood.

When she realized that someone walked next to her she got a better grip on her walking stick. The hard wood made for a wonderful weapon and she would be fine with employing it if the need arose.

The footsteps were heavy and the shadow of the figure moved with a lumbering gait that she recognized.

"Darsken! I did not expect you to travel here." Was there joy in her voice? Yes, there was. She did not see her brother often enough.

He looked her way in the perpetual darkness of the storm's cold cover and smiled brightly. "I am asked for help by my little sister, I come as quickly as I can."

He moved closer and without saying a word raised one arm and swept back his cloak. As she had many times before, Daivem moved towards him and felt his burly arm pull her closer still until she was nestled at his side. The cloak fell against her and drew her into a nest of warmth that smelled of home.

"I have missed you, Daivem."

Her arms wrapped around his solid waist and she squeezed hard enough to make him grunt. "Oh, I've missed you, too."

He looked around the area and back at the fallen

tree. "We should leave here and move faster. I feel this will worsen."

Not far away another tree groaned loudly and swayed to one side.

Daivem nodded and they stepped away from the world, into the Shimmer. There they stayed as they walked on, and Daivem told her brother what had happened in this reality.

CHAPTER TWELVE
THE COLD

Brogan McTyre

The He-Kisshi came, soaring through the dark clouds, spots that danced and drifted on the horizon until, suddenly, they were closer.

Harper called out a warning and the rest of the men came above decks, Faceless among them, towering over even the tallest.

Brogan took one look at the situation and shook his head. "And why don't the bastards close in?"

"At least one of them will, if only to demand we surrender you." Jahda bellowed to be heard over the waves and the wind. The ship was still moving steadily enough but the waters were choppy and the sails creaked through the build up of ice. Several times the remaining sailors had climbed the masts with heavy wooden sticks and risked their lives to beat the sails until the ice broke away and scattered over the deck.

Brogan had only been on a few ships in his life and never in this sort of weather. He was fascinated by the risks they took, and heard second-hand that under most circumstances the ship would have turned back. Apparently, the crew was terrified of suffering the same fate as their crewmates. He was satisfied with that answer. They had to get to the realm of the gods and to his knowledge there was only the one way.

"Let them come," he said. "When they do, we kill them."

"They are Undying." Jahda stared at him. "You have been granted a gift. Do not use it foolishly. Gifts such as yours are not known for lasting forever."

"Then we hurt them very badly."

Jahda nodded.

Harper pointed rather than spoke and they watched as one of the shapes drew near. Instead of landing on the deck, the thing settled itself close to the top of the tallest mast, hovering just inches above the wood.

It waved a hand and the winds died away. There was no mistaking the correlation of the action and the resulting calm. In seconds the waves slowed down and then stilled. The ship was adrift on a placid sea.

Brogan held his hand near his axe, but did nothing else.

The He-Kisshi stayed where it was and slowly turned its head, as if seeking one shape in particular. Finally it settled on Brogan. From this range it was only a cloaked shape. There was no sign of what lay hidden in the cowl.

"Brogan McTyre. The gods demand your death."

"Come get me." His hand found the haft of the axe.

"I do not come for you. I am here to let you know that you will die. I do not need to touch you to kill you. I merely need to let you know you will never reach your destination, Godkiller."

Brogan's lips twitched into a half-smile. "Godkiller. I rather like the sound of that."

Harper snorted, even as he slipped an arrow from his quiver and prepared it. He did not say anything, but Brogan heard his amused condemnation just the same.

To his right Faceless stared at the Undying.

The creature did not bother with Faceless, but continued to focus on Brogan. It shifted then finally settled on the wooden perch and Brogan could see the thick, clawed toes of the thing as they sank into the wood. The entire boat shifted with the change in weight.

"You will not reach your destination, Brogan McTyre. You and everyone on this ship will die before then." As the thing spoke it finally stopped looking his way and turned its hooded face to the skies. Above it, far above it, several forms now hovered over the ship, drifting like carrion birds, in a slow and steady circle.

The clawed hand of the thing touched the wooden mast for a moment and then let go. Where the pads of its hand had pressed to the wood, the color changed. The brown of the seasoned oak became first gray and then white, and that stain began to spread. The air was already bitingly cold but it became colder. The stain continued to grow and what looked like steam came from it. No. Not steam. The very opposite, in fact. The wood groaned and sighed as frost bit deep into it and spread faster. In mere seconds the whole of the mast was frozen solid and the vapors continued to rise even as the stain spread faster still. The wood screeched and swelled. The Undying dropped from its perch and spread its wings, rising on a burst of air so sudden that it staggered everyone but Faceless. Harper had been prepared to loose an arrow but never had a chance as he was too busy recovering.

Seconds, that was all it took, and the ship's mast let out another deep groan as the frost thickened and covered even the areas where ice had made itself at home.

The frost raced down and touched the deck and then went further still. From below decks the sounds of voices crying out drifted their way, Laram's chief among them. A moment later the horses let loose with their own noises.

Harper aimed a second time and loosed.

The He-Kisshi rose higher and then let out a scream as Harper's arrow drove into its throat. One clawed hand grasped at it, and the thing slipped in the sky, dropping toward the ship. Harper hit it with two more arrows as it struggled to remove the first from its thick neck.

It let out an enraged roar and flew toward Brogan's best friend, but before it could reach him Faceless lashed out and caught the shape in his long arms and pulled it toward his chest.

Oh, how it struggled and growled, trying to break the grip and failing. Faceless made no sounds as it pulled the form closer still, wood-like fingers spreading and sinking into the thin fur of the Undying until the flesh beneath ruptured and blood flowed.

The shapes above the ship dropped then, falling

like stones and then adjusting to spiral down toward the wooden deck, even as the frost painted that wood a bitter white.

Brogan moved his boots lest the vile stuff overtake him. Faceless stayed still and squeezed harder at the Undying even as frost grew on his body. The skin of his unusual companion grew white, but still Faceless continued to hold the struggling form, squeezing until bones creaked and then broke in his impossible grip.

One of the things came down to aid its captured brethren and Harper planted several shafts in the body with the aid of two of the others. The remaining He-Kisshi were wiser. They did not land and they stayed out of arrow range as well.

Harper added two more arrows to his work before the Undying rose out of range. One by one it pulled the arrow shafts from its body and cast them down into the waters. Each arrow that dropped steamed in the cold air and even in the dark of the overcast sky, Brogan could see that they, too, had frosted over.

And each of the arrows that struck the waters hissed as it made contact. They splashed down and did not sink as they should have, but instead floated and skimmed along the surface of the sea. Each of them trailed lines of frost wherever they moved.

The frost thickened and the waters slowed, growing white across the surfaces touched by the fallen missiles.

Harper spat, his lean face set and furious.

Brogan stared on, his mouth open in the cold air.

Faceless let out a sound and his skin cracked where the frost was the worst. Despite that, he did not release his prey and the Undying let out a screech as the arms constricted even more. Something cracked loudly and the chest of the He-Kisshi caved in. Blood vomited from the oversized mouth.

The shape in Faceless's arms sagged and moved no more.

Still the waves slowed and finally halted. The air grew bitter, cold enough that Brogan feared frostbite.

Roskell Turn, slight and shivering, began to chant words. Moving his body in an effort to stay warm, perhaps, or as part of whatever it was he was attempting.

The Galean cupped his hands around his mouth and exhaled. The air that came from him stretched and writhed like a wineskin filled with wriggling fish. It grew larger and he took that moving, seething thing and shoved it into his coat, shivering violently as he did so.

The He-Kisshi came closer, staying just out of arrow range, and one of them settled at the top of the mast again.

"You will die. All of you."

Brogan smiled. "And so will you." It was not a kind smile. He was not in a kind mood. If he had any say in the affair, the Undying would join the gods in their fall from power.

He intended to have much to say on the subject.

The Undying circled the ship, high in the air, in most cases.

Faceless took the broken thing he'd been fighting and cast it out onto the waters where it lay on the hardened surface, wings fluttering in the harsh winds.

While they waited, the dead thing slowly stood and staggered, still broken but no longer dead. Brogan could see it mending and loathed that talent.

"All of you will die!" The thing on the mast screeched the words and then rose into the air, rising higher and higher as it spiraled into the clouds.

Brogan looked around and spotted what he wanted. The ship was equipped for long voyages and that meant sometimes resupplying from the offerings of the ocean itself. He had seen the harpoons earlier and asked one of the remaining sailors about them. There were ten of the things and each had a line attached. They would throw them at whatever fish they could find, or the dolphins that sometimes danced in the waves near ships. If they caught something in lean times, the crew managed to eat.

As the one standing on the frozen waters started to spread its wings, Brogan took aim and hurled the harpoon. His aim was true and the force of the throw was good enough to let the barbed end puncture its belly. Already wounded and nowhere near at its full abilities, the thing fell again and shuddered.

Brogan grabbed the thick rope, braced his foot against the frozen railing, and began hauling his new prize toward the ship. Harper did not help. Instead, with no encouragement needed, he notched an arrow and waited.

The thing about his mates was, as surely as he could count on them to come to his aid, he could count on them to use their brains. Laram, who had every reason to hate him, was still below decks, but a few of the others made themselves useful and grabbed his rope, joining in tugging his prize aboard.

The other Undying had been circling but they once more dropped lower, even as Brogan and two others began pulling the He-Kisshi's dead weight up the side of the ship, grunting and straining.

Like as not they'd have never gotten the thing onboard, but Faceless came over and helped. He had at least the strength of a dozen men, and when he pulled the body fairly leaped to join them.

The other Undying came closer this time and Harper stared blankly at them. His face was serene and his eyes were soft and when he breathed there was a sense of peace and balance that came from him.

His aim was true and the first arrow stuck in the side of an Undying's "hood," drawing blood and a scream from the thing.

Brogan looked down at his bloodied prize and drew a large knife. "I've skinned one of you! I'll skin another!"

One of them spoke, "You cannot kill us all. And we will come back. You no longer have the power of Walthanadurn to aid you."

Brogan shook his head. "Are you so sure of that? Would you like to test it?"

"The protections you were granted by the gods are gone. They no longer want you as a sacrifice. They merely want you dead."

The thing gestured and the wind that hit Brogan threw him back as easily as he might throw an infant. His footing on the ice was precarious at best and gone in an instant. He staggered and then hit the frozen deck, grunting at the unexpected impact. His blade slipped from him as he sought to stop the wind from casting him away.

Faceless watched him slide, head tilted and likely considering what to do. Harper did not waste time with thought. He drew and loosed an arrow, and a second later the cloak around Brogan's shoulders and neck stopped moving. The arrow drove deep into the deck and held the thick fur. Brogan grunted and shivered as the winds continued unabated. His attempts to stand were failures.

He saw Jahda moving but barely had a chance to recognize the man before the harpoon he was carrying cut the air and struck the wind caster. The barbed tip slid through wing and arm alike and the He-Kisshi let out a shriek and the winds stopped.

The skies above rumbled and shook and lightning cast false daylight across the ship, the sea, and the distant shoreline. The He-Kisshi screamed, "I'll kill you all!" The beast reached with its other hand and pulled the harpoon through the bloodied arm, grasping the area under the barb and hauling the shaft of the weapon further along, until it was freed.

Faceless stepped closer to Brogan and he felt an inordinate rush of affection for the creature. This was not its battle and yet here it stood, ready to fight beside him.

The He-Kisshi lashed out. It threw the harpoon aside and spread the fingers of both hands. The hairs on Brogan's body stood on end, and breathing became a challenge. He knew that he was as good as dead. That was all he needed to know. Perhaps the creature would strike them with lightning. Perhaps with another assault of wind.

Instead of dying he saw the He-Kisshi explode into flames. One moment the creature was ready to attack, and the next fire licked across the whole of its body.

Anna let out a scream of her own as her hand caught fire. He hadn't even seen the woman come to the top deck, and now she fell to the wooden planks and waved her hand furiously in an effort to quell the flames licking at her fingers and trying to run higher up her arm.

Next to her Roskell Turn stepped closer, as if to protect her, and at the same time he cast something into the air. It looked like a handful of pebbles, but they rolled in the air and rose, soaring in a widdershins gust of wind that lifted them higher until they faded from view, rising as high as the other Undying.

Whatever he'd thrown into the air made itself known. Flashes of light made the sky as bright as day for one moment and then the He-Kisshi were falling from the skies to crash into the frozen waters.

Faceless looked at the creatures on the ice and took in a massive breath. It looked as if the creature was thinking of how to attack, but instead it merely stared at the closest of the Undying.

Roskell dug in his pockets, eyes wide and face a mask of panic. Brogan grabbed at another harpoon, desperate to find a weapon to take out the creatures before they could attack again.

Whatever the Galean found, he threw it toward the waters and then ducked. Something dark rushed through the air and scattered toward the He-Kisshi. A moment later the skies were filled with lightning that danced across the frozen waves and found each of the Undying and caressed them with electrical tongues. The air roared. The sea broke. Frozen waves exploded and then melted in the heat of the electrical storm, sinking the Undying even as they burned.

Jahda grabbed at the man who was supposed to be piloting the ship and pointed to the north. The man nodded, eyes wide and terrified, and then reached for the wheel.

Jahda gestured and called out words that Brogan could not hear. The sound of thunder still drowned out everything else.

The sky changed. One moment there were clouds and afterimages from the lightning and the next a hole ripped into the world directly ahead of the ship. The hole was filled with impossible lights in colors unknown to Brogan. The ship fell into that maelstrom of seething lights and a moment later the darkness was gone.

Nausea caught hold of Brogan and dropped him to his knees. The impact was painful but the feeling in his guts was worse. He had eaten bread and cheese a few hours earlier and that meager meal forced itself from him. All around him the people on the ship seemed to suffer the exact same fate. The only one unaffected by the change was Faceless, who looked around at the fallen, his nearly featureless mask of a face revealing as little of his thoughts as ever.

Brogan felt his body shake but could do nothing about it. Even his attempts to continue looking around were thwarted a moment later. He closed his eyes and fought against the wrenching of his stomach, but to no avail. His body was crippled by dry heaves for several moments.

And then the nausea and pain were gone and the waves slapped at the ship and cold air that was much warmer than they'd felt a moment before moved across Brogan's flesh.

When he opened his eyes properly and looked around, he saw everyone doing their best to recover.

Faceless looked at him and moved closer. "You are unwell?"

"I'm alive." It was enough for the moment. A glimpse over the side showed that the waves were moving and gave no sign of the Undying.

"We are alive." Jahda nodded his head and climbed to his feet, leaning heavily on the railing.

"What happened?"

Jahda looked around some more, even as he answered. "I moved the ship. I have begged a favor and had it granted. We are further along our journey than we were. I cannot guess by how much."

"What did you do?"

"As I said, I have begged a favor. I moved us from where we were. The Shimmer provided the aid. I do not know that I could ever do that again." His voice was weak, shaken.

Brogan opened his mouth to answer but shut it quickly when he saw the shape far above them. One of the He-Kisshi. There was no doubt.

It did not come closer, but instead hovered a moment and then moved on. The masts groaned and Brogan looked up to see thick ice forming on both of them. A moment later the ice spread down the masts to the ship itself. For a moment he thought the attack was done, but no, the cold came again with a vengeance.

Jahda spoke. "There's no escaping this. If we stay here, we will be frozen like this ship. We must leave."

Brogan shook his head. "And go where?"

Jahda shook his head. "There is only one place to go."

Within minutes the crew and Brogan's associates were all following the same trend and heading for the water. The ship groaned and creaked and steamed as the ice took it inch by inch at a slowly increasing pace. What had been frost became a thick layer of ice.

Anna favored her burned arm. Roskell Turn once more pawed at his pockets and the satchel he carried until he found what he was looking for. He cast a powder toward the waters and Brogan watched as the waves where he had gestured mimicked exactly what the Undying had done. The waters calmed and then froze. The ship continued to freeze and the water did the same and as quickly as they could the entire group disembarked. Two of the crewmembers lowered a plank and then they tried to draw the horses from the inside of the ship, but despite their best efforts they failed.

Brogan and company stood on frozen water and looked on as the ship turned white and then shattered. Around them the ice continued to do its business and grew in a widening circle.

Brogan tried to find something to say, but there was nothing. He had no words. Oceans did not freeze. Ships did not become ice. That said, he stood on the ice and looked at the ruins of the ship, with absolutely no idea how they were going to reach their destination.

CHAPTER THIRTEEN
WHAT DEMONS DEMAND

Beron

The pain finally stopped. It did not fade away, but instead merely ceased.

Beron opened his eyes and looked around at the world Ariah had made for itself. The bodies of countless people still littered the ground and hid under foliage that crept across the land. Vines and blossoms and trees were everywhere and some bore the oddest fruit he had ever seen. Not far away the heavy, head-shaped fruit on one massive hardwood moaned and cried as the winds blew across their faces. Blind eyes wept nectar and strange bugs greedily crawled across faces to drink their sweet tears.

Madness.

All of Ariah's world was filled with the dead and the things that fed on them, but it was disguised to look beautiful.

Ariah stood near him, once again clothed in a human guise. He smiled as he examined Beron.

"Can you move, Beron?"

Beron nodded and then frowned. Though he wanted to move, his body seemed incapable for a moment. He looked down and saw that his body was not what he remembered. There were two arms, and he had a torso, but lower down, there was more of him. His body was–

"What did you do to me?"

"I made you better, Beron. I made you larger and stronger."

As Ariah spoke it changed shapes again, this time to reflect what Beron himself now looked like. There were four legs and a broad, powerful body. His shape was similar to a war dog, sinewy muscle and claws and thick fur.

"Ahhh..." It was all he could manage to say. He had never been a vain man, but he had always been a man – and now?

Ariah sighed. "All that I have given you can be replaced by what was there before, but for now, learn to use your new shape. Learn to appreciate the power."

Beron closed his eyes and swallowed. "You can remake me as I was?"

"Of course. After you have settled matters with my enemies and helped Brogan McTyre in his quest."

"Why do I now help him?"

"Because the old gods must be put away, and he is the best option for that."

Beron nodded his head.

Slowly, he tested his new limbs. They obeyed his commands, but he had to make certain he knew what they were doing and so he walked carefully and did his best to observe the new shape of his body even as he grew accustomed to it.

"I feel the strength of this body, but I cannot manage this feat alone. I will need another army."

"You have one already, waiting for you. You will have another when you leave here. I prepare them even as we speak."

Around them the trees creaked, the vines rustled and the bodies of the dead remained where they were.

Beron felt a shiver run through the whole of his new body.

"You will not wander alone, Beron of Saramond. You will have an army of devoted soldiers. They will answer to you for so long as you answer to me."

Beron lowered his head in submission.

Always there are those who rule and those who are ruled. He could accept following a god that offered him power and weapons, and who trusted him to fight for him.

He stretched his new body, pleased with how quickly, even changed, it became a familiar form. He had learned to walk at an early age, but feared that acquainting himself with this form would take too long. He was happily mistaken. In a matter of moments he walked smoothly despite the change of gait. He had no doubt in his mind that the quick adaptation was another gift of his new god.

"You are too kind to me, Ariah. I will always serve you, and gratefully." He spoke the words. He meant them.

Ariah stepped aside to show a feast laid out on a

table grown from the very plants. "Eat and gain your strength. Soon enough I will send you out to fight for me again. Do not fail me, Beron. I am fond of you, but there are limits to my patience."

Beron nodded and moved to the table. Fresh meats, fresh fruit, an abundance of cheeses and breads, all awaited him. Sweet wines and potent ales were provided to wash down each part of the feast.

While he ate, the lord of the pocket world spoke and told him what was expected in the coming battles. He listened, and asked questions, and prepared himself.

When the meal was finished Beron moved away from the table and watched as it dropped slowly into the ground, consumed by the plants that carpeted the area.

"I will not fail you, Lord Ariah."

Ariah smiled. "Go. Move from this place and know that I am watching over you." Once again the demon lord offered him sword and spear and shield though none had been brought back with him that he knew of.

Beron bowed once, formally, and then moved. As he walked, he heard the sounds of his army rising from the ground. He looked back only once and was horrified by what he saw. That was good. That was excellent, really, because if they scared him they would terrify his enemies.

The Sessanoh

The male Grakhul prepared the sacrificial pits. Not far away two of the He-Kisshi watched, but said nothing.

That was enough of a warning. The preparations were methodical and precise, lest the gods take offense.

After three days, the Undying rose into the air and rode the winds toward the north and east.

The Grakhul relaxed, but only a little; the gods always watched and would know if they failed in their efforts. Urhoun sneered at the skies and contemplated what must still be done. There would be sacrifices required. Currently a hundred of the Grakhul children remained among them, working and cleaning the entire area. They would be sacrificed within the next few days, their sanctified blood used to honor the gods and prove the loyalty of the Grakhul. The gods were merciful. The gods were good.

Urwaquo, a man who was not known for his skittishness, came close and pointed to the top of the mountains above them.

"There are horsemen up there."

Urhoun frowned and scanned the hilltops. "Where?"

"South and east. They are riding single file." He pointed. "There." And so it was. He saw the horsemen this time and scowled. "Do we not have guards posted?"

"We do, but they have made no sounds." He nodded. If the men were still alive, they would be punished for their failures.

"To arms, but quietly. If we have new enemies here, let them learn of us as our blades carve them apart."

Urhoun found his own curved blade and strapped it to his arm, locking the chain in place. No one disarmed the Grakhul without removing an arm.

The chain was held in his hand to stop it rattling and he moved, climbing up the side of the hill surrounding the Sessanoh with his companions as the word was spread. It did not take long for them to prepare. None of the Grakhul were without their weapons nearby and all of them longed for battle after being denied for so long.

The gods had frozen them in place, but never truly left them asleep. For centuries the Grakhul had wandered the world in their dreams, often more aware than those that had been left awake. They had seen Pressya and Lomorride, the lands to the south where still more people followed the will of the gods. They had seen other lands too, further south still, where the gods were unknown as yet. The people in those places would be taught their place when the gods willed it. Until then they remained ignorant and lived as animals.

When he crested the hill Urhoun rested on his belly and looked into the valley below as best he could.

There were so very many of them. He did not know who they were, only that they moved into formation and waited. Many of them bore strange markings on their flesh and he squinted as he saw them.

The skies were not darkened by clouds here and he could see them clearly enough to know that there were easily three to every member of the Grakhul.

There were more of them coming still, moving single file over the mountains along several paths that led to the valley where his men were supposed to be watching and waiting. Urhoun did not see his guards and doubted that they were alive.

Torpuah, one of his longtime friends, asked, "What will we do?"

"There is no choice in this. The gods want the Sessanoh sanctified and protected. We fight."

"When?"

"When a few more of us have gathered. They have advantages in numbers. We have advantages from position. They must climb the side of the mountain or follow the narrow trails."

Even as he spoke, however, the first of the men below began moving up the three trails leading to the Sessanoh. None of the paths were particularly wide, but they were wide enough for a horseman to maneuver with ease.

Urhoun cursed under his breath and then spoke louder. "Call to arms!"

The three men closest to him called out and even those who had not yet been alerted reached for weapons and moved toward Urhoun. They were warriors. They would fight.

The horsemen came much faster than he'd anticipated. Much, much faster. They rode hard up the winding paths and even as his men gathered their weapons they broke over the crest of the hill and started down the other side, each of them ready with a weapon and moving quickly out of the way of the ones following behind.

The first of his men to reach the attackers died with a battle cry on his lips and a sword through his skull and eye. The men closest to him were warriors, true, but they hesitated as the blood flowed.

Urhoun let out a war cry of his own and charged

toward the closest trail. The riders there could not slow down, did not dare if they wanted to avoid delaying the whole of their army, and so he attacked as quickly and savagely as he could, hoping to block the flow of riders coming into the Sessanoh.

It was his misfortune, though he was unaware of that fact, to choose King Parrish as his first target.

Parrish dropped from his horse even as he deflected the blow, and caught Urhoun's long hair in his free hand. Urhoun tried to pull back and his enemy ripped brutally at his hair, twisting his head to the side and using the pommel of his short sword to strike Urhoun in the temple.

Urhoun swept the chain at the end of his sword and slapped it across the man's leg. The man let out a hiss of pain and let go of his hair. Urhoun staggered back and dared a grin at the respite. The next second he was backing away again as the swordsman came for him, the weapon in his hands moving in a series of short, brutal strikes that Urhoun was hard pressed to fend off. While he focused on the sword, his attacker kicked out and caught his leg at the knee. The joint bent the wrong way and agony ripped through Urhoun. He stumbled and felt the blade cut across his free arm. Blood ran warm in the cold air and Urhoun let out his own hiss of pain.

It was a game, really, a dance of sorts, and though he was out of practice and had slept frozen in ice, Urhoun still knew the rules of that dance. He stepped in hard and fast, taking advantage of the close proximity to leave his enemy's sword out of the equation.

The stranger smiled at him, a baring of teeth

worthy of a hunting wolf, and moved in closer himself, shoving back against Urhoun with surprising strength. In his experience humans were not overly strong, but this one, despite being lean, was hard with muscle and savage in his demeanor. The man pushed harder still and Urhoun pushed back and–

One moment he fought against a powerful opponent and the next he was sailing through the air, trying to understand what had just happened. When Urhoun hit the ground it was at a bad angle and he felt his left shoulder soar into agonies the likes of which he'd never experienced in his life.

His enemy did not bother with finishing him off, but instead called out to his horse. The beast moved aside and let more of the riders through.

Urhoun tried to rise and let out a yelp of pain. His arm refused to move, but the effort to try making it follow his orders was enough to leave his vision gray and his ears ringing.

The horsemen kept coming. Urhoun looked around as he tried to recover, and saw more and more of the riders charging through the opening, their steeds plowing past anything that got in their way, including his men.

The man he'd fought climbed back on his animal, making the task look easy, and then called out in their strange language, gesturing with an arm. The riders moved, heading toward the Sessanoh, sweeping their weapons at anyone in their way. They had spears, they had swords, and they had other weapons that he could not clearly see. Wherever the riders went, his people fell, bloodied, damaged, or dead. They did not die alone. Most fought hard and died with honor, but they died just the same.

Urhoun rolled over and whimpered as he slowly climbed to his feet. The world faded to gray twice more but he finally stood. Around him the battle moved on; the riders continued pouring into the area and hacking down his people as if they were wheat before a farmer.

Without lifting his sword, Urhoun closed his eyes and called out to the gods, begging assistance from the He-Kisshi or any other available source.

When he opened his eyes the man who had ruined his arm stood before him. His face was painted with drops of blood and his body glistened with sweat.

Not a hundred yards away he saw the man still fighting, still killing, but he stood before him as well.

"I am not King Parrish. I am the god Parrish serves. I am Theragyn, the Master of the Cauldron. Speak to your people and they could be spared this. They will die now, serving gods who do not care about you, or you and yours can pledge yourselves to me and be tested within the cauldron. Prove worthy and you will reap great rewards."

"The gods cannot be defied."

"They can. They are. Join me and you will know glories the likes of which you did not know existed."

"The gods are the gods." He shook his head. "They are unforgiving."

Theragyn smiled sadly even as the man who looked like him drove his blade deep into Urwaquo. The blade punched completely through the man's chest.

Theragyn said, "You can still save them."

"The gods cannot be denied."

"So you keep saying." Theragyn reached out and touched Urhoun's hand gently.

The pain was immediate. The pale white skin where Theragyn had touched turned black and withered. As Urhoun watched, horror growing in his heart, the blackened flesh continued to grow, the small patches reaching toward each other and spreading.

He gasped and screamed. The pain was so massive that he forgot all about his dislocated shoulder for the moment and tried to move again. Where the flesh had blackened, the skin ruptured, releasing gray, decayed meat and blood that was already coagulating.

Urhoun tried to scream again, but failed as his lungs rotted within his torso. He stood for a moment longer as the agonies of living through his death worked their way through him.

In moments he was dead and he saw nothing more.

His people did not last much longer.

Parrish

There were casualties, yes, but that was to be expected. Men died and were injured. Horses were wounded and a few were struck lame enough that killing them was a mercy. The bodies of the fallen were burned in fire, cleansed of their sins in this life by purification. The corpses of the enemy were hauled to the great holes in the ground, and per Theragyn's demands, they were gutted, bled and then cast down into the pits.

Parrish smiled. He was exhausted. He felt wonderful.

All around him the Marked Men and the soldiers worked hard to finish the tasks before them.

Not far away he saw Theragyn waiting, looking exactly like him, a smile on his face.

Parrish stepped closer and crossed his arms over his chest as he bowed. "All you would ask of me, I will gladly do, my lord."

"You serve me well, Parrish."

"What would you have us do now, my lord?" He knew that there was more. There had to be. The gods themselves were getting involved in the conflicts.

"Rest for the night. In the morning I will move you to another place. The war grows, Parrish, and we will rule all if we are wise."

"Then let us be wise, Lord Theragyn."

CHAPTER FOURTEEN
PATHS TO WAR

Opar

The trail was still obvious, but at least the fires had faded away. The charred remains of woods and towns and prairies all showed the continuous path to the north.

Opar rode on, mostly spending time in his wagon, but occasionally riding a horse to stop himself from being alone with his thoughts.

The gods had decreed that he would serve them and there was nothing he could do about that except choose to die. That was not a choice he wanted to make and so he did not.

The Undying said that the enemies would follow this path, or that they would meet those enemies by following this path, but the cold was almost crippling. The sun had not shown itself in days, the winds cut harshly across the landscape and the rain that fell froze on contact with, well, everything.

Edinrun could still be returned to him, that was

what the Undying claimed. Still, he had seen the bodies, mountains of corpses burned into smaller mountains of ashes and bones. The buildings alone would do him little good without his citizens.

And yet here he was, riding for the northlands, and through the ruins of what had once been neighboring kingdoms. The course shifted away from where he knew Saramond had been, because the place where the city used to be was no longer there. The seas had swallowed the land, wiping it away with ease.

The trees around them creaked with the weight of building ice, and from time to time they could hear a powerful crack as something broke under the weight.

Not surprisingly, the soldiers were grumbling. None of them wanted to be there. They might have even run away, but the fear of the gods kept them loyal where the promise of gold failed. Gold only bought things. Gods could make or break whatever they chose.

Rithman coughed into his hand. Opar looked his way, annoyed but doing his best to hide it. "I'm not trying to aggravate you, cousin, but we're running low on supplies."

"Of course we are." He hadn't even considered the need for supplies. There were others who usually handled those affairs for him, but there were no stores to take from, no merchants from whom they could make purchases. "Nothing to hunt around these parts, is there?"

"Everything is dead or dying." Rithman shook his head. "We've no equipment for fishing, though that would be our only choice I think."

"So tell the cooks to work something out. Make

nets, or harpoons, or whatever they need. Catch fish. The gods say we move this way. They do not care if we are fed. We have to take care of that ourselves."

Rithman nodded. "What we saw was real, wasn't it?"

"Oh, yes. I would rather you remember that, too. Forgetting is only going to cause us troubles."

Before Rithman could respond, a horn shattered the relative silence. The guards had horns for a reason. Opar did not expect an attack, but it was always best to be prepared.

The area around them was dark. They had torches to light their way but they did not illuminate the nearby woods.

Another horn blasted a warning and then a third.

Rithman moved away from the entrance to the wagon and strode across the frozen ground, calling orders.

Opar could hardly do less. He hastily pulled on his boots and grabbed his cloak. The sword and scabbard came along as well.

The winds outside the wagon were worse than he'd expected. His skin fairly let out a yelp of its own. Still, he had to do this. The king needed to lead his armies and the gods were making demands.

So be it.

There was chaos outside the wagon, but it was the chaos of order being forced upon an army. The men lined up with their squads and battalions in short order. The horsemen were quick, the footmen were quicker. They were not completely silent, but no one called out who was not supposed to, and so they heard the sounds soon enough.

There was the sound of the wind, the sound of the rain pattering down and beneath those sounds came the odd rustling of things moving that were simply not human.

The noises were too low, for one, and they scratched and hissed and moved slowly, where a boot would have sounded like a drumbeat.

Opar's skin shivered at the notion. There was nothing to see in the darkness.

"What has been seen?" he asked Rithman as he moved closer to the man.

"Nothing that makes sense, my king. There are no soldiers but the forest moves."

"The forest?"

"The trees have been shifting with more than the wind."

"You've summoned the whole of my army to fight the trees?"

"No, my liege." Rithman's voice had an edge. "We've called the army to prepare in case the trees are merely a sign of something different."

It wasn't the time to chastise his general in front of the troops, but if there proved to be no reason for the congregation of forces, he intended to let Rithman feel his anger properly.

Not a hundred yards away, at the edge of the great swath cut across the area, something cracked and one of the trees let out a long moan before it came crashing down.

Most of the soldiers standing in the path of the falling monolith cleared out of its way before they could become fatalities. A few did not. They let out cries of pain in some cases and were far too silent in others.

Rithman called for four squads to move the tree aside. It was a large thing, to be sure, but the men began the task and soon had the thing rolled most of the way off the actual path.

And while they were so engaged, the enemy attacked.

The sight made no sense. Near as Opar could tell the attackers were wrapped in vines and leaves. He squinted to see better in the darkness, but to no avail.

The soldiers let out battle cries and screams and drew weapons as the attackers clubbed them with blunt tools or pierced them with what looked like sharpened sticks.

The lightning danced through the clouds and gave brief moments of better illumination. What they showed were the sort of images that led to madness.

The attackers were not wreathed in vines, but seemed made of them. Muscles and sinews of green were wrapped around faded, yellowed ivory. Skulls and bones showed through the leaves, though there was no sign of actual flesh. Each of the things was an impossibility, and no two were quite the same. Several of them carried thick bones as weapons. Most were blunt, but a few were broken off into sharp edges.

The things attacked with savagery. They swept their makeshift weapons around and clubbed at Opar's soldiers, cracking skulls and impaling flesh. The men tried to fight back, but they were panicking. They'd seen storms tear a city apart, but none of them, not even Opar himself, had ever seen plants and bones attack a person before.

Rithman was good. He called for backup and made certain that his men followed the orders given. He also drove forward on his horse and brought his sword into the conflict. When he saw that little damage was caused by the weapon, he changed tactics and used his shield's edge to shatter bone and pulp green flesh.

Through it all, the sound of rustling leaves and creeping vines were the only noises that the enemy made. Opar stared on, slack-jawed.

"Where is Opar?" The voice bellowed from within the ranks of the plant-things and Opar flinched. The thought that the things might speak was terrifying.

Instead, a different nightmare came forward. From the waist up, he looked like a man, heavily scarred with dark brown skin. Below that he could not be certain exactly what he was seeing, only that it had four legs and wide feet with heavy claws. Whatever else he could say about the thing was lost in studying the sheer size. As humans went, the torso and arms were massive. As four-legged creatures went, it was larger than his warhorse.

"Opar! Come to me! Surrender and all will be spared!" The voice was loud, to be sure. He trusted the thing calling to him as far as he trusted the servants of the gods. There were more of the He-Kisshi, however, and so he decided not to surrender to this new thing.

Instead he pointed to Rithman and said, "Help me kill that beast."

Opar was not a coward. He was frightened by things that should not have existed, but that was wisdom in his eyes. Not foolishness.

He climbed aboard his charger and drew his sword. The plant things might not bleed, but what he looked at seemed flesh and blood. That was enough.

While the soldiers did their best against the plants, Opar and Rithman charged the monstrous thing that led them. The two had fought together, trained together and worked together for many years. It was easy for them to circle the beast and keep it off balance.

Whatever it was, it looked to Rithman first and then to Opar. While it was busy with Rithman, Opar risked a slashing attack across the thing's flank and drew first blood.

He did not expect it to move so quickly, however, and barely managed to parry the return attack with a spear thrust. The beast was powerful enough to nearly unseat him.

While Opar did his best to deflect the spear, Rithman attacked with all that he had, defending his kin and his king. His horse reared up and came down on the side of the odd creature, hooves cutting across the ribcage and leaving bloody marks.

The thing immediately turned all its attention to Rithman, screaming incoherently as it thrust with its spear, and then the lower half of the creature reared up and slashed with thick claws against the neck of the man's horse. The roan never had a chance to defend itself as its throat was torn away.

The dying horse fell forward and so did Rithman. He did not fall far before being impaled on the spear. Opar's cousin coughed blood and reached for the weapon thrust through his chest, but did not get far before he collapsed.

The monstrous thing that had killed Rithman screamed again. He was saying words, but his rage made them gibberish.

Opar took his chance and drove the tip of his sword into the thing's side as it turned toward him. The blade was almost pulled away, but Opar held tight and watched his sword cut a fearsome wound.

The spear took him in the shoulder, driving deep and cutting through muscle before it rammed into bone. Did Opar scream? He didn't know. His entire world focused on the pain, and he simply could not tell.

The sword dropped from his hand. He watched it fall.

The pain was still too big for him to care. It dwarfed everything else.

All around him in the semidarkness the men he commanded fought on, some fell and others continued their charge against an unholy enemy. Opar grunted as the hellish half-man wrenched the spear from his shoulder and tossed him to the ground as if he were a rotten head of cabbage.

The half-man stared down at him for a moment; fury painted its face into a mask and then slowly he smiled.

"Opar..."

He couldn't have denied the truth just then even if he'd wanted to. Opar nodded his head once before the man's sword came down and finished what the spear had started.

Beron

Beron raised the severed head of King Opar over his head and reared up, screaming Ariah's name. His body rushed with renewed energy and the army of things offered him by the demon lord shivered with the same rush of energy.

A moment later they renewed their attack on Opar's people, cutting at them savagely. Men died easier than the things that served as his soldiers and Beron grinned in pleasure at that thought.

If Ariah wanted him to kill an army of fools, then he would do so.

Around him the plant-things moved, defying the cold that should have destroyed them. Glistening bones shifted within their forms, and soldiers rushed in against them only to die. Beron felt no pity for the people. They were as insignificant as slaves. They stood between him and his destiny. He would rule over the ruins of this world before he would surrender to others. His god was with him and that was enough.

How seldom the world agrees.

The first of the He-Kisshi dropped from the sky on wings that fluttered and snapped instead of flapping. He did not understand how the monsters could fly, but he recognized them well enough. The Undying were the stuff of nightmares. Of course, these days, so was he.

"You dare defy the gods?" The thing hissed the words and as it spoke the winds died down to let it be heard.

"Fuck your gods! I found a better one!" Beron

flipped the spear around in his hand and prepared it for a proper throw.

"Then you are a fool!" The creature landed on the ground and immediately reached for the whip on its belt. Beron, who knew exactly how much damage a whip could cause in the right hands, grew alert.

"Your gods would destroy the world because one man offended them! I will serve a god that would stop them! Your gods have ruined my life!" He screamed the words, barely aware of how angry he was. "Your gods took all that I have and Ariah offers better!"

The He-Kisshi came closer, and despite being larger and better armed, Beron felt fear in the center of his guts.

"I will see you fall before me, Beron of Saramond."

"I will kill you before you can, or I'll take you with me." He spoke as bravely as he could, looking into that dark hood filled with teeth.

"You. Are. NOTHING!" The whip slashed across the air and caught him with a sudden fiery pain across his left nipple and down to the edge of his belly. Many might well have stopped at the agony, but Beron had been tortured and beaten before. Instead he charged forward, and threw his spear.

The weapon had been crafted by Ariah himself, and it ran true and on target.

The He-Kisshi caught the weapon before the tip could penetrate flesh. In all his life Beron had never seen a man move that fast. Of course, the Undying were not men. They were the voice of the gods, the will of the gods personified.

The Undying cast the spear aside and moved

forward; its entire body shivered with rage and the mouth opened wide in a violent hiss.

The whip came around a second time and caught Beron on the side of his face, opening a scintillating line of pain from his nose down to his chin, and splitting his mouth open in the process. Teeth shattered beneath torn lips, and Beron roared. He knew he should have been crippled by the new agonies, but he was not. Ariah had blessed him.

As the thing had charged toward him, so he now moved forward, sword in one hand and shield in the other. When he reached the Undying he smashed into the creature with all of his might, the shield pushing the horrific thing backward.

The Undying staggered, screeching its indignity. Beron pursued, his sword hacking downward to strike at flesh.

And the accursed thing caught the blade with its hand. Skin bled and bones were cut, but the weapon came to a stop in that grip.

"Enough!"

One word was all he heard and then the arc of white lightning moved through the He-Kisshi and into his sword too fast for Beron to process properly.

He had been rebuilt as a weapon. He was far tougher than a human being and he knew that. He'd been cut deep in his side, and the whip had opened fresh wounds. Still, the electricity was more than he could hope to prepare for.

Heat fried his flesh and his eyes alike. His hair burned away and the claws on his four feet melted into the ground. The whip had hurt, but this? The lightning coursed through his veins and boiled the blood inside his body. His heart exploded. His lungs collapsed into burnt ruins within his chest.

Beron did not die.

He wanted to die. He would have begged Ariah to take him if he could have formed words, but his torn, shredded lips had been burned away.

"You would follow a new god? You would replace me and mine as the voice of that god? So be it. Let us see if you are truly undying."

For one moment there was peace, as his life slipped away.

When he opened his eyes, he saw Ariah standing above him. His god was not pleased.

"No, Beron. There will be no death for you. You are *my* Undying. Go. Kill my enemy."

An instant later Beron was back in the very same spot as the He-Kisshi began to move away from him, prepared, like as not, to finish off his forces.

Beron gave himself one heartbeat to panic at the thought of never dying, never escaping the pain of combat.

Then he charged forward on his four powerful legs and brought his sword down on the shoulder of the creature that had killed him. His roar echoed across the frozen trees. The scream of the Undying reverberated back as he cut the creature nearly in half.

"Never turn your back on me, He-Kisshi!"

As he watched, the tormented flesh began to seal itself. He did not give the beast time to mend and instead hacked into the head of the thing, cleaving the obscene mouth in two and them stabbing several more times in an effort to blind all of the tiny eyes that surrounded that maw.

As it shivered and bled before him, the head cut in twain, the lightning flickered again and the winds came back full force.

High above he saw the shapes of other winged things moving through the clouds, their shadows painted on the storm by the lightning that swept the heavens.

There were more of them. Many more. He hacked into the creature on the ground before him, finishing the grisly task of cutting it completely in two. When he was done, Beron grabbed the closest piece of the thing and threw it as far as he could. They were Undying? Fine. He would make the task of living one they had to earn.

Three of the obscenities dropped from the clouds.

The plant things that served him, the humans that fought them, all noticed this time when the He-Kisshi came.

"You would kill one of ours?" Again, that indignant tone, as if the notion of being defied was nearly impossible to comprehend.

"I would kill all of you!"

The cowled shape did not carry a whip. Instead it simply moved backward a step or two and left a thick fog in its place. The fog may have started in that spot but it did not stay there. It grew outward at a nearly impossible rate, blinding Beron's eyes to anything he might have seen.

"Where are you, coward?" Beron grinned and challenged the beast to fight.

"Here." The response came from behind him and he had long enough to know he was dead before his life ended.

Ariah did not speak this time, but instead made a casual gesture and tossed Beron back into the world.

The He-Kisshi were waiting this time. Two of the creatures stood near each other, a few feet from where he had last died. He saw no corpse and remembered being back in Ariah's realm. Perhaps he would ask for an advantage at his next death and see if he could be moved elsewhere.

A flick of a wrist and the new Undying sent a whip around his neck. The weighted end of the thing slapped across his windpipe and crushed it.

Before he could die, however, the other one breathed a cloud of white at him that quickly froze his skin and the weapons Ariah had once again provided him with.

He felt his eyes freezing within his skull and then he was dead.

"I grow weary of this, Beron." Ariah's voice was not offended so much as bored. The handsome face that looked at him was fraying at the edges and the true face of the demon threatened to show itself to him.

"Can you place me in a different location, Ariah?"

"No. There are rules. The He-Kisshi may not be reborn in new places and neither can you. I moved you once before, but it was exhausting. Do better. Kill them."

"They can control the elements themselves! Wind,

and fog, and lightning. Fire, from what I've heard and frost from what I've felt."

"Then kill them faster."

An instant later he was back in the same place again, and the Undying stood before him.

Before he could speak, or even truly get his bearings, something drove into his spine where his humanoid self and bestial self met. The pain was even larger than he'd have imagined possible and his death was fast.

He had not even finished dying yet when the shape of the He-Kisshi that had killed him moved past in a streak and attacked Ariah.

Whatever the Undying did, it took effort. The body of the thing warped and bent as the very air around it was torn asunder amid a crash of tinder and a flare of lights worthy of a bonfire. Whatever barriers held the worlds apart, the creature tore through them.

The demon lord was powerful, to be sure, but it was also caught off guard by the savage attack of the Undying as it forced its way into Ariah's realm.

Lightning ripped across the land, burning plants and shattering bones as it moved. The fury was horrifying, and Beron closed his dying eyes lest the light burn them away, but there was no escaping the noise of thunder tearing the skies apart.

And there was no escape from the sound of Ariah's rage and pain as the creature attacked him.

Beron was not as dead as he'd expected. He heard Ariah scream and heard the Undying howl in pain.

The winds grew furious and the rains that struck

his body froze on contact with both him and the ground around him.

The plants that Ariah had created froze, sealed in a sheath of ice. Beron opened his eyes and dared look upon the devastation. Ariah no longer bore any semblance to a human shape. It was a massive form, twisting in on itself as it fought against the Undying. The claws of the thing tore into Ariah's warped flesh and drew what could possibly be blood again and again, but it suffered greatly in the process. The wings of the thing were burned away when Ariah struck back, and bone showed through its hide in several places. Still it fought, and Beron tried to move but could not. If he were truly Undying, he was more limited than the beast before him.

Interlude: Desmond Harkness

Seven days. They had walked for seven days along the edge of the ruination, looking at the waters as they continued to rise, and staring at the ruins of things that could only be gods.

Bump said, "I'm hungry."

Desmond nodded. They were both hungry and the waters tasted of the sea, and the rain was cold and wet and miserable. If the man complained any more there was a real chance that he would kill him.

"I know you are hungry. And tired. And sore."

Bump looked his way with a half-smile on his tired face.

"It's only fair. Each and every time you whine about your wife, I will whine about something else."

"I have not been 'whining about my wife.'"

"Oh, gods, yes, you have."

"I've been wondering if she is dead." He shot Bump a withering look.

"We'll find out when we find out. In the meantime be grateful that we are alive."

"I'm as grateful as I can be." Desmond gestured at the world around them.

"Not so. You have your legs and your balls. That's a blessing."

"Blessings are offered by gods, you jackass." Desmond spat the words. "Do you suppose the gods are offering us protection when they've set out to have us killed for helping Brogan?"

He thought about mentioning his feet, but knew the man was in the same situation. The soldiers that had captured them a week earlier had driven nails through their heels to slow them down. It had worked to a certain extent, but when the seas came crashing against the mountains he and Bump had made a run for it, and managed to survive.

He had no idea how. The mountains themselves had shook, and a skeleton that was absolutely impossible had shattered the mountains and then attacked something even more horrifying in the ocean before collapsing into the waters.

Through it all they had run, or hobbled as best they could. That was all there was to it. They had fled for all they were worth, sleeping when they could manage and doing their best not to freeze in the horrid weather. Now they walked close to the sea, not because they chose to, but because the land was slowly being swallowed and everything lower than them was already gone.

"See that, do you?" Bump pointed out into the water, his eyes squinting.

They were lucky enough in that now and then a rift in the clouds showed them the waters and offered hope that the end of days was not completely upon them. They even saw seagulls now and then, though none had come close enough for them to hunt, even if they'd had so much as a dagger between them.

Desmond squinted, felt the blisters on his face tighten with the expression and then nodded. "Boat."

"Only one we've seen in days!"

"We shouldn't even see a fucking boat, Bump. The ocean isn't supposed to be here."

"Perspective, lad. It's all perspective. We see a boat. That boat sees us. I can tell because it's changing course."

"Like as not we're to be someone's food at this point."

Bump laughed and slapped Desmond's arm. He was also good enough to catch Desmond when he nearly fell off the rocks and into the waters below.

"Try not to be so depressing. You're beginning to sound like Harper."

The boat came closer, and at a good clip. The winds helped it along as it changed course to skim along the shoreline, and finally Desmond allowed himself to hope.

And when he saw the woman maneuvering the craft he even managed a smile, though it split half the remaining sores on his face.

"Darwa! What are you doing out here?"

The old woman huffed and shook her head. "Looking for you, you damned fool. Your wife would never forgive me if I didn't bring you along."

"You've seen my Anna?" His heart hammered in his chest, desperate for news.

"I have not! But I know where she is heading. You and your fool friend can come down here, I'm not going up there for you."

He very nearly sent them both over the side in his haste to reach the boat and the old Galean who had taught his wife half of the sorceries that she knew.

Bump yelped a few times but did his best to keep up, and in a few minutes they were swimming through shallows to reach the boat.

It was larger than he'd first thought, or at least it seemed that way as they climbed aboard, Bump first and then Desmond.

Both of them were soaking wet and shivering.

Darwa was an older woman, but she was also in surprisingly good shape if her strength was any indication. She hauled Bump aboard and then Desmond, and her grip was like iron.

"There we go." She was wearing a thick fur coat and looked impossibly warm.

She said something, he had no idea what, as the words hurt his ears, but a moment later a stiff warm breeze was blowing past him and filling the single masted sail of the small boat, launching them toward the north at a speed that scared Desmond senseless for a moment. He relaxed when the warmth penetrated the cold that had become his world.

"I cannot thank you enough, Darwa." He dared a second smile. The witch woman knew things and among them was the fact that his Anna was still alive.

She grunted and then reached into a heavy bag. What she pulled out was more than should have fit. She started with heavy fur cloaks, and followed with dried meats and a skin of wine. They were silent and grateful for a while as they chewed the hard meat and sipped at the wine, which was sweet and helped warm them further.

Darwa spoke as they ate. "We head to the north and we have a long way to go. I can keep the worst of the storms away, but there are many threats ahead of us."

Bump asked, "What sort of threats?"

Darwa gestured at the sky and then the sea. "The gods are angry and they are scared. They will find anything they can to aid them in stopping Brogan McTyre and all of his friends and that includes both of you. They want you dead."

Bump opened his mouth and then closed it.

She said, "So why don't they just kill you?"

He nodded and took another bite of dried meat.

"Galea wrote that in order to protect themselves the gods placed themselves in a different realm, a place where the people and things here cannot touch them easily. That place is hidden away in dangerous waters, and it is hard to find and harder to enter. The Undying and the Grakhul are here to make sure that the will of the gods is done without them ever having to enter this world or allow others to enter theirs."

"Are they that afraid?"

Darwa squinted at him and Desmond thought he saw a smile on her face. "I do not know the answer to that. They might just as easily be lazy, but whatever their reasons, they hid themselves away and made surrogates to do their bidding."

Bump nodded his head. He eyed the woman with what looked like actual longing. Desmond said nothing. The woman was not a beauty but neither was she a wretch. He could have pointed out that she was, according to her own words, much older than she looked, but he opted not to speak of the matter at all. It was not his place.

"Darwa, do you know my wife's fate?"

"Do you mean to ask if Anna is alive? She is." The woman nodded her head and then swept back her brown hair when it fell in her face. "Alive and unharmed, though I expect she has been changed by what she's seen."

Desmond frowned at that, ready to ask another question. Instead of giving him the time she pointed to the monolithic corpses nearby.

His frown deepened but he said nothing.

Around them something moved in the dark waters and they saw lights, faint at first but coming closer. Darwa hissed her irritation and then made gestures in the air. Their boat stopped moving and the winds settled.

The lights came closer still, taking forms that strained his eyes with their illumination and their design both.

"Stay still, you fools." Darwa was glaring at Bump as she spoke.

For a few minutes they remained as quiet and still as they could while the forms moved around the area and then slowly spiraled away into different parts of the vast ocean. Finally, Darwa nodded and once again made gestures. A moment later the wind picked up and the boat surged toward the north, shifting around the impossibly massive dead things in the water.

"They don't smell." Bump was staring at the massive skeleton and the thing pinned under it. Despite his attempts, Desmond could not quite comprehend what it was. It had scales, and fins and teeth, and what might be an eye stared up at the clouds. The parts did not add up for him.

"They will, but it will be long after you've died. Gods don't rot easily." Darwa said the words in an offhand manner and Bump frowned, considering them very carefully.

"Those are gods?"

Darwa nodded.

"Then what were those things in the water?"

"The God with a Thousand Names has children. Those were a few of them. They seek anyone connected with the man who killed their mother."

"And that would be?"

"Brogan McTyre."

Desmond could think of nothing to say. Neither could Bump. They moved silently through the dark waters, often staring at the dead impossibilities resting to their north and, eventually, west.

CHAPTER FIFTEEN
CONFLICT

Brogan

"Are we going to walk to the Gateway?" From anyone else the question would have been frustrating at the very least, but it came from Faceless, who very likely had no idea where they were going or how far it meant traveling.

Brogan nodded his head. "I don't know that we have any other choice. The horses are dead. Frozen solid inside the ship." So were a few crewmembers. Laram had made it above decks but three others had died in the attempt to get away from the He-Kisshi and their damnable abilities.

Jadha had moved through the entire ship looking for survivors and found none. When the man returned from the ship his face was grim and his normally cheerful demeanor was somber. Whatever had happened inside the ship was something he would not speak of. It was also something that disturbed him deeply.

The group was as bundled as they could be and once again Anna and the other Galean – it took him a moment to remember the man's name – Roskell Turn, had done something to keep them, if not warm, at least not frozen. Their breaths barely even showed as steam when they exhaled.

"Ship!" It was one of the remaining crewmembers that called out and pointed to the south. At first Brogan saw nothing in the darkness but the shape made itself clear soon enough.

It was a ship, and larger by far than the ruin they had been forced to abandon. There was a name on the side, but the shadows and darkness hid that away as well as any colors the ship might have been flying.

As they watched the ship came closer and the skilled crew slowed it, turning the sails into the wind until the vessel came to a rough halt.

Faceless stared at the ship with no expression, though there was little in the way of features to offer any. Anna stared as well, and most of the crew. Brogan looked along the deck to see if he could find any faces. Finally one showed itself.

He had met the woman before, but at the moment her face filled him with dread. His actions had caused massive damage to the world around him and the loss of her city was likely the sort of thing that Hillar Darkraven would not forgive easily.

It would be a shame to have to kill the lady. She had always been friendly enough when they met.

The crewmember that had spotted the ship called out in his language and someone from the other ship called out in response. Within moments there were boats being lowered into the slush-filled waters.

Brogan walked over to Jahda and spoke softly. "Do you know Darkraven?"

"We know each other."

"Are you friends?"

"We are not." He looked at the boats coming toward them and shrugged. "Neither are we enemies. We respect each other's position."

"Let's hope that continues."

Jahda looked his way and nodded. "It will."

"Yes?"

"Of course. Even if she is pursuing you, and I suspect she is, when this is all done she will need a place to stay and the Kaer-ru are the closest lands that will support her shipload of people."

Brogan nodded his head and sighed. "In the meantime, I expect we should all be prepared to fight." He needn't have wasted his breath. A quick scout of his surroundings showed that all of the people with him were checking their weapons. Several of the men, Harper among them, had already prepared their bows and were eyeing the approaching boats with wariness.

The boats did not take long to reach them. All seven of them.

There were more people on those boats than there were survivors from the ship. It was not a comforting thought at all.

They came ashore en masse and approached the same way, led by Darkraven and the largest woman Brogan had ever seen. Darkraven was not angry in expression. The other one was.

"Which of you is Brogan McTyre?" Darkraven's voice was smooth and calm.

"That would be me." Brogan took one step forward.

Darkraven looked and slowly nodded, recognition showing itself. "You have made powerful enemies."

"That I have. I've killed a few of them, too."

"That he has." Jahda spoke calmly.

Darkraven nodded and even managed a very small smile for the man. "It's good to see you are alive. I had doubts after all that has happened."

Jahda returned the facial expression and did little else. "You are very far from home, Hillar."

Her smile grew larger. "The world is my home. What choice do I have?" Her eyes looked toward Brogan. "Someone sank my city."

"I assure you it wasn't me." Brogan forced a smile of his own, knowing full and well that it was not pleasant.

"You are Brogan McTyre. You started a war with the gods." Hillar spoke as calmly as ever. The longer she uttered words, the less he trusted her.

"Not at all." He took two steps forward and the lads moved forward with him. "They started the fight. They took my family. I am returning the favor."

"You would kill the gods?" The woman laughed at him.

"I already killed one. Check with your Scryer."

"I can't. She's gone mad."

"And do you suppose that might be for a reason?"

"Enough of this!" The large woman walked forward and stepped past Hillar Darkraven. "Come with us so we can surrender you to the gods!"

"And where are you going to take me?" Brogan kept his smile and tightened his grip on the axe. The woman was heavy with muscle and well-scarred. She did not act like a courtesan. She moved like a warrior.

"Wherever the gods decide." She moved closer still and stopped only when she realized that Harper was tracking her motions. He was easily in range to hit her and well out of the range of her massive sword.

"Stanna, isn't it?" Harper spoke casually but there was nothing about his stance that reflected the same tone. His eyes were locked on the woman and his half-smile, the one so many women found attractive, was locked in place.

She was unimpressed.

"You escaped me in Torema. You'll not escape out here."

Faceless moved. It was a fast thing, unexpectedly and terrifyingly swift. The giant figure turned on his heels and ran to the right, reaching into the darkness and grabbing at something. A man screamed and was lifted high into the air. Faceless held him aloft for a moment and then slammed the shape into the ground. From several yards away Brogan heard the sound of bones breaking.

Several of the boat people started talking at once and Darkraven looked on, studying Faceless as if seeing him for the very first time.

"Why is it attacking?" The woman seemed surprised, but not overly so.

"Ask him."

Faceless threw the man toward Brogan with unsettling ease. He hit the ice and slid bonelessly.

Definitely dead. "He planned to attack. He was carrying blades and had them in his hand." Faceless held a small collection of throwing knives out for Brogan to see.

"There you have it. He was protecting us."

Darkraven's smile dropped a few notches. "I did not order anyone to take lives."

"Then perhaps you should see who else believes they are in command of your people."

"There are many people who want you dead."

"She's got you there, Brogan."

"You're not helping, Harper."

The big woman, Stanna, spoke up. "Come with us, let's just have done with this before it gets any worse."

"We've an agenda. It does not involve surrendering to anyone." Brogan spoke as clearly as he could. "Go home. We'll be along when we've finished what needs doing."

"No home to go to," Darkraven shrugged. "That's part of the problem as I recall."

"Find a new home. If you are here for me and mine, you'll fail."

"We have you outnumbered."

Jahda spoke up. "Leave here, Hillar. He's under my protection."

"You would defy the gods, Jahda?"

"The gods have gone mad. I will see this finished one way or the other."

"Torema is gone!" Her calm demeanor cracked for a moment.

"And killing him will do nothing to bring it back. Move on. Go to Kaer-ru. There is land aplenty and we can sort this out later. For now, however, we have things we need to settle to the north."

The arrow came from a great distance and at such speed that Brogan barely saw it. He called out to Jahda and the man had enough time to start turning before the point of the missile took him in his chest. The ice was slick and the impact was heavy and Jahda fell to the ground with a grunt.

Harper cursed, changed his target, drew and loosed. The darkness was not complete, but Brogan saw no one.

"Enough of this!" His voice boomed across the ice. "Back to your damned ship or I'll see all of you bleed."

Darkraven made a gesture and her people attacked.

They came from different directions. Apparently there were many more of them than Brogan had initially believed and they were intent on taking him and his.

Faceless stepped closer to him and protected his right side. Faceless, who now had nostrils that were clearly defined on a nose that was more than a lump. Also, his brow was more clearly noticeable. The changes were subtle, but they were there. Laram, who barely looked at Brogan these days, who certainly did not speak to him, took his left and Harper stayed where he was, along with the other archers, doing their best to end anyone else who stayed in the distance.

Once the fighting started, they were just shapes. If he did not recognize a face, Brogan defended and attacked as if the enemy was before him.

Not that long ago in the grander scheme of things, Anna Harkness had made a pack of dogs disappear.

Now she made them come back, and as Brogan watched the animals charged into the midst of his enemies, scattering several of them as they attacked.

Hounds growled and bit. Men and women alike screamed as the animals appeared, startled or torn into by their teeth. Brogan did not know or care how Anna managed her sorceries at that moment, but he was decidedly grateful for them.

He took advantage of the situation, wading into the fight. The axe was heavy and it was deadly. He used the weight to knock aside the first sword coming for him and then spun his entire body around to cleave into the attacking man's face. There was little more than a gasp of pain before the man was dead.

They came in a wave despite the dogs. Worse, not all of them were fighters. Some of them were cutthroats and that was a different sort of matter altogether. The warriors were direct. Cutthroats tended to sneak in where they could.

To prove his point a woman with a severely scarred face appeared on his left and, before he could warn his friend, Laram had a dagger shoved through his neck. He staggered back, his hands moving to stop the sudden, violent flow of blood that jetted from the wound.

Laram, who had always been a good lad and always been dependable in any situation, died in seconds, his eyes wide and his mouth gaping as he tried to breathe.

He hoped if there was a place where the dead gathered that the poor bastard would find his Mearhan again.

Brogan turned to the woman and swept his axe

toward her, but she backed away before he could make contact, and in the darkness of the cold night she vanished amidst the crush of people and animals.

One of the dogs let out a yelp of pain that ended abruptly. So did one of the people screaming obscenities.

The fighting blurred. There were people crushing themselves into the combat and others backing away, wounded and bleeding or simply too scared to continue on. That was the thing about fighting – some were made for it and others were not.

Somewhere along the way Harper had released his bow, and drawn his swords. He danced in close and took Laram's place, his face still locked in that vulpine grin of his. His hooked sword cast another man's weapon to the side and the second blade whisked in and opened a wound in the same fellow's throat. He blocked another attempted attack and grunted at the force of the blow.

Not far away Stanna caught a man with her sword and then kicked his corpse free of the blade, her eyes locked on Brogan. She intended to take him down and he intended to remain on his feet.

Faceless caught two of the attackers and lifted them in his hands, grunting as one of them struck his chest with an axe once, twice, and then a third time. Each blow left a scratch but nothing substantial. The man with the axe screamed and then let out a worse sound as Faceless crushed his captured arm into a bloody pulp. He threw the man into another one of their enemies and then concentrated on the other fighter in his grasp. Brogan sensed a certain grim glee that came from the creature.

The dogs took several of the enemies down before archers ended them. Roskell Turn was doing something, muttering to himself and making gestures, but if those motions did anything at all, Brogan didn't have time to study the situation.

The sword blow from Stanna nearly knocked his axe away. The woman swept the sword around for a second attack and Brogan retreated, stunned by her sheer strength and savagery. She was a controlled force, and he felt each blow she sent his way as he deflected them. He grunted and moved back, and she came forward calmly, efficiently doing her best to remove his head from his shoulders.

Harper was nearby but no longer mattered. Faceless was on the other side and he too ceased to be important. It was all he had to fight this woman and not lose. Stanna moved and he danced with her, keeping himself safe and trying to find a way in, past her nearly flawless defenses.

Metal clanged on metal and Brogan reached for his short sword, only to change his mind as the massive blade she carried clashed against his axe with bruising force.

The woman looked at him with a face carved from stone. There was no fury. There was no anger. There was just her unsettling level of skill and her strength.

Brogan kicked her in the leg with all of his might. She wasn't expecting it, or didn't seem to be, and winced as the pain ran up her thigh. Never one to ignore an advantage, Brogan shoved himself into her while she was off balance and sent her stumbling.

The woman caught herself at the same time he brought the axe around. She parried, but the blow was powerful indeed and the sword slipped out of her grip.

There was no time to smile or jeer. She came for him, ignoring the lack of weapon, and hit him hard enough to take his feet from the ground.

He hit the frozen surface and swept his leg at her ankles. A moment later they were locked together on the ice, doing their very best to beat the other to death.

Tully

The notion, near as she could tell, was for Darkraven's forces to distract Brogan McTyre and his people while the Blood Mother took care of actually killing their mutual enemies. Theryn seemed perfectly content with that plan and set herself up with her elite followers. While the rest of the attackers were settling in boats, they'd scaled down the side of the ship that was hidden away and then made their way to land when everyone else was distracted. It might not have worked in many circumstances, but the perpetual night out on the sea helped.

Tully knew what she was supposed to do. She was supposed to stay on the ship.

She followed Theryn instead. Despite her best efforts, she had not been able to get any of the Blood Mother's ilk alone. Had she, they'd surely have died. Either they were too aware of her presence on the ship, or they were simply damnably lucky.

So it came to this. Temmi was moving with the rest of the fighters, but they'd decided somewhere along the way that Tully was too fragile to join in.

The black clothes came in handy enough when she descended to the ice.

She'd watched and waited and did nothing. Once again, the team of lieutenants was very good at what they did and they made it impossible for her to get close without being spotted, right up until the nightmare thing that stood with the enemy spotted Rik and grabbed him.

Rik had been a friend. He'd even risked his life to help her escape from Hollum when Theryn was ready to peel the skin off her body.

That didn't stop the monster from breaking him like an egg.

Kem fired an early shot and hit a tall, dark man in the chest. A second later an archer for the other side buried an arrow in his face for his efforts. He never even let out a sound, just fell back on the ice, dead.

That was when the chaos started in earnest. The Darkraven gave out her call to kill everyone and the battle began properly.

Tully stayed out of it. She had specific targets in mind.

Naza, the scarred woman she had once called sister, was moving amongst the enemy like a mist, cutting and slashing when eyes were turned away from her, and then reappearing elsewhere.

Tully had one advantage and that was simply that she knew where to look, and how to see the other woman. A small toss of her wrist and the blade planted itself deep in Naza's hamstring. The woman let out a yelp of pain and tried to find the source of her sudden agonies. The man who'd killed Kem earlier with a single arrow shot had switched to using two swords instead. One of the weapons had a hooked end and caught Naza's arm even as the other blade slipped in and filleted her guts.

He was past in an instant and moving through the crowd with the same sort of grace and stealth. That left Theryn herself and Choto to consider.

Choto let out a hoarse scream as the monster with the others caught her and bent her backwards until her spine snapped.

Theryn's knife buried itself in Tully's hand when she was still trying to find the woman. The pain was massive, but no larger than what she'd been trained to withstand.

Theryn, the Blood Mother, earned her name in Hollum. She'd been a leader among the Union of Thieves and she'd specialized in assassins and cutthroats more than she did burglars. But she also understood the benefit of endurance and had taught all of her "children" to survive the harshest situations through pain management. It was one thing to run fast or climb walls, another to be perfectly still while crouching on one leg or holding onto a windowsill. Tully had learned the hard way the benefit of endurance, and that meant overcoming cramping muscles and extreme discomforts.

All of which meant that Tully moved fast and pulled the small blade from her hand without blacking out or screaming.

The Blood Mother was on her even as the blade came free.

Theryn did not waste time with words, but instead hammered at Tully, driving her backward with a thin sword in one hand and a curved nightmare blade in the other. The curved piece was deceptive – it could reach farther than Tully wanted to think about. The other sword, while thin, was hard and sharp and would cut her open with ease if she were caught.

Tongues of steel tried to taste her, and Tully retreated, having no other option. She could either get in too close for the weapons to cut her, and try her luck with the very dagger that had bloodied her hand, or she could back away and stay out of range. Neither was the easiest notion at the moment but until she could get a better grasp of her own weapons she didn't see that she had much of a choice in the matter.

Her foot slipped on something wet on the ice and Tully went down hard. She was, however, a fine student of the woman trying to kill her, and she rolled quickly out of the way as Theryn tried to slice her into gobbets.

Sometimes friends are the most amazing things.

She did not know where Temmi came from, only that the girl came at Theryn like a charging bull and sent the Blood Mother stumbling across the ice, pinwheeling her arms and trying desperately to keep her balance. Say what you will about ice, but it's a sight harder to stand on than most ground. The Blood Mother slipped at last and crashed onto her side. Temmi started toward her but Tully called out a warning and circled carefully.

Throwing knives. The first one went into Theryn's leg. She let out a grunt and rolled over, ignoring the curved blade and throwing a thin leaf of a blade in return. Tully watched it coming and moved out of the way, narrowly avoiding the blade aimed at her chest.

While she was doing that, Temmi ran forward and kicked Theryn in the face. It was a solid blow, and the target of the kick smashed backward, her face bloodied.

Temmi wobbled on the ice but kept her balance.

Tully threw a blade and watched it skip off the leathers Theryn was wearing.

Temmi did not have knives. She had a short sword. Theryn came up with a dagger in her hand and Temmi hacked down with her weapon of choice, cutting the woman's bicep to the bone. All the training in the world means nothing to a muscle that's been chopped away. Theryn's hand dropped the blade. She looked up at Temmi with fury in her eyes.

Temmi swept the sword the other way and cut half of Theryn's face off. Nose and cheek and chin all blossomed blood and the woman fell back, screaming. Even in the near-darkness, Tully could see bone.

Temmi did not take any chances. She brought her sword up again and chopped down, burying the blade in Theryn's chest. Possibly the most lethal woman that Tully had ever seen was dead. It was not at her hands but she was all right with that. She had never wanted the woman's life, only her freedom from the demands the woman made.

Not far away Stanna let out a roar and slapped down a man almost as tall as she was. He hit the ground and rolled before getting back up.

Even closer in, Hillar Darkraven was proving why she was worthy of leading a city of criminals. She was bloodied and battered but she was still fighting and her elbow drove into a man's throat before she shoved a knife into his heart.

The night skies screamed.

The winds that had been steadily pushing at all of them suddenly drove down like a hammer blow and all around her the people who had been fighting found themselves hard-pressed to stay on their feet. Tully herself was thrown sideways and rolled across the frozen surface.

It had to be the He-Kisshi. Tully's heart seized at the thought. Ever since she and Niall Leraby had escaped the sacrificial death planned for them, the same undying beast had stalked them again and again. It had killed Niall and now it was coming back for her, ready to make her vanish as surely as it had stolen him away from them.

All around her the fighting stopped.

Only three figures were standing. First was the faceless thing that had killed at least three people she knew of. Next was a dark-haired woman covered in enough cloaks and skirts to hide away any real features aside from her face. And finally a short, dark man who looked around with a furious expression.

"This is over!" The short man had a thick accent that she recognized as Galean. Not the He-Kisshi after all, but instead a sorcerer. She was relieved. There had been a time when she would have been terrified of the man and his possible skills, but in comparison to the Undying he was a minor threat. He could be killed if it came to that, the same could not be said for the hooded servants of the gods.

"Go back to your ship and leave here." The man's voice was clear enough. "Do not make us punish you with your lives."

Hillar Darkraven looked at the man with a murderous glint in her eye. She did not like being told what to do and she surely did not like being thwarted. Tully didn't have to know the woman better than she did to understand that fact about her.

"You speak as if we have a choice in this matter." Hillar's voice was remarkably calm, despite her expression.

"You do." The man stared levelly at the ruler of the world's largest dead city. "You can leave or I can kill all of you."

"You can't kill all of us."

"Would you test me?" The small man stepped closer, but rather than being foolish enough to get within range he merely looked at her and watched as Hillar suddenly turned red-faced and began to cough and wheeze. She was not breathing, that was obvious. Her face reddened even more and she fell forward. Had she been standing, she would surely have hurt herself in the fall.

One heartbeat, two, three, four and suddenly she was gasping. Her watery eyes rolled briefly and Hillar coughed again before taking in a deep breath.

"I don't have to kill all of you. Only a select few. The rest will take my words and hold them closely."

Hillar stood back up slowly, panting and resting her

hands on her knees as she steadied herself.

"Or I could have you killed." She looked his way and slowly stood to her full height, which was not overly impressive.

"We are done now." The voice came from elsewhere and Tully shifted enough to see the speaker, the man Darkraven had called Jahda. He was bloodied but not dead.

Hillar stared at him and he stared back. It was a silent fight, strictly mental, and Tully had seen that sort of combat countless times over the years.

Hillar finally nodded. "We retreat!" She looked at Jahda and then at the man Stanna had been fighting. If that was Brogan McTyre, the man who had declared war on the gods, he was slightly smaller than she'd expected but looked the part of a crazed killer. "You've no ship. You've no way out of this frozen waste, and we'll certainly not aid you."

The red-haired man spat red phlegm and smiled. He had a wolf's smile: a promise of death and little else.

"Go to the Kaer-ru. You'll be safer there, Hillar." Jahda spoke softly, his body not standing as tall as it had before. The arrow was gone from his chest and he held a press of fur against the wound.

Hillar nodded and turned toward the boats. Tully started moving toward them as well, careful to avoid being seen. She would climb the side of the ship and be done with it. Temmi stared at her for a moment, her face a mask of unasked questions. Tully would have to explain. That was all there was to it. They were friends, and the girl was kind enough not to report her for her actions. That did not mean she wouldn't expect answers.

Stanna looked hard at the man she'd been fighting. He stared back with a matching expression.

A decent number of people headed back to the boats, but almost the same number was left behind, dead or dying. It was the end of the world, and few seemed at all interested in burying the dead.

Brogan

They made a bonfire for the corpses. They weren't savages and Laram had been a friend and very nearly a brother.

Harper stared at the fires and asked, "Do you believe that death ends the journey? Or do they move on?"

Brogan spat. "I've no care at this point. If there is a journey it's different for the dead and the sacrificed. Mine were sacrificed. According to the old stories that means they are food in the bellies of the gods." It was a lie, but only half a lie, really. He had hopes. But little belief left to him.

"Yes, but Laram and that Mearhan girl. Maybe they'll finally be together."

Brogan nodded his head. "We can hope. He deserved that at least."

"He was a good lad."

Brogan looked at his companion. "What's gotten into you, Harper? When did you become sentimental?"

"The world is likely ending, and even if we save it, it's very changed from what it was. Most of the civilized places have been scrubbed away by the gods.

I suppose I'm missing the world we knew."

Brogan nodded. They were silent for a while and then he said, "We need to be on our way. I can't even say how far we have to travel. I just know we've no ship and a long way to swim."

"Hmm. Maybe the Galean can do something about that."

"Anna?"

"No, the true Galean. I expect he has more power than he wants to show us."

"I can hardly force him."

"You can ask." He pointed with his chin to where Jahda and the man were in discussion near a small fire. Not long before, the Galean had been helping the taller man with his arrow wound, cleaning and binding the spot. "Or you can wait for him to do it for you."

Brogan sighed. It would certainly be easier to let the man handle his work for him, but then that wasn't going to get him where he needed to be any faster, especially if the king of the Kaer-ru didn't ask the right questions.

He walked toward them and both men looked his way.

Roskell Turn said, "We need a way to get where we are going."

Brogan nodded. "That seems to be the challenge."

"I've been talking with another Galean. She is trying to reach us. It may be a day or two, but she had transportation for us."

"And what will we do in the meantime?" Brogan gestured around. "We are standing on ice and the land is not close enough that we can dare swim."

"No," Turn agreed. "That would go poorly. But there are ways around this and I should be able to help at least that much."

"Why are you helping me, Roskell Turn?"

"Is there a choice?" The man smiled. "We live or we die. In any event, the books of Galea tell tales of the gods that you have not seen. Among those tales are stories of how the gods come around and how they leave. They are always violent tales." The man shrugged. "The signs are there, Brogan. The time has come for the gods to fight or fall. We are here to see this event but there's nothing we can do to stop it from happening. The old gods and the new will fight as they have before."

Brogan shook his head. "No. The old gods will fall. I will kill them."

Roskell nodded his head. "That you will try, and possibly succeed, I do not doubt, but when the gods fall there will be others who want to take their places."

Brogan nodded his head. "Then I suppose I will kill them, too."

The expression on Roskell Turn's face said clearly that he wasn't sure if Brogan was jesting. He chose not to explain himself.

Roskell spoke again. "Brogan, the Books of Galea were written because the gods chose to answer questions from one of their most faithful servants. They told the truth to one person and she, in turn, wrote those truths down. They told Galea how to manipulate the world, how to bend the will of the world to their bidding, but it is not an easy task. It is not easy because the gods are not generous by nature. They make demands, they insist on sacrifices." He raised his hands and shook his head. "Not that I need to tell you, of all people, about that. What I mean is the gods did these things to prepare Galea and her followers for the world that will come around. The world has always worked the same way. The gods are born, they grow in power and they replace those who came before them. This does not happen often. It does not happen without change. The mountains were built when the last gods fell and they have been shattered with the death of a god. This is not a small thing."

Brogan frowned. "I know this."

"I don't think you do. You have been given the power to touch the gods by Walthanadurn. He blessed you with this ability. That does not mean you will easily kill the gods. You had a hand in the death of the god of the seas. But that still leaves four deities left. Even if you manage to kill them, and that is a task that I do not think you fully understand, the demons will come along and have their say in this. They will rise to take the place of the previous gods because that is their nature. Your nature is to fight against any who would hurt you. Their nature is to seize the power they have sought for so very long."

"I don't care. I will stop them if I can."

Roskell stared at him, his mouth working to find the right words.

Despite his injury, Jahda chuckled.

Brogan spoke slowly. He needed to make his point. "We have had gods for too long. They do nothing but make demands. If they cared, if they did anything at all that aided us, I could see their purpose, but they do not. They make demands. They take. They take some more and then they do it again. I have been given a chance to change that and if I can, I will. I might fail. I very likely will fail, but I will try just the same."

He looked at the two men and squatted.

"I do not understand all that the dead god did, but I can feel the differences in me. It is more than the ability to touch the gods, though that is enough, I suspect. I feel the world differently. I see and taste and hear things that were never there before." He frowned, and shook his head. "It would be easier to show you than to tell you, and I have no way to show you." He shrugged. "The dead god did something to me. I know that. I know that there is more that must happen before I fight the gods and I believe that the weapons I need are close by, but I have to find them and possibly even shape them. They will be strong enough to kill the gods. I will be strong enough. What makes you think I can't kill these demons you speak of? They are younger, weaker gods and I am doing their work for them. What makes you think I can't finish this task the way I see fit?"

"Brogan, the gods are not only about strength, they are about fighting with actions and with thoughts, they are about strategies as generals are about strategies in wars. To them we are parts of the game."

Roskell Turn shook his head and pointed with one finger, tapping Brogan's broad chest. "You are a fighter. But you are also a part of the game. One or more of these gods and demons likely set you as a player without you ever knowing. Your family was chosen for sacrifice? All of them, yes?"

Brogan nodded. His stomach tightened again at the thought.

"It is likely that god or demon, one of them or more than one, chose you and used your family to involve you in this conflict."

Brogan nodded. He leaned in closer to Roskell and spoke very carefully. "I have reasoned that out myself."

"You have?" The Galean seemed surprised.

"Oh. Yes. That is why I will kill all of them before this is done. I do not know which of them decided to involve me or kill my family to make it happen, but if any of them are to blame I will kill them all to have my satisfaction. Better no gods at all than gods that would do that to my family."

CHAPTER SIXTEEN
THE WAY TO REDEMPTION

Myridia

The fish were plentiful and the Grakhul ate while they waited, guarding the Gateway between the worlds.

Myridia felt stronger than she had in many, many weeks. It wasn't only the food or the waters of home, she believed. It was also the radiance from the Gateway that bathed them constantly.

There was no time for savoring the feeling, however. There was a war coming and they would be prepared. The times when they might have rested were filled with practice and drills.

One of the He-Kisshi had also returned and watched over them, perching high on the Gateway and often staring into the distant, dark seas or into the ocean. The lightning that ripped away from the Gateway never had any impact on the creature, but instead actively avoided it.

When the hooded shape drifted down to the area where Myridia swam in the cold waters she turned her attention to it immediately.

"I am Dowru-Thist."

She lowered her head in acknowledgment and then waited for a response.

"You are honored, this day. The gods are entrusting you to release their devoted followers from their slumber."

Myridia frowned. "Which followers? Where do they sleep?"

"The Hahluritiedes. It was they who reshaped this world into the image the gods desired. They have followed the gods since the creation of this world and they have slept since the fall of Walthanadurn."

"Where do they...?"

"They rest far below the Gateway. You must swim to find them. You will know them when you see them."

Myridia felt a nervous ball form in her guts. There was nothing said that should have caused it, but everything that was spoken made that unsettled energy grow.

Without another word she sank under the waves, beckoning with her hands for the others to follow. Most listened, a few remained behind, unaware at first that she had gestured. She did not correct them. Mostly she wanted Lyraal. The woman was there, as always, at her side.

They swam downward for a few moments before she slowed and drew Lyraal to her. "We are to awaken creatures I have never heard of."

"We can hardly know the will of the gods, unless they inform us," Lyraal shrugged.

"There is more to this. I feel it in my innards. I fear there is something we are not being told."

Lyraal stared at her for a long while without speaking and then moved her hands in a flurry of gestures. "The gods command us and we follow. That is the way it has always been, Myridia, but you have changed those rules several times now."

"What do you mean?"

"You kept us with your humans. You made us travel with your troupe in the hopes that you would be closer to Garien. You have acted within your desires, not the desires of the gods, on several occasions. Do not question them now. It is not the time. The world as we know it is ending and you would continue to question the gods."

Lyraal was angry, she could sense that. The quick, nearly stuttering movements of her hands as she signed her words, that, too was an indicator.

Her own frustration came through as she responded. "If you feel that I have done poorly as a leader, then why do you follow me?"

"I follow you because you are wiser than me, but you are not listening to the voice of the gods. You are questioning what is supposed to be, as if there is a choice."

She stopped for a moment to consider, and then finally replied.

"We traveled half a continent to find out that we were not supposed to be the guardians of the Sessanoh. I am partly to blame for that, yes, because I listened to Unwynn when she said we should go to the Mirrored Lake and prepare the way for more sacrifices, yes, but the Undying told us similar and never mentioned that others would be sent to do the same thing. We were given a choice: become mates to the Grakhul who were sent along, or come here and fight the enemies. Did I make the wrong decision?"

It was Lyraal's turn to look confused as she considered. Around them the majority of the Grakhul swam in a circular pattern, slowly descending but taking their time while the women who led them debated.

"I do not know."

"I do. I chose not to be a servant to men who think they can make our decisions for us. I am not a broodmare. I am a warrior, and a priestess."

Lyraal nodded.

Myridia continued. "Either you trust me as your leader or you do not. If you do not, then ignore me. But if you do trust me, then you need to help me. I fear we are betrayed again. I fear we are asked to do something that will cause us harm. I have no reason to believe this except that my guts say it."

Far below them the ground swelled in several places. Silt and dirt that were not touched by the raging seas in the distance remained as a cover for the monolithic shapes resting in the shadows of the Gateway.

From this height they were little more than forms half-hidden in shadow.

Still, those uneven shapes filled Myridia with dread.

Lyraal looked upon them and seemed unimpressed.

"I was uncomfortable with the Grakhul who came from the west. I am more uncomfortable with these shapes. I do not trust that waking these Hahluritiedes is a thing we should do."

"It is the gods who tell us this. How can we deny the gods without being damned to a death beyond the worst pain we have ever experienced? It is the gods who have ruled us and shaped us, Myridia. How can we defy them?"

And there was the crux of the problem. She could not defy the gods. She had never defied the gods. Throughout her life she had been driven by the desire to please the beings that had created them all and given them purpose.

And yet...

The idea of following this order sent shivers through her entire being. She knew it was wrong. She knew it would cause disaster. She knew she could not defy the gods.

Without any more thought she swam down, heading for the closest of the vast shapes. They were larger than she had expected, several hundred feet in height each. In the scope of the world they were tiny but so, too, the Grakhul.

Her hands touched the silt and pushed it clear and as she did so the others followed suit, brushing away centuries of accumulated sand and covering. It was not hard; the substances had not sealed the shapes, merely hidden them from sight.

Clouds of debris washed away from the forms, revealing them slowly. They were not humanoid. They were other things, other shapes. Some had limbs and others had fins. Some were serpentine and others could not easily be defined.

That they were of the gods was clear. They bore the essence of the gods and, like the radiating energies from the Gateway, they seemed made of the divine.

She could not understand her fear. Surely these were creatures designed by the gods to serve a holy purpose.

Lyraal looked upon the shapes with awe. She did not touch them so much as she stroked and caressed. All around her the Grakhul followed Lyraal's example, crooning softly to the glory of the hidden shapes as they were revealed. Truly, these were a power to be revered.

And yet, Myridia still felt the dread, the tightening of her innards. Even as she looked upon the forms that the gods had left here, signs of their power and potence, even as she allowed her webbed fingers to caress the unmoving forms, she knew that something horrible would happen if they continued.

Lyraal and several others began to sing. Their voices carried through the waters, echoed across the ground and the shapes slumbering beneath the Gateway. Myridia did not sing, she did not dare. Fear ran through her entire body and she moved back from the forms as they started to awaken.

The first of them shifted, the second breathed and slowly, oh, with agonizing slowness, they all began the task of waking up from their endless slumbers.

Myridia shook her head and if she had been capable of crying tears in the water she surely would have, for even as she started ascending she understood what was causing her fear.

They had been asleep for endless ages. Surely when

they awoke they would be hungry.

A few of her followers looked her way and signed their confusion, but Myridia did not respond. The gods had made their decree. The Hahluritiedes were needed and she and hers were to awaken them. She could not tell her people to flee, but she could not stay herself. Her love of the gods was surely flawed. She had denied the need to mate with the Grakhul of the west and now this.

Myridia swam upward, moving away from the Gateway and heading south. Lyraal's song carried on for a very long while. It only ended when her friend began to scream.

Behind her, far away now, the creatures that the gods had used to shape the world woke up and feasted, as the gods had planned.

Was she to be condemned by the gods? Possibly, but she could not turn back. She dared not. The gods had surely gone mad and were punishing the devoted.

The gods had demanded she die for her sins, whatever they might be, and she had defied them. There was no place left for her in this world and yet, she refused to leave.

Myridia defied them and swam away, her heart breaking with every move she made and every wail of pain and fear she heard from her beloved sisters.

Interlude: Daivem Murdrow

The dead were everywhere and they were lost, tormented and suffering. War did that. The gods sometimes claimed the dead, but in this case they either could not or simply chose not to. That was the trouble with traveling between worlds. Her brother, Darsken, had warned her that traveling the worlds could cause confusion and he was not wrong. He seldom was, much as that notion annoyed her.

The darkness did not bother her, and the bodies of the dead were merely debris in her eyes. The spirits of the dead were the parts that mattered, though from time to time they tried to cling to their corpses as if the rotting flesh held answers they had not yet realized.

The soldiers she had been following were dead. The king she had met was no longer among the living. Not all of their spirits lingered but those that did she gathered and added to her collection.

For generations on end the Louron who were trained to do so had done exactly what she was doing. The Inquisitors sought the people who killed without reason and tried to help the dead along the way. Most, like her brother, were wiser than she was and only aided one at a time. Some, like Darsken, gathered the souls of the murdered, took a small payment from them and solved their deaths when they could. Daivem was not satisfied with that. She never had been and she suspected she would not live much longer if she continued to gather all the spirits she found and store them away.

The wooden walking stick was designed to aid her in holding the energies of the dead but there were limits and she was rapidly pushing beyond what could be stored. A water jug will only hold so much before it overflows, but this was not the same thing. She could continue to push the dead into the carefully crafted receptacle and they would not spill out. They would stay, but if she continued to push them into the staff, it would be more like a skin than a vase. The wood would eventually fracture and release all that she had gathered.

The problem was the same as before. She had no idea what to do with them. They were dead. They were restless and if they were left where they were, the possibilities of them tainting the land were strong. Many lands had haunted places where the dead had been left too long in pain, and had festered like a rotting wound. That was what she hoped to avoid.

"I don't know why I am trying." She reached out and beckoned to a soldier's spirit. He had died badly and was afraid. "I have no place to keep you."

She said the words but they were a lie. She knew why. Watching the dead suffer was not something she could do.

The shape that drifted down from the skies was not a complete surprise to her, but she was not comfortable with meeting one of the Undying.

The wings of the thing fluttered for a moment and then it pulled them close until it looked like nothing more than a man in a hooded robe. She was not deceived.

"What is it that you do?" The voice was soft.

"What I must to offer peace to the dead."

"Why do the dead need peace?"

"Why do any of us need peace?" She looked toward the creature as it shuffled slowly closer.

The feet of the thing touched the frozen earth and seemed unaffected. "How can you stand the cold?"

she asked.

"I am Undying. Cold. Heat. They are minor inconveniences." It tilted that odd head and studied her intently for a moment. "Where do you come from? You are not of this world."

"I have followed the Shimmering Path to where I am called. I am from Louron."

"Louron." It seemed to taste the word. "You are among the untouched."

And there it was. The tone she had been waiting for. The gods had never spoken to her or her people in this world that she knew of. They had never attempted to force themselves on the Louron, or if they had, they had found them unpalatable.

"I follow the Shimmering Path."

"This path of yours, can it truly take you to other worlds?"

She nodded and pulled another spirit closer until she could wrap it into the energies held within her walking stick. "I am from another world. I travel here because the dead call to me."

"The dead belong to the gods."

She looked toward the thing and sighed. "If the gods would take them, then they should take them now, before they rot like fruit and ruin the ground where they walk."

"They cannot simply take the dead. The dead must be sacrificed."

"These dead have not been sacrificed. They have been killed."

"These dead were following the orders of the gods. They have been taken by demons."

Daivem nodded her head. “They speak of the plants and the bones.” She pointed to the closest lump of frozen vegetation. “They speak of dying for a cause they did not understand.”

“There is nothing to understand. They were servants of the gods and the gods do not need to explain themselves.”

“I do not judge. I merely observe.”

The hooded shape nodded. “That is wise.”

She said nothing and the creature continued to look on as she did her work. Several minutes passed in silence before it spoke again. “If the gods demand the lives you take, will you offer them over?”

“This realm belongs to the gods. Who am I to defy them?” She was not completely certain if she spoke the truth.

The Undying continued to watch her. The clouds above roiled and spilled snow and ice. The storm grew more powerful and she pulled her hood closer to her face and looked around the area. The bodies of humans and demonic servants alike were motionless and slowly the white buried them.

“Will the gods ruin this whole world?” she asked.

“The humans here have not done as they were told. Those who offended the gods are still alive, and so the gods continue to punish all.”

“Who will worship the gods if they kill all the people?” She frowned in thought even as she asked the question.

“That is the challenge, I think. The gods prepare to remake the world. If the people are all dead, there must be a new people to take their place.”

She said nothing to that. What could she hope to say? Gods had their own rules.

After another long silence, the creature spread its wings and she felt the winds pick up as it was lifted into the air. "If the gods demand it, I will take what you have secured."

"If the gods demand it, I will let you."

Without another word the Undying rose into the air and faded into the darkness.

Not long after that Daivem heard a more familiar and welcomed voice.

Darsken Murdrow spoke softly, "That is an unusual creature."

"That is a messenger of the gods, sent to see what I am doing with the spirits I have gathered."

He nodded his head and frowned. "I have spoken with the Grand Inquisitor. He does not feel you should be here."

"I go where I must."

Her brother's frown deepened. "Agreed, but you take great chances and as your older brother I would rather you not. In any event, he says you should find Jahda, who has lived here for many years."

"Where is Jahda? I have seen no sign of him."

"I don't even know him. I cannot help."

"I'll find him." She shrugged and then pulled her cloak closer – the cold was savage now, and only getting worse. The sun had not shone in days, hidden away by clouds. Darsken seemed unaffected, but Daivem was beginning to think the cold would never leave her alone again.

"I cannot stay. There are things I must handle back

in Fellein. There are... dark things happening."

She nodded and started to speak, but he interrupted.

"Please, Daivem, do what you must and then come home. This world. I don't think it will last for long, I think the gods here have decided to end it and that is a good reason to leave."

"The dead–"

"Are dead. Help them if you can, but if there is no world they will find a way. That is what the dead do, my sister. They find their way."

In many ways her brother was wise, but they did not agree on how much help the dead needed. She was more likely to help them than he was.

He chuckled. "I know that look. Help them if you can, but go to Jahda. He knows this world and you do not."

"Is he trained in the ways of the Inquisitors?"

"I do not know. I believe he is. He is a king here. Go to him. Take his advice and then come home." He shivered. "Come home to where it is warm and the damned sun knows how to show itself."

For just a moment he leaned in close and his lips pressed against her temple. Then he was gone.

Jahda. It was a name. She would talk to the dead and ask a favor of them and they, in turn, would continue to get her help.

She knew what they wanted, of course. She had asked. They wanted revenge. That was always the case with the dead who died violently. They almost always wanted the satisfaction of revenge.

Of course, most of them wanted revenge against the gods who punished them.

She wasn't quite sure how she could manage that, but she had to try. Perhaps Jahda could work out the details where she was failing.

Stanna

"What the hell was that?" Stanna paced. She was restless and she was angry. They'd had their enemies in their grasp and instead of winning the fight they had retreated.

She knew the reasons. They just didn't matter.

"They had Galeans, Stanna." Hillar shrugged her shoulders and then slipped out of her cloak. "I did not expect Galeans. They almost never leave their island and when they do it's mostly to work as healers."

"Had I known I'd have put a spear through the little fucker's skull!"

"And I'd have loved to see it, but you did not know. You will know for the next time."

"The next time?"

"We're hardly finished." Hillar looked her way and chuckled. "This is not nearly over. We have retreated, but we have not run away."

"What do you mean?"

"You're a slaver, not a sailor. There are no stars to guide us, but we will find our way. We are heading north again. We will find the place that Brogan McTyre and his scum are trying to seek. There are only a few things to look for this far north and I suspect they do not look for what is left of Saramond. We have a ship and they do not. We will find what they seek before they do and, when we get there, we only have to wait until they show up and we will kill them. You can kill their Galeans first."

Stanna nodded and calmed herself.

"Brogan McTyre. I had him in my hands."

Hillar nodded. "And he had you. I saw that fight. I did not think there was a man alive who could fight you and survive."

"I am very good at what I do. There are others who are just as good."

"We suffered losses. We suffered a great deal of losses." Hillar's voice softened. She was not happy. She was also the sort whose voice seemed calmer when she grew angry. Stanna bellowed her rage. Hillar whispered.

"I expected better from the Hollumites."

"Aye. And so did I. Theryn's reputation for death was not a mild one and it was well-earned. There was a reason I allowed her on the ship."

Stanna nodded. She was a slaver, and she understood the tricks of the trade, but she had always preferred honest combat to the sneaking efforts of backstabbers.

"How long until we see them again?" Stanna looked at a bruise running across the back of her hand, where the red-bearded bastard had blocked a killing blow, and scowled. She wanted him dead. He had, regardless of his intent, altered her entire world. Temmi was a nice plus, she could hold that girl forever, but almost everything else had gone the wrong way.

A bell sounded faintly, three times. Each strike of the bell was cut short, meaning it was no mistake. The alarm was given that one of the Undying was nearby.

As at least two of her friends were sought by the He-Kisshi and since one of them that she'd beheaded might well hold a grudge, Stanna took the warning seriously.

Hillar looked her way. "Are you worried about the Undying?"

"We do not always see things in the same light." She did not offer extra information. That would be foolish. Hillar was her employer and trustworthy enough, but the woman was also known for keeping only the secrets that she found convenient. Let her know that a particular person was targeted by the Undying and that somebody became a method of bargaining if the need arose.

Hillar nodded. "I am uncomfortable with them myself. They tend to make threats more than they keep promises."

"They follow the gods and the gods are ending the world. I have doubts that they will stop even if the right people are killed."

"Well, if they leave us the rest of the world, I can possibly live with that."

Stanna shook her head. "I have never had much need for gods. They have never had much need for me. Still, I would rather they leave the world for us."

"So we do as they ask a little while longer and then we find a better place to be."

"Pressya," Stanna sighed. "They say the lands there are open and there are only a few towns. We could build a new city, I think."

Hillar smiled. "I like the way you think."

"I will find a place to live and be happy. Or I will

take Brogan McTyre's place in the fight to kill the gods."

Hillar frowned. "Carefully. I have never seen the ears on a He-Kisshi, but they have a way of hearing more than they should."

Stanna patted her sword, the Bitch, and said nothing.

Beron

Beron crawled back into the world again, his skin steaming from his time in the heat of his master's realm.

The He-Kisshi were long gone. In their stead he saw ranks of soldiers. They were human, and they were familiar to him. He recognized the colors and the coat of arms for King Parrish of Mentath. He also recognized the writing on the flesh of the Marked Men.

There were columns of soldiers and scores of Marked Men, and then there was Beron, alone on his side of the equation. He stood unevenly on his human legs, not certain how or why Ariah had decided to remake him in his own image.

A lean man, shorter than he and yet powerfully confident, looked at him and nodded. None of them were smiling. Not a single one.

He nodded back. He had never met Parrish, the king of the Mentath, but he recognized him from the descriptions he'd heard.

"You are Beron. You are the priest to Ariah. I am Parrish. I am the priest to Theragyn. We are allies in what comes next."

Beron nodded. He did not smile, either. "And where are we to go?"

"North of here. We follow the path the gods were good enough to offer your enemies."

Beron looked around and saw the frozen remains of the creatures he'd led and the humans he'd killed along with them. It was possible that a few on either side had survived but he had his doubts.

"And what do we do?"

"What we must in order to serve our new gods."

"Have you a horse? I'd rather not walk this entire distance."

Parrish gave a half-smile. "I expect we can find something."

The beast he was offered a few minutes later was one of the finest animals he had ever seen. Powerful, graceful and dressed properly for the weather with a thick coat and armor in the right places. He climbed aboard without any difficulties and the animal held his considerable weight with ease.

"You did this?" Parrish pointed to the remains of the battle that could be seen beyond the ice and snow.

"I had help."

"Truly?"

"The Undying did their part to kill me."

"And yet, here you are."

Beron thought back to the He-Kisshi that Ariah had torn asunder. "With one less of the vile things here to cause us troubles. But I expect they'll come when the time is right."

"I am certain of it. We have been prepared for them."

"Truly?" He frowned at the thought. He'd believed himself well-prepared until the Undying showed up and ruined all of his plans. Again.

"Our master has studied these things and understands there are ways to finish them once and for all. We have but to wait for the right moment. This, too, is part of the plan to end the gods."

Beron shook his head and tried to hide his smile. "There are plans in place?"

"There have always been plans. Ten times the gods have punished their children for daring to speak out or make plans. They have imprisoned and tortured to make clear who rules this world. What they have not done is convince those they punished."

Beron nodded his head.

Parrish continued, "They have only cemented the need for change."

He was not completely sure that Parrish was accurate in his assessments, but he nodded again, just the same.

"Well, I expect we'll have an answer soon enough. The He-Kisshi like to interfere. They've already had their share of conflicts with me and with you, I would wager."

"It's not a wager I'd take. I know the results. The Undying have already interfered and caused me to kill a favored son in order to appease the gods."

Beron, who was sure he had several bastard sons and daughters, merely nodded. If his children were placed before him, he'd not know them from a hundred others. He'd sampled his share of slaves over the years and never felt a need to see if they spawned afterward.

"We should be on the way."

Parrish gestured with his hand. "We move that way."

Beron nodded and kicked his horse into step with the king's own. They each represented a god. That meant, as far as he was concerned, they were equals.

"How far away are they?"

"The Undying or the people we are supposed to support?"

"Either. Both."

"In both cases I do not know."

"Then we should ride faster, lest we miss the opportunity to serve our gods."

Parrish looked at him for a while, an odd smile on his face, and then nodded. A moment later they were moving again, riding toward the north and following a path that had, so far, led only to death.

CHAPTER SEVENTEEN
THE LUXURY OF GUILT

Brogan

Anna sat near one of the small fires and warmed herself. The air was bitterly cold and she had bundled herself into more layers than seemed possible. Worse, she still managed to catch his eye, even buried under a mountain of furs and clothing.

Brogan sat down near her, carefully looking into the flames.

"What?" She, too, looked at the fire.

"Thank you. That's all. I wanted to thank you for your help with the ship earlier. The people from it, I mean."

She shook her head. "What choice? If I'm ever to find my man, I have to stay with you, as he will surely find you before he finds me."

"Oh, I think he'd be more likely to look for you, Anna. I'm not as significant to him as you are, I'd wager."

"You are easier to find than I am."

"How do you suppose?"

"If we were both rocks thrown into the same pond, you would make a bigger splash."

"I don't understand." He frowned. There were times when the woman made no sense to him. Then again, that was true of most of the women he'd met. That was why his Nora had been so very special.

"You are a very loud man, Brogan. You have made an impact on the world that is larger than most have ever seen and you are not done yet."

"Not by choice."

She looked his way with an expression that was a perfect mix of humor and contempt and it made him very uncomfortable.

"What?" Did he sound defensive? Yes, he did. He didn't care for that, either.

"You stride like a giant. You, who have fought gods and Undying without flinching. You, who have fought slavers, cheated slavers and killed slavers without fear of consequence. You walk the world as loudly as you can and you revel in it, even if you don't like to admit it."

Brogan shook his head. It wasn't true.

"I'd rather be at my house, enduring another winter. Waking next to Nora and listening to my children complain that there is nothing to do and all of my stories are old and heard a hundred times."

Anna's face softened then. "I know it. I understand it. I would like the same for me and my Desmond and yet here we are. Desmond is missing and yours have been given to the gods."

He felt the tension in his face and knew his

expression was not kind. For a moment he wondered if there was any kindness left in him. It surely did not feel that way.

"I'll take them back." His voice was little more than a breathy sigh. "I'll have them back, or I'll die trying."

"You see? I am worried that my husband might be dead. You are worried about whether or not you can take your family back from the gods. I make a splash with my thoughts, but you create gigantic waves with yours."

"I will not apologize for hating the gods, Anna. I will apologize for any troubles that Desmond has walked into, and if he is gone I will grieve, but I'll not apologize for hating the gods for what they've done."

She stared at him for a moment and shook her head. "I'd expect no less from you, Brogan."

"I am sorry for any pain I've caused, Anna, and I am grateful to you, but I'll not stop."

"Nor would I ask you to."

He nodded his head and stood. "I expect the Undying to show soon. They have little choice at this point."

"How do you mean?"

"They've sent people and the people have failed. What other choices are there?"

Anna looked at him as if he had surely lost his mind. "There are choices you can't begin to know."

Brogan frowned. "Are there other things that serve the gods beyond them?"

"You act as if I have the answers to all the mysteries. In my years studying the Books of Galea I learned one thing above all others, and that is simply that the gods have given answers, but they have not told the whole of the truth with the stories they shared with Galea. They are filled with secrets they did not share and never would."

He started to ask a question and then stopped himself. Of course they held on to secrets, just as he would if he were training a dozen men as soldiers. They would learn a lot from him, but he would never give away everything he knew and understood.

"Aye. Well said."

"I do not know what they will bring forth next, but the gods have options you have not seen and they will bring them to bear if they have to. Still, I expect you are right and that the Undying will be their next choice."

Faceless came toward them, his body little more than a silhouette in the darkness, but as he came closer more of him was revealed and the changes he was going through became more prominent.

"What are you becoming, Faceless?" Brogan asked the question without malice. He was simply surprised.

The shape of the thing was different. Leaner, taller, and the skin that he thought resembled the rough bark of a tree was smoother now, as if that same bark had been sanded and oiled into a fine sheen.

"I do not know what I am. I cannot know what I am becoming. I only know that I am not like you or the others around us, Brogan McTyre." Despite all the changes, there was still no mouth to speak of. Faceless had hands that moved easily now, and his feet had developed toes. The rest of him was changing as well, looking more humanoid, though now the body was closer to gaunt. The top of the creature's head had changed. There were hints of texture now, as if a sculptor had decided to test whether or not to add hair to a form that was mostly finished, and remained uncertain.

Still there was little by way of a face: two holes where eyes might fit and an indication of a nose.

"You keep changing. It is interesting to watch."

"You change as well. Your hair grows longer. You grow leaner."

He nodded. He had no reason to shave in the cold and all of them were leaner: there was food, but not as much as any would have liked.

"Where do we go, Brogan? I do not know what I need to know if I am to help you."

"We travel to the north. There is a place where, if the stories are true, I can face the gods."

Faceless nodded as if that answered all of his questions. A surprising thought, as far as Brogan was concerned. All the notion did for him was to add more questions.

"They are coming!"

Brogan didn't recognize the voice, but he called a response. "Who is coming?"

"The Undying! Three that I can see."

Brogan looked to the skies, but saw nothing.

Faceless shook his head and pointed with a finger that had not been fully formed and separate when they'd met. Where he pointed was the ground, not far away. The ice was still there and they were all cold, but somewhere along the way in their travels they had found land and not just frozen water. That was for the best when one considered what the Undying could do.

They walked slowly, their feet settling in the growing snow and sinking a few inches with each tread. He could only assume the things were Undying. They were hooded and walked without concern for the cold.

They moved for him unerringly and he stood and prepared himself, his hands resting on the hilt of his sword and the handle of his axe. He would not be taken by surprise.

Faceless looked at the things and tilted his head for a moment.

Anna looked on, her face growing more and more worried as they continued to advance.

Finally, the creatures stopped moving, just at the edge of the warm glow from the fire. Their faces were lost in shadow, but he had seen enough of them to remember what they looked like with their vast mouths filled with teeth.

"Have you come for a reason?" Brogan did not waste time guessing what the creatures might be inclined to do. So far, they had shown themselves to be arrogant and dangerous. He had not made any effort to become friends with the things and certainly had no plans to do so now.

"The gods would see you dead, Brogan McTyre."

His hand gripped the axe harder. "Yes, you've made that clear enough."

"We have come to make you an offer. Give yourself to us and the rest of your people will be spared."

He laughed. "Spared? To do what? Try to live on

this frozen waste until the food runs out and the cold kills them?"

"The world is not dead yet. It can be spared. All you have to do is offer yourself to us and we can settle this."

Anna shook her head, surely meaning to say something, but one of the He-Kisshi looked her way and the entire form seemed to shiver with anger.

Brogan stared hard at the thing until, after several seconds, it looked back his way. "I have no reason to trust that your word is a bond."

"You dare?" The one that had stared so hard at Anna Harkness spoke to him.

Brogan almost laughed as he answered. "Truly? Have you not seen what I am willing to dare?"

The first that had spoken called out, "Enough, Ohdra-Hun. We are not here to fight with anyone. We are to seek a peaceful end to this before it is too late."

Brogan shook his head. "I think not. I have come this far and I will not stop."

"That is foolish on your part. You cannot hope to survive."

The one called Ohdra-Hun also spoke. "You will die. You cannot face the gods."

"I already killed one of yours, and I've heard that's impossible." He made sure to smile as he spoke.

Ohdra-Hun let out a hiss and stepped forward. The other two He-Kisshi called its name at the same time but it didn't seem to care. "You stink of deception!"

Brogan scoffed. "You come here with promises of peace that you never planned to keep. You come here with plans to kill me, and you say I stink of deception?" He was barely aware of the axe in his hand. Had he considered it carefully he still wouldn't have understood exactly how it got there. Some instincts were simply stronger than others.

Brogan shook his head. "You say you come in peace? Then leave the same way. If you try to attack, I'll kill you as I did the other who crossed me."

Ohdra-Hun stepped forward again and this time its hand reached out to grab at Brogan.

Brogan stepped back and caught the thing at the wrist. The skin was hot to the touch, dry and hard and lightly furred. He found the contact repugnant.

The Undying moved forward and pushed into him, the strength of the thing unsettling and more than he expected. It lifted him easily from the ground. And Brogan kicked it firmly in the center of its chest and staggered it backward.

The thing recovered quickly and came forward again, furious, hissing.

Brogan brought his axe around and caught it cleanly in the chest, opening the flesh and splitting the breast. Ohdra-Hun swept both of its arms around, the claws bared and ready to rend flesh. Brogan stepped back, dodged the attack. He had battled the things before but had allowed himself to forget how resilient they were.

"Enough!" Both he and the Undying were thrown aside. Brogan rolled, scurried to catch himself before he was blown too far, and managed to get to his feet with an effort. Ohdra-Hun rose from the ground with a roar that shook the hairs on Brogan's head and echoed off every surface. It turned toward the other two of its kind, but stopped itself from attacking them.

The other two spoke in unison, "You would offend the gods with your anger, Ohdra-Hun?" The Undying settled itself, head lowered in a mockery of shame.

"This is your one chance to save your friends, Brogan McTyre." It was the first of them that had spoken. "The gods are not often forgiving."

Brogan shook his head. "Neither am I. My family was killed. There's nothing more to say."

Ohdra-Hun seemed to swell as it took in a deep breath, but rather than saying or doing anything, the creature simply stood its ground.

"My family was taken. They were not returned. I don't care what the gods offer. They've offended me and I'll see them dead."

"Then you are a fool. We leave you now. When we return it will be to kill you."

There was nothing to say. He couldn't have thought up a proper response to that on his best days, and those were long gone in his opinion.

The He-Kisshi stepped away, turning one after the other. Ohdra-Hun's wings fluttered enough to show the chest wound it had received that was already half-healed. Brogan did not have that advantage.

They walked away, unmolested by any of the remaining people. Brogan considered attacking and decided against it. They came under conditions of truce and they left the same way. The only exception was Ohdra-Hun and it had already been reprimanded by the others of its kind.

Harper came closer, his bow held casually in one

hand. The odds were better than good that he'd been waiting to wound or kill the things had the situation gotten any worse.

"So what was that then?"

"A lie. I could have surrendered and all of you would be free."

Harper nodded. "That's certainly a lie. They'll kill me under any circumstance. I'm a traitor to their way of thinking."

Brogan looked away from his friend. He could find no answer to the comment that would take away the sting of what he'd already asked of Harper and what the man had done for him in an effort to save his family. There simply was no proper response.

Harper slapped him on the shoulder. "We've discussed that already. I'd not have done anything differently, Brogan, so stop thinking on it."

Brogan nodded and said nothing else.

But he thought. He thought about his dead family and the people who had died since he'd started his mad war against the gods.

He wouldn't stop. He had no choices left if he wanted to save anyone. He believed that with all of his being. The gods lied. Their servants lied. There was nothing else to it.

How many had died?

How many more would die?

Brogan's teeth clenched and his fists followed suit.

For a moment he'd almost allowed himself the luxury of guilt.

There would be none of that.

Faceless looked his way, and Brogan noticed but

did not care. His anger roared to life again inside of him, a furnace that had, for a moment, almost been extinguished. He had not started this; the gods had, or perhaps demons had used him to start a war. In the end he did not care. The path was laid out and someone, somewhere, had decided that his family had to die. He would punish that someone. He would kill that someone if he could, regardless of where that individual stood or lived.

"You are angry." Faceless spoke to him without guile.

"I am very angry."

"Why?"

Brogan shook his head and then bared his teeth in a smile. "Because all that I loved was taken from me, and the reasons do not make sense."

"Is that why you want to kill the gods?"

"No." He looked at Faceless and stared into the pits where eyes should be. There was something there now. Not just light but something more. "And also yes. I want revenge for what happened. I also want to make sure it never happens again."

"How could it happen again?"

"Faceless, the gods have been around for no one really knows how long. They have always demanded sacrifices. They have never granted anything in return. If you hear the oldest legends, there are tales that the gods have punished people many times for not obeying them. Whole cities, entire kingdoms, destroyed because someone dared say 'no.'"

Brogan looked away for a moment to find the words and finally looked back. "They've killed countless people just to punish a few. And they're doing it again now. I defied them. I tried to save my family from sacrifice and I failed. You understand that? I failed and still they punish the world."

He moved, because standing still no longer made any sense to him. "My family died and I suppose I went a little mad. I decided to pay them back in kind. They took all I had and I tried to take all that they had. I killed... I killed a great many men. And I dragged off all the followers of the gods that I could find to sell as slaves.

"I still don't feel bad about that. I suppose I should, but I do not. The people I took, they killed my family. They declared war on me the second they took my family from me. And I accepted the challenge. The people around me, they're here because they have no choice. They might even believe the way that I do, that the gods have to be stopped, but mostly they have no choice. They can help me stop the gods or they can die as surely as the land around us is dying or dead."

"What did the gods demand?"

"They demanded my life. They wanted me and my friends to sacrifice ourselves, or they wanted others to sacrifice us, mostly as a form of apology, I guess."

"And you did not want this?"

Brogan laughed. "No, lad. I most certainly did not. Even if I did want it, they'd only do it again. I was just told that the gods, or possibly the demons, probably chose me. They took my family to force my hand." He spat. "I am only a piece on a gameboard for them."

Faceless shook his head. "Then you will fight them because of this?"

"No. I'll kill them for this. I'll make sure that they never do this to another. That is my mercy. That is my kindness. I will stop them or I will die trying."

"Even if everyone with you has to die?"

Just that quickly the anger cooled a bit. Not enough to extinguish it, but enough to make Brogan consider the consequences of his actions.

"I've no choice now. The gods have called for war and I have answered. If you or the others want to leave, I understand, but I must finish what I started. There is no choice in this for me."

Faceless nodded and stood so still that he nearly appeared a statue. After several moments he finally spoke. "I think I am here to help you, Brogan."

"Why is that?"

"Because I am drawn to you. Because there is a voice in my head that I hear without my ears, that says I must stay with you and protect you."

"Truly?"

Faceless nodded.

"Then I suppose I shall accept that help, my friend." He said nothing more than that, but he found himself wondering exactly what, or who, had sent the creature to join him.

Brogan looked toward the Galean and wondered if the man might have an answer to that question. Now was not the time to ask, but possibly soon.

CHAPTER EIGHTEEN
THE GATHERING STORM

Myridia

Myridia slept as best she could and though the cold did not bother her, she shivered.

There were things that mortals were not meant to know. First was that their gods lied. Second was that their gods did not care. Those thoughts weighed heavily on her. She had spent her entire life in devotion and service to the gods. She had studied their history and learned all that she could of the world, the better to please them.

And, ultimately, she had to believe that she had failed the gods.

"Oh, Lyraal..." She longed for her friend.

Because she could not be a part of her old world any longer, the world that the gods had destroyed, she swam to the south. Her plan was to go until she found another land, or until she was struck down by the gods for her insolence. She swam deep below the surface, the best to avoid being seen by the He-Kisshi, who would surely want her dead on behalf of the gods.

The waters to the north looked no different, but they were colder now. The gods had killed the last of her tribe. She and hers had been ordered to sacrifice themselves to the Hahluritiedes, the shapers of the world, according to Dowru-Thist, who had no reason to lie unless the gods told it to. The lies made her ache and made her angry.

There could only be one reason for awakening the things that she could think of. The world would be re-formed. Likely all that lived in the world would be erased and there was nothing she could do about that.

The water around her was as dark as pitch. She sang softly and listened to the echoes to better find her way.

There was little to run across. The ocean was deep here, and even as low as she was, the bottom was farther away still.

Perhaps the gods only intended to rebuild what had already been destroyed. She could not know. They had no reason to tell her. She was, after all, little more than food.

Bitterness ran through her, and Myridia scowled.

Rather than dwell on the betrayal, she swam as hard as she could, ignoring the pull of the sword strapped to her back and the drag of the current that very nearly seemed to call her back to the north.

The gods had betrayed her. That was all there was to it.

The light she saw coming from the south was enough of a warning. Myridia watched on and stopped moving, making herself as still as possible to avoid being noticed in the perpetual night of the deep sea.

The glow was bioluminescence. The skin of the creature gave off a faint silvery light that she would likely have never seen under most circumstances, but in the nearly perfect darkness their skin was like a beacon.

Were they her people? No, but she could sense that they had been once upon a time. Their faces were different, far more bestial. The lips were gone, replaced by brutal rows of sharp teeth. The claws on the webbed hands and feet were too long, too thick and at least as deadly as the razored teeth.

They were not Grakhul, but they were. There was enough left to let her know that they were females and that they had once been her people. Now they moved through the waters seeking she knew not what, and every sense she had told her they were deadly and would kill her.

She was not a coward. She was merely not ready to die. She was not ready to die for uncaring gods.

Myridia waited until the stream of glowing figures had moved past her, and then she headed south again, her anger growing to overwhelm her sorrow.

Her people were dead because the gods had commanded it. She was alive because she defied the gods.

How then could the gods be right if their actions destroyed everything she had ever cared about?

Distant lights in the sky above the deep waters eventually caught Myridia's attention. She swam to the surface mostly because she needed a distraction from her thoughts.

The clouds swirled and coalesced to her right, above the land mass that she and her sisters had moved past when they were heading for the Sessanoh. Not far away, she thought she could see the remains of the small town where she had captured her sword.

Perhaps it was morbid curiosity, but Myridia swam for the shoreline and then climbed out of the waters, feeling the steady flow of briny liquids dripping down her back from the covered blade.

Unwynn settled against the small of her back as if it had always been there.

She walked, heading along the rocky shoreline until she found a path leading inland. The skies remained dark, but occasionally a flash of light showed those clouds gathering in intensity. They swirled and rushed and the lightning continued to hammer the sky, beating it into a frenzy of activity.

There. The small town where she and her friends had stolen horses, stolen weapons and started their trek across the land proper was to her right. All was dark.

She made her way to the town, frowning. There should have been something, someone, but there was nothing.

For half an hour she examined the buildings. They were devoid of life, but not of people. The half-decayed remains lay scattered about. Most had been done in with violence and it took her a while to realize that the very people in the town had committed the murderous acts. She didn't have to wonder why. They made it clear. It was women and children who were slaughtered. They were, mostly, killed in their sleep with a single stroke of a blade across the throat.

Murdered. Possibly to spare them the end of the world and the long death that starvation would have caused. Or murdered because the few men who were not similarly killed were offering them as a sacrifice, for all she knew.

In any event, the town was dead. The rest of his people joined the man who'd died at her hands, and the air was oppressive with regret or the ghosts of the dead.

"I do not believe in ghosts." She told herself that simple lie and hoped it would warm her. It did not.

Myridia found nothing of value. No food, no water, no clothes that she wanted. After a while she turned back to the waters and headed on her way.

Within minutes of leaving the spot the skies broke open in a cascade of lightning that shook the earth and showed clearly the great funnel cloud that descended on the small town. It took seconds for the winds to shred the buildings and cast the remains of man and beast alike into the air and out of sight.

The storm continued to rage, to blast the surface of the land clean and she nodded her head, feeling her lips tighten into a harsh line.

It was likely an act of the gods. The Hahluritiedes wanted a clean palette to draw a new world upon and so they erased all that had been before. There was no doubt in her mind that the storms would grow even worse as they reached areas where there had been people or there still were struggling survivors.

To the south then. That was her decision. She would travel south and swim past this damned land in the hopes that she might find other, better places beyond the scope of anything she had ever seen in her life. And if she failed, so be it, but she would try just the same and if she came across survivors, people who still lived and struggled, she would advise them to do the same.

The waters were cold, but not so harsh that she feared freezing to death. Swimming helped, of course.

Above her the lightning still played in the clouds, the waves still slammed themselves toward whatever shoreline they could find and occasionally a boat or ship passed by as she continued her trek. There were not many, but there were a few.

Myridia was alone as she had never been before. Her people were gone. Her gods had abandoned her. Still, she did not cry. She moved, losing herself in the waters and in the course of events.

Brogan

The rain was replaced by ice. Brogan pulled his clothes closer to his body and huffed warm breaths across his hands. The fires were dwindling. There wasn't enough to keep them burning. The only good news was that Anna still managed to find food for everyone. He pondered how that was possible, but decided it best not to consider the contents of her bag too carefully.

Jahda helped and so did the remaining crew of the dead ship. They were adept at fishing, even in the cold, it seemed, and so there was fresh meat. He would always prefer beef or mutton to the supplies he was given, but Brogan was grateful for the food.

The weather aside, he did not like waiting. Two attempts at reaching the actual shoreline had failed and the men who had made the attempts were now close to the largest remaining fire and doing their best to dry off completely.

Never let it be said that Brogan was a complete fool. He learned from their examples. He turned to Jahda at one point and asked, "Is it true that you and your people can walk across water?"

Jahda shook his head. "We have ways of traveling, but they do not allow me to move a dozen people over water without getting wet. We have to wait."

Brogan nodded and then shrugged. Patience was not what he preferred but he could accept the need from time to time.

"I have never waited for a boat before. I usually just walked to the docks and paid for service."

Jahda looked out at the sea. "That is a bit more challenging these days."

Brogan nodded.

"No docks. But Roskell has assured me our ride will be here soon and I have no reason to doubt him."

"Same here." Brogan turned his attention to Jahda. "You have both come to my aid and I thank you for that."

"There is little by way of choice, my friend. We allow the world to burn or we help control the fires." There was no judgment in the comment, merely a statement. Brogan found himself oddly grateful for that fact.

"There has never been a choice for me. If a man took my family I would have fought to get them back. A king? The same. A god? The same. Anyone who thinks there was a choice was not present when I found out."

"I have heard the stories of what happened and what you did in response. Tell me, how do you justify selling the Grakhul into slavery?"

Brogan actually laughed. "I don't. I had two choices. I could kill them all or I could sell them. What mattered to me was that they never do to another family what they did to mine. I felt slavery was a mercy."

Jahda stared at him for a long moment and nodded.

"Judge me as you will. I'll call it madness and grief. I didn't want any more blood on my hands. I did not want to kill innocents. The women and children had done nothing to me, but I was not going to leave them where they were, the better to sacrifice others."

"I do not judge you, Brogan. I seek to understand you."

"Ask your questions and I will answer them." He shrugged. "That I owe you at the least."

"What will you do if you manage to stop the gods?"

"I do not know. I haven't thought that far ahead. I only know I don't want the gods taking anyone else."

Jahda nodded.

They stayed silent for a while as the winds continued their ominous howling and the frozen rain rattled and danced across everything. Jahda pulled his hood closer, and shivered in the cold.

"How does this end, Brogan?"

"With me dead and the gods dead. If I'm lucky."

"Do you wish to die?" The man from Louron frowned.

"No. But I can't see any other ending for this. If I survive long enough to kill the gods, I don't expect there will be anyone celebrating my continued life."

"You might be surprised. I know many people have had family taken from them over the years. Not many are fond of the coin for a life idea. Most would rather have kept their family."

"That sounds like a truth, but I expect most would rather still have a home."

"There is that," Jahda sighed. "You have heard Roskell Turn say that this was all inevitable."

"I don't care," Brogan shrugged. "As I have said already, I'd have done the same regardless of who took my family from me. If that makes me wrong, then I am wrong and nothing will change that."

Jahda nodded. "I do not think you are wrong." He leaned in close. "I also do not think that your friend without a face is as innocent as he would like you to think."

Brogan looked toward Faceless. He and Anna spoke and others listened. The creature was staring at another of the small blazes around which the group had gathered in fragments. His face had some form, true, but in comparison to the others he was nearly featureless. Anna said something that made the creature laugh and it was joined by several others.

Brogan said, "The Undying will come for us."

"Yes. They have already said as much. That does

not change my beliefs about your friend." Jahda spoke softly but firmly.

"I know. And I'll listen to your caution, but for the moment he is one of the only things I've ever seen that could hurt one of the monstrous creatures and they are still many and we are still a small gathering."

"We have no choice but to fight if they show themselves, but we are not as powerless as you might think."

"I never said powerless." Brogan looked at the man and shook his head. "I said we are few. If they come in force, it's possible that they will take us. You saw what they did to the ship. If they have a chance to strike us the same way, we might not have any choice in this."

Jahda frowned and looked off into the distance. "Someone is coming."

Brogan turned and looked in the same direction and then rubbed at his eyes. "I see nothing."

"Look more closely." Jahda's long finger pointed at the very thing that made Brogan rub his eyes. There was an odd flickering in the distance. Not a light source so much as a distortion of what little light existed. On very hot days he had seen similar pools of reflection on the ground, false images that looked like mirrors or water, and disappeared as one got closer.

"What is that?"

"That is someone walking the Shimmering Path."

"The what?"

"It means one of my people is coming closer."

In seconds a shape appeared, neither close by, nor very far away. The figure was buried in a heavy, hooded cloak and if he had not been warned he might have suspected a He-Kisshi of trying to sneak closer. The shape seemed almost to have three legs but Brogan reasoned out a walking staff of some sort. No. Shorter.

Jahda stood up and crossed his muscular arms. Brogan stood, too, and rested his hand on the haft of his axe. It had been a long while since he'd moved around without being ready to grab a weapon.

The woman who walked their way was young and dark-skinned and had features that were as alien to his world as could be. She had very broad lips and her hair looked like Jahda's, only longer and more unkempt. Whereas his braids were organized and meticulous, hers were an explosion filled with afterthoughts in comparison.

She stopped in front of the leader of the Kaer-ru and stared up at him, one eye half-squinted shut as she examined the man. His hands moved to his hips and he smiled down at her, as he might smile at a mischievous child.

When she spoke, Brogan understood not a single word, and when Jahda responded the same remained true. Their noises were a singsong of gibberish, but it was a pleasant chaos.

Both looked his way and the woman's dark eyes scanned over him from head to toe. Her facial expression was still half a smile but the other part was a hard scrutiny hidden beneath the pleasant expression.

"You are the man who wars with the gods?" Brogan listened to her voice, considered the expression on her face and then nodded.

She nodded back and actually smiled. "You do not look insane."

"I've been called worse." He shrugged.

"I am told that you will need help. I am here to offer my assistance." She stepped closer. She was tall for a woman, and substantially taller than Roskell Turn. "I am not sure what I can do, but I have been told to work with Jahda, and he in turn says I should work with you."

"What do you do?"

"I help the dead."

Brogan stared for a while, trying to read if she was jesting. "I am not dead. Not yet."

"I would be surprised if you were. Most corpses are not so active."

He thought about the towering skeleton of Walthanadurn. "You might be surprised."

Jahda laughed out loud and a moment later Brogan and the girl were both smiling.

"Daivem Murdrow, this is Brogan McTyre. Brogan wants to kill the gods. Daivem wants to help the dead. She has brought a great number of them with her."

Brogan looked around and frowned. There were no dead for him to see. He decided to simply let the problem go – if she could help, he would take the assistance. If she was crazy, well, he was the one who wanted to kill gods, and that said little for his possible sanity.

CHAPTER NINETEEN
PLANS CHANGE

Tully

The ship moved through the half-frozen waters at a solid clip, and slowed only when they saw the lightning lighting the skies to the north.

Tully stared at the lights and frowned. From what they were saying, the home of the gods lay in that direction and Brogan McTyre was planning to attack them. She had no idea where that sort of information came from and little desire to find out. The man wanted the gods dead. That was interesting.

"What are you thinking?" Temmi stared at her and then used a very large knife to cut an apple in half. She cored the first half and without asking tossed it gently toward Tully. Tully caught it, nodded her thanks and bit into the sweet fruit in one motion.

"That maybe this Brogan McTyre has the right idea." She muttered the words through her bite of fruit.

Temmi looked at her as if she had suddenly sprouted feathers.

"Hear me out. The Undying want me dead. They want you dead. The bastard that has pursued us has killed your family and our friend and has no intention of stopping – and he serves the gods. If the gods are dead, our problem is solved."

Temmi snorted laughter and chewed on her apple. As with Tully, the words were muttered through the food in her mouth. "That's lovely, of course, but I don't know as one man can kill the gods."

"I don't either, but if he did, he'd be doing us a favor. That's all I'm saying. Sooner or later the He-Kisshi will come for us and if they find us above decks I expect to die as quickly and badly as poor Niall did."

Temmi scowled. "We don't know he's dead."

"I felt him die in my soul, Temmi. I felt him die as surely as I felt my mother when she died." Tully's voice was soft. It was a lie, but it was the sort of lie few people could argue with. It wasn't so uncommon to feel a loved one's death. Tully had simply never had a loved one to die on her.

Temmi nodded. "So what of it? Will you betray Stanna like you did the people from Hollum?"

"That wasn't a betrayal. I already told you that. It was living to see the next day. However dark that might be."

Temmi nodded and said nothing. If she had decided to report what she had seen, Tully had no doubt that she would already be dead. Stanna might well have forgiven her, but there was no hope that Darkraven would have been so understanding.

"No. I'll do nothing that would hurt Stanna or you. I'm just not sure how I should side when the gods want me dead. I was to be a sacrifice, I already told you that."

Temmi nodded and chewed at her apple before she answered. "I know. I know all of this and I agree. I never want to see the Undying again, myself. It might be I need to have a chat with Stanna about all of this."

Tully closed her eyes on the blizzard of fear that attacked her stomach at the notion. Stanna was a friend, yes, but she was also a slaver, and a mercenary and currently working for a woman who wanted to see Brogan McTyre dead for a hundred different reasons, not least of which was the loss of her city.

"I'm not a fool, Tully. I'll consider this carefully and if I bring it up I'll do so quietly."

"I just... I just want peace, Temmi. I am so tired." She sighed. "You're the only friend I have left. I watched one of my best friends die the other day and the rest of the people I used to call friends were among those I helped kill in order to save myself." She looked at Temmi and wiped at the tears threatening to burn her eyes. "I am so very fucking tired."

Temmi moved closer to her and put a hand on her shoulder. It was an attempt to comfort and Tully knew that. After a moment Temmi leaned in and gave her a proper hug and she hugged back, sniffing. Her muscles relaxed just enough to let her know how much tension rode through her and then she was pushing back from the contact. No one was allowed to get close in Hollum. The only ones that ever did were the ones that survived, and they were rarities, indeed.

The bells came again. The Undying were in the air near the ship, or, worse, they were on the vessel and speaking.

Temmi once again got a wide-eyed expression on her face that said she'd been caught. Tully understood exactly how she felt.

Was it curiosity or something worse? Tully wasn't sure she'd ever know, but she found herself moving up through the bowels of the ship and then upward, heading for the top deck and the captain's quarters. There, if she was lucky, she might see the Undying and hear what it wanted.

Hiding was her gift. She did it well.

Tully crept carefully into the cabin, moving through the open doorway when everyone was looking at the He-Kisshi. She had seen enough of the beasts that she never wanted to see one again, and yet she, too, was nearly mesmerized by the beast. It should not have been so intimidating, especially when seen from behind. And yet there it was, a hunched, high-shouldered shape with a hood. It looked like it was wrapped in an old fur cloak that had long since gone to seed. It smelled of cinnamon and other rare spices and it looked slowly at Darkraven, Stanna, and several others that Tully did not know as well.

"There are people among you who have offended the gods or their servants. I would have those people brought to me." The voice was cold, bitter and very familiar.

Stanna scoffed and shook her head. "There is no one on this boat that has offended the gods, but a few might have offended you in the past."

"I am a servant of the gods. I am the voice of the gods. My word is as law."

Tully shifted carefully, looking at the shape while doing her best to remain quiet. Was it the same one? Possibly. She could not say. For a brief time the flesh had seemed raw and new around the head that had been severed and had regrown, but if this was the same beast, that was no longer the case.

"One of the people on this ship was chosen as a sacrifice by the gods and escaped."

Stanna laughed a second time and shook her head. "And to what end do the gods want that sacrifice now? If they have it, will they stop destroying the world?"

The creature shook with rage, its hands opening and closing, showing the vicious claws that ended each finger.

Darkraven shook her head. "Enough. Give me a name. If you have a name, perhaps we can help you. If not, leave."

"You dare!"

Darkraven snapped her fingers and three of the men around her raised short, powerful crossbows and aimed them at the thing. "I am done. You and your damned gods have destroyed everything I own. I owe you nothing. You are not welcome here. I 'dare?' Yes. I do. Because I'm finished listening to you and anyone else who sets out to ruin me."

The He-Kisshi moved. It took the distance between itself and Darkraven in a heartbeat and had the woman by her throat. The claws sank into skin and Hillar screamed in pain even as she drove a blade into the guts of the creature. Blood flowed and the thing let out a hiss as it spun toward the closest of the crossbow wielders. The bolt came from the weapon and drove through the arm of the beast, impaling the forearm and forcing the creature to let go of its captive.

Hillar fell on her ass.

The thing screeched and tried to dodge the two crossbow bolts that drove into it. One struck the darkness of the hood, and punched through the back of the creature's head. The other struck where the heart would be on a person.

Stanna and the Bitch moved forward. The sword cut the thing open from its hip up to the neck and through the shoulder in one swing.

Hillar climbed to her feet and glared at the remains. "Bind it in ropes. Tie the ropes to an anchor. Drop the anchor into the blasted seas."

"It'll come back." Stanna looked at the remains. "I cut the head off this thing before."

"It'll take time. By then maybe we can have this finished."

She turned away from the dead thing as her men started to follow her orders. Stanna moved with her, the two of them ready to have another discussion about the gods knew what.

The flesh of the He-Kisshi opened up and slithered up one of the men who'd shot it with a crossbow. By the time he was opening his mouth to scream the He-Kisshi had been reborn. It was not a bloodless transformation. The guard's body made wet noises as the thick hide of the Undying constricted over it and sealed around the surprised man's shape.

Though she tried hard to see everything, the entire violent action was too fast. What she did see made Tully let out a scream of shock that was lost under the noises of the Undying and the mercenary alike.

"I grow weary of these games." The Undying reached out again and this time when it grabbed at Hillar Darkraven, its claws peeled the scalp from her head like the rind off an orange.

The woman who had once owned Torema let out a shriek of agony as the blood flowed down her face. Before anyone could move, the Undying threw the screaming woman against the cabin's wall, shattering bones and wood alike.

It moved, and the next man in line, who was busy drawing his sword and casting aside his crossbow, died as the creature drove a fist through his chest, shattering bone and pulping internal organs with the force of the strike.

Stanna stepped back and prepared for combat in the close quarters. Her sword stayed close to her side, bared and bloodied and seemingly hungry for more.

The Undying shook the body of the dead man from its arm and turned its hooded face toward the last of the three men who had shot at it. The man was justifiably terrified. He tried to run and failed. The man made two paces before a sudden wind blasted through the room and hurled him toward the Undying. Stanna's short hair whipped around and Tully was actually staggered by the force of the wind, her hiding place revealed in an instant.

The man twisted in the air and tried to find a way to escape but the Undying was ready and caught him with those vile claws as the winds made its wings snap and flutter.

It turned toward Stanna and let out another loud

hiss as it ripped the man in its grip in half.

Stanna backed away, shaking her head. Tully did the exact same thing from the other side of the cabin.

The blood-soaked He-Kisshi threw the ruined portions of its prey to each side as it came for Stanna. "I remember you..."

Stanna didn't waste her time with words. The Bitch's tip slammed into the creature's chest and she let loose a battle cry as she lifted the thing from the ground and drove it into the wooden wall next to where Hillar lay slumped and bleeding.

Again, the thing screamed as it tried to stop the massive sword from pushing any deeper into its body. Stanna did not wait for it to recover. Instead her other hand came forward and she drove a heavy dagger into the beast's head. The blade punched through flesh and bone, the point running into the oversized mouth like a new, shiny, bloodied tooth.

Still it fought. The body was pinned to the wall, but the legs were free and they rose up, sweeping the air, trying to claw open Stanna's stomach or legs. She shifted her body and stepped back half a foot, narrowly avoiding having her thigh ripped open by the heavy claws. She pulled the blade from the head and slammed it home again in a new spot. The He-Kisshi roared and reached out with long arms.

Stanna grunted and pressed the hot, leathery body into the wall.

Tully watched on, horrified.

Stanna let out a battle cry again and brought her leg up to kick the thing in its bloodied guts. The vast mouth and head of the He-Kisshi lunged forward and

Stanna pulled her leg back, narrowly missing getting her foot bitten off.

Tully moved past the other woman, pulling her daggers out as the thing lunged and tried to force its way up the sword sticking it to the wall.

Blood flowed from the heavy wounds in the nightmare's belly and it moved closer to Stanna even as she tried to kick it back again. The claws of the He-Kisshi's foot caught the leather of her pant leg and ripped the thick hide open. Thin trails of blood opened and wept on Stanna's knee and calf even as she pushed her body into the thing again and shoved it further down the sword.

Tully's first dagger drove into its neck and blood flowed freely.

The second dagger cut three fingers from the hand of the beast as it reached out to tear Stanna's face from her skull.

That vast, dark mouth lunged for Tully then, ignoring Stanna completely. She backed up and stifled a scream as the teeth slammed together in a hard WHOMP. Her hands scrambled for more daggers from her collection and caught one of her larger blades instead. She brought the weapon up as a guard against those damnable teeth, and the tip of the thing opened a new, deep gash across the maw. Those eyes, dark and shining, glistened amidst the blood and studied her as the mouth tried for her again.

Stanna let out an inarticulate scream and drove her own knife's blade into the thing's neck again, a third time, and a fourth, before it finally turned to bite at her.

Stanna threw herself back as it lunged forward and once again slid up the blade that had it impaled against the wall.

This time she shoved the whole of the long knife's blade into the damned thing's mouth and down its throat. If the blade hadn't pinned something vital, she would surely have lost her hand as it tried to bite.

Finally it stopped moving and let loose a sigh.

Stanna stepped back from it, carefully, eyes wide and very alert, her body shaking with her gasping breaths.

"That thing died easier the last time."

Tully shook her head. "They do not stay dead. Not ever."

Stanna nodded her head. "Do not leave here. Do not touch that thing."

"I had no intention."

She waited four minutes or so before Stanna came back with a very hefty blade and an axe to boot.

She watched as the woman cut large portions of the thing away. Each limb was cut away from the others. The vast leathery sails it used for wings were removed and separated. When she was done Stanna took the head and hurled it into the ocean.

Stanna took the body one piece at a time and the crew watched her, some horrified and others simply awestruck.

Over the next hour as they moved along in the ocean, a limb at a time was tossed into the waters and finally the heavy torso of the thing was wrapped in cloth, bound in the ropes intended to tie the whole body together and then thrown over the side as well.

"I don't think it's dead."

"Neither do I, Tully, but I expect it will take a while for the fucking thing to mend."

"What do we do now?"

"I don't know." Stanna moved back toward the cabin that had been Darkraven's office on their journey, and walked past the woman's broken remains. There was a desk with a heavy oak chair. She took that spot and rested her head in her hands. "I prefer to let others do the thinking, you know? I prefer to just follow orders and make certain that things get done."

Tully nodded her head. "Who was Darkraven's second?"

"On this ship? Me."

"You have seen how the gods work. You have seen what they are willing to do."

Stanna nodded her head and looked toward Tully. "And?"

"They will not save the world. They will keep destroying it."

"You were almost sacrificed. I can see where you might have a set opinion."

"But I don't. I didn't. I just… I think that Brogan McTyre is right. The only way to stop the gods from ending the world is to stop the gods." She moved her hands around. "I've no idea how, but he seems to have a notion or two."

"You want to join the madman who started this?"

"I want to live through this." Tully spread her arms wide. "Whatever this is. I want to live, Stanna. I am tired of running and hiding. I want to live."

Stanna stared at her for a long while. Her eyes were

unreadable in the gloom of the cabin. "They'll come for us. The Undying."

"The one you killed? It came for me several times. I think it's the one that took Niall from us."

"I remember it," Stanna nodded.

"There are others. I don't know how many, but they will come for us."

"Then I suppose we should find the bastard McTyre and work together to end this madness."

"And if someone doesn't agree?" She was thinking about the people left on the ship. Many had fought against McTyre and his people already.

Stanna stood up. "If they want to argue, they can go into the waters, too." The way she said it, Tully had no doubt she'd hack them apart first and enjoy the process.

The He-Kisshi

Ohdra-Hun drifted into the depths. He was not conscious, not in any way that would have made sense to a human being, but he was *aware.*

He knew that the others came for him. They moved from their places around the wasted lands and further away and they came as quickly as they could, desperate to make sure that no more of them were lost to the universe.

Uthl-Prahna was dead. Gone. Impossible though it seemed, he was lost to them forever. So, too, was Lidin-Throm, who had attempted to punish the demon Ariah and been locked away or destroyed within the prison that was the demon's home. They could not tell for certain what had happened aside from the fact that it was gone, removed from the world. The balance of their world was damaged a second time, so, yes, the He-Kisshi congregated where the remains of Ohdra-Hun had been cast into the waters and they dove deep, sliding below the waves and moving through the water on wings made to cut air or water with ease.

It did not take them long to gather the remains. The challenge was finding a new host. The land around them was barren, stripped of all worthwhile life.

They traveled to the south and found more travelers soon enough. The ship was smaller, overcrowded with survivors desperate to make landfall. They were lost. The clouds made navigation a challenge and the He-Kisshi moved around the ship for several minutes before Dowru-Thist dropped down to the deck and looked at the people there. They were, understandably, nervous.

"You are starving."

One of the men nodded his head.

"You would have food?"

"Yes. Please."

"You would find your way to land?"

"Yes. Oh, yes, please." The one that spoke was brave enough to look Dowru-Thist in the face. Most of the others refused.

Dowru-Thist reached out and pulled a young boy toward him. The boy was at the cusp of puberty, nearly perfect for their needs. The boy screamed, of course, and his mother came forward to beg. The man who had spoken on behalf of the people called out and two men held the woman. They would listen and survive or they would be punished by the Undying as had always been the way.

With a gesture of his hand Dowru-Thist reached into the sea and drew it into the air. Several shapes swam in the waters he summoned and when he gestured, the bounty of live fish splashed down on the deck of the ship. The desperate, hungry humans worked quickly to capture the thrashing beasts.

While they did that, and the woman cried for her child, the man who had spoken looked to Dowru-Thist and shook with fear. He was wise.

Dowru-Thist pointed his finger to the south. "Head in that direction. You are two days from land." The man nodded and bowed, falling to his knees in gratitude.

The boy in his hands squirmed and tried to break free, but could not. Dowru-Thist made certain his grip was solid and then rose into the winds that he summoned. It was a short distance to reach land where they could collect the pieces of their fallen brethren.

Within twenty minutes the process was complete, and Ohdra-Hun lived again. It roared its rage into the airs and prepared to rise but this time Dowru-Thist and two others stopped the tirade.

"Enough. You have given into your rage too often, Ohdra-Hun. It is now time to be calm. We will destroy all that lives on this world, as the gods have demanded. They have woken the world-shapers and all that is here will soon be replaced. You will have your revenge. Now is the time to stop Brogan

McTyre."

Ohdra-Hun staggered around and the others watched, ready to attack if need be, though they had no desire to do so.

Finally their brethren relaxed and nodded. "It is time, Dowru-Thist."

"We go now. We will kill the fool who would kill the gods and who killed our own."

They rose as one, and moved high into the air. They did not need to seek Brogan McTyre. They knew where he was. The gods told them.

The gods were scared.

The He-Kisshi did not understand fear. It was not a part of their nature.

Brogan McTyre

The land to the west vanished. North and south of where they were the land continued on, but to the west storms came along that brought vast funnel clouds, and those clouds hit the earth and pulled it away.

"What is happening?" Brogan couldn't see who asked the question.

Roskell Turn answered. "The gods are removing the world from existence. That is their way." His voice was soft and solemn.

If the world were a drawing in the sand, then a giant was erasing that drawing in broad strokes. He thought back to the skeleton of Walthanadurn and shook his head. That was all he could think of as he watched it happen. Brogan held his axe and sword and stared at the land as it was destroyed, fully aware that there was nothing he could do to stop the decimation.

Where the distant silhouette of the land had been, there was now nothing but a vast expanse of water.

It was upon this endless stretch that the boat showed itself. It came from the west slowly. Perhaps it came swiftly but it seemed to take a very long time. The tiny shape grew in size until finally he could see it was a boat, but even then, the details were nearly impossible to make out in the darkness.

Anna Harkness cried when she saw the figure of her husband, Desmond, on the vessel. She did not scream or weep but instead stood up and danced from one foot to the other impatiently as tears ran silently down her face.

Brogan smiled for her reunion, and if a part of him envied Desmond that joy, it was only natural in his eyes. His Nora was gone, after all.

Desmond looked like a hound tied to a tree. He wanted to run, to leap, to swim the icy waters if need be to get to his woman, but the slow fire of reason kept him on that unusual boat as it came closer.

And the boat was unusual. For all the world it looked as if the woman piloting it – was it Darwa? He thought so – had made it from the roof of a Lodge. It was always possible. The woman had been living in a Lodge when last he saw her. The structure was half-buried in the earth as he recalled, but that meant nothing. Galeans were, as he was learning, capable of many unusual feats.

Darwa looked his way and nodded grimly. She seemed incapable of smiling. He understood.

The odd-looking vessel thudded against their island of ice and broke a portion of it away.

"Be swift about it. We should be leaving here." Darwa's voice cracked like the ice as she spoke.

Brogan nodded and grabbed his meager supplies. He also grabbed Anna's as the woman had set aside any semblance of caution and hurled herself into her husband's arms. Desmond caught her and staggered a bit, but kept himself, and his wife, upright. They hugged as madly as any couple ever had, and that included Brogan and his Nora.

Brogan looked away and felt his jaw clench. He carried the bags onto the boat, swaying with the waves and the rocking of the thing. Yes, it was part of a Lodge, but it had been changed. The Galean had either reshaped the thing or used her sorceries to change it; he did not know and did not care. It held their weight with ease and he was grateful. When all the others were aboard, Faceless stared at the vessel for a long moment and then reached his hand into the air above it. The air crackled and Brogan thought he saw something happen, but whatever it was, it occurred too quickly for his eyes to fully recognize it. Faceless pulled back quickly, a wince forming on his nearly featureless face.

"Hurts," he said as he looked at his fingertips.

Darwa nodded. "I have warded this vessel against demons. You are a demon, or a servant of one."

Brogan frowned, but before he could say anything, Anna broke away from the deep and passionate kiss she was giving her husband to take in a breath and speak in Galean to the other woman. Whatever she was saying, Roskell Turn agreed and nodded to prove it.

"Enough." Darwa shook her head. "I have warded this boat for a reason. Neither the gods nor the demons of the world need travel with us on this mission."

Faceless looked at her, expressionlessly.

Brogan ground his teeth together and said nothing. The situation was very simple, really. The witch was the only chance they had of getting where they needed to go. Faceless was a demon? That was merely confirmation in his eyes. He had expected as much all along. What else could the thing be? It certainly was not a god. At least he did not think it was a god. The only ones he'd seen were much larger.

"They say this creature has helped you and kept you alive, Brogan McTyre. Is that the truth of it in your eyes?"

He nodded once. "Faceless has defended me several times, including from the He-Kisshi."

Darwa's expression changed as she looked at Faceless. She grew sterner still and her eye twitched as if she had just smelled a dead skunk. "Come aboard. Know this. If you do anything I do not like, I will revoke my protection from the wards and you will burn."

Faceless looked on for several seconds and finally reached out to the air again. Brogan could see the scorch marks on the creature's hand. This time when it touched the air nothing happened.

Faceless climbed aboard and said, "I believe you."

"Then you are wise," she spat.

A moment later the boat lurched forward at a higher

speed than Brogan would have thought possible. He held on tightly and so did the rest. Faceless staggered and barely caught himself from falling into the waters.

Anna and Desmond folded over on each other and settled in a spot where they could hold themselves and simply be together. Brogan looked away. He saw Harper watching him. Harper said nothing. That was, perhaps, for the best.

Bump made noise. It was what the man did when he was around other people. He laughed, and he talked and he told tales of what they had been through and Brogan listened, though he said nothing.

They traveled to the north. The boat made a deep wake as it rode along, and Brogan faced the direction they traveled, looking at the distant lashes of lightning that marked his destination.

He could not say how far away they were, only that he could now see the light from the Gateway.

Darwa said, "You should prepare yourselves. The Undying will certainly strike before we can reach the Gateway."

Brogan nodded. He'd been thinking about the He-Kisshi and how to handle the situation. This was not the sort of thing he wanted to deal with. This was not the sort of combat he wanted. He wanted to fight and kill the gods and everything else seemed like a distraction.

Harper looked at the Galean and asked, "Will poisons hurt the damned things?"

"Some might. They can heal from most anything but poisons might work. If they are the right sorts."

"I've serpent-tongue, red hendrique and firewort."

"Firewort. The other two might slow them, but firewort will kill nearly anything that ever walked the lands."

Harper nodded.

"Of course it won't keep them dead, and if they see the arrow coming they can bend it on the air and send it back."

Harper nodded again and considered his options silently.

All around him the people on the boat prepared themselves. There were two exceptions: Desmond and Anna spoke to each other softly with worried expressions, and Jahda spoke with the woman from his land, the two of them having a serious debate if he could judge by their frowns.

"I thought you'd warded this boat from demons." Bump said the words even as he sharpened one of his long daggers.

Darwa shook her head. "They're not demons. I can't ward against them. I've tried several times in the past."

"Well then, what good are you?" The woman turned her head sharply to glare at Bump and he laughed. After a moment her expression softened into a smile. Brogan shook his head. Bump often seemed to push for his own death. How he was still alive was one of the universe's great mysteries in Brogan's eyes.

The winds picked up again and Darwa moved her hands, spoke softly, and then nodded in satisfaction as the direction of the winds bent to her will.

"I can warn when they get closer, if they are not trying to hide themselves." She reached into a bag around her waist and fished out a blackened something that she promptly put into her mouth and started chewing.

Brogan looked away.

They'd come soon. He would do his best to be ready. There was no choice in the matter.

Enemies that would not die added to his troubles heavily.

"How is it that they are undying?" He looked toward Darwa as he asked the question.

"It is by the decree of the gods. They can do anything, Brogan McTyre. They are gods."

He nodded his head. "Your books of Galea say nothing about them?"

"Only that the He-Kisshi are the voice of the gods. They are the 'Divine Collectors,' meaning they gather the sacrifices and decide who is to be taken. They make decisions for the gods and speak for them in many matters. They can only be killed by the gods themselves, and that will not happen."

Once again Brogan's jaw clenched as he considered the Undying.

"Do you suppose it hurt them when I killed one of their kind? Truly killed?"

Darwa didn't even bother looking in his direction. "I know it did. You helped kill a god and one of the He-Kisshi. You have enraged them and wounded them deeply. That is why the rules have changed, Brogan. That is why they no longer care if you are sacrificed."

She gestured to the west where the land was gone.

"They are erasing the world. At least this part of it. Most of the cities are gone. The kingdoms of man have fallen. If there are people still alive in the land, it is something they will soon settle."

"How?"

"You still do not understand, Brogan." Darwa turned her head to face him completely and her eyes locked on his. "They are *gods*. There are some things they *will* not do, but there is little that they *cannot* do. They have summoned the Hahluritiedes. Galea says that these creatures are what is left of previous gods. They were stripped of their will, their minds, and made into servants. They shaped the lands around the world and created all life as you have seen it. The Hahluritiedes created man, and made horses as they are. They lifted mountains into the air and cut rivers across the world. They are the makers of all that you have ever seen."

She shook her head. "They are the source of all that has made this world."

"Are they?"

Something about the way he asked that question caught Darwa's attention. "What are you thinking?"

"If they made the world, if they will unmake it, then what can't they do?"

"They can't think for themselves. They have no minds. They cannot act without being ordered."

"Yet you say the gods have all the power."

"The Hahluritiedes were gods once. They are all that is left of the gods who survived the last change of power." She shrugged. "You have seen for yourself that gods are hard to kill. They still have power that can be used by the gods."

Brogan nodded and longed for a place where he

could sit and contemplate the creatures that were remaking the world.

Wishes seldom come true.

Darwa looked to the skies and sighed. "The He-Kisshi are coming for you, Brogan. For all of us."

Brogan nodded his head and stared at the waters around them. "Land would be better."

Darwa nodded in response. "I can do nothing about that."

Jahda sighed and then called out, "I might be able to help."

The girl, Daivem, shook her head. "No. It can't be done without hurting yourself and you know it."

"It can. If you help me."

Darwa scowled. "If you are going to do something, do it soon. They are coming fast and they will use the waters to kill us all."

"It would be easier to shed this world." Daivem spoke and Brogan heard her, but he had no idea what it was she spoke of.

Jahda shrugged. "Just the same."

The two of them stood and whatever it was they did, the world went mad.

CHAPTER TWENTY
DESTINATIONS

Daivem

Jahda asked much. He wanted her to use the dead to save the world. She had no notion if that was possible, but after a long discussion she conceded that there might be something to his plans.

That was one thing. It was another to consider what else the man wanted.

The Shimmer was not a gift given lightly. It cost effort and it risked the chance that the power behind the Shimmering Path might well reject them and cast aside the abilities they had been granted. That was a real risk and more than one of the Louron had been lost along the way.

And now he wanted to move the entire boat.

Of course he was right, but that did not make her happy.

Of course she helped. That was her place in this. She had been told to come to the man and listen to his wisdom.

The Shimmering Path was always there. Opening the way to it was the challenge. She offered her help, but let Jahda determine the course.

In moments the air before them rippled and then split.

There was no warning for the others. There was no time and it was a relatively short jaunt.

The boat shuddered and the people on it stumbled, all save Jahda, Daivem, and the demon-thing they called Faceless.

Several of the people on the vessel made exclamations and two actually asked the gods for help. Daivem suspected those prayers would go unanswered.

The world around them shifted, stretched, changed.

Jahda led the way, pushing the Shimmer to aid him, asking, demanding, begging and cajoling. Once again the power that had helped the Louron on many occasions worked to their benefit.

It was only a few minutes to reach land. During that time the others on the boat cried out or held themselves and each other. A few of the people on the boat looked ready to vomit, but none did.

Brogan McTyre looked on, seeming unaffected. He had been altered by contact with the divine, she understood that, but it seemed that he was changed more than she would have expected.

Then they stopped, the front of the boat rapidly pushing into a rough shoreline. The wood scraped, and the whole of the vessel halted, leaving those standing with little choice but to move a few paces or fall down. Some did fall just the same. There was only so much room.

Darwa, the Galean who had rescued them from an island of ice, climbed out of the vessel with confident steps and called over her shoulder, "Move fast. They're coming and they will be here soon."

"Who?" The man who spoke meant nothing to Daivem. His face was unfamiliar.

Darwa turned her head sharply. "Have you heard nothing? The He-Kisshi. The Undying come to end us all. Be fast with gathering your thoughts and your weapons. We live or die by them now."

The man nodded and pulled a harpoon from under his cloak. The tip was all she'd seen previously. The rest had been hidden beneath his furs.

The He-Kisshi came. They would kill anyone who stayed. She thought very seriously about stepping into the Shimmer until it was all taken care of.

They waited perhaps fifteen minutes and then Darwa called out that the Undying were approaching.

The creatures came swiftly, looking like vast birds, wings outstretched and holding on the wind.

The creatures, ten by Daivem's count, dropped like a murder of crows and landed in a circle around the area, none of them close by. They did not need to be any closer from all that she had heard.

Darwa and the woman who'd nearly tackled her man moved together and Roskell Turn joined them. Three people who studied the Galean books. She had no idea what they could do against the He-Kisshi.

One of the hooded forms took three steps closer. "Galeans. By tradition you are respected by the gods. They have long honored Galea and her followers, seldom choosing from yours as sacrifices. Why would you place yourselves with Brogan McTyre?"

"You are ending the world." Roskell Turn spoke softly. "What choice if we would live?"

"If you leave here now, you will be spared what is about to happen."

Three of the small gathering of humans nocked arrows and drew back their bows. They did not wait for a signal, but loosed their weapons in fast succession. The first arrow was deflected with a gust of wind, but two others found their targets. One left an Undying hissing in fury. The other was a different tale.

The He-Kisshi growled low in its chest and reached for the shaft that pierced it. Before its claw wrapped around the protruding arrow, it stopped and staggered backward. The growl became a shriek and the thing fell back, stumbling until it collapsed on the ground.

All of the He-Kisshi turned to stare as one of their own fell and then thrashed, the motions not coordinated in any way. The thing screamed and twisted, its feet clutching at the air, his hands clawing at the frozen soil.

"Ellish-Loa. What befalls you?" One of the others moved forward and then stopped as an archer let loose another bolt. The creature moved with unsettling speed and dodged the missile. It gestured with a hand and the archer was knocked back by a wind strong enough to throw the man nearly twenty feet. He hit the ground hard and rolled several times before coming to a halt.

There was no horn sounded, but there may as well have been. The attack came fast after that.

The loudmouth called Bump drew two long blades and ducked backward, fading into the night. The darkness was nearly complete and he vanished from her view. Whether or not the Undying could see better was not something Daivem knew.

The archers took aim again and started their attacks. There were more than she'd expected. Seven arrows sought flesh and found it. As had happened before, one of the He-Kisshi fell screaming to the ground and did not rise. She had no idea which of the archers was using poison, but could think of no other reason for the creature to fall so suddenly.

One of the things turned and opened its taloned hands. A moment later fire arched through the air and caught Roskell Turn even as he was gesturing at the very same beast. Whatever he had planned, it was too late. The He-Kisshi was faster. Roskell let out a scream as the fire ate the clothing on his chest and arm and boiled the flesh on his face. He tried to cry out once more, but inhaled only fire.

The Galean could not escape the flames. In moments he was dead, his body lighting the area.

By that time Brogan McTyre had attacked the closest of the creatures, and they were engaged in a hard battle. It might be that the He-Kisshi could control the elements but it also seemed likely they had to concentrate to do it. From a distance they were at an advantage but the Godslayer was using an axe large enough to cut a man in half and he was apparently skilled at it. The blades hacked into furred flesh and the creature retreated, doing its best to block a flurry of slashes.

Not far away the first of the things that had been poisoned twitched violently and started to rise, but did not get far. The man with the harpoon drove the weapon through its opened mouth and out the back of its head, pinning the creature in place. He did not stay around to see if it was properly dead, but moved on, taking a club from his belt.

The creature that fell on him drove the man to his knees and started clawing meat from his chest and shoulders. The man did not last long.

Darwa flung a black dust from her hands and the dust glowed a sickly green as it covered one of the Undying. The creature did not so much as utter a sound before it fell to the ground, stiff as a tree stump. A low keening noise came from the He-Kisshi as the unearthly glow grew brighter. In moments it stopped breathing and collapsed on itself.

The battle raged on and Jahda moved closer to her.

"You should get away from here. What you carry is precious."

She shook her head. Part of her felt the same way, but she wanted to witness the battle. Her curiosity about the Undying was a potent thing.

Roskell Turn's spirit rose from the ashes of his body and without even thinking about the situation, Daivem stepped closer and took the spirit into her grasp. "I think I'll need you."

She felt no regret, no loss over his death. They had met only briefly and she had not been nearly as interested in him as he in her.

No spirit rose from the dead or dying He-Kisshi. She expected as much. The essence of the creature stayed with the flesh, the better to ensure a return to life.

One of the hellish beasts struck the ground and a tremor shook the earth beneath them. A moment later the rocky soil split and heaved itself in two separate directions. The He-Kisshi were unaffected, but everyone else staggered and three of the men – islanders and members of the ship's crew, she was certain – were swallowed by the ground before it abruptly snapped shut.

The math was simple. There were only a dozen men left and four of the Undying were wounded or dead, but that wouldn't matter when they came back from the end of their lives. The He-Kisshi had the advantage. Even those who had fallen to poison were already recovering. They were in pain, to be sure, and in one case the thing let out a scream and died again, but they were recovering. In time the people would die to the divine. That was almost always the way.

When the horns sounded, all of the people in the fight – Undying included – looked to the west and saw the coming army.

Daivem had heard of the Marked Men, but was not certain she had ever seen one before. The whole of the group seemed made of the infamous soldiers. They bore markings on their flesh, some barely seen because of cover, but others with the stained flesh covering large portions of their faces and necks.

They came on warhorses, and they rode hard and fast, their weapons drawn.

As one the humans scattered. No one with even the sense of a fool wanted to get crushed under the war beasts. Archers spread out and lined the area, still riding their horses and men with lances charged forward, lowering the great, wooden poles and charging straight for the Undying.

Daivem saw Brogan McTyre from the corner of her eye and saw the smile that bloomed on his face. It was as savage an expression as would be expected on a feral dog.

The creatures were surely too arrogant for their own good. Most of them stood their ground as if shocked that anything would consider attacking them, even when they were engaged in a battle already. Three of the things rose into the air, clearly wise enough to know when an army was attacking. The rest stayed in place. The ones that flew into the air were struck by dozens of arrows, the shafts quivering in ruined flesh and blood sluicing away from the wounds.

Most crashed to the ground and immediately climbed back to their feet. One of them ripped the arrows from its flesh and shrieked its outrage into the air, only to get impaled by a lance and then trampled by the horse and rider sporting the weapon.

The Marked Men were fearsome in battle, every claim about their abilities being proven in Daivem's eyes. Alone they would have been formidable, but together they were coordinated and following orders. Archers did their part, lancers struck true and as the Undying fell still more soldiers came forth, cutting, stabbing, and hacking until the bodies were broken on the ground, and cut into separate parts.

Daivem could see the creatures trying to rebuild themselves, but the Marked Men prevented it. They kept the pieces separated and carved the hides from the beasts, peeling them away like the rind off rotten fruit. The thick hides were then kept separated, often by soldiers who drove iron spikes through the flesh and pinned it to the ground.

There were ten He-Kisshi. There were hundreds of soldiers. The work was grisly and grim and the Marked Men were determined. In reality it was the work of minutes but it seemed much longer. The hands of the Undying were impaled to the ground. The legs were handled the same way. The heavy, bloated torsos were opened and more spikes pinned the remains in place. The head of each of the creatures was pressed down so that the wide, deadly mouths were crammed into the soil and then they, too, were impaled with long iron spikes that were hammered into the rough earth. The wings were cut away and they were fixed in place as well.

When it was finished, the Marked Men moved away from the bodies and stood guard around them. Their horses, well-trained she had no doubt, were glad to be away from the bloodied trophies.

Daivem watched on as one of the Marked Men rode closer to Jahda and then bowed formally with a smirk on his long face.

"Jahda. It is good to see you again, my friend."

Jahda looked back and nodded. "I have to say I have never been happier to see you, King Parrish."

"My lord, Theragyn said to meet you here. He said you would have need of us, and so here we are."

"I think, perhaps, it is Brogan McTyre who has need of you. He is the Godslayer, not I."

Parrish looked toward Brogan without much searching. The lack of light was no longer a problem as the soldiers began to build bonfires from supplies they'd brought with them. The winds continued to howl, but slowed when Darwa once more worked her sorceries. She might not be able to change the weather – and for all Daivem knew she could – but she at least curbed the worst of its raging appetite for destruction.

Brogan McTyre and King Parrish eyed each other for a long moment even as the king rode his horse closer.

Brogan stared, hands still holding his bloodied axe and sword, as the man approached. When the king climbed down from his horse, Brogan finally set his weapons in their respective places on his belt.

"You killed a god?" Parrish eyed him carefully.

"I had help." Returning the measuring stare Brogan said, "I remember you. From when you tried to kill me and all the other defenders in Stennis Brae."

"Different times."

"Aye. The world wasn't ending."

"I talked with your king about that, you know. He made me see the reasons for what you did. I'd have likely done the same."

"A surprising number would have. My only regret is that I did not save them."

"No regrets about starting this?"

McTyre smiled. "It wasn't me. I didn't steal an entire family away."

Parrish smiled back, and Daivem knew they were testing each other's mettle with words. "Still, the world has been changed by you."

"If you wish to have your say with steel then have it, but I've no desire to debate with you regarding my actions. My family was my world. I would have done the same a hundred times in order to save them and the rest of the world be damned."

Parrish's smile faltered. "The gods made me sacrifice my boy in order to save my country."

"Do you love the gods so much?"

Parrish spat and sneered at the notion.

"Then you made the wrong decision."

"You've no place speaking to me like that." Parrish took a small step forward. "I'm a king."

"I think you're a fair way from your throne." McTyre gave not an inch. She would have been surprised if he had. She'd never met a Godslayer before but expected they were made of strong stuff.

Jahda stepped between them, his body a barrier between weapons. He should have been terrified, but he was calm, or at least he managed a good facade.

"That is enough. There will be no fights among us. We have common enemies that should be taken care of before we indulge in petty conflicts."

McTyre threw that grin of his and walked away, not bothering with any more discussions. Not for the first time, she suspected the man might be mad. To be fair, most people who sought to fight gods very likely were.

Stanna

The Scryers had all gone mad. Darkraven had hoped they'd get better, but they only worsened.

Stanna, now in command of the ship and the people on it, grew tired of their screams and had them cast over the side into the dark waters. No one argued. If the truth be known, they were all just as tired of the sounds of the seers' screams and scared of what they meant.

Temmi sat with her in the captain's cabin and the two of them ate a meal together. Both Tully and Temmi had joined her when she offered them space. There was no denying that there was safety in numbers. Stanna did not believe there was a person on the ship that could beat her in a fair fight. She also didn't expect there were many who would be obligated to be fair about any situation as the end of the world loomed closer.

Just an hour ago they'd seen a giant treading across the land. There had been a few cloud shapes in the past that had certainly seemed as if they might belong to giants, but this was different, they could see the thing. It was not human in shape. It was different enough that looking at it for too long made the eyes hurt and the mind want to scream.

As it walked along the ground the world around it changed. All hints of vegetation vanished and the land grew oddly level. The winds coming from the shore offered a stench of ashes and rot. The air was ripe with decay and worse.

The land was changed by the passing of the thing and Stanna felt a knot of fear in her guts the like of which she had never experienced before. Was it a god? She did not know and did not want to consider the possibility too carefully.

"Shame about the Scryers." Temmi spoke casually and Stanna looked her way. When Temmi used that tone of voice it sometimes meant she wanted to pick at verbal wounds until they bled. Stanna was not in the mood.

"Get it out of your system." Stanna didn't quite growl, but it was close.

Temmi shrugged. "Be nice if they could have told us what that thing was or where we are going."

Stanna shrugged. "I don't know, and don't care, as long as it leaves us be. And we are going north."

Temmi looked disappointed. She was in the mood for an argument. Stanna was not. There were a hundred things she had to take care of constantly, one of the reasons she always preferred to be near the top of the command chain and not at the very pinnacle. Now there was no choice and the crew was grumbling a great deal. She'd heave a few over the sides if she had to, but for now the loss of the maddened seemed to have reminded folks that she was in charge.

"There's another one." Tully had been so silent that Stanna forgot about the woman. She was looking out the porthole and staring at the distant land, where there wasn't much to see. The clouds were too heavy and even the lightning didn't offer much illumination.

Only now that wasn't true.

Stanna grunted and stood up, moving across the cabin to the same spot as Tully. The small blonde moved aside, letting her see the world beyond their ship.

There was a figure and it was possibly even larger than the last. It moved slowly, each stride seeming to take too long, but that was only because they could only see the legs of the thing, the rest was hidden in the clouds. Could she have guessed a size? No. There was nothing to compare it with. All she could safely say was that it was too large to make any sense in the grander scheme of things.

Light ran through the thing like lightning through the clouds. Flashes of different colors rippled through heavy flesh and moved on, even as the thing continued to stride.

A small flash of color caught her attention and Stanna looked to the left, close to the edge of the ship, where something pale moved over a wave, heading straight towards them.

She did not speak to anyone, but instead grabbed the Bitch and left the cabin, heading for the upper deck.

There was a light rain falling and it was cold enough to make her regret not grabbing her cloak first. Saramond had been warm. Her homelands had been cold. There was a reason she chose to live in Saramond.

In the waters, riding along the waves, she saw a strange creature. It was white-skinned and looked like a blend of fish and woman.

"What are you supposed to be?" she called to the thing and pointed the Bitch's scabbard at it to make sure it knew she was speaking directly to it.

"Grakhul." It spoke after some consideration, but she suspected the words were truth.

"Are you drowning?"

"No. I came to warn against going north."

"What is to the north?"

"More of those things. The Hahluritiedes."

"What do they do?" Stanna looked at the thing moving across the land again and frowned.

"Remake the world. They serve the gods."

Stanna stared for a moment and then pointed to the creature in the waters. "So come aboard, Grakhul. I would hear more about these things."

She looked around for a rope with which to help the creature climb aboard but needn't have wasted her time. It went under the water and then came up like an arrow loosed from a bow. It had to scrabble for a moment but the creature made the deck of the boat and settled itself on naked feet.

The transformation was not subtle. In a few moments the thing went from fish woman to pale woman. Strapped to its back was a massive sword, on the scale of the Bitch, and the fish-beast stood shivering on the old wooden planks.

"Come with me. We'll find you a warm place and you can tell me what you know." She let the woman go first and offered directions as needed. The sword the Grakhul carried was not one she wanted at her back until she knew the woman better.

It didn't take long to reach her quarters and both Tully and Temmi stared long and hard at the pale, naked woman. The difference was that Tully looked at the woman as if she might be daft, and Temmi let out a squeal of happiness and ran toward her without hesitation.

The pale woman looked at the approaching girl as if she'd lost her mind. Then she smiled and opened her arms.

Temmi ran into them and hugged her, not the least bit worried about the fact that her co-hugger was naked.

"I had thought you long lost to us." The Grakhul whispered the words and held Temmi.

Temmi held her back and talked into the woman's pale hair. "I'd heard you were all dead."

"Almost all."

Stanna stared hard at the pale woman. She was a fish. Then she wasn't. She had a sword but no clothes. Oh, yes, this one would be interesting.

There wasn't a great deal to eat left on the ship – the stores were now guarded at all times to avoid theft and the men who did the guarding were among her most trusted lieutenants – still, she sent Tully to fetch a plate of fruit and cheese from the stores and offered them to the woman after she'd settled in near the brazier and they'd found her a blanket to wrap herself in. The sword stayed where it was.

Temmi called the woman "Myridia." The name meant nothing to Stanna.

Within an hour they'd caught up on all that was significant and Stanna was asking questions about the nature of the giants they'd seen. "They are rebuilding the world, but first they will erase it."

Stanna heard about the struggles of her people and how they had finally been offered up as food for the giants.

"The gods have sent their faithful servants to their deaths?"

Myridia nodded. "We have failed in our purpose."

She looked down at the ground. "First we were to prepare the sacrifices. Then we were supposed to prepare the Sessanoh for the new sacrifices. Then the gods decided we were to be the mates of others like us, but very different in mindset. We have always been the leaders of our people and they wanted us to submit to men we have never seen and be their mates without question. When I said no, they sent us to fight Brogan McTyre, and then, instead, they sent us to wake the Hahluritiedes. I only realized that it was a sacrifice of us all when I saw them waking and knew they would be hungry. If I had stayed I would have died along with my sisters."

She knew that look well enough. Had seen it on the faces of slavers a few times. There was a question in the woman's mind about whether or not she had made the right choice.

"So what do you think to do now?"

"I hadn't thought beyond getting away. I saw your ship and wanted to warn you off from what waits north of here."

Stanna nodded and looked toward the flames in the brazier. "We will be going north. Brogan McTyre wants to fight the gods. The Undying have attacked my friends many times. I don't think we can run from them forever and sooner or later they will attack and win unless we have vanquished them." Myridia looked ready to interject but Stanna held up a hand. "I know. They are Undying. The gods bring them back again and again. If the gods are gone, the Undying go with them."

"You cannot fight the gods. You cannot touch the

gods. They are beyond contact."

Stanna smiled. "Brogan McTyre killed a god. He can touch them. We will help."

"He *killed* a god?"

"That is the story I have heard. The news was so grave that it drove the Scryers mad."

"Do you have a Scryer on this ship?"

"Not any longer."

"That is for the best. The He-Kisshi can use Scryers to find their targets." Stanna smiled at that.

"In any event, we go north. I cannot send the ship in the other direction and as you can see the land is not safe. The Halle–"

"Hahluritiedes."

"Yes, those. They are changing the world and we cannot risk going ashore where they are."

Myridia nodded.

"So we go north. We will fight with this madman and we will hope to win."

"You cannot fight the gods." Myridia sounded adamant.

It was Temmi who spoke up. "Truly? The fuckers killed my family. One, just one of the He-Kisshi killed my mother, my father and my brother because they stood between it and the woman who got your food. Tully ran. Others ran, Tully is still alive, and I am still alive because Stanna stood up for us and because we fought for ourselves." Temmi did not yell, but she stared hard at the other woman, her eyes wet with unshed tears. "You broke away. You ran away. You defied them. What else will you do before you fight them?"

"I–"

Temmi brushed away whatever she was going to say. "My family served faithfully for generations. You used to sing to me when we visited. You used to play with me when we were both younger. I did nothing wrong, but my family died. You did nothing wrong and yours were sacrificed to feed these Hahluritiedes." She jabbed a finger that tapped Myridia's chest through her blanket. "You want to swim away, go and do it. I'm done with that. I've watched everything I ever knew in this world get ruined by the gods. I die fighting them, then at least I die for a cause. I won't run to another land and have them change that, too."

Myridia grew silent and sullen. None of them spoke for a while until finally the pale woman said, "I will go with you."

Temmi nodded and leaned in closer to the small fire.

The ship continued to rock slowly in the heavy waves. The winds continued to howl. In the distance giants moved and reshaped the world away from what Stanna had known her entire life.

Without another word she rose and grabbed her oil, her whetstone, and a rag. The Bitch needed her edge sharpened. The fighting would begin again soon enough.

CHAPTER TWENTY-ONE
THE PALACE OF THE GODS

Harper

Harper knew the way. He had traveled the path to the Grakhul no less than fifty times in his life and even without the stars he could see the Gateway and knew what lay there. Or at least he thought he did.

They climbed once more into the boat and rode into the waters. The vessel was decent in size but certainly not large enough to hold Parrish and his army. The man seemed unworried. So did the massive slaver who had placed a bounty on their heads.

Beron looked at Harper and at Brogan both, but said nothing. He didn't need to. His expression made clear what he thought of the two of them. Given a chance he would kill them but for now they worked together. That was the way of things for the moment. It would change in time, especially if the slaver had anything to say about it.

Harper did not care. He would keep an eye on the man and make certain that his back was never to his blades.

Beron did not smile. He said nothing and he didn't need to say anything. That he had been cheated by Brogan and company was a matter of fact in his eyes. The circumstances did not matter. He had paid a fortune for the Grakhul and the He-Kisshi had demanded that the pale people be freed.

He was different now. When they'd met in Saramond the slaver had been beyond confident. He purchased the slaves offered and never hesitated for a moment. He had given over a fortune and done so without concern. He had been the law on his land and he knew it.

Now he was in a different situation. He was not the one in charge but he still stood with confidence. He was not a soldier. He was a commander, just not the ultimate voice in the chain of command.

What the man likely did not know or did not care about was that he and his had tortured several of Harper's friends. That was a slight that had not been forgotten and would not be forgiven. Harper made sure that Brogan knew what Beron had done as soon as he safely could.

Desmond looked at the slaver with rage in his eyes but did nothing. He was not a fool. He touched the scars on his face and looked at the man, but never said a word.

Bump either did not care or simply did not recognize the slaver. Likely he did not care. There was also the chance that he was simply biding his time. It was hard to say with the short man. He was known for his skills with knives, not for his predictability.

Brogan looked at the slaver and shook his head. "Whatever your plans, if they involve vengeance keep them to yourself."

Beron towered above the man, but nodded just the same. "I am not here to fight you. I am here to fight with you. That is what my god demands of me."

Brogan shook his head. "Why are you so eager to serve another god when the last lot have made such a mess?"

Beron laughed deep in his chest. "Loyalty has its rewards."

Faceless chose that moment to come closer and look down at the both of them. He said nothing but he caught Beron's attention.

Beron stared the creature over, memorizing him, perhaps, or trying to understand the mystery of the thing that stood before him, returning his scrutiny. Brogan looked from one to the other and said nothing.

His expression did not change by much, but it did change. He made a decision without saying a word.

Whatever his choice, it was one that Harper would follow. Brogan had begun this insanity. He would see it through to the end and Harper intended to be there with him the entire time.

"Madness," he whispered. And he meant it. They fought gods. Even if they succeeded, most of them would likely die before the battle was done.

Darwa called for everyone to go and looked toward Parrish. "We can take perhaps five..."

"No need. We will meet you when the time is right." Parrish smiled at the woman. "We will be prepared."

Darwa nodded and called again for everyone who

was going on her boat to join her. Brogan nodded his head and moved toward her. Harper moved too, but was careful to keep his eyes on the slaver. They were not colleagues. They were not friends. He did not trust Beron not to hold a grudge. Few men seemed capable of following their gods blindly and even the most devout were only human.

Beron did not attack. He did not say a word, but merely watched as Brogan and his peers left the shore behind.

It was only after they had cast off and moved to the north that Harper realized Bump was not on the boat.

He said nothing about that fact.

Brogan

"That man does not like you." Faceless was direct.

"I'd be surprised if he did. I sold him a lie and he paid for it dearly." Brogan thought about that long and hard. The notion refused to leave him be. He had done many bad things in his life, but selling the Grakhul was not one he regretted. The slavers deserved any pain they endured, based on what they did for a living. He'd seen first hand how they treated their property and he'd known going in that there was a chance the slavers would not be happy with what they bought.

"Why would you sell him a lie?"

He doubted the creature fully understood the concept of lies.

"Because I was angry. The gods killed my family and I wanted them to suffer. I killed all the males of the Grakhul and then I sold the women and the children to Beron. I told him they came from far away, and that I'd purchased them as slaves. He used to sell slaves before the world started ending. I made a great deal of money. The gods wanted their people back and took them from him."

"Did you know they would do that?" Faceless tilted his head and studied Brogan's face carefully.

Brogan shrugged. "I did not. But even if I had, I wouldn't have cared. I wanted those people to suffer. If I had been wiser maybe I would have killed them all, but I wanted them to know my pain, to suffer as I did with the losses I felt. And I wanted to make sure they could no longer make sacrifices to the gods."

Faceless nodded very slowly. In the darkness, his face almost looked normal.

"I sense a change coming over me, Brogan. I will not be the same soon."

"Aye? And what will you be, Faceless?"

The creature looked around for a moment and then looked back at him. "I think I will be a weapon for you to use against the gods. Like your axe, or your sword, but designed to cut the flesh of gods."

Brogan frowned at that notion. "I can't see me swinging you over my head, if I'm honest. You're a bit too large." He meant the words as a joke, but Faceless seemed to take him seriously.

"As I said, I will change."

Brogan felt a nervous shiver in his stomach. "Do you know how, or when?"

"I cannot say. I will remain with you, Brogan McTyre, but I will not be the same."

He had grown rather fond of the creature. It was supposedly demonic, but had never been anything other than kind to him. Still, he would keep his eyes open and see what happened. If he could find a weapon that would wound the gods, all the better.

"Where do we go, Brogan McTyre?" The woman, Darwa, spoke harshly. He had never heard her use soft tones.

"The Gateway of the Gods, according to Harper. It's supposed to actually be the way to visit the lands where they live."

"It is indeed, according to Galea."

"I intend to kill the gods."

Darwa nodded. She was near the front of the boat and he walked closer to her. "Yes, you said that before. I have seen no sign that you've changed your mind."

"You said I needed to find the weapons I needed. Have I found them?"

"You have. You can now touch the gods, as we have already seen. There is a weapon coming to you that will aid in this quest. If the signs I've seen are correct, that weapon is a gift from the demons who mean to overthrow the gods."

"That is not a comforting notion."

"Nor is it meant to be. They'll take the place of the gods. It is what demons do."

Brogan stared out at the dark seas, watching as the occasional flash of distant lightning made the waves visible before vanishing.

"I don't want more gods. I don't want more of the same."

"You can touch the gods. You can touch the

demons, too, but I don't think you are strong enough to kill them all."

He said nothing.

"I don't think you are strong enough at all, Brogan. They have something that you do not, they have sacrifices."

"I'll not kill anyone to make me stronger." He pulled at his beard as he thought. "Can demons be sacrifices? Can gods?"

"I've no idea. Possibly, but who can say with such things? I have never seen anything in the writings of Galea about either. And believe me, I am one of the best read among the Galeans."

Brogan shook his head. Roskell Turn was dead. That was something he was still trying to absorb. The man had not been around him long, but he had helped him on his path to revenge.

Of course, a great number of people were dead. More than he could likely count in a day. More than he ever wanted to count.

Guilt tried to rise inside of him and Brogan shoved it angrily away. He did not start this war. He would end it. That was all.

"What waits on the other side of the Gateway, Darwa?"

"It is said that the gods offered many answers to Galea because they loved her. They did not love her that much. That is a secret they did not share."

"Whatever happened to your Galea?"

"She wrote her stories down and she died."

"The gods didn't love her enough to keep her alive?" The words were meant as a barb. He couldn't quite resist. There was a bitterness in him that anyone was so important to the gods when his family was seen as little more than a meal.

Darwa chuckled and shook her head. "They loved her too much to keep her around for eternity. The Undying, they are designed to live for eternity and not care. Humans are not made that way. There have been tales of immortals before and the one thing they all have in common is that the endless seasons eventually drove them mad."

"And yet the gods are happy with their immortality and fight to keep it."

"That is their nature."

Brogan spat into the waters.

"We are hours from where you want to be, Brogan McTyre. This would be your chance to rest before we reach the Gateway."

"I cannot sleep. I am not tired."

And that was the truth of it. He had closed his eyes several times since returning from the tomb of Walthanadurn, but he had not slept deeply even once and he was not tired.

"'Those who are touched by the gods are never quite the same,' according to Galea."

"And she was touched by the gods?"

"Of course."

Brogan nodded his head.

"So are you, Brogan."

"What's that then?"

"You are touched by a god. Walthanadurn chose you for his revenge."

"A dead god chose me?"

"As you were already told, gods never truly die."

"Then where are the remains of Walthanadurn? Still stuck in those old bones of his?"

"He is with you. He chose to help you and that required all that was left of him."

She said more, but he did not hear her words. All that was left of the god resided within his body? The thought sickened him. He was grateful for the chance to fight his enemies on a level field, but that he was tainted by a god was disturbing. He wanted to fight the gods and now, in order to do so, he was infected by the very beings he meant to slay.

"Do you hear me, man?"

Brogan shook his head. "Say it again if you will."

"I said he is dead. He is not listening to your thoughts. He cannot celebrate your victories and call them his own. Gods cannot die, but they do, just the same. All that is left is the remains. Like the bones you saw and watched collapse, all that remains of Walthanadurn is what held him together. What he gave you is a gift, Brogan. Not a curse."

"How do you know what I think?" The Galeans unsettled him at the best of times.

"There's no sorcery here. I see the look on your face and I understand your concerns. Walthanadurn is dead. He cannot come back to life. The Hahluritiedes are what is left of other gods. Gods that died or were killed. They have more left of them. Think of it like this: the Hahluritiedes are like candles that have mostly burned away. There is still wax. There is a wick. They can be lit and they can cast light across the world. Walthanadurn was nothing but a wick, no candle. The god was murdered and he died violently. He died and remained because he was once a god. There was less of him than of the Hahluritiedes, and according to the Books of Galea, there is no mind left to the creatures. They are merely power that obeys.

"Walthanadurn gave up what little remained inside of him that you might have your revenge."

Brogan nodded his head. Still, his hands clenched and his teeth ground against each other at the thought.

"The gods will not welcome you, Brogan."

"What will I face?"

"There is no way to know. The gods have kept some secrets to themselves. If they had kept more, you would not be as prepared as you are, and yet there are more things that must happen."

"Like what?"

"You are able to touch the gods. They can touch you, as well. You must have a proper weapon to fight them."

He thought of Faceless's words but said nothing. "Like what?"

"The shape is unimportant. If you would fight the gods, you have to have a weapon that can touch them as you can, or you just use your bare hands." That thought actually made him smile. He'd delight in breaking their bodies with his hands if he thought he could manage it.

"Do the gods have weapons?"

"Oh, yes. They do. Sepsumannahun broke his great sword when he killed his father, Walthanadurn, but he did once have that sword. All of the gods will surely have weapons."

In the distance, closer than he'd expected, Brogan saw the arch that was the Gateway of the Gods. Lightning licked across the surface, danced along the edges, and ripped into the clouds above. It was still a long way off, but the brilliance of the electrical flares seemed like sunlight after so long in the semi-darkness.

"How does this end?" Brogan spoke mostly to himself.

"How else? With violence and death."

Beron

The thought of letting those bastards leave unharmed cut at Beron more than he wanted to admit. More than he wanted to ever think about. In the world left to them now, money and gold meant nothing, but that wasn't the point. They'd cheated him. They'd sold him worthless property and then run away before he could do anything about it.

He wanted the whole lot of them dead.

"No." The one word rang through his skull loudly enough to make the slaver wince.

"But–"

"They are nothing. All that you have lost will be as nothing when this is all done, but for the present time Brogan McTyre and his companions serve a purpose. He is the Godslayer as he was meant to be the Godslayer. He is to kill my enemies for me and I will be free of my prison and I will rise up and have dominion over this world. When that happens, you will serve with me as you have served faithfully until now, but you must forsake your revenge for that to happen."

Beron closed his eyes and felt the way his hands clenched with the desire to crush McTyre. Still, he nodded. "As you wish, Ariah."

In an instant Beron felt the world shift and when he opened his eyes he stood once again within the domain of Ariah. The air was thick with the scent of rotting blossoms. The trees were redolent with their bizarre, writhing fruit and the ground was nearly hidden under a carpet of fallen petals. Ariah himself stood before Beron, dressed in intricate armor. The filigree showed serpents and vines intertwined. His sword looked exactly like Beron's. "The gods must fall. His is the hand that should slay them. He is the weapon the demons have forged for that reason."

"The demons? Not just you?"

Ariah allowed a small smile that was as beautiful as the rising sun after days of darkness. "There are many demons. There are ten locked into this world. Three of us have worked together to make this happen. Together we will rise and strike, when the time is right."

Beron said nothing to that. What could he say? That his was the sword that should serve the demons? He'd been serving as best he could and so far the cost had been high. His mind tried to slip past the moments when he was bloodied, cut, torn and slain. Still, the memories lingered. He closed his eyes and felt the Bitch hacking through his neck. Stanna was a terror and he'd always known that. But she beat him in combat and he'd always known in his depths that he could take her.

His heart had lied to him.

"Then what would you have me do, Lord Ariah?"

"You are my eyes, Beron. You are my strong right arm. You serve me already. Without you, I would not know where to send the armies of Theragyn. Without you I would not know what Brogan McTyre was doing and how to aid him if aid he needs. In a moment I will call on you again. I will send you and the Marked Men to wait at the final battleground."

"The final battleground?"

"The Gateway to the Gods. You will wait there for Brogan McTyre. You and the Marked Men will ride into combat with him and make certain that he lives long enough to face the gods."

His stomach felt like it was falling over the side of a cliff.

"I am to enter the land of the gods?"

"That has always been your destiny, Beron. You are my right hand. You are the sword that smites my enemies."

Beron blinked and was once again in the darkness. Fires burned around him and the Undying lay dead, hacked into pieces and literally nailed to the ground, their various parts twitching, but unable to rejoin.

"First, however, I give you a gift." Ariah's voice was soft and sweet with promise.

Beron frowned, uncertain what the demon meant.

"Take your sword. Drive the tip into the skull of each of the Undying."

Beron walked to the first of the He-Kisshi heads and did as he was instructed. The blade drove deep and the sudden rush of energies was as sweet as honey pouring into him.

The He-Kisshi mouth opened and closed in a silent scream. The countless round eyes around that orifice shuddered and then burst like overripe fruit.

In seconds the energies were gone and the head turned gray, the flesh and the fur alike, leeched of their vitality.

Without hesitation Beron walked to the next of the severed heads and repeated the action with the same results. The charge of energies poured into him and the vile head of the thing lost its color and motion.

The power was delicious. The hammering of his heart was a song.

Soon enough the last of the creatures was treated to the same kiss from his sword. When he looked around, none of the bodies moved at all, and the flesh on all of them had gone a dusty gray.

Parrish looked at him, a puzzled expression on his face. "What have you done?"

"What my god asked of me."

Parrish stared at the ruins on the ground for a long time without speaking.

Finally the king said, "It's time for us to move on, I think."

Beron smiled. Every part of his body sang with the power he'd taken in which, he knew, was only a small fraction of what had passed through him on the way to Ariah.

"Lord Ariah will provide us the passage we need." He looked at the king and smiled. "He will guide us to where we need to go."

To make that point, Beron walked over to the horse he'd been given and climbed into the saddle. A moment later Parrish nodded and did the same. Within minutes his followers joined them. The fires were still burning and in their light Beron could see the decomposing remains of the He-Kisshi. Even immortality did not mean much when the gods readied themselves for war, it seemed.

He did not need to think about where to go. Ariah provided that information. Beron rode to the north, moving at a steady pace. When the time was right, the world around him shifted.

The land he walked on was frozen, and the ice was a thick impediment to moving quickly, but the horse continued on and the Marked Men followed after him, led by their king.

The Gateway rose above his head. He had heard of the landmark, of course, but had never seen it. Why in his life would he have ever had a reason to go that far north, or to stand on so small an island?

The strip of land was enough to hold all the horses and then some. Above him a thick bridge of stone rose in an arc, and from that stone lightning reached for the clouds and did its best to cut the skies into shreds. The lightning did not move downward, for which he was grateful.

In the center of that archway the air was warped. It did not clearly show what was on the other side, but instead rippled and flexed into distortions that hurt Beron's eyes. The wind in the area seemed to come solely from that distortion and the air coming from it smelled of summer.

In the waters around them he could see the pale faces of creatures unlike any he had ever seen before. They seemed part-human and part-fish, with dark, dead eyes that stared dispassionately. He knew them for what they were, creatures gifted him by Ariah. They were not the same as the pale females he had been given before. These were not the Iron Mothers. But they were something similar and he had no doubt that they had a connection to his god.

This, then, was his army.

The creatures stayed in the waters, but they sang to him. The words did not matter. He did not understand them, but he knew they were his to command and that they were loyal to him and to Lord Ariah.

Beron looked upon the waterbound creatures and knew that they were good. When the time came, they would serve and they would help him reshape the world in Ariah's image.

Amen.

CHAPTER TWENTY-TWO
PREPARING FOR WAR

Daivem

Daivem and Jahda spoke a great deal. She found him utterly fascinating. He had spent over half of his life on this world and had immersed himself in understanding the politics of the kingdoms, the customs of the people and the ways of the gods here. She had traveled to this place only because the dead called to her. When she said as much to the man who was as powerful as a king, he had laughed and said the same was true for him. The dead had called and he had listened, which was often the way with the Louron, wherever they traveled.

"I don't know why the dead called me. There are dead everywhere, but the ones here? Theirs are the voices I heard."

Jahda nodded and smiled. "You hear the dead because you want to hear them. That is the way with our people. You can claim that they call out to you but if you do not listen the voices fade in time. They become a whisper no stronger than the sound of the tides."

Daivem frowned. That was not the way of the world to her reckoning.

"I know that look. I have seen it many times. You are trained as an Inquisitor. That means you have not ignored the calls of the dead. You have chosen to listen. Some inquisitors choose who they will listen to. They train themselves not to hear that whisper. And that is all it is, Daivem. As long as you ignore it, it will never be more than a whisper. You said your brother is an Inquisitor, too, yes?"

She nodded her head.

"Yet he is not here. He is not running after the sounds of the dead's whispers. He is, instead, listening to the sounds of the dead only when he wants to hear them. He uses necromancy to listen. He has decided that the whispers are too confusing." He smiled. "You should learn from him. If you follow this path too long, you wander off to a dozen worlds and maybe you forget how to wander back. I followed those whispers when I started here and then I shut them away and concentrated on what I thought was more important."

"What was more important than the voices of the dead?"

"The voices of the living, of course." He shrugged. "The dead have moved on. They have lived their lives. The living are still trying to find their way. None of us ever has an easy time of that quest, child."

Daivem frowned a bit but considered his words.

"You have listened to the dead here. You have been drawn to them and I can *feel* them in your Inquisitor's staff. You hold the power of entire cities. Of armies.

Holding onto that is not dangerous yet, but it will be if you are not very careful."

She nodded her head. She had already thought the very same thing.

"The He-Kisshi say that the dead belong to the gods."

Jahda nodded. "They would. They have delivered the living for sacrifice for as long as they have existed. They take the living to be given to the gods. Those living are sacrificed and the gods do whatever it is that they do with those souls." He smiled warmly at her. She smiled back, because he had that effect on her and most people. He was kind and that kindness was infectious.

"So you disagree?"

"I think the dead belong to the dead. I think we have a long tradition of trying to help them. They get caught sometimes, as you know. The dead get lost in details. 'Why did I die? Who killed me? Have I done all that I could?' They ask these questions and then they fade away. They become nothing but echoes if they are not helped."

"I haven't helped them. I'm merely moving them."

Jahda smiled. "Help is not always easy to see. You have taken them from the places where they were lost. You are moving them, yes, but you have to ask them or yourself, where do they want to go? What do they want to do? When you find that answer, you will know how to handle the masses you have taken on as a burden."

What he told her was not something she did not know. Rather it was something she had forgotten that she knew. The dead did not choose to linger in the world. They were confused by it.

Daivem smiled and nodded.

"Thank you, Jahda. You are wise."

"Well, I suppose that is why they told me to act like a king for the Kaer-ru." He smiled.

"Did you not ask to rule?"

"No." He frowned. "I was just foolish enough to say that I would."

"What would you do with the dead, Jahda?"

The man stood up and stretched. He was astonishingly tall. His eyes looked out toward the Gateway, which was now only a short distance away. The lightning caressed the skies and almost everyone was looking toward the place where, if he had his way, Brogan would be fighting the gods.

"The dead are dead. I would ask them to serve the living and help fight the gods."

Daivem stared long and hard into Jahda's eyes, trying to solve the mystery of his words. He smiled in return.

"How?" She whispered the word.

"That I cannot tell you." He stared once again at the growing arch of the Gateway. "Perhaps," he said, "you should ask the dead."

She listened carefully to his words and then she did exactly what he suggested.

Niall Leraby

In his dreams he had a body. He walked along the shade-touched forests of Edinrun and sampled fruit from the orchards. Sometimes, when he was blissfully lucky, the girl, Tully, walked with him and offered him a smile.

In his dreams they even held hands, and he was fairly certain that if he risked a kiss, she would kiss him back.

Life had left him a coward, and he knew that. But he had done his best to be a good person.

Death was different. He had no idea where he was. There was no contact. No touch, no taste, no sight, no sound. Nothing but his memories and his imagination, which, to be kind, was not currently his friend. He knew there were others around him, all around him, but few of them could be seen or touched and the few he could hear sounded mad with grief.

Really, death was not at all what he'd expected.

When he thought for too long he forgot all about the small pleasures of life and focused far too much on the last moments of his existence.

He felt the claws of the He-Kisshi sinking into his flesh as the thing soared high into the air, dragging him along for the ride, an unwilling participant in a nightmare flight.

And then it released him to fall, fall, fall.

The anger surged through him again at that notion. When he was alive there was only the fear. Now, after the end of his world, that fear grew hot and glowed like the sun.

The woman who'd spoken to him before spoke to him again now. She said, "Do you want revenge?"

There was only one answer, really. The gods and their servants had ruined his home, killed his family, made him suffer through several personal hells, driven his people insane and tormented him before casting him down to the frozen earth.

"Yes." It was only one word, but it echoed.

No. No echoes. There were other voices added to his and they all seemed to agree. Yes. Revenge. That would taste sweet indeed, after an endless span of being lost in his own thoughts. Had anyone told him he'd died only a handful of days earlier, Niall would surely have laughed bitterly at the jest. Time had long lost all meaning.

Yes. Revenge. It was a lovely notion.

Faceless

There were many questions that Faceless could have answered, had anyone considered asking him. Where did he come from? There was a place to the south of Stennis Brae, and north of Mentath, where, if one waited patiently, a city sometimes rose from the lifeless soil. Once, not all that long ago in the grander scheme of things, a man named Garien and his troupe of performers got lost there. Some of them came away unharmed, the rest were taken by shadows.

It was from that place that Faceless came. He walked away from the area days after Garien and his people trod across the sands, and he followed a call to find and enter the crystalline prison that held the body of a dead god.

The vast cavern held no mysteries for him by the time Brogan McTyre showed up. He had been there for well over a year, moving in the silence and shadows and studying the vast corpse that filled the entire mountain.

During that time, he seldom thought. He was never created for deep considerations. He was designed to wait for Brogan and to assist him if needed. He did both in short order and joined the man in his quest.

Many creatures remain uncertain of their purpose, but Faceless knew his from the moment he was dropped into the world.

His purpose was to serve Brogan McTyre, first as a comrade and then as a weapon.

He felt the change starting before any visible signs showed. He could not have explained those sensations, not really. He lacked the skills.

Had anyone asked him why he was chosen he could have explained that he was literally created to serve as a weapon for Brogan McTyre. He had been drawn from the blood of Druwan, who walked in darkness and who cried shadows. He existed solely because Druwan wanted to help the Godslayer and thus help free herself from the prison where the gods had so long ago locked her away.

Druwan was his creator and he was faithful to her. He was also created for Brogan and thus was faithful to him.

No one asked him. Though in some cases he was simply not asked in the right way. Druwan loved riddles. No riddles were asked, nor were any solved. He simply did as he was told.

The boat of Darwa crunched along the shoreline of the Gateway and several of the people onboard staggered a bit as the vessel slowed to a stop against solid land. Faceless knew it was time. His very sentience would be an offense to the gods but his body was a different matter.

"Brogan."

The man looked his way with a small grin of curiosity. He had learned much by observing the red-haired man. He had learned facial expressions and what they meant. He had not learned all of them, of course. That might well take lifetimes that he simply did not have.

"Yeah. Faceless? What can I do for you?"

"It is time for me to go."

Brogan frowned. "What do you mean?"

Before he could speak an answer, Faceless reached out and caught hold of Brogan's arm. His fingers gripped the forearm of the man, as he had seen the man do when meeting with a friend. The fingers gripped lightly.

"I will miss you, I think."

Brogan frowned again, confused.

And Faceless changed.

He lost his consciousness.

His body transformed.

Brogan cried out in pain and surprise.

And Faceless died.

Just as he was meant to.

Brogan

Brogan felt the pain lash through him like a bullwhip cutting through his body from the inside. It started at his hand and expanded from there, growing through his flesh in seconds and fading almost as quickly.

He'd been looking right into Faceless's eyes, noting that there was more in those hollowed spots than mere darkness. The creature had grasped his forearm and given a proper shake and then changed.

Had the creature once looked like wood? Yes. But he had changed and grown smoother as time went on, losing his rough, nearly barklike texture.

Several of the others, Anna and Harper among them, moved toward him with worried expressions, but he waved them back. Whatever was happening, he didn't want to risk anyone else getting hurt if this was truly an attack. And he did not think it was.

What had been the flesh of the oddest companion he had known moved, flowed, rippled across the distance between them. The change made him think of molten wax as it just starts to grow firm again. There was heat and there was movement and then the figure he'd grown accustomed to moved up his arm in a wave of tingles that changed from mildly ticklish to feeling like he was being stung a thousand times wherever the mass touched him.

It only lasted long enough to elicit a gasp. Then Brogan saw the odd fluid wash up his arm and across his chest. Not all of it, only a thin layer. The rest stayed in his grip and warped and shifted, the weight changing several times as it stuck to him.

The stuff flowed under his shirt and across bare flesh. It seared its way across his entire chest and torso, over his back. It flowed up to his neck and stopped short of his jaw.

His knees grew weak, but Brogan held himself up.

The weight of the stuff was obvious, but spread out as it was, he did not feel crushed by it. Instead he stood and compensated.

When the sensations stopped, Brogan let out a second gasp and did his best to recover.

And then he considered what had just been done to him.

His flesh was still there, of course. It was merely hidden beneath a sheath of armor that fit across his chest and stomach like a second skin. One arm was covered in the stuff as well. It snuggled close to him and didn't seem to have the sort of joints he would have expected from armor. It fit like a glove. And where there should have been bulky spots, there was instead a series of seams that moved together over elbow, and shoulder, and wrist. The stuff was scaled like a snake's hide.

More of the same substance – what had been Faceless and now decidedly was not – was gripped in his hand. The shape was slightly off, but familiar. His hand held an axe. It was large, and it had two blades and the balance of the piece was spectacular. The haft and the blade alike were of a dully-gleaming dark metal.

He did not think as he tested the weapon. He merely let his body work through a few exercises. The balance was as perfect as he suspected. The armor did not hold him back at all.

Darwa stared at the armor. Her finger poked it several times.

He asked a question with his eyes and she scoffed. "I've no answers for you here, Brogan McTyre. This is nothing covered by Galea in her many writings."

Brogan studied the blade. It was very sharp. It looked capable of carving through a man with ease.

Perhaps then, it might even cut a god. That was, of course, the purpose of the stuff. He had no doubt at all of that.

Harper looked at the armor and frowned. "Are you hurt, Brogan?"

"No." He shook his head and frowned. "I don't think I am."

Anna studied the stuff with the same sort of curiosity Darwa showed, only she was more direct. She pulled the shirt away from his arm and moved her hands over the hard surface coating his skin. He did not feel her touch, of course. She touched the armor. Part of him, no matter how hard he tried to suppress it, wished that he could feel her hand on his arm.

She was not his. She never would be. He was not hers. He never would be. He reminded himself of those facts and looked away, toward Desmond. The man was looking back at him, a worried expression on his face.

"Did that burn, man?" Desmond's voice was thick.

"There was a sting, but it's gone now."

Harper spoke, "Along with Faceless?"

Brogan nodded, his face pulling into a frown at that thought. "I don't understand it, but I think that was what he planned all along."

Anna shook her head. "I don't claim to understand demons or gods, either. I just know they do things their own way."

"Let's get to shore. You have company waiting for you, Brogan McTyre."

As Brogan moved toward the edge of the boat and prepared to walk across onto the land, he spotted the others waiting for him. Beron the slaver, Parrish the king, and the Marked Men. They were a small army and they claimed loyalty. He would take his chances.

The first foot he settled on the land around the Gateway rested on cold, damp rock. It felt good to stand on solid ground. Nothing about the waters was comforting to him. He was raised in mountains and spent most of his life on foot or on the back of a well-trained steed.

The air here was unsettlingly warm. All the way toward the island the cold had bitten deep, moving past furs and cloaks and biting at any bared flesh. Now, however, the furs and layers seemed stifling. Was that the armor? He had no idea but doubted it. As he looked around others showed signs of adjusting to the new temperature, and the Marked Men still wore cloaks, but were not as heavily protected from the elements.

Parrish looked his way and nodded. He returned the gesture. The man might well be a king, but he was not the king of Stennis Brae and there was no allegiance owed.

Beron offered a curt nod of his own. He was not happy to be standing so close to Brogan and he certainly wasn't pleased to deal with the man who'd cheated him as an equal. Brogan understood. Were they on opposite sides of the dilemma he'd have felt the same way.

There was nothing to be done about it, and so Brogan ignored the man aside from nodding in return. He would watch him, but there were bigger problems in his world just now.

"So that's the Gateway." Harper spoke with grudging awe. The towering archway was the source of the warmth they felt. It spilled out in a constant, slow breeze, and as they stood beneath it, light began to come from the distorted air.

"What is that?" Brogan asked the question as he squinted a bit.

Anna shook her head. "Looks to be sunrise."

"Sunrise? Here?"

"No, Brogan. Sunrise in the home of the gods." She was not being bitter. She was simply surprised. "That warmth, that breeze, that light, they all come from a different place. They come from where the gods reside."

Brogan spat upon the land. "How very nice for them."

Parrish pointed. "We've company."

Brogan looked and sighed. He'd seen the ship before. "That would be Hillar Darkraven and her people. They don't agree with what I'm doing or what I've done."

Parrish chuckled. "Neither do I. And yet, here I am."

"Think you can make her see reason?"

"Unlikely, but I'm willing to try." The man's smile annoyed him. Most everything about Parrish annoyed him. Old grudges did not die easily.

Still, he nodded his thanks.

There wasn't much to be done, but wait. He needed time to prepare himself for the fight, if truth be told. It was not a regular combat that he was headed for. There were gods involved. He planned to win, but that didn't mean he expected an easy fight.

One of the Marked Men moved forward and spoke softly to Parrish. The king nodded and spoke back, frowning.

"Is there something wrong then?" The question came from Harper.

Parrish shook his head rather than responding. His face was no longer quite as amiable.

Beron scowled. He looked over at Brogan and studied the weapon in his hand, but said nothing. He then looked at Brogan's companions and frowned more heavily. Likely he was noticing the lack of Faceless. Brogan chose not to enlighten him about anything. The layer of armor that ran close to his skin was snug enough to feel like it belonged right where it was. It felt completely natural against him and that part actually bothered him as much as what the armor had been made from.

Faceless was gone and would not be coming back. That should have bothered him much more than it did. He knew that, but could not change the fact.

"So what are your plans, Brogan McTyre?"

"Right now, I'm waiting on a ship. If they want trouble, they'll have plenty."

Parrish nodded his head, but did not look pleased. That fact bothered Brogan not at all.

"After that, I think I'll have a meal and then perhaps go to war with the gods."

Parrish stared at him without a word, but that annoying smirk of his had fallen a bit and that was a lovely thing.

"We can discuss any plans after the ship is handled." Brogan had no desire to discuss anything with the man but if they were supposed to help him, he supposed it was inevitable.

They only waited a short time before the vessel turned and then dropped anchor. By the time they'd settled in on the narrow strip of land and started a few small campfires, the first boat was rowing over with several armed figures.

The waters around the boat rippled in ways that made no sense. Something was under the water and staying close, near as Brogan could tell.

The massive woman who'd fought him earlier was among the women on the boat. There were several, including a pale woman who could only be Grakhul. She stared at him with open hostility. He did not waste his time returning the glare; he had larger matters to attend to.

When they reached the land, one of the women, a muscular, short blonde, hopped out and into the shallows, pulling the boat along. Two of his own broke from the ranks and helped, though both kept wary eyes on the folks on board. It wasn't hard to drag the boat close enough to let others ashore.

"I'm Stanna." The redhead looked at him and then looked askance at Beron. "Didn't I kill you?"

Beron fairly growled, "I'm harder to kill than you think."

If she was worried about the slaver, she hid it well.

"Hillar Darkraven is dead. I've commandeered her ship and those of us I discussed matters with agreed it's better to side with you than against you. We're here to offer you aid."

"You want to help?" He spoke the words slowly and tried to savor them. The last thing Brogan had expected was assistance and yet here was a second small army willing to side with him against the gods.

Not that it would matter. They wouldn't be going with him.

The redhead laughed. "We don't want to help. There's no choice, you fool. You've killed a part of the world. If we want to live on what's left, we have to do something about it."

Brogan felt himself smile. "At least you're honest about it." He sighed and stretched. "I intend to eat first. Then I'll see about killing the gods."

The pale woman looked his way and continued her glares.

When he grew tired of them he pointed at her. "I know what I did to your people. I know what you did to mine. You want to kill me? Best do it now. I'll be busy later." He stared hard at her, eyes unflinching, his arms close to the weapons he carried.

"When this is over," she replied. "When you have finished your war on the gods, if you are alive then, we can discuss whether or not you need to keep breathing."

"What is your name?"

"Myridia."

"When this is over then, I will meet you on the field of battle. You might need to wait in line as I expect several of these people would like me dead. But just now I'm needed."

Without another word he moved toward the closest fire, ignoring the glare spilling out from the home of the gods.

Within ten minutes he was eating his final meal and preparing himself for whatever might lay ahead. He ate cheese. He ate bread. He drank water and considered wine before deciding against it. His stomach was having enough trouble with the meal already and he wouldn't invite worse disasters if he could avoid it.

Those were already planned for the day.

CHAPTER TWENTY-THREE
THROUGH THE GATEWAY

Stanna

"Well, this is madness." Temmi was scowling as she looked at the gathered soldiers eating food. Mostly she was scowling at Brogan McTyre.

"Madness? More than anything else we've seen?" Tully spoke. She was watching, too, half-expecting any of the vast number of people to charge at them and start swinging blades. It was that sort of tension.

Stanna reached into her bag and pulled out four dried figs. Hunger was starting to get to her and she wanted her head level.

"You're talking about them eating?" she asked through the mouth of fruit she was chewing into.

"Gods, you're doing it too!" Temmi actually glared at her.

"Don't be a fool. Your body needs food to stay strong. Your mind needs sleep, your body needs food. You're wise about it, you handle both before you fight."

"My body needs to piss," Temmi responded. "Always does right before I know it's coming, or during if someone surprises me."

Stanna nodded. "Yeah. I can see it. I've had more than one time I needed to empty myself during a fight. Damned uncomfortable, but not a priority."

She looked at the gathered masses. Marked Men she had seen but never fought. Beron? Well, he was dead. She'd cut his blasted head off and here he was alive again. That meant sorcery of some sort. She'd not trust him. That he'd been trying to kill her had put a strain on their relationship in any event.

"Are you listening to anything I'm saying?" Temmi's voice was an angry buzz.

"Are you going on about how insane everyone is to be eating?"

"Well, yes."

"Then I'm not listening. I would kill for some mutton. Or a good steak."

Myridia was staring out into the waters, horrified. "They were my people once."

Stanna look at the other woman. "And now they aren't." The pale woman looked her way and seemed genuinely offended. "Listen. First thing that happened when this war started was the world started ending. I feel for you. I know you are in pain, but hear this and hear it clearly. The whole land where I was raised and where I've lived my entire life is ruined. It's either under water, burned away, or destroyed by those giants that the gods sent out to clean away everything."

Stanna paused to take a sip of ale from her skin

while the woman stared at her.

"We've all lost everything. It's a war and we're stuck in it. We've chosen sides and we're readying for the final fight. We're fighting gods and whatever they might have hidden away from us. That's it. We're likely all dead by this time tomorrow, so you may as well stop looking at the worst of it and prepare to draw as much blood as you can before you die."

Tully nodded her agreement and Temmi looked like she wanted to fight about it but couldn't find a good argument. Myridia nodded.

"I mean the ones in the water. They used to be my kind. Now I don't know what they are."

Stanna shrugged. "Ugly. They're damned ugly. And I wouldn't trust them if I were you. Like as not if they are serving Marked Men or Beron, they are tainted."

"Tainted?"

"By demons."

"Demons hate the gods?"

"Of course."

"Then they are allies."

Stanna laughed and slapped at her thigh. "That's a good notion. Hadn't thought of that."

Tully dug into one of her pockets and pulled out dried beef. Stanna stared at the hard lump like it was the finest thing she'd ever seen and Tully grunted, broke it in half and threw part of it her way.

Stanna smiled and then popped the piece into her mouth. Enough spit and it would be palatable.

"So what are we going to do?" Temmi's voice was small.

"We're going to remember what the gods have

done and go do our best to kill them."

"Don't you have to have a special weapon for that?"

"Don't know. I guess we'll find out. So far the Bitch has cut everything I've used her on." She shrugged.

"Why aren't you afraid, Stanna?"

"Nothing I can do about being scared, except forget the fear is there. I have other matters to attend to and fear gets nothing done."

Beron came toward them.

Without missing a beat, Stanna lifted the Bitch from the ground near her and drew her from her sheath. "Beron."

"Stanna."

"You wanted to discuss matters?"

"I have been given protection by my new lord, Ariah. He has a fondness for good warriors and I could arrange a similar pact for you if you are interested." He eyed the Bitch warily, which was wise.

Stanna chewed on her dried beef for a moment while she considered his words.

"What's the price then?"

"Loyalty."

"That's hardly a price at all."

"Well, there might be sacrifices."

"Isn't that what started this whole mess?"

Beron frowned at her, lost.

"Sacrifices, Beron. Giving gods a meal instead of making them work for it."

Temmi laughed. Tully snorted. Myridia was not amused.

"I've no need to call another being master. Never have, never will."

Beron shook his head and moved away, seemingly disgusted.

"I'd watch that one," Tully said.

Stanna shrugged. "He was never very trustworthy. He's also nowhere near as good as he thinks he is at fighting."

A few of the other ex-slavers were close enough to hear that. Rhinen laughed out loud and looked her way.

Stanna smiled back and kept chewing on her bit of dried beef. It was almost time to die and she wanted to remember her last meal fondly.

Parrish

Parrish looked at his soldiers and wondered how many of them would be alive soon. They had been made better by Theragyn, but the gods had their own ways and they were going to another world. Each and every one of the Marked Men had been to another world. He knew that, he understood it even if the notion sometimes made him want to panic. They had been remade by Theragyn and that only happened in the demon's domain. His new god had explained that to him, but this was different. They were going to a place where Theragyn could not go. He was a powerful being but he was limited by the very beings they were attempting to fight.

Demiro, one of his best, moved closer. "We are ready, sir. The soldiers have been fed, the horses are rubbed down and calmed." The horses, well-trained as they were, had followed orders through the entire course of events. They did not, however, seem to like walking between worlds. Or demons, for that matter. It was an effort to get them to remain calm. The men had their orders and did their work. Their horses were important, and frankly they were harder to train properly than men were.

"We follow the orders of Brogan McTyre. When he leaves we all leave. Tell everyone to be ready."

Demiro nodded and moved back to speak to the rest of the leaders. There would be no time for playing foolish games. They were going to war, a proper war, for the first time in years.

Not all the training in the world was going to guarantee success.

Parrish closed his eyes and concentrated on Theragyn. The voice was still there, the presence was still there, but it was soft and distant. Still, he was eased by the thought that his new god was ready.

"I go soon to serve you, my lord."

"Your life will be a song of glory, Parrish. You will rule over all the lands when we are finished." The voice soothed him.

The tension left his body and his mind cleared. Theragyn always had that effect on him.

"They'll fall, my lord. I'll see to it."

There was no response, but a wave of euphoria moved through him.

It was time. He saw Brogan McTyre stand up and head for the Gateway. The rest of his people rose as well.

One of them, a woman with mouse brown hair and a thin build, reached out her hand and spoke words at the base of the vast stone archway, and the lightning that had been caressing the sky since they reached the area – though, he noted, not causing thunder – ceased.

It was time.

He had never been so scared in his entire life. He had, after all, abandoned the very gods they were likely going to meet.

Harper

Harper looked around at the people moving in close to the portal leading to the home of the gods, and sighed. There were too many of them and if even one decided to end this madness before it could be finished, he didn't know for certain that he could stop them.

Harper was not as trusting as some. It might well be that every person in the entire area was telling the truth, that each and every one of them was here solely to help Brogan achieve his quest. However, it might also be, just as easily, that any of them planned betrayal. To that end he'd already asked the archers to remain ready.

Brogan was not trusting. He was just cocky. He'd fought a god and won, which would likely add to anyone's confidence.

For that reason, Harper was going to fight for the both of them.

He'd had a long while to consider whether or not his prayers might have caused any sort of troubles for Brogan and his family. The question of whether or not his jealous desire to have a life more like Brogan's could have made the gods choose the man's entire family to sacrifice had twisted his guts for most of the time he'd spent walking this planet after the gods decided to end it. If he let it, the thought would eat at his brain as surely as the giants walking the planet ate the land. In the end he would likely never truly know. He also decided that the answer was no. The gods had never answered a prayer of his in the past. They'd just taken as they saw fit.

Still, he'd make certain Brogan got his chance to end the madness once and for all.

The white-haired Grakhul woman continued to glare at Brogan's back. So did Beron, when the slaver wasn't looking directly at Harper and promising bloody retribution with his eyes. None of it mattered.

Even as he contemplated the many folks who wanted his best friend dead, the woman, Darwa, touched the edge of the stone arch and started speaking in a language he had never learned. Galeans did not, as a rule, like to share their secrets. Anna Harkness touched the stone of the archway as well, and began keeping pace, saying the same words, though it took her a moment to fully keep up with the woman who'd taught her much of what she knew.

When the two voices effectively became one, the true show began.

At first they managed to quell the lightning. Then the view from within the opening in the arch changed. The distortion lessened and then vanished, showing a clear pathway through a field of grass that was tamed and taught to grow at the same speed. He'd never seen the like in his life.

The world beyond the Gateway looked too perfect. The colors were too bright and the castles in the distance all seemed as if they'd never had so much as a bird shit on their stones. Perhaps none dared. Perhaps there were no birds because the gods did not like them. He could not say and did not want the knowledge of how the gods thought.

That way, he was certain, madness waited.

There was a sudden shift in the air, and the winds that had been chilling him suddenly grew warmer. The breeze was strong enough to push his cloak back and ruffle his hair.

Ahead of him, Brogan let out a deep sigh and nodded his head.

Not but one second of delay and then Brogan stepped across the threshold of the archway and vanished from sight.

CHAPTER TWENTY-FOUR
WAR TORN

Brogan

The land beyond looked too perfect. For that reason, Brogan did not trust the image he was seeing. It was a promise of paradise, perfect weather, tended lawns and vast palaces fit for, well, for gods.

There were five of the vast structures, though one of them now lay in ruins. He could see it in the far distance and part of him understood that what he saw was once the home of the god of the seas, the very thing he had destroyed along with Walthanadurn. He knew that the castle had fallen at the exact same time as the god had died. There was no question of that in his mind. He knew, because somewhere inside of him, what remained of a god knew.

Crossing through the barrier was easy. He only had to walk forward. As he stepped through the weather changed. There was heat now, and there was a hard, bitter wind.

What he expected to see was the truth laid out

before him. What he saw was exactly that, and the truth was not pretty.

There were still castles in the distance, but they were not as perfect as one might expect. They were ancient, and though the mortar and brick held, all of it looked decayed and well into the days of ruin after the best of everything had passed.

The skies were not as blue as a robin's egg. No, they were almost as dark as the cloudy caul that served as skies back in his homeland. The breeze that struck him smelled of rot and ruin. The perfect lawns he'd seen were diseased and what grew there was certainly toxic in nature.

As with all things, he was certain, the gods lied. They showed a promise of paradise for any who might be brave enough to venture into their world, but the reality was like a badly scarred face behind a mask of beauty.

Perhaps the gods were once perfection and glory, but all that remained was decay and the vestigial memories of what they had been.

And between him and those rotted castles? Well, there he saw the armies of the gods.

They waited in ranks that were too vast to comprehend. It was likely that Brogan could never count as high as the servants of the gods numbered if he spent his entire lifetime doing nothing else.

They were brutes. Of course they were. What they wore offered no glory to their masters, only a promise of death and destruction. Great breastplates and chain beneath and leather and enough armor to slow any mortal man down. They wore it with ease and they moved with purpose, their equally oversized warhorses prancing impatiently – ready, it seemed, to do battle.

The faces of the creatures were hidden away in helmets that showed only a space for their eyes to see. Each soldier bore a sword and a shield, and weapons designed solely for the purpose of killing. Their heavy arms were thick with fur, and where there was bare flesh it was coated with warts and scales. They were not human, but they mimed the part well enough.

Brogan looked upon them and felt himself smile. This he could understand. He may not live through it, but he could fully comprehend the reason for their existence. They were here to stop him. He was here to get past them and reach the gods themselves. He would not be stopped by them. He would not be stopped.

Brogan roared and charged forward, running toward the first of his enemies. As he stepped deeper into the realm of gods he felt the energies within him catch fire. His arms were strong and the axe he carried seemed to weigh nothing. The armor on his body, pressed close to his skin, changed as he moved, grew thicker, developed coarse markings, yet still seemed weightless.

The soldiers who faced him were in perfect marching order. Each and every one standing at attention, riding a steed that carried them with ease.

The first of his enemies had no time to flinch before his axe was driving the creature's helmet down into his neck and shoulder, carving a trench into the great metal facade. He fell from his horse and the animal toppled, crashing to the side.

An empty suit of armor astride a hollow horse. Brogan scowled, confused by what had just happened.

Behind him the first of the Marked Men came through, riding horses and prepared for war. He looked back toward them for a moment and frowned. This was not what he expected. This was not the war he'd planned for.

The armored soldiers on their armored horses moved. A moment before, the armor had been empty and the horses had been hollow, but now, without any apparent change, they came to life.

As Brogan stared, the ranks of soldiers in the service of the gods raised their weapons, prepared their shields and started toward the Marked Men.

The Marked Men, in return, raised lances and shields as their mounts began the charge.

With Brogan in the area between both forces.

He backed up, shaking his head. Whatever had been going through his mind, the reality of the situation got the better of him and he retreated, moving between the ranks of Marked Men and letting them have their place in the combat.

When he could, Harper came closer. "Is this the part where you planned to fight the gods all alone?"

"I didn't expect an army, I also didn't expect that army to play games."

"What do you mean?"

"I attacked first. I hit a hollow suit of armor on a false horse."

"They're gods, Brogan. They're hardly going to play by your rules!" Harper had to yell to be heard as the Marked Men and the armies of the gods clashed. It was not a balanced fight at all. There were far more of the gods' soldiers than of King Parrish's trusted warriors.

Still, lances versus swords; the first wave of attacks went to the Marked Men, who unseated a great many of their enemies as they charged forward. Soldiers from both sides were unhorsed and fell to the ground. As they tried to rise, more of the riders came forward and knocked them aside or trampled them. Brogan watched on, considering if there was a way he could enter the fray.

Harper shook his head. "Do you think it would be wise to fight these men when you already have gods to battle? Don't be a fool."

He shot a withering glance toward his best friend and Harper shrugged it aside with ease. "One of these fools cuts off your head, you'll do no one any good."

Harper was moving to the side, seeking a way past the masses. He wasn't having much luck. There were hundreds and hundreds of fighters near them and the clash was growing as more of the Marked Men came through.

"I'd planned on doing this alone."

"I have no doubt, but it can't be handled that way, Brogan. There are too many here that want to see this end as much as you do."

"So how am I supposed to reach the gods through this madness?" He was yelling himself now as the battle continued.

Parrish himself came toward him, a small faction of Marked Men spearheading a wedge of horses and soldiers pushing through the melee, intent on reaching him.

Harper pointed at the group. "I expect he plans to help."

Though it had seemed for a moment that the soldiers of Mentath would never stop entering the fray, they did, in fact, run out of fresh reinforcements, and faster than Brogan might have liked.

The battle grew louder and moved closer, as the hordes of the gods smashed through the ranks of the Marked Men. Though he had not truly engaged any of them yet, they seemed intent on reaching Brogan.

Parrish shook his head. "I've no idea where you plan on going to reach the gods, but I can try to get you closer to those distant castles."

"I expect it won't matter." Brogan shook his head and spat. "I've no idea how many soldiers they have."

Parrish shook his head and offered a hand. "Climb aboard. We'll do what we can."

There seemed little choice. The fight was coming their way and without a horse and a barrier of some sort, Brogan would be struck down. His initial arrogance had been just that, arrogance. Sooner or later someone would strike him down if they could find him. It was just that simple.

Harper moved, sliding past him and striking at one of the armored creatures coming for Brogan. His swords were fast and brutal and he pushed the thing down from its mount, his weapons striking a dozen times before the thing could try to climb to its feet.

There was no choice. Not really. Brogan took the

offered hand and climbed aboard the warhorse behind King Parrish.

Within moments Harper was lost in the background as the Marked Men forced their way into the battle and bashed at the servants of the gods. They met resistance quickly and soon the wedge formation began to soften and fall apart as the soldiers were entangled in combat.

Brogan growled. "This is madness!"

"You wanted to fight the gods, McTyre! Did you think it would be easy?" Parrish swung his sword and hacked down on the thick arm of one of his enemies. The sword did its work and the thing let out a bestial shriek as flesh and bone alike were carved in two.

Brogan's axe cleaved through its head while it was defenseless. The impact was brutal, but nothing he was not prepared for.

In the distance behind them the Gateway flared again and again as more people came through. The slavers from the ship were arriving, and they attacked with abandon, hacking and cutting at the things that fought the Marked Men. Perhaps the attack was unexpected, it was hard to say with any certainty. All Brogan knew was that the armored things were pinned for a moment between two groups, a pincer maneuver that had them retreating in short order.

Brogan smiled. Adrenaline soared into his body and it was more than just that. He'd been caught many times in the song of combat. The body's desire to wreak violence upon an enemy. He'd fought against Parrish and his people in the war against Mentath. He'd sold his sword a hundred times, and it was almost always a guarantee of violence when he rode in defense of merchant wagons.

This was different. He was in the home of the gods and whatever had been done to him, being there seemed to make him stronger. A sword clashed with the armor he wore and skittered off harmlessly.

"Come to me, you bastards!" He roared the challenge as Parrish fought ahead of him and his own weapons fell to the left and right. The warhorse was a brute and its hooves came down again and again on the mounts of the enemies. Blades came for him and he deflected them with ease. His reflexes seemed far greater than they should have been and he smiled as they charged across the battlefield, cutting a path through the enemy that none of the others seemed capable of keeping up with. The Marked Men fought well, but not well enough. It wasn't long before Parrish and Brogan were alone in a tide of the enemies.

Parrish breathed harshly, his lungs working like bellows. Brogan was at ease in comparison, his movements unaffected by exertion, his strikes as smooth as if he were merely chopping at weeds in the yard of his old home.

The home he'd shared with Nora and the children long ago, it seemed. The home that was gone, destroyed by his own actions, surely. The mountains moved and a dead god rose and whatever was left of his home in Stennis Brae was likely rubble, not that it mattered.

That home had been important once. His family had been important. His head throbbed with the loss of both, but he shook it off as best he could, and blocked a blow meant to take his head from his shoulders.

The horse under him collapsed.

He had no idea what had been done, but the animal stumbled and fell without a sound and in seconds the ravagers they fought were on the poor creature and it was not getting back up.

Brogan fell, and pushed himself away from the saddle and Parrish. The horde came in closer and attacked, but the armor he wore protected him from most of the blows and his sword did the rest. He should have been aching, exhausted and panting heavily, but none of that was true. None of that mattered. The energy kept pumping into him as he fought against the armored nightmares, his axe denting or cutting armor with each blow.

He was not falling, but there were so many of them. Sooner or later they would take him down.

Parrish rose up and let out a hoarse roar, his sword hacking brutally at one of the enemies, his eyes rolling with panic as he realized the exact same thing. The blows were easily deflected. The horseman drove forward on his mount and slammed into Parrish, forcing him down and under the hooves of the beast. The king of Mentath did not die gently, but was instead mangled as the steed pounded into him over and over, breaking bones, tearing skin and pulping muscles.

Parrish fell back and did not rise again.

Brogan moved on, nearly lost in a sea of horses and riders.

His heart hammered now, not because of exertion, but because of fear. The thought that he might fail had only been an abstract concept until now. Now, he had to find a way past the hordes serving the gods or he would never have a chance to exact his revenge. He needed that revenge, too. He needed to end the gods. It was all that mattered any more. That thought scared him almost as much as the notion of not having his satisfaction.

"Face me! Face me, you damned cowards!"

The gods did not answer, but more of the armored soldiers crushed toward him, a wave of men and horses determined to see the end of him.

Stanna

The war came on hard and fast and Stanna met it the same way. The Bitch cut deep again and again and she danced away from the worst of the blades. The enemy was well-armed and sported serious armor, but their protection made them slow. A blade bit into her shoulder, but not deep enough to stop her. She grunted, moved, brought the Bitch around, and drove the heavy blade into the visor of the thing facing her. The blade was true and rang against the back of the great helmet. The warrior fell back, dead. Stanna moved on, reaching out with her free hand to grab a horseman's cloak and use it as a means of hauling him from his ride. By the time he hit the ground she had already killed him.

The next in line nearly took her head, but she ducked enough to survive the attempt.

Beside her Temmi screamed and slashed and managed not to get herself killed though her blade did not manage to inflict as much harm.

Tully slipped in, cut and retreated, her eyes wide and her face a study in controlled panic. There were joints in even the finest armor and Tully found them, driving her curved daggers in hard and then backing away before most of the enemies could retaliate. Most. She was already bleeding in several places, but like Stanna, she managed to avoid fatal blows.

The slavers did what the slavers had always done. They attacked with sheer brute force and numbers. Rhinen led one faction, hammering at the enemies and managing not to get himself killed. Several of his followers were not as lucky and he wasted not so much as a breath on them. They lived or died as they had always lived or died. There was no time for anything else.

Argus proved what a man with a spear could do, bashing and stabbing and unseating his enemies in a constant dervish of activity. He was not alone. A dozen other spearmen worked with him and they worked more in unison than Rhinen and his group. That was one of the reasons Beron had always trusted and admired the man.

Beron was nowhere to be seen and that made her nervous. She didn't much like the notion of him sneaking up on her when she wasn't looking. There was nothing to be done for it at the moment.

A breeze was all the warning she had as one of the armored things raised a single-bladed axe over his head and hacked toward her skull. She brought the Bitch around and ducked in close. Her blade met his wrists, cutting deep and stopping the axe's forward motion. His own strength did the rest and the bastard screeched as his hands fell free from his wrists. While he screamed, she used the pommel of the Bitch to dent his helmet into his skull. A return stroke cut deep into his neck and she moved on, looking to her left. Argus came close and impaled a man intent on attacking her. The spear bent but did not break under the mass of the thing that fell from the horse and then crashed into the ground, spear-tip buried deep into meat and armor alike.

He was still pulling the spear free when one of the hellish brutes rode him down. The hooves of the horse slammed into Argus and, as he staggered the rider's shield edge shattered his skull.

Stanna managed to get out of the way of the same horse and rider, but it was close and she felt the bruising blow across her left shoulder blade as the shield smashed into her.

Tully vaulted onto the back of the horse and drove her dagger into the base of the rider's neck before she fell free on the other side. It looked like she just stepped up, landed her killing blow and then stepped down on the other side. Stanna knew she'd have failed if she ever tried the same maneuver.

The rider flopped from his saddle, dead, and Tully lurched to the right as another rider came, aiming to take her down.

She dodged the attack.

Temmi, who was stabbing her sword into a man's side, was not as fortunate. The horse struck her a staggering blow and she fell to the dirt with a loud smack. Rhinen was there a second later, hauling the girl out of the muck. Temmi shook her head, or the force of Rhinen's movements shook it for her, it was hard to say.

No time for distractions. Stanna turned to the side and blocked another attempt to carve her face from her head. An elbow caught the man in his thigh and then her shoulder caught his hip, sending him off the saddle as the horse went past. The beast's flank caught her and sent her stumbling, rolling and then crawling to her knees as the fighting continued.

She might well have died then, but the pale Grakhul woman, Myridia, was there, her sword a black arc as it caught a man moving on Stanna. The blade was as sharp as she'd expected, and opened the man and his breastplate from left to right. He did not fall down and die. Instead he drove the point of his own sword through the pale woman's left forearm, nearly severing the limb.

Myridia let out a gasp and fell back, holding her sword, though Stanna could not imagine how.

A moment later the rider dropped his weapon and collapsed.

Stanna looked around and saw more of the same. The attacking riders were everywhere and they were savagely efficient. It was a matter of time. Something had to change soon, or the last attempt to save the world would die as surely as the people trying to do the saving.

Daivem Murdrow

The fighting started before she moved through the vast Gateway, and it didn't seem likely to stop. The land of perfect beauty that she'd seen was gone, replaced by more decay and darkness. She found herself wondering, not for the first time, if there was any part of this world that was not already dying.

The Marked Men drove forward into a vast sea of soldiers and then were overwhelmed by the crushing weight of that sea.

They fought hard and they fought well, but they likely never had a chance, the numbers against them were too great. As soon as they died their spirits were ripped away from them and drawn back through the Gateway. She saw them struggle against the pull, but it was too powerful. Whatever deals they had made had sealed their fate in any possible afterlife. She had captured the life force of many of the same sorts of soldiers in Edinrun, but that had been a place sealed away by the gods and this place had a portal leading back to the world where they had lived their lives.

A good distance ahead of her she could see Brogan McTyre fighting. He seemed more alive than the people around him. His axe and sword moved, cut, cleaved. The armor on his body deflected most of the blows thrown against him, but in time he would fall if nothing changed.

Jahda sighed. "He will never reach the gods if this continues."

Daivem nodded her head and pressed her lips together. "We have to reach him. Too much can go wrong from a distance."

Jahda nodded. A moment later he faded from view, moving into the Shimmer. She'd been afraid that special gift of her people would not work here, but it did. Perhaps the gods were unaware, or unable to stop it, perhaps they simply did not care. In any event, she stepped into the Shimmer and followed Jahda as he moved along. If only they could simply move to new places without first examining them, how much madness could have been avoided?

The world around them was still there, but just set aside – they could see everything around them, but could not interact. Soldiers on both sides fought and were struck down, though the tide was very much in favor of the gods. It was their land, after all, and they made the rules.

When the armies of the gods fell, there was no release of a spirit. They were not living things in the truest sense, more likely simulacra, given exactly enough life to serve and die.

She moved past them and followed Jahda. He stepped back into the real world before her and almost immediately was engaged in combat. His hard staff blocked a brutal blow and he staggered back before catching himself. The armored foes were everywhere and they were driving toward Brogan McTyre, doing their best to take him down.

The man was a fighter and he was touched by a god, but that did not make him immortal. He was bleeding in several places, those unprotected by his armor, though most of the wounds seemed superficial.

His mane of red hair was disheveled, his beard looked like a chunk of it had been cut away by a keen blade, and his eyes rolled with madness and rage. Still, the axe came down and cut through soldiers. The sword parried and thrust and cut deep again and again. Something had changed since he'd come here. Perhaps that bit of him that was marked by the presence of a god was more alive here, in the place where gods ruled and dwelled.

"Watch yourself, woman!" Jahda yelled at her and pushed her aside, blocking a cut meant to remove her head.

There was no time for guilt. It was time instead to do what she could for Brogan McTyre.

The man prepared to fight gods and had been given that ability, but they had an advantage over him. He was not truly a god. He had not spent eternity gathering the lives of sacrifices and hoarding that energy.

That was where she came in. Daivem moved quickly, dodging past one of the dark armored warriors of the gods and leaping to get closer to Brogan.

"McTyre!" Her voice almost broke. "I've something for you!"

The red-haired man let out a grunt as he brought his axe down and cut a soldier's head free of his body.

"I'm busy, lass!"

Rather than argue, Daivem reached for him and touched his shoulder. He was panting now, and sweating from exertion in the places that weren't cut and bleeding. Up close she could see that his armor was breaking in several places: not dented like metal, but chipped and cracked like stone.

Her fingers touched flesh and Daivem in turn touched her wooden walking stick and released what she had held inside. The feeling was like a river carving a channel inside her, there could be no chances taken, not in this place. So the energies had to use her as a conduit in order to make sure they reached the right place.

Souls. Spirits. Lives. Ghosts. By any name they were energy and they flowed into Daivem, giving her miniscule glimpses into their experiences and lives. Soldiers who fought, children at play, lovers lost and found, and a thousand others all ran through her, leaving a fading memory here and there. Niall Leraby, the man she found dead in the snow, who had called out so furiously for revenge, roared as he passed through her body. He howled his fury at all that would never be, at all that had gone wrong and still more. He echoed inside her louder than the rest. He wanted revenge against the gods and he intended to have it.

All of the dead she'd encountered in this world, the spirits she'd gathered on battlefields, and in cities that were dying, in pocket worlds designed to torture the citizens of Edinrun and the soldiers who dared investigate that haunted, lost place, all of them pushed into her and from her hand into the body of Brogan McTyre.

When she had spoken with Jahda and asked his advice, that was what he had suggested. If a man touched by gods wanted to fight gods, he had to have the same advantage as them. He had to have sacrifices to offer him the necessary energies.

The difference here was simple: Daivem had asked if they were willing and the dead had said yes. Anything to end the gods who had ruined them and taken so much from their loved ones. Anything at all to have their say at last.

Brogan McTyre roared. His eyes bulged in his head and his skin reddened as if touched by hours of sunlight.

He did not move away from her, truly, she doubted he could move at all. He had never been prepared for this sort of spiritual contact and even Daivem, who had trained for many years, had trouble keeping hold of herself as the energies of the dead ran through her.

For Brogan McTyre it was surely a hundred times worse.

Beron

He was moving closer to McTyre when the woman touched the red-haired bastard and did something to him. Beron had no idea what was happening, only that for the moment McTyre was incapable of defending himself.

When the man ran into the realm of gods, Beron followed. He kept a distance and he watched and he defended himself from the madness of the soldiers waiting for them all.

Brogan McTyre was chosen by the demons to fight the gods. Beron found that notion maddening. The cheating bastard who had started the end of the world was supposed to gain all the honor and glory of defeating the gods, clearing the way for Ariah and the other demon lords to ascend and become something greater. There was no doubt in his mind that somewhere along the way, that sort of glory would reflect back on the western bastard who had taken everything from Beron, deliberately or not. His world was in ruins. Brogan McTyre did it. His fortune was gone and his empire crumbled. Brogan McTyre caused it.

The thoughts haunted Beron as surely as the gods tormented the demons in their prisons. As surely as Beron himself had tormented endless slaves in his time.

Brogan McTyre needed to die and he needed to do it soon. Beron would take his place. Beron would earn the glory. Beron would prove himself to his new god, Ariah. He would show himself worthy of being favored.

The slip of a girl touched Brogan McTyre and whatever she did seemed to paralyze the man.

There would never be a better time for taking care of the situation.

Beron started forward, holding his sword at the ready. He had been patient and now he would be rewarded.

The first blade cut across the back of his thigh, severing the hamstrings. His leg gave out immediately and he fell forward, more shocked by the lack of control than anything else. The pain came along a few moments later, nearly blinding in its intensity.

The second blade jammed into his throat, stopping him from speaking or screaming out his anger. Blood ran in a hot stream down his neck, to his chest, slipping past his armor with ease.

That second blade stabbed again and again even as he fell forward. When Beron tried to rise, a booted foot kicked his arm out and dropped him back to the ground.

"Stay there, friend. Just lie down." The voice was harsh, the message clear. It wasn't meant as a kindness.

Beron tried to stand again, but instead dots of blackness swam in front of his eyes.

The voice was bitter. "You killed a lot of my friends, Beron of Saramond." The blade this time pressed against his eye. "I don't much like you." A second later the blade was pushed deep and there was an explosion of pain before the darkness dragged him away.

He saw the man who killed him, had seen him before, in fact. He had been among the captured allies of Brogan McTyre. Short, thin and balding. He tried to remember the name that went with the face but there was nothing.

And then there was Nothingness.

CHAPTER TWENTY-FIVE
GODHEAD

Brogan

The woman with Jahda touched him and he warned her away and then the entire world changed. Whatever it was she did to him it was potent and explosive. His body felt hot and feverish. His senses twisted. He could hear too much, see too much, feel too much, and though it was overwhelming it was not the first time he'd felt this way.

The last time a god had touched him and changed him. This time it was more than that. This time there was something inside of Brogan that changed.

There had been times in his life when Brogan thought he would surely die of the cold, and one occasion where he very nearly drowned in a river. His body felt like he remembered feeling when he stepped into warmth after that bitter cold and when he sucked in fresh air as he surfaced on the river, only more so.

The exhaustion that made his muscles shake faded away. The aches where blades had scratched or even cut him vanished. His body surged with energy and Brogan let out another scream.

And then he changed.

Harper

They came from everywhere and for a while all Harper could think about was not dying. It was exactly that simple for him. Do not die. The good news was that he'd become very adept at not dying over the years. Mostly the trick was not getting hit. To that end Harper dodged, blocked and moved on, doing his best to keep his eyes on Brogan at the same time. The man was fast, he had to give him that. Of course, the horse he rode away on made that part easier.

Harper did not have a horse. That luxury went away when the ship he bought was ruined by the Undying.

He didn't let that stop him. He saw the woman touch Brogan. Harper saw his best friend twist and twitch for a moment, even as he once again lashed out at an enemy getting too close.

Behind him Daivem Murdrow dropped to her knees as if exhausted. Her face hung too low to the ground for him to clearly see her expression. Not that it mattered. Brogan dominated his attention, because as he moved forward again, he changed. That was the only way to put it. One moment Brogan was Brogan and the next he was growing.

Brogan cried out, demanding that the gods face him. He very nearly roared the challenge as he had before; the difference was that this time his voice carried like a peal of thunder. He walked forward and moved away from Daivem. And as he strode, he grew. His blade slapped across a soldier and sent the man sprawling as if he'd been hit by an enraged bear.

The battlefield shuddered and the soldiers around him, creatures surely chosen by the gods for their ferocity, retreated. The ground shook where Brogan walked and everyone around seemed aware of it. Fighters from both sides slowed and then stopped fighting. It wasn't a matter of choice. Brogan's presence was overwhelming. Harper had known the man his entire life and had never been afraid of him, never worried the man might kill him, but he worried now.

Brogan was no longer merely Brogan. He was more than that in a way that Harper could not easily define. He was a dangerous creature now, no longer human. He was scarier than the He-Kisshi, and the Undying had been terrifying. He was larger than he should have been, true, but it was more than that. It was simply that he was dangerous, that he was more *there* than any mortal being could be.

One of the fighters for the gods charged forward and lashed out at Brogan. The sword shattered as it struck him. Brogan looked around and waved his arm, and to the last, the fighters lined against him collapsed. They fell from their horses and the horses flopped to the ground, just as suddenly useless.

Brogan demanded again that the gods show themselves and fight.

This time, something responded.

Stanna

The fighting stopped. It was not a gradual thing, but happened all at once. The warriors on both sides felt the change in the atmosphere that marked the change in Brogan McTyre. There was no way to define what had happened, but whatever it was, it was bigger than mortal combat. They couldn't have ignored the change any more than they could a tidal wave.

Then the soldiers collapsed. As one they fell and did not stand again. The silence was a potent thing. The few remaining Marked Men and those who'd survived looked around in shocked silence.

Temmi joined in, holding her head. She had taken a mighty blow when the horse sent her sprawling. Next to her the pale woman still bled, the wound deep enough that she'd need proper patching, but Myridia still stood and that was a good sign.

Tully moved about, panting, wild-eyed and wary. She had no desire to be attacked and was actively looking for potential enemies.

Stanna stopped caring about what was going on with her friends and associates at precisely the same moment that Brogan McTyre started growing. It was not subtle and it made no sense in her world perspective. The man physically changed, doubled in size and then doubled again in the space of a few heartbeats.

She thought her eyes were playing tricks on her initially, but no, he grew and he grew a great deal. Stanna, who was notorious for not being afraid of anything, stopped and stared, her mouth agape, as the man who planned to fight the gods grew enough to make her feel like a newborn in comparison.

He stepped, and he grew. Another step and he grew still more. A dozen strides and he was still looking larger, though she knew he was physically moving away from her vantage point.

He stepped and grew again.

Stanna looked away and closed her eyes, needing to consider this for a moment.

When she looked again he was farther still in the distance and if she had to guess was close to one hundred feet in height.

"Face me, you bastards!" McTyre's voice was the same, but louder than seemed possible.

Around her others were reacting to the transformation, confirming that she had not lost her mind. The ground vibrated with each step he took, his weight enough to leave an indentation with every stride.

Beyond him, she knew, there were five castles, each stranger than the last. One was in ruins, the others were in poor shape but still stood. The stone constructs were ancient, as old, it seemed, as some of the ruins that had marked areas where the gods had punished people before. The stones were weatherworn, the ground around them barren of life, or left with little but lichen to show that life still existed.

That did not mean they weren't occupied. From the closest of the structures something came forth. It was too distant to understand at first, a small speck from a far away building.

And then the damned thing did as Brogan McTyre

did. It walked and as it drew closer, the thing changed shape and size, until it was taller than McTyre.

Temmi said, "What is that?" She was squinting to see the thing in the distance.

Tully answered, "I think it's a god."

Whatever it actually was, it changed as it moved and looking at it hurt Stanna's mind.

CHAPTER TWENTY-SIX
BATTLEFRONT

Brogan McTyre

He was not alone, he knew that, but Brogan felt in control of his body and that was enough for the moment. He wanted to get a better view while staring across the almost level landscape and even as he thought that, he rose in height. He grew enough that, if he had let himself think about the transformation, he would have been terrified.

The power moving through him was invigorating and intoxicating. He wanted to laugh at the way his body changed to suit his whims, and he had to force himself back from allowing too much change.

Was this the power of the gods? To recreate themselves so easily? Could he alter the world around him with only a thought? The fallen enemies he walked past made him think so.

Something came from one of the keeps ahead of him. He knew it was a danger when it stepped in his direction, he could feel the power coming from the thing. He swept his axe into a ready position and continued moving on.

If this were a god, he'd kill it and savor every second of the combat.

The shape changed. It walked like a man, but the body was too thick with muscle, too broad through the chest, and the face was reptilian. Brogan had never cared for the gods, had never learned their names or wondered if they looked like people. It had never mattered.

The eyes of the thing glared violently red, and it carried a whip in one hand and a sword in the other. The whip cracked out across the distance between them and Brogan felt the weighted tip of the thing cut across his chest.

The armor he wore shattered with the impact, falling away from him like fragments of ice sliding down in an avalanche. No damage was done but the force staggered him.

The face of the thing opened in what might have been a snarl. There were rows of teeth, sharp and dripping fluids.

Brogan moved fast, charging his enemy. He felt his teeth bared in a smile and shifted the sword in his hand until he could sweep it toward the monster's face.

It reared back too quickly for him to make contact, and Brogan spun, brought the axe around and buried it in the thing's side. Meat parted, skin split and the reptilian nightmare let loose a scream of agony that was loud enough to shake the air.

The sword in the monster's hand thrust at him

and scraped flesh in a white-hot line of pain. Brogan grunted and kept pushing forward. Near as he knew the only way to kill a thing was to keep hitting until it fell. God or no, it would feel him and it would fear him if he had any say.

Apparently, it felt the same way. Black blood drooled freely from the wound in its side but the thing came again anyway, smashing into Brogan and lifting him into the air.

He rolled as he hit, his body crushing shapes beneath him. There was no thought of whether or not those shapes were his companions. Brogan focused solely on what was happening in the combat and everything else would have to wait.

Brogan made one knee and felt the whip lash out again, this time the damned thing wrapped around his arm just below the wrist and stung him even as it pulled his sword arm down.

Brogan rose up and charged again. The whip was a dangerous weapon, to be sure, but not meant for closer quarters.

His body smashed into the scaly bastard facing him and both of them tumbled. The face of the nightmare was next to his, and its teeth became the main focal point of his vision as the thing opened its mouth and tried to bite him in the face. The haft of his axe took the blow instead and several of the teeth shattered on impact with the grip.

While the damned thing was working out what had just happened, Brogan used the hilt of the sword in his other hand to take out one of the creature's eyes. Blood flowed much more freely from that wound and the feet of the god caught him in the stomach and kicked him toward the sky. Brogan soared and then fell to the ground, rolling as quickly as he could to get back to his feet.

By the time he was standing, so was the now one-eyed monster. Five steps and they were back in conflict. The whip that the creature used was still wrapped around Brogan's arm. He was grateful that it had let go of the weapon or it could easily have staggered him with a hard pull. As he ran the whip fell loose. As he clashed with his enemy, the axe came around again and hacked into the ribcage a few inches lower than before.

He'd have been celebrating if the bastard's sword hadn't met with his leg at the same time. Both came away from the collision bloodied and furious. Hot warmth flowed down to Brogan's boot and he pushed forward. The cut was deep but not enough to cripple.

God or demon or other, the thing looked down at the cuts in its side. While it did, Brogan came down with the axe on the top of its head and cleaved the heavy skull open.

No matter what the nature of the beast, few things continue on without a head. The creature dropped fast to the ground and its entire body shook violently. Brogan planted the blade of the axe in its head four more times before it stopped convulsing.

There was no time for celebration. As the thing finally stopped moving another roar came from further along the battlefield, and something dark came forth from its keep.

Brogan did not wait. He moved in that direction,

sweeping his axe around in an arc. The wound in his leg knitted shut amid a series of painful itches. The flesh was solid again after only a few steps. Brogan grinned and charged toward his enemy.

Harper

"What the hell was that?" Harper watched the dead thing on the ground. It did not move. It did not breathe. That was a blessing in his eyes.

Blood flowed freely from the massive wounds on the gigantic form. The blood did not rest easy, but trembled as the body cooled.

"That was a god." Darwa spoke softly, her eyes locked on the same subject. She squinted. "I believe that was Hepset-Hamu, the River God. There are only a few descriptions of any of the gods, but he was supposed to have the skin of a scaled serpent."

Harper nodded. "Then what in the name of all that is right in this universe is that?" He pointed to the dark shape that was growing larger even as they watched. It had the form of a man, but the head was obscured by a thick caul of black smoke or mist. There were hints of a face within that constantly shifting mask of darkness, but they were only hints.

Darwa shivered and wrapped herself in her arms though the air was warm enough to elicit sweat. "That is Gla'Eru'Wrath the Light Eater. All that is dark and hidden in darkness is the domain of Gla'Eru'Wrath. It is also the death dealer."

The thing drew a sword and swept that long-bladed weapon in a full circle around its body. As the blade was wielded the air behind it rippled, turning dark wherever the sword has been.

"What?" Harper stared, uncertain as to what, exactly, he was seeing.

"Gla'Eru'Wrath's sword devours light and leaves a rift between worlds. To be cut by that blade is to be forced between two worlds. It is death."

"Do you think you could have warned Brogan about that before he had to meet it in combat?"

Darwa grinned, but there was no joy in the expression. "He wouldn't have listened. He is far too arrogant for that."

Brogan

The shape of the thing seemed very nearly made of shadows. Against the backdrop of dark clouds and harsh winds its face was hinted at but not seen. It was dressed in dark armor and bore a heavy cloak. Far more importantly, it carried a massive long sword that had better reach than Brogan's sword or axe. If it hit first there was little he'd be able to do to avoid being cut in half. The figure stood still as he charged and Brogan watched that cursed blade. Behind it more darkness moved along the path the blade had taken.

Brogan slowed down. He did not trust what he was seeing. He could not.

"Will you not fight me?" The words were not spoken aloud, but forced themselves into his head like thrusts from a rusted dagger.

He shook his head to clear away the question.

"I'll fight you. I'll just not make it easy for you."

"You will die either way." The voice continued in his skull and Brogan shook his head to clear it. The shadow-maned form swept the vast sword around as easily as a dandy from Edinrun might a thin rapier. "You have offended the gods and you have killed two of my brethren. It is time for your end, Brogan McTyre."

"You killed my family!"

"Your family never mattered. You never mattered. You are merely food to be harvested as we see fit." The thing moved closer. "My name is Gla'Eru'Wrath. I will kill you now."

"Your name is shit, and I'll wipe you off my boot, you prick." He grinned again as he prepared for the fight. Let the bastard come to him. Let him think he had a chance, but this was for Nora and the children. This was what he lived for now. This was all he wanted of the world, a chance to kill the sadistic bastards that had taken from him without remorse.

That hint of a face lost in darkness scowled and then the armored giant was charging, coming his way and actually growing even as it moved.

Brogan stood his ground as the thing came closer. The feet hit the earth hard enough to cause vibrations. The very ground cracked under each gigantic tread.

And Brogan waited, breathing deeply and preparing himself.

Gla'Eru'Wrath was twice his size at least, and grew larger as it came. Brogan wasn't sure that was to the god's advantage. He had reach, but if he could not strike Brogan down with one blow, he'd have a chance to retaliate properly.

On the other hand, he definitely had reach. The giant swept back his sword and the eyes within that vast cloud of a face squinted as he took his swing.

Brogan saw the strike coming. Trouble with a truly big sword is it's devilish hard to hide an attack. The advantage of course was one good strike and you'd likely cut a man in two.

Brogan dove to the side, rolling past the immense blade. The air behind its edge wailed as it was sliced open and Brogan saw the wound that was cut between the worlds.

He had no idea how these things worked. He was still trying to accept that he had passed between realms, but the air trembled and then the sword hit the ground and split the foundations of the world as easily as his axe might split a log for a fire.

The ground crackled and the rend in the fabric of the land raced toward the Gateway and the people he knew and cared for. The bodies of dead soldiers and Marked Men alike collapsed into that rift, and plummeted through the clouds to land the gods alone knew exactly where. More importantly, the dead lizard thing fell through the tear in space and Brogan saw the rivers of blood falling from the thing that rained down as well.

Part of him wanted to know where they fell. He never had the chance to see as the ground sealed itself after a few seconds.

That was for the best. He had no desire to be thrown through that hole himself.

Even as the tear formed between the worlds and the fallen dropped across a dead land, Brogan rose up and stabbed his enemy in the chest with the points of both axe blades. The tips cut through the hard armor and punched into whatever passed for flesh on the deity. Gla'Eru'Wrath had not recovered from trying to cut Brogan in half; he was still off balance. Brogan used his own weight and shoved the axe harder, and in the process he grew again, matching the height of his attacker. The growth was effortless. He barely had to think about it.

The god's sword fell from his grasp and Brogan pushed again, grunting with effort as the double tips of his axe blades punched deeper into torn armor and meat alike.

The body of the god opened still more and cold, shadowy filth spilled from the wound and bled down over Brogan's hands, slicking them and chilling his flesh.

He pulled the axe free, and shoved his short sword into the smoking face of the god. Tendrils of midnight wrapped around the blade but did not stop it from cutting deep into whatever lay beneath.

Gla'Eru'Wrath cried out and Brogan pushed harder, stabbed deeper into the head of the deity. The sword blade bent, and after a moment the metal shattered. What was left was a jagged stub of blade and a hilt. Brogan drove that edge into the god's face, pushing with all of his strength. He could not see the wound he made, but he felt the cold flow of viscera that came from it.

Gla'Eru'Wrath caught Brogan by the neck, both gauntleted hands wrapping around his throat, the thumbs seeking to crush his airway.

Brogan's axe wielding arm swept up and across the two hands of the god, knocking them aside before the thumbs could find good purchase. As the arms were slapped away, the broken sword blade crashed into the god's throat, driving deep into tender flesh and carving a trench that bled still more cold blackness into the air.

Gla'Eru'Wrath spoke no more, but instead coughed and backed away, vomiting ichor from whatever passed for a mouth in that black shroud around his head.

Brogan pulled back and stabbed again, again, and again, each time feeling flesh and bone against his hand and what remained of his sword.

Gla'Eru'Wrath let out a throaty gasp and fell forward, crashing into the ground. The black cloud around the god's head bled outward, slowly swallowing the body of the dead thing. By the time it was completely consumed, Brogan had moved on.

There were more gods and he didn't trust that they would wait patiently for him to reach them.

He was correct in that belief.

The arrow caught him in his shoulder and cut through meat to vibrate in the bone. The pain was exactly as fearsome as he might have guessed, and Brogan let out a completely involuntary yelp of pain.

His eyes looked at the arrow for a moment and then tracked the path it must have taken to find the archer. She was tall and slender, and had gray in her hair. She was an attractive woman, or at least chose to show herself that way. Whatever the case she pulled another arrow and drew back her bow in one fluid motion, exactly the sort that made him envy Harper whenever he saw the man prepare to kill.

Whatever the case, the bow was drawn and the arrow loosed. It came toward him in a blur that he didn't think he could block.

CHAPTER TWENTY-SEVEN
THE BLOOD OF GODS

Harper

The woman's form was flawless.

Before he could ask Darwa said, "Mahnsatepusamu, Queen of the Gods and God of the Storm and the Hunt. She is the very finest archer ever."

"Then why did she miss?"

Darwa looked away for a moment to stare into his face. "Harper, she did not miss. That was her way of warning him of his impending death. Also, the Books of Galea state that she likes her enemies to suffer."

"Brogan can't dodge an arrow."

"Nobody can who is not very lucky."

"Why don't they attack together?"

"The gods?" Darwa looked toward him and shrugged. "Why does he attack the gods?"

"Because he means to kill them, of course."

Darwa nodded. "And why does he attack alone? Why not bring a dozen people like you with him?"

"He said he cannot."

The Galean shook her head. "He does this alone because he wants the satisfaction of killing them. Whatever else he might claim, that is the truth of it."

Harper nodded his head.

As they watched, Brogan stooped down to capture the smoldering sword left behind by the last god he'd battled. The goddess loosed another arrow and by sheer blind luck Brogan was lowering himself to grab the sword's hilt as the arrow ran across his back and skittered harmlessly off his armor.

He winced as he hefted the blade. The black aura around it continued on, smoking and leaving a black trail whenever he moved it.

The archer frowned, disapproving. She said something but the words were unknown to Harper.

Darwa said, "She's chastising him for using her brother's weapon."

"I don't think he cares." Harper shook his head.

Brogan said, "I don't care!" His voice boomed out across the battlefield.

The body of Gla'Eru'Wrath had liquefied; all that remained was the hollow armor and a jet-black residue that oozed slowly across the surrounding area.

"They fight him alone for the same reason, I suppose. They want to prove that one mortal is not enough to cause them fear. They want to kill him themselves, to prove they are the strongest." She shrugged. "That, or they are simply not speaking to each other. Sometimes the gods squabble."

That was all the time Harper had to waste. His friend was fighting gods, after all.

All around him the remaining humans talked and

watched. Not a one of them thought to attack. His best arrow shot would never reach the archer fighting Brogan, and even if it did none of them had been touched by a god or granted the ability to fight one.

The massive redhead slaver came closer, nodding to him and looking at Darwa. "You are Galean?"

"Yes, I am." She didn't look away from the fight. Mahnsatepusamu pointed a finger at Brogan, while he held the sword at the ready and ignored the wound in his shoulder. Or, rather, tried to ignore it. Harper knew his friend and human anatomy well enough to know he was suffering.

"What is that stuff?" She pointed to the pool of blackness spreading from the dead god's armor.

"It is the blood of a god."

"What does it do?"

Darwa turned away to look at the woman. "It's blood."

"Yes, but it's the blood of a god. I have been told that the shards in the Broken Swords were the blood of a god, or possibly the remains of a sword. Didn't Brogan McTyre have to do something with those before he could take on the power to fight a god?"

That got Harper's attention.

Darwa looked at the woman and slowly a smile spread across her face.

"That was the blood of a dead god and it required great rituals. This is the blood of a dead god and I have no idea what it might do if you touch it."

Stanna frowned and considered that for a moment. "One way to find out." With that, she started walking across the battlefield. Three others walked with her.

One of them was Grakhul. The other two were young and likely as foolhardy as the giantess.

Harper sighed and watched them walking. Then with a second sigh, he started to follow.

Ahead of them all, Brogan charged at the archer, roaring out a battle cry as he went.

Brogan

His shoulder burned where the arrow still rested against bone. He could not take the time to pull it free, as he could feel the barbs of the arrowhead moving within the meat of his arm. Instead he reached, bent the arrow and then let out a muffled scream as it finally broke, leaving a few inches of haft sticking out of him.

His previous wounds had healed. This one did not, perhaps because the arrow was still in his flesh, perhaps because whatever the woman from Louron had done earlier was wearing off. He had no idea how any of this worked, only that he had a small chance of killing the gods and intended to take it.

She had another arrow drawn back in her bow and was watching as he tossed the last one aside.

Her eyes were dark and gray as the storm clouds and her lovely face may as well have been carved from stone.

"I will kill you, Brogan McTyre. You leave me no choice."

"I will kill you. I have a choice, but I want your death. I want to make you scream, and bleed, and die."

The arrow came straight for his face. There was no way he could possibly dodge it. The sword swept before him, a vain attempt at blocking the missile. He was too fast, and the sword crossed in front of him too soon.

The black streak that followed after showed him what was left of the Broken Swords as it ripped a wound between the worlds. The great bodies of Walthanadurn and whatever it was they had killed together were clear to him. The arrow was not. A moment later he understood that the opening between the worlds had swallowed the arrow. Had he the time to look he'd have likely seen it crash against the mountains themselves.

There was no time. The woman was aiming again already.

The sword in his hands was a burden on his bleeding shoulder, that was a fact, but it was also keeping him alive. He ran toward her and she stood her ground and loosed another arrow, aiming for his chest this time.

That was wise. It made him move about in a way that was decidedly uncomfortable and made him hiss at the pain.

It also made him angry, but he held that inside. No use in the anger getting the better of his common sense and so he shoved it aside for the moment.

He swept the sword around again and moved to the side. The air split as it had before and for a moment he saw the raging clouds above his homeland and one of the gigantic things that was reshaping the world. Had he his way the arrow would have punched through the monster's head, but he couldn't see where it went.

By the time he recovered from the swing, the god was once more letting loose her arrow. This time he was too close to even attempt to block, so instead he spun his entire body with the sword and brought it across her body from her left shoulder to her right hip. The bow was in the way, whether she attempted to block or not, but it did not matter. The sword cut through the bow and then deep into the archer who used it. The muscles between shoulder and neck split in two, and her collarbone followed. The archer screamed in pain as the blade kept cutting and, behind it, that maddening trail of black followed. As he finished his swing everything above the trail of the wound fell away. Neck, head and one arm, drawn through the hole cut between the worlds.

The lower portion of her body fell, spilling hot blood across Brogan in the process. He did not care. He was soaked in blood and it didn't matter. All that seemed important was that she was dead, as dead as his family.

If he thought he might have a respite before the battle continued, he was mistaken. The last of the structures before him shuddered and exploded outward as the god that rested there rose and announced itself.

What were gods? From what he'd heard they were the same as demons, only stronger. They were, perhaps, more mature versions of the demons. He had no way of knowing, he truly did not care. All that mattered was that they had to go. They had to be removed, they had to die; in order to save the world, yes, in order to save people from ever being sacrificed, certainly, but mostly they had to die because they had taken from him. They had stolen away the joy in his world and he intended to return the favor before he died.

The thing in front of him did not want to take one form, it seemed, but preferred to change constantly. One moment it looked like a man and the next there were odd shapes spilling from it, writhing tendrils that snapped and shivered. A moment later and he was looking at a figure that seemed sculpted from muck, barely able to hold itself together. Another heartbeat and another form, this one crystalline and shedding large blades of crystal even as it moved toward him. Another moment and the form was a towering serpent that seemed made of iron. It slithered forward and hissed through teeth that glittered blackly.

Still it moved, and still Brogan watched. This was not like the others, this was more powerful, and there was something familiar about the feel of it, even if there was nothing about it he had seen before.

"Enough. You have done enough. Stop now."

It changed again, taking a shape he knew very well. It looked at him and studied him with eyes he had seen before.

There were few people alive who could possibly make Brogan hesitate. Harper was one of them. Harper stood before him, however, in all his glory, that damnable smirk of his still in place.

"You're not Harper." He stared into Harper's eyes and Harper stared back, every single detail flawless. He wore the same clothes, he carried the same weapons, though he had not drawn any yet.

"I am Sepsumannahun. I am the God of Gods. I am the slayer of Walthanadurn and you have angered me."

Brogan nodded. "Let's be done with this, then."

The god did not move. He did not need to.

Brogan felt his bones start to break within his body. The pain slammed through him and swallowed him whole.

Harper

Stanna reached the blood first and after only a moment of hesitation she reached down and placed her hand in the black fluid.

She frowned. "Nothing. I feel nothing but sticky muck on my palm."

Temmi said, "Well, what did you expect? It's dead now, isn't it?"

Tully frowned. "I'd have thought something would survive. It was a god, after all."

Harper looked at the three companions and contemplated whether or not they were all going mad. Not just them, but him as well. He'd expected that something must surely still be there, that some sort of power might still exist. Why else would it be there? What purpose could it serve?

The woman who'd touched Brogan before walked closer, frowning.

"What does it do?" Harper asked her, wondering if she might have an answer.

"I think it is all the spirit left of the god that he

killed." She frowned. "It's trying to speak to me, but I don't think I know what it wants."

There were several others moving closer now. They had seen people moving, people leading, he supposed, and decided it was a good time to gather together again.

Jahda was among them. The man still carried that same soft smile on his face and Harper wondered if he even knew any other expressions.

Jahda closed his eyes and tilted his head.

"It does not speak a language I know."

The Grakhul woman nodded her head. "It speaks the language of the gods. They would not bother to speak any language but their own."

Jahda nodded as if that made perfect sense.

"Does anyone here speak the language of the gods?"

It was Darwa that answered Jahda's question. "No. That is forbidden. But understanding the language is only a matter of training."

She looked at the vast flow of shadow-dark blood and then squatted before it. Desmond called out from behind him and Harper looked, knowing what he would see already. Anna walked closer to the Galean, her face set. She was terrified, he could see that, and as well she should be – they walked in a forbidden place and stared at the remains of a god. No matter what happened, it was likely that they would never leave here the same as they entered. The lands around the Grakhul home had been poisoned by the gods. How then could this be any different? The land was bleak, as nearly lifeless as the nameless keep of the

Grahkul. He had been trained to stay away from the poisonous lands around that keep, as had his father and his grandfather before him. This, however, was something far worse. This was a land fllied with the power of the gods. Was it deadly? Probably. He did not know for certain, but he suspected as much.

Harper frowned. In the distance the last of the gods moved toward Brogan. The others had all had form, but this one was merely a massive pillar of bright white light that undulated and occasionally spat out streamers that looked like tongues of fire licking the air before they pulled back. Brogan seemed nearly hypnotized by the glowing shape.

"I don't know if touching the blood is a good idea." Harper spoke up and saw the frown on Stanna's face deepen. "The land around the Grakhul was tainted."

The Grakhul woman spoke, "That is from where the gods punished our people for not listening to their decrees. They cast down a demon on that land."

"And yet I have heard at least two people say that demons are the same as gods. So how is their blood different?"

Darwa scowled. Anna frowned, and the Grakhul woman shook her head. "If the gods wanted us dead, we would be dead."

In the distance Brogan let out a roar of pain and his body convulsed.

"It might not be able to help us, but would it help him?" That came from the smaller of Stanna's companions. He thought her name was Tully, but he had only learned their names from hearing them called, and it was impossible to say for certain.

Darwa stared at Brogan in the distance. He was fighting against something, struggling as if he'd been bound in chains, and his wounded shoulder bled freely.

Darwa shrugged. "Possibly. Who can say?"

"You can," Harper answered. "You've read your books. Will it work?"

"I am not sure that what you want can be achieved." Darwa scratched absently at her chin and closed her eyes, thinking.

Daivem stepped closer and held her hand over the black substance. She looked back at Jahda. He shrugged and spoke to her in their own language. It was a short exchange, not angry but urgent, between the two of them, and Harper wished, not for the first time, that he had learned how to speak like the Louron.

Daivem finally grew impatient and planted one hand in the substance. Her entire body stiffened as she touched it, and then she shook her head, trying to break the contact. "It's... I don't know if I can do this!"

"Do what?" Harper looked at her and considered reaching out to help her break away, but between them was Jahda and he knew her better. Perhaps if he decided it should happen that would be for the best.

Jahda leaned down and shouted at her in her own language. A moment later she nodded and held her carved walking stick in her other hand. The wood swelled, as if it had soaked for days in water, and she let out a groan loud enough to make him worry for her safety.

"Do it!" Jahda roared the words into her ear and Daivem nodded. He saw nothing come from her or her wand, but he felt it. It was a cold wind cutting across a hot desert. The air nearly steamed from the chill it carried, and Harper felt his flesh crawl.

Whatever she was doing, she was stealing from the dead god and aiming whatever she had stolen directly at Brogan.

She was either helping him, or she was killing him and there was no way for Harper to know which.

Brogan

Brogan screamed again as the changing shape in front of him continued to kill him without so much as bothering to touch his flesh. Bones broke, muscles convulsed and agonies like he'd never imagined smashed through him, dropping him to the ground. Even the impact with the earth was a new level of pain, as bone burst through flesh and scraped against the rocky soil.

"You are meat. You are little more than a meal, but now you have killed my family and I will destroy you over the course of eons." Sepsumannahun spoke slowly and Harper's teeth were bared in a sneer of contempt. "You are angry because your family died? They were bred to die! You are all cattle!"

Brogan tried to move, but nothing worked. His muscles were shredded, his fingers twitched without any real chance of flexing, and his breath came in shuddering gasps.

From the distance something screamed as it cut

through the air. He could not see it as it was behind him, but he heard it. The sound was a wail of fury, a primal scream.

Whatever it was that moved toward him hit his body and sent him rolling across the ground.

Energy washed into him, freezing his muscles and then warming them again. He felt the anger of Gla'Eru'Wrath and knew what it was that was happening. He was absorbing the dead god much as he had absorbed the essence of Walthanadurn. The difference was, this was not deliberate on the part of the god and his defeated enemy was furious about being used this way.

He reached to his shoulder and clamped his teeth together as he gripped and then forced out the arrowhead. The world waved in and out a few times in the process and it was all he could manage not to vomit on himself.

Brogan thought about being healed and it happened. The pain was impossible to ignore and he wept through it, but in seconds he was whole again and Sepsumannahun was looking at him, wearing the face of a shocked Harper.

"What have you done?"

Brogan didn't answer. Instead he stood up as quickly as he could and grabbed his weapons. The sword of Gla'Eru'Wrath and the axe that had been Faceless filled his hands.

Sepsumannahun snarled and reached for him. He carried no weapons and likely did not need them.

There was exactly one advantage that Brogan had over the gods and it was a simple one: he knew how to engage in combat and it seemed that they did not. Even the best of them was awkward and clumsy, in comparison.

He had spent half his life on the field of battle. Perhaps they had not.

Sepsumannahun reached for him, and Brogan drove the point of Gla'Eru'Wrath's blade through his chest, through the place where a heart would be in a human being. Harper looked back at him, wide-eyed and shocked. Brogan left the sword there, and while Harper/Sepsumannahun looked on, Brogan caught him across the side of his face with an axe blade.

Flesh and bone fell away. Harper's face collapsed and bled. Brogan did not let himself think, did not have time to consider what happened, but instead struck again and again, while Sepsumannahun screamed.

Deep inside of him Walthanadurn roared in satisfaction. The sword in Sepsumannahun's chest did what it seemed always to do and opened a rift between the worlds. Did it hurt the God of Gods? He prayed it did. Certainly it seemed to, as the shape of Harper wavered and collapsed into a field of nearly blinding light.

Three more strikes of the axe as that light flickered and flared and started to extinguish, before a dozen tongues of fire lashed out and cut at him.

Brogan felt the power he'd absorbed pulled from his body. He understood what was happening. The god was hungry, starving, and it wanted to protect itself from death. Surely the same energies that had let him heal himself would work even better for a deity.

Brogan shook his head. The sword was still buried in that light. He could see the hilt. His hand reached out and grabbed the weapon. Flesh burned on his hand and he growled as he pulled, twisted and sawed with the unnatural blade.

Sepsumannahun let out a sound that was not even close to human and the entire being shook. The ground beneath it burned, melting and changing colors, glowing redly as Brogan continued to saw the sword through the wound he had already made.

More tongues licked away from the god and cut trails of agony across his body. Where each touched, his skin split and burned.

Brogan raised his axe up high and brought it down on what appeared to be a column of light. Like the sword, the axe struck and stayed in place.

Brogan screamed. He could do no more. His arms burned, his flesh cooked, and his bones felt like they'd been replaced with molten lead.

The god was dying and that was almost enough. He wanted to see it die. He wanted to feel it. And so, Brogan reached out with his arms and wrapped them around the tower of fiery brilliance. He held on as tightly as he could, felt his hair burning, his beard catch fire and his flesh broil in the heat of a dying god.

For the second, or was it the third, or perhaps the millionth, time, he felt himself dying, seared and blinded and burnt beyond the ability to heal himself. His lungs felt like they were filled with hot coals. His flesh was stung and ruptured and ruined.

Sepsumannahun let out a final wail of pain and then collapsed, knocking Brogan off his feet at the same time. Brogan held on to the falling god, unwilling to let go, needing to feel the thing die. This was revenge. This was all he had left.

The hilt of the sword burned into his chest. The axe fell away, dropped somewhere nearby but he could not see it or feel it, only hear the clatter it made.

Because he was not dead yet, Brogan willed himself to recover from his injuries. At first there was nothing, but then, slowly, the pain flared up again as raw nerves mended themselves, and burnt flesh healed from trauma.

His lips moved. His eyes blinked. The vision was there, but not fully mended. His left eye saw better and he stared at the remains of Sepsumannahun. They looked human enough, though the flesh was bloodied and torn. The god looked old, withered, frail, and dead.

Brogan continued to heal though the process was slow. He managed to stand up, though his legs ached and his knees were weak.

Near as he could tell the god was dead.

That did not mean his fight was completely over.

He walked toward the Gateway, toward his companions and the way back to their world. As he walked, he felt the differences in his body. He made massive strides but did not travel as far with each step. His body was shrinking, falling back toward a more human size.

Behind him the sword of Gla'Eru'Wrath continued to do what it had always done and the body of Sepsumannahun let out an odd sighing sound as the chest of the thing collapsed on itself, taking the hilt of the sword with it. A moment later the body flopped to the side, exposing a massive wound in the chest. There was no sign of the sword.

The world went gray for Brogan and he fell to his knees first, and then on his face.

CHAPTER TWENTY-EIGHT
GODS OLD AND NEW

Daivem

There was nothing left to do, so she let the walking stick fall from her hand.

For over a decade she had held that stick daily, working her hands over the wood, making carvings and corrections as she needed, listening to the voices of the dead as they told her how to work the wood and make it better.

The stick was charred now. Not ruined, but weakened. She had never tried to hold the power of a god inside it, but she had used it to channel that power and the staff was not quite up to the task.

Neither was she. When she was a child she'd seen a man hit by lightning. He had burned from the inside. She had done the same, or it was close enough that she could not tell the difference. Inquisitors are trained to deal with pain, but this was different, this was crippling agony and she simply could not hold it inside.

Daivem let out a wounded cry and fell back on her ass in the dirt.

Jahda was there in an instant, his hands seeking to find spots where contact did not cause her agony. His success was limited.

"We go through the Gateway soon and then we return home, Daivem. I may come back here, but you are done with this place and these gods."

She took no comfort in his words.

Stanna

Stanna shook her head and watched the madness of gods falling and a mortal man stumbling back through the battlefield where he had done the impossible and killed the deities they had been forced to worship their entire lives. He crashed to the ground and Stanna spat, and then started running toward him. Brogan McTyre had just killed the gods. He had fought them and slain them and now he was defenseless.

And like Brogan himself, Stanna understood that the fight was not yet finished.

She was not alone as she started for him. Harper ran alongside her, and so did others she did not know. Of those she did recognize, white-skinned Myridia was the fastest.

Brogan McTyre lay face down, panting in the dirt when they finally reached him. Myridia looked at the man but did not touch him. Her eyes were wide and she was gasping in deep breaths. Her hands were at her sides and seemed incapable of staying still.

Stanna looked down at the man and felt a confusion

she did not expect. It wasn't quite fear. He was too battered for her to be afraid of him, but there was something akin.

"How is he still alive?" Temmi asked the question.

Harper Rutkett ignored the question and turned Brogan over. His eyes looked hard at the face of his friend and then he placed a hand over the man's mouth and nose, frowning. "He's breathing. He's alive."

The Galean spoke up, "The gods are dead. The new gods will come now. The demons from the world we left behind, they will take this place and make it their own." She looked over her shoulder and then around at the others who were still gathering. "We should not be here when that happens. They will want to feast and we are food."

"How long will it take before they know?" The woman who spoke meant nothing at all to Stanna.

"That the gods are dead? They likely already know that. They will come soon if they can. That is their nature." The Galean shrugged her narrow shoulders and frowned. "We should leave. Grab him and take him from here, but we should leave before it is too late."

Brogan McTyre opened his eyes and sucked in a deep lungful of air. His voice was raspy.

His eyes looked at all of them, moving wildly, and he shook his head. "Leave here. It's not over yet. I can feel them coming."

"Feel who, Brogan?" Harper spoke softly, still crouched over his friend.

"The new gods. They're coming here."

"Then let's go."

Brogan McTyre pushed away the hand that tried to help him up and shook his head. "I'll not be going, Harper."

"What?"

"One last fight for me. One last time. I have to kill them before they can take this place, whatever it is."

"What are you talking about, you fool?" The Galean's voice was not unkind. "There have always been gods. There *must* be gods."

He looked at her and shook his head even as he pushed himself up from the soil. "Why? So that they can do the whole damned thing all over again?"

"That is the nature of our world, Brogan McTyre. We live by the decrees of the gods. They make the world as they see fit and we live in it."

"No!" He shook his head. "No more! I meant what I said before, no more sacrifices." His hands clenched and he took three steps, pointing toward the Gateway. "Go. Get away from here. I'll kill them all as soon as they arrive. They'll die by my hands."

"There's not enough of you left, fool." Stanna spoke softly.

"There's enough." He stared at her, daring her to disagree. "I can feel them inside me yet, the gods. They want out, but that's not for them. They're dead and I'm alive and that means what's left of them is mine to use. It's not much, I'll give you that, but it might be enough."

The Galean spat. Still, she turned and headed for the distant rift between the worlds. "In any event, I will not be here when the demons arrive. The knowledge of Galea must be preserved and that is now my duty." She did not turn and look back, but started walking and kept walking.

A moment later the woman whose name she did not know nodded her head and looked toward Brogan. "I have to go with her, Brogan. Me and Desmond. I must."

Brogan McTyre's face betrayed him for an instant. He felt something for the woman, though he had lost his wife only recently to the gods themselves.

He said nothing but gestured with his hand. "Go with them." Harper stared, his jaw working, the smile she'd almost always seen on the man's face missing as well. "See them safely through," Brogan insisted. "I am not coming home."

"I'll be taking my chances here, with you."

"No!" Brogan's voice was hoarse and it broke easily.

"We would all like a better world, Brogan McTyre. Not just you."

"Watch them, Harper, get them home."

Harper shook his head. "Bump'll do that for me. Won't you, lad?"

A shorter man, the one she'd seen walking away from Beron's corpse, nodded his head. "That I will." He stared at Brogan for a moment and then gave a small wave and turned. A moment later several others left with him.

"You've lost your minds." Temmi shook her head. "You killed the gods. Killed the He-Kisshi from what I hear. But something has to rebuild the world."

"There's already something down there to do that. Don't know what they're called, but they're supposed to rebuild. Maybe they'll handle it and maybe they won't." Brogan brushed the dirt from his legs and stared at Harper. "You should leave." His eyes looked around and found Stanna. "All of you."

Stanna snorted. "What will you do with these demons?"

"I plan on killing them."

"With what?"

He pointed back the way he'd come. "My axe is there."

Stanna nodded. She looked at Temmi and then at Tully. "Go on with you then. I'll be along when I've talked sense into this lot."

Temmi nodded. "Just be quick about it." She started away, muttering to herself and holding the back of her head where she'd taken the worst of the blow to her skull. She moved as if she were drunk. Stanna hoped that resolved itself soon.

Tully eyed her for a moment, not saying anything and then finally spoke. "You can't fight demons. You're only a person, no matter how strong you like to think you are."

"I know what I am." Stanna smiled and then swatted the girl on her backside. "Get on and watch over her. She's not nearly as fearsome as she likes to think." Tully looked like she might say something else, but then she closed her mouth and nodded. Was there a chance the girl would shed a tear? She thought not. Still, the girl looked away and then she started walking, catching up with Temmi, but not too quickly.

They moved into the distance, a small gathering

of people, some she knew and some she had never known. Standing with her were two men she'd done her best to finish in battle. She'd failed in both cases and that was rare. Aside from them, there was one last Grakhul. One last servant of the dead gods.

"Do you really think you can fight these demons, Brogan McTyre?" She eyed him as she asked the question and he nodded before finally answering.

"Aye. I'll kill them. Or at least most of them before I die."

"What of the things remaking the world?"

It was Myridia that answered. "The Hahluritiedes." The Grakhul looked at Stanna and squinted. "They are the shapers of the world. They follow the orders of gods."

"And if there are no orders?"

"Then they sleep."

"And if there are no gods?"

"Who can say? There have always been gods."

Brogan spat. "No more."

Stanna rolled her eyes. "Yes. That is the plan."

Myridia sighed and unsheathed her sword. In the distance, far from where they stood, there was a disturbance. The ground shook and the air let out a screech as something began forcing its way into the realm of the gods.

"Just as well," Myridia said. "The gods lie."

Stanna nodded. She had no idea what the woman was talking about. Nor did she care.

"Something is coming." Harper shook his head.

Brogan McTyre nodded and grinned. He made a gesture and the axe he had dropped was in his hand.

"You've still time to run. The lot of you. I'll hold it back."

Harper and Stanna snorted their responses at the same time.

It was nearly military precision. They stepped around and made a square, each covered by the warrior at their side. No words were spoken.

None were needed.

The first of the demons came crawling from the ground, a shadowy form that writhed and hissed as it moved to the surface.

It was not human. It was a beast, to be sure.

But it was not a god, either, at least not yet.

There were four of them and only one of the demon lords, so far.

Those were the sort of odds that Stanna could accept.

The thing noticed them and let out a shuddering scream that made her teeth ache in her head.

Stanna drew the Bitch and stepped forward into a proper battle posture. Her smile matched that of Brogan McTyre.

ACKNOWLEDGMENTS

Special thanks to Tessa Moore, my beloved, for believing in me. Thanks to Charles R Rutledge and Cliff Biggers, who have helped me in countless ways! More thanks than should be possible go to Penny Reeve, Nick Tyler, Marc Gascoigne and the entire crowd of Robots! You folks do so much that no one ever sees…